The author left school at fourteen years of age, then attended night classes studying shorthand/typewriting and book-keeping which she was employed doing until she was twenty years of age. She then enrolled as a student nurse, and qualified as a state-registered nurse at 23 years of age. She later became a nurse tutor until she retired at 69 years of age. She had her first novel published by Austin Macauley Publishers when she was aged 79. This is her fifth novel to be published by them. She is married with two children, six grandchildren, and six great-grandchildren.

I would like to dedicate this book to my husband, Ian, and my family who, without exception, believed in my ability to be successful in having another book published, in spite having a few setbacks along the way.

To my daughter, Jayne, who so willingly put her own work on hold innumerable times, in order to help me with the laptop. To my granddaughter, Natalie, who in Australia typed some chapters for me, while listening to my very low voice on tape in Northern Ireland. To my daughter-in-law, Susan, who read my manuscript and gave me such encouragement to send it off. To my son, Malcolm, who also gave me such encouragement and who, so spontaneously, came up with the title.

Norah Humphreys

WE'VE BEEN KIDNAPPED— HAVEN'T WE?

AUSTIN MACAULEY PUBLISHERS™

LONDON • CAMBRIDGE • NEW YORK • SHARJAH

A CIP catalogue record for this title is available from the British Library.

ISBN 9781035848782 (Paperback)
ISBN 9781035848799 (ePub e-book)

www.austinmacauley.com

First Published 2024
Austin Macauley Publishers Ltd®
1 Canada Square
Canary Wharf
London
E14 5AA

20240416

Chapter 1

Monica sat quietly gazing around the room she was in. She thought it was beautiful with its large picture window overlooking the garden and the orchard beyond. The actual shape of the room was uninspiring, just a large square room with its two doors, one leading to the bedroom, the other to the bathroom. The walls had been painted a soft pale green colour and pink velvet curtains were draped in perfect folds on either side of the window. A pink carpet stretching from wall to wall blended in perfectly with the decor. Two large comfortable sofas upholstered in a delightful floral mix of green and pink occupied a large part of the floor space but left room for a folding table and three straight back chairs suitable for mealtimes.

Monica realised that at this moment in her life, she would never appreciate anything quite as much as this room and her presence in it. She found it hard to believe that this was where she was going to be living—herself and her darling son. This would be their home and it was all thanks to the kind man whose advertisement she had answered just two short weeks ago.

She had answered several advertisements in the last three weeks with no success even though she had attended interviews. When she saw the one where a live-in child-minder was required by an elderly gentleman to look after his daughter aged four, she applied at once even though she did not hold out much hope of being interviewed. In all the other interviews, when people heard she had a child and was a single mother, they soon terminated the interview. The day of her interview with Mr Wallace, she applied some light make up, something she had not done for months. She looked critically at herself in the mirror in the bedroom—a bedroom a friend had offered to her when she was literally homeless. Now, as she looked at herself, she thought she looked all right, considering what she had been through in the past couple of years. She knew she looked too thin but there was nothing she could do about her weight loss. She just hoped that she would not look as if she would be unable to cope with a girl of four years of age.

The fact that she had good references from both her previous employer and her minister gave her a degree of confidence. After all, she had worked as a nanny for a young professional couple before her marriage and had close dealings with young children at her local church and Sunday school. The man that was going to interview her lived in the same town as she did. His address on the letter she received from him asking her to come for an interview told her that. She knew the area quite well; it was renowned for being the most prestigious district for miles around.

On the afternoon of the interview, Monica had taken the local bus across town and got off at a stop she thought would be near where this gentleman, Mr Wallace, lived. She found Circular Road without any problem and made her way along the footpath while looking for number 10. It was quite an imposing house, Monica thought briefly, as she made her way to the door to ring the bell. She knew she was much too preoccupied to notice anything—she was only thinking of her interview.

She was taken aback when the door was opened in response to her ringing because the person who stood there was not like an elderly gentleman as had been advertised. This man, although not in the first flush of youth, was certainly not what she would have termed elderly. Elderly surely meant someone at least sixty years of age. This man who had just opened the door looked to be no more than forty to forty-five years old.

"Mr Wallace?" Monica enquired hesitantly and then went on more confidently, "I have an appointment for an interview at three o' clock today." She did her best to appear calm and professional. She needed to be successful here today.

"Yes, you must be Mrs Scott, please do come in." He smiled in a welcoming manner. "If you just follow me down the hall to the second door on the right there." He closed the front door quietly behind her then, indicating the door at the end of a large formal hallway, led the way a few steps to where Monica was to be interviewed and from where she would learn by letter three days later that she had been successful. Also, in the letter he asked her to come back to meet his daughter and he would then show her the accommodation she would occupy.

8

She had no way of knowing, when she took up the offer of looking after Jennie Wallace, how much she would need the refuge of the annexe he had told her was hers for the duration of her employment.

Chapter 2

After he had shown Monica Scott to the front door and reassured her that he would let her know in a few days if she had been successful, Edward Wallace returned to his study where he had interviewed her a short time ago.

He sat down on the seat by the window which overlooked his rear garden, but he wasn't really noticing his shrubs or lawn, he was thinking about the girl he had just interviewed. From the moment he had opened his front door and saw her standing there, he sensed a vulnerability about her and some sense of grief pervading her. She was however very composed throughout the interview and when he asked if she had any dependents, her appearance seemed to become more alive and she replied to his question with a smile on her face, "I have a son, he is seven years old," she hesitated and then went on, "but I was made homeless a short time ago. You see, my husband was killed almost two years ago in a horrific road traffic accident, a drunk driver was responsible. So any savings we had were soon used up."

She gave a loud sigh and her voice trembled as she went on, "So I have had to put him in a children's home—until I have found a job, that is. So, it is very temporary." She hurried on, "I have proof I was married; I am not just a single mother I am widowed, Mr Wallace." And she withdrew a large brown envelope from her handbag. "This is my husband's birth certificate and death certificate." Monica was having difficulty keeping her composure.

Edward Wallace took the brown envelope from her and then handed it back to her without opening it. "I believe you, Mrs Scott. So please don't ask me to read them, I have your references here," and he indicated the envelope Monica had given him earlier in the interview, "I do intend to read these, I assure you." And he smiled reassuringly as he spoke. Then as he rose from his seat, indicating the interview was over, he went on in the same reassuring way, "I will be in touch in approximately four to five days' time, Mrs Scott, certainly no longer."

They left the room together and as he opened the door for her, he asked her how she had travelled for her interview.

"I got a bus across town, there is a bus stop close by and I know there will be one coming along shortly."

"Good, I thought perhaps you had walked here, your address on your letter told me you lived on the other side of town."

"Yes, a friend of mine let me have a room while her other friend, who actually lives with her, is away visiting her mother in England."

As Edward thought back to all that had been discussed between them, he thought of her, a young widow with her son in a children's home. It was a home he knew had a very good reputation. It was run by some Christian Organisation so no doubt the boy would be well looked after. Then he thought of the widow herself. She must be heartbroken, what she had come through following her husband's fatal accident and then being in some accommodation or other which no doubt she would have to leave when her friend's friend came back.

Edward also felt very guilty now that in his advertisement he had said he was an elderly gentleman. It was obvious by the look on Monica Scott's face when he opened the door to her that she was quite taken aback by his appearance. Although he was relieved to know he did not actually have the look of an elderly gentleman as he had quoted in the advertisement, he still felt ashamed that Mrs Scott was, to say the least, puzzled by it all. Perhaps she thought it was a printing error, he certainly hoped so.

However, he assured himself, he had had good reasons for doing what he did. After his last experience of employing someone who turned out to believe that he was really looking for a wife or even a mistress, he wasn't taking that chance again. That same girl had been difficult to get rid of, threatening him with the law and prepared to swear that he had raped her. However, thanks to the help he received from his good solicitor, she had eventually decided he was a lost cause. But he felt guilty now when he thought of Monica Scott—her making a pass at him would, he thought, be very unlikely. There was no doubt Monica Scott seemed to have some qualities he admired.

One other thing he had noticed during the interview, she did not make him feel under pressure to offer her the position out of pity. Apart from that brief spell of speaking about her husband and son, she had remained quiet, calm and factual throughout. He realised she did not want to get the job out of any pity anyone had for her but on her ability and fitness for the job. Indeed, he must write to her tonight, offer her the position and post the letter first thing tomorrow morning. The offer of the position would be based on her experience and he would also state a day and a time suitable for them to meet. She needed to meet his daughter and see the accommodation she would be living in.

Chapter 3

Monica answered Mr Wallace's letter immediately she received his offer of the post of governess for his daughter and confirming his offer of accommodation for her and her son. He said he would need to see her soon to go into some details regarding his daughter, Jennie, and he would show her the annexe of the house which would be her home for the duration of her employment with him. He suggested a day and time on the following week for Monica to come and perhaps she would let him know by return if this arrangement suited her. The meeting next week to finalise everything would be with a view to Monica starting her employment two days later. He also told her that when she came next week, he felt she should move into the annexe the same day in order to be settled in prior to commencing work.

Since getting the letter from Mr Wallace, Monica had carried it around everywhere with her. She just had to keep reading it again and again. Today, she had brought it with her to the second appointment with him. She still found her success hard to believe and she needed the letter just to be sure there was no misunderstanding about her post. Now, as Mr Wallace showed her around his beautiful home, Monica was able to appreciate the whole beauty of the place, the gardens with its array of beautiful flowers, while indoors the soft mellow tones of paint, furnishings and curtains gave the place a very welcoming, comfortable feeling. Today was so different from her first visit when she had been too anxious about the interview to notice anything. As they went from room to room, Mr Wallace explained that he had a housekeeper who lived in and it was she who kept the place spic and span and made him his food.

"She will, of course, clean the annexe regularly too and do some shopping for you when you need it. Her name is Agnes Finlay," Edward paused for a moment and then went on, "I think it might be better for your relationship with Jennie if you were addressed by your Christian name. Mrs Scott sounds very formal, and it is not really formality I want for Jennie." Then he hastened to add,

"But if you have any objections with that, I will go along with her calling you Mrs Scott."

"Oh no, Mr Wallace, I think I too would prefer if she called me Monica." She hesitated, anxious to reassure him, "I know, in Sunday school I was called Mrs Scott but that is a very formal setting, a one-to-one teaching experience is quite different." Monica smiled by way of confirmation.

"That's settled then. Now, when do you go to collect your son from the Melton House?"

"I have arranged to collect him at two o'clock tomorrow afternoon." Monica's face was transformed as she spoke. Edward saw that the mention of her son's name lit up her face and totally transformed her demeanour. He realised that the woman in front of him must have endured some deep heartache with the loss of her husband, when just the mention of her son could remove some of the suffering from her expression.

"Well, I will leave you to settle in. If there is anything you want and if you have any questions, please do come through, I will probably be in my study."

"Thank you for everything, Mr Wallace, and for this lovely annexe, it is so perfect for Christopher and myself."

"Yes, I think it is ideal for you both." And Edward smiled as he made his way out of the annexe. "I will be expecting good results with Jennie, you know."

After Mr Wallace left her, Monica got to her feet and made her way into the kitchen to make some tea before going to ring the Melton House about her collection of Christopher on the following day. She hadn't seen him now for three whole weeks, she had to make do with just ringing the home several times because the Christian Committee didn't agree with people visiting very often, they always told her it upset the young boys and girls. She did let them know she would be collecting him at two o'clock tomorrow. Two o'clock was the time arranged but it seemed such a long time away. The whole evening dragged before her, but she would make herself a leisurely tea and spend some time in the bedroom. She wanted to make sure that everywhere was cosy and welcoming for Christopher and she intended to put his favourite pair of pyjamas on his pillow. All of that should help pass the time. It was a pity she couldn't put his favourite teddy out, he had taken it with him to the home, but she did have his red tartan pyjamas Santa had brought him for Christmas.

Last Christmas had been a very difficult time for Monica, the savings she and Thomas had had were slowly dwindling away and she seemed to have little

14

or no prospects of finding a job despite having applied for several. Thomas had always been so optimistic about their future maintaining there was no way they were going to spend the rest of their lives in a rented house. That is why he had been so eager to save as much as he could but with Monica not working and rent and such like to pay, he never could save as much as he would have liked. And then the accident.

The accident in which a drunk driver came out of a side road when Thomas was returning from his work in his solicitor's office and hit him with such impact that he was flung around the road, narrowly missing another car. He never recovered consciousness and died a week later. He was 32 years of age, and it would be two years in October since the accident. Almost two years of grieving for the loss of her darling husband, worrying about Christopher and his loss and a time firstly of uncertainty and then despair as the money finally ran out and Christopher and she were facing eviction.

But now, things were so much brighter for her and her son and she believed that Thomas was smiling down, happy for her success.

Chapter 4

Melton Home was situated in four acres of grounds off the Hill Brook Road in Lisburn. It was a true Georgian house with its unique front door and deep sash windows. It was approached by a wide sweeping drive which was so pale and bare that it gave the whole place a sense of desolation and emptiness. It was only when someone stepped inside that there was any feeling of welcome permeating the place. The main hallway was very large and airy, and a magnificent sweeping mahogany staircase was the centre piece of the whole room. Several soft aged settees were placed against the walls which gave the place a sense of comfort and timelessness.

Several doors led off to various rooms. There was a reception room, an office, dining room and a communal playroom. This afternoon there was an important meeting in the Melton Home, Jill knew two men from the very top of the Christian Committee were coming out at two o'clock to discuss some of the children and their progress and future. That was as much as she knew, she was only filling in for Mrs Foster, the matron who had rung this morning to say she was sick and asking if Jill would sort out the meeting for her. So here, Jill was in the office, she had just set out carafes of water and glasses on the table. She had put the children's register on the desk and placed immediately and pens beside it. She also had a sealed envelope which Mrs Foster had told her to give to the senior man when he arrived.

She just hoped everything would be all right as she had never had direct dealings with these men before. It had always been Mrs Foster who had to spend time with them when they came, which was quite infrequently. They seemed to leave all the running of the place to the matron and the staff. So, the fact they were coming today when Mrs Foster wasn't here would be the very first time that Jill could remember.

She heard the car arrive at exactly the time they had arranged but then they were always very punctual, and Jill often wondered how they always managed it. As she opened the front door for them, she put a welcoming smile on her face, greeted them by name and then quietly directed them to the office where she had everything waiting for them.

"Mrs Foster, is she joining us?" Mr Baird asked as he opened the envelope and examined the contents.

"Oh, I am sorry, Mr Baird," Jill hastened to tell him, "Mrs Foster is unwell this morning and unable to come in. I am deputising for her." Jill indicated the letter. "I think she explains everything in there that is what her husband told me this morning when he brought the letter to me."

Mr Baird did not answer Jill immediately, just pulled out a seat and sat down and indicated that Mr Jenkins, his partner, and Jill do the same. Then he looked directly at Jill for the first time. "And your name is?"

"My name is Jill Corken and I have been employed here for three years," Jill answered. Mr Baird had obviously no idea who she was. "I am employed as a carer here." And she indicated the playroom across the way and the dining room.

"You know the children well then?" Mr Baird asked.

"Oh yes, very well," Jill replied.

"I see from this list we have only five going from here, three boys and two girls." Mr Baird indicated the letter laying on the desk beside him, "Is that right?"

"Going? Going where, Mr Baird?" Jill was astonished by what this man was saying. She had had no mention of the children going back to their parents or going to any other home for that matter. "I don't think any of the children are moving at present, I am sure of that."

Mr Baird looked at her questionably and then he gave a little laugh and a strange sort of secretive smile and went on, "Oh, we are sending some of the children for a couple of weeks' holiday by courtesy of a kind benefactor and Mrs Foster has given me names of those who would be most suitable; it is all here, in this letter. Their ages range from four years to nine years."

Jill was dumbfounded with this information; why on earth had Mrs Foster not told her about this turn of events? "A holiday, I didn't know." Her voice she knew sounded quite hoarse.

"We wanted it to be a surprise for the children." Will Baird was secretly congratulating himself on thinking so quickly about a holiday. Obviously, Mrs Foster had confided in no one about this development in the children's welfare.

"Mrs Foster has written five names here, Ms Corken. One boy aged nine, one aged seven and one other aged five. She says it is important that two of the boys are not separated as the five-year-old depends on one of the other boys so much. The two girls are younger, both four-year-old." Will Baird studied Jill closely as he continued speaking, "I will leave it with you to let the children know to get their belongings together. They will be collected around 6am tomorrow morning, as far as I know." And now Mr Baird seemed in a hurry to close the meeting indicating to his colleague that the meeting was over. "If there is any change in the arrangements, we will let you know, Miss Corken."

"Where are they going on holidays, Mr Baird? I need to be able to tell their parents if they visit or ring up," Jill said and then went on, "unless of course Mrs Foster has already told the parents about the holiday." Jill was hopeful that this was indeed the case, otherwise the parents would be calling, knowing nothing about this holiday.

"Well, I really can't answer that." Will Baird sounded abrupt and quite cross, he realised, but he just wanted to get away from Melton Home, he didn't need any more questions.

"This holiday has just been decided and arrangements completed for tomorrow morning. So even Mrs Foster would not have known much about it especially where it was going to happen." He put a huge smile on his face but, Jill thought briefly, that his smile did not seem to reach his eyes.

"We will leave you to tell the five children the good news. They will be delighted; I am quite sure. They would never have been on a holiday before." And with that, Will Baird proceeded out of the office with Mr Jenkins meekly following him. Jill brought up the rear and after seeing them off the premises proceeded to go and find the children and tell them about this holiday. It was only as she was climbing the stairs to begin the task of getting five children organised with some of their belongings, she realised that Mr Baird had not answered her question as to where exactly the children were going on holiday. What clothes she was going to put together for these five children when she didn't even know where they were going?

At the same time, the children concerned only possessed a few garments anyway. Indeed, she might have to supplement them a little to make sure they were respectable and, even more important, clean and comfortable.

Chapter 5

Monica did not sleep well on the first couple of nights in her new apartment. She was so excited about seeing Christopher again and bringing him home here. Several times during the night, she switched on the small lamp which sat on the bedside table separating Christopher's bed from hers. Eventually, she had to resort to her old trick of counting sheep in order to try and fall asleep. Then she awakened suddenly, the June summer sun streaming in through a chink in the curtains, and on looking at the clock, Monica realised it was nine o'clock in the morning. She was glad she was not starting work this morning as she would be arriving late for her work, and how would that have looked on her very first day? Now, as she slipped her feet into her slippers and pulled her dressing gown around her, she found she was looking forward to meeting Mr Wallace's daughter. It was he who had suggested they wait until Christopher was with her before she should meet Jennie. Monica thought this gesture of Mr Wallace was very considerate of him and suggested to her he must be a real family man.

She spent part of the morning tidying Christopher's and her bedroom and cleaning the kitchen and bathroom. She intended to leave early to collect Christopher because she wanted to shop for some groceries before collecting her son. She had just finished writing her shopping list when there was a knock on the kitchen door. When she opened it, a grey-haired, plump lady with the deepest blue eyes Monica had ever seen stood there. She smiled openly at Monica.

"May I come in? I am Mrs Finlay. Edward said he had told you all about me."

Monica smiled back as she opened the door wide and nodded. "Yes please, Mrs Finlay, do come in. My name is Monica Scott." Monica indicated the lounge. "Let's go into the easy seats. Would you like a cup of tea or coffee? Mr Wallace left some provisions in for me until I get to the shops." A thought struck Monica, "Was it you who left the pie and all the other provisions?"

"Yes, it was me." Agnes Finlay sat down on the seat by the window. "On Edward's instructions, of course. He is a very thoughtful employer, I can tell you,

Monica. Both of us are so lucky to have found a job with him." Agnes looked around the room as she spoke. "You have the place very tidy. Edward would like that—he is a very tidy man himself."

"Well, this apartment is such a pleasure to tidy, Mrs Finlay, it is so lovely and cosy and so suitable for my son and myself," Monica replied.

"Tell me about your son, Monica," Agnes said, and Monica knew by her expression and tone of voice that Mrs Finlay knew she was a widow.

"My son is called Christopher. He was seven years of age just last November. He normally attends Brownlee School, but for the past four weeks he has been in a temporary children's home as I had no house for him until now. So today I go and collect him from the home at two o'clock." Monica's voice broke as she spoke.

Although Agnes knew Monica was close to tears, she answered her in a cheerful voice, "Isn't that wonderful," and she smiled warmly as she spoke. "I'll look forward all afternoon to meeting him. Boys of that age are so manly I think, don't you, Monica?"

Monica smiled gratefully at this woman who had so quickly found a place in her heart.

"Right, tea or coffee, Mrs Finlay?"

"I will have tea and one of those digestive biscuits I bought for you yesterday, and please just call me Agnes, as I will always call you Monica."

"Alright, Agnes it is then." Monica made her way into the kitchen to make the drinks. She was back shortly with a tray containing two cups of tea and a plate of biscuits which she placed on the dining room table. Agnes rose and joined Monica at the table where they sat in companionable silence having their tea and biscuits.

"What time did Edward ask you to come through to meet Jennie this afternoon?" Agnes asked as she set her coffee cup back onto the tray.

"He told me to come into him at three o'clock and then I start work with her tomorrow morning."

"What will Christopher do?"

"Mr Wallace said Christopher should join Jennie and me for some lessons to keep up to date. He thought it would be a good way for the two children to get to know one another." Monica went on, "I know school is out for the summer, but I was glad to hear Mr Wallace wants to include Christopher in the lessons as he is a bit behind in his school. And Mr Wallace tells me Jennie is too."

Agnes was tempted to tell this girl sitting before her what she knew of Edward Wallace's marriage and subsequent divorce and his nightmare experience with his last governess. But she decided not to, it sounded a bit like malicious gossip, and she felt she would be disloyal to Edward by telling his problems.

"I agree, Monica, Jennie needs to concentrate a bit more than she does and perhaps working with your son will help her do just that." Agnes rose from her seat. "I'd better go and get some work done, but thanks to you, I have nothing to do in here." Agnes made her way to the back door of the kitchen. "But please do not think you always have to have it spic and span. I will give it a thorough cleaning every week for you. And if at any time you can't get out to the shops, just let me know what you need." Agnes hesitated on her way out. "I'll see you very soon and your son too, of course, Monica. I look forward to that and all the best in your new post."

"Oh, thank you, Agnes." Spontaneously, Monica went over and threw her arms around Agnes. "It is so lovely to meet you," she said with deep feeling.

"And you too, dear," Agnes said gruffly on her way out, raising her hand in a goodbye.

Chapter 6

It was a beautiful warm June afternoon and the sun beat down on Monica's face as she made her way to the bus stop. She looked up at the town clock as she waited at the stop, it showed one-thirty and Monica knew the bus must be along shortly to take her to be reunited with her son. The journey was a merely fifteen-minute ride to the stop nearest the Melton Home.

As Monica alighted from the bus and began the short walk to the home, she realised she would be a little bit early to call for Christopher. But if he wasn't ready to go when she called, she wouldn't mind waiting in the hall. Somehow, she didn't know why, she'd prefer to wait inside the home and put in the time there as lingering about the Hillbrook Road or the Melton Drive until two o'clock.

A young, slim, fair-haired woman opened the door in response to Monica's ringing the bell. Monica had noticed the girl on a couple of occasions when she had visited Christopher, but she'd had no dealings with her. The girl was smiling brightly at her as she greeted her with a brief hello.

"I'm Mrs Scott," Monica said, "I am here to collect my son, Christopher. I am taking him out today."

"Please come in, Mrs Scott, my name is Jill Corken."

"I haven't actually met you before although I've seen you working hard around here," Monica said as she stepped into the hall.

"Mrs Foster is off sick at present, so I am standing in for her. We will just go into reception, and I'll have a look at Christopher's record for you." Jill Corken was at a loss as to how to handle this situation. This lady had arrived at the Melton Home expecting to take her child out of here, but he had been collected some eight hours earlier and taken on a holiday. Where to, Jill had no idea. She had tried ringing Mrs Foster several times this morning but could get no reply, she must be in bed still feeling sick. She had even tried to contact Mr Baird but was told by the receptionist of the Christian Community Centre Head Office that he was unavailable. Now this dilemma. She had to be totally honest with this woman now standing before her.

"There has been a bit of a misunderstanding, Mrs Scott." Jill looked directly at the woman. "The truth is Christopher has been sent on a bit of a holiday with four other children this morning." She went on quickly, "I think it is for a couple of weeks, but it was all arranged by Mrs Foster, and she is, as I have just said, off sick at present. I did try ringing her several times, but I got no answer."

The despairing expression on Monica's face was quite frightening to Jill. "Please, try not to be alarmed, Mrs Scott, it is only a short holiday, I am sure," by way of reassurance Jill went on, "There was just the five of them and Christopher was chosen because little Joe Totten is very attached to Christopher and Mrs Foster didn't want to separate them." Jill sensed that Mrs Scott was relaxing a little. "Christopher is very kind to Joe and looks after him all the time you know," she added quickly. "So I am sure they will have a good time. I know it is disappointing for you that you aren't taking him home but perhaps you could ring later. Meantime, I will try and find out where they have gone. Perhaps then you could go and see him there, if it isn't too far of course."

Monica stood quietly looking at the girl in front of her. She was so shocked at all she had just heard that she could scarcely take it all in. She just knew Mrs Foster had known when she was coming to take Christopher home. So, could she not have sent someone else in his place on this holiday? But then he went with his friend Joe. And now when Monica thought of him, of how good Christopher was with his young friend, some of her tension eased and she partially understood why her plans had been overlooked.

"I did not know they gave the children holidays," Monica continued. "I did not read anything about holidays in the information I have about the home."

"Maybe it is just a new idea, Mrs Scott." Jill hurried on, "Well I have been here three years, and this is the first holiday any of the children have had since I came. I am sorry for your disappointment, but I will be in touch as soon as I know anything of their whereabouts. If you ring me tomorrow morning hopefully, I will know something then." As an afterthought, she asked Mrs Scott if she would like some tea, she looked so cold and still. The information she had received this morning about her son must have been such a dreadful shock for her.

Monica replied, "No thank you. I will just return to my apartment, and I shall definitely ring you tomorrow."

Chapter 7

"Joe, don't be wandering off on me, sure you won't?" Christopher tightened his hold on Joe's hand as he spoke, "Miss Corken told me this morning to look after you and take care of you. That is what I need to do, Joe."

"This is a big boat, isn't it, Christopher?" Joe spoke in a quiet tone and Christopher had to bend over to hear him. "I have never been on a boat. Have you?"

"No Joe, I never have. My dad took Mum and me to Newcastle twice for holidays and we stayed in a caravan. But on a boat, never." Christopher said, "So this is going to be a good holiday I think, don't you?"

"As long as you stay with me, Christopher but I'd rather my granny was here with us. Why could she not have come too, Christopher?"

"I'd rather my mum was here too, Joe, but I suppose if the home is sending us then they wouldn't want our mums and grannies." Christopher looked around the ship as he talked to Joe. Although he had never been on a ship, he knew Joe, he and the other children were in the deck of one now. He had seen boats and ships in story books and read lots about them. But he never thought they'd be such a size, big enough to make him feel a bit scared. But he must not let Joe know that, because he knew Joe was very timid and easily frightened and Christopher being scared might scare Joe even more.

It was only yesterday evening after they had had their tea and had gone up to their dormitory to get ready for bed that Miss Corken had told them about the holiday they would be going on the very next day. She had then insisted that they must go to bed early because they would have to be up and ready to go at six o'clock in the morning.

"Two girls and a boy of nine from the other dormitory will be going too, Christopher, so you will all meet up in the dining room in the morning." Jill Corken was anxious to make this outing as organised as possible for the five children, "And Christopher, I want you to look after Joe at all times, will you do that?" Christopher looked over at his friend Joe sitting ever so quietly on his bed.

"I'll do that alright, Miss Corken, I will," then he added, "Does my mum know I am going?"

Jill hesitated for a moment, "I am not sure if Mrs Foster told her or not, but I will let her know, don't worry, Christopher."

Christopher slept soundly that night and the morning came so soon they found it very hard to try to get out of bed, but Miss Corken had been so kind and calm about everything, helping them wash and dress and then carry their bags down to the dining room. Then she had gone back upstairs to help the two girls and the other boy with everything before joining Christopher and Joe. All the time telling them how lucky they had been to be picked for a holiday.

She gave them toast and orange juice insisting they were not going anywhere without something to eat, especially so early in the morning. And now here he and Joe and the others were on this huge ship and Christopher wondered where they could be going. Maybe being on the ship was just going to be part of their holiday. It seemed hours ago since they left the home in a small bus which had arrived so early this morning for them with a kind man helping them out with their bags and into the bus. He explained in a softly spoken voice that they would be going to a boat but on their way there, they would be stopping to collect other children who were going on holiday too.

They stopped at a couple of places and eight children from one big house had boarded the bus with a lady who seemed to be helping them. Then they stopped again outside another huge house and four children and a man came over and climbed up the steps and sat down. The man then helped them put their bags in the racks above them and went over to a seat beside the lady and man who had helped earlier.

Now, this evening, Christopher was glad Miss Corken had made them the toast for they had had nothing to eat since and he was very hungry. But the man who had driven them here, who seemed to be their carer had told Christopher a short time ago they would be going for something to eat very soon. As Christopher was beginning to wonder when exactly they would eat, the kind man appeared beside them and he told all the children he had collected that day in the minibus to come with him.

"We are going to join the children you see over there," and he indicated two other groups Christopher had noticed earlier, "and we will be going into a dining room to have something to eat. Later I will show you where your cabins will be," and he smiled reassuringly at them and then roughening Joe's head of blonde hair he said, "I know you like to be with this young fellow here so I will make sure you are not separated from him. Now," he went on, "let's go in and get some food."

Joe and Christopher had plates of sausages and chips which were piled quite high and afterwards they were given drinks of juice and a jam bun. Then when they were shown to a cabin with two bunk beds in it and Mr McGrath had left their bags and clothes in the cabin, Christopher decided they were going to have a great holiday, and said so to Joe, who nodded in agreement as he climbed into the top bunk, claiming it as his. Then, on Christopher's orders, he sought out his pyjamas from his bag and Christopher did likewise. Soon the gentle swell of the boat in the calm waters had lulled the boys to sleep.

Chapter 8

"Oh Mrs Finlay—I mean Agnes—I know I should be happy for Christopher being chosen the way he was for this holiday and especially being trusted to look after another young child, but…" Monica had difficulty telling Agnes Finlay about her afternoon, she was just so disappointed and upset that she did not have her son by her side and she knew she probably would not see him for another couple of weeks. "I was so wanting him here with me, I know I should be grateful, but I can't help how I feel." Monica put her head in her hands and sobbed, loud wracking sobs which shook her whole body.

"Monica, it is such a disappointment for you, I would know that." Agnes sat beside her and held her close. "Why on earth did someone not let you know about this? It would have made everything much easier; I believe it would. Surely somebody knew about it?" Agnes thought about how Monica looked forward to bringing her son home only to be told he was away on holiday; Agnes thought the girl had been treated very shabbily but she would not upset her anymore by saying so. But when she looked at Monica Scott, she did feel very angry about it and would just love to go to that home and say how she felt. But she couldn't do that, Monica Scott was priority for now and she must be encouraged to renew her optimism and look forward to seeing her son very soon.

"I am going to make some tea, Monica, and then later I will bring you a plate of dinner." Agnes gave her a quick hug. "I am quite sure you could not face making anything, so don't you worry about it. And do you know?" Agnes continued in a firm voice, "having Jennie to look after and to teach will be good and the time will soon pass and then you'll see your son again." Agnes gently removed her arm from Monica's waist and went into the kitchen to make the tea and get some biscuits. When she came back into the lounge, she was relieved to see Monica seemed much brighter and managed to smile as she accepted the tea and biscuit Agnes gave her.

When Monica spoke again, her voice was much stronger, "Do you know, Agnes, I am really looking forward to working with Jennie tomorrow. I love children, you know. And it will keep my mind off everything until Christopher is safely back." She added more soberly, "I do wish I knew where he was, but Miss Corken told me to ring tomorrow and she would let me know, that is if she is able to get in touch with Mrs Foster, the matron. Did I tell you the matron was off sick and that is why I wasn't told?"

"Yes, you did tell me that, Monica, and I hope she will be back when you do ring, and you will be able to talk to her personally without having to get indirect messages."

"Oh Agnes, you have been so kind, and I am looking forward to everything here, especially with my darling Christopher."

Agnes smiled, "That's the spirit. I too am looking forward to your company my dear. Now this evening, after I bring you dinner, you need to have a relaxed night, and I will see you in the morning."

Monica wakened suddenly and she thought she had overslept but was relieved when she looked at her bedroom clock to see it was only seven o'clock, she had a few hours to have breakfast and prepare for the day looking after young Jennie. She was quite amazed this morning that she now accepted so easily that Christopher was on a holiday with some other children. Monica now felt it might be better if she had a few days alone with Jennie in order to get to know the little girl and for Jennie to get accustomed to her. Probably her son's holiday would only last a week, she did hope so. Anyway, she would be ringing Miss Corken later today to find out exactly where the children were. Then she would be able to content herself, settle into her new job, get to know Jennie, and look forward to Christopher coming home.

The day flew by for Monica, she found Jennie to be a sweet, timid child who nevertheless seemed keen to learn and hung on Monica's every word. This endeared Jennie to Monica, and they quickly developed a rapport between them. When lessons were over it was lunch time, then the afternoon was taken up by spending an hour in the playroom, building blocks, and making cut outs of paper dolls and their clothes as creativity seemed to be of great interest to the little girl. After that the two of them went outside for a walk in the wonderful grounds of the house and here Monica did her best, although her knowledge of plants was limited, to teach her pupil the names of the flowers she herself knew. Tomorrow then she would spend some time drawing the flowers and teaching Jennie how to spell the names of the simpler ones. They were so intent on watching a huge bee circling a bunch of beautiful white daisies that neither of them heard Mr Wallace approach.

"So, this is where you are then, Jennie?" When Monica looked up and saw her employer standing smiling, she was somewhat relieved.

"I thought I should try to teach her the names of some flowers, this is such a beautiful garden, but I only know a few myself," she explained.

"I have gardening books in my study, Monica, I will look for an elementary one this evening, that may help you." He smiled broadly at her now, "that is a good idea you have, to get her interested in nature." He went on as he looked at his watch, "It is now some ten minutes after four and as I always spend time with Jennie before tea, ending your day around four will suit us fine."

"Thank you, Mr Wallace... I mean, Edward." Monica hesitated over the name. "I need to find out where my son has gone for his holidays," she hesitated, "Agnes told me she would tell you the latest on Christopher."

"Yes, she did, Monica. It is just a pity someone did not let you know he had been chosen to go." Then he went on, "But he will be back soon I am sure, and you will be well settled in by then."

"Thank you for everything. Edward." Then Monica bent down and hugged Jennie telling her she would see her in her school in the morning. Later that evening, Monica learnt from Miss Corken that the children were in the South of England, in Southampton no less, and would be away for two weeks.

29

Chapter 9

"Joe, Mr McGrath has just told me we will be getting a train this morning. He said we are in Liverpool." Christopher had no idea where he was or where this place, Liverpool, was either, but Mr McGrath—he had told Christopher his name a couple of days ago—had told him if he or Joe needed anything and couldn't find him to just ask somebody.

"Mr McGrath says we are going by train to a seaside place, he thinks it will be our holiday place, somewhere called Southampton." Christopher began helping Joe get his pyjamas, toothbrush and flannel back into his bag. "But he says to look on the train ride and the boat we have been on as part of our holiday, Joe." Christopher proceeded to gather up their two bags. "We are to go and get our breakfast. Mr McGrath says he will wait for us and the other children on the deck and take us to the dining area, then he says we will be heading for the train." Then as they were walking along the deck a thought came to Christopher. "Have you ever been on a train, Joe? I have a couple of times to a place named Cork to see my granny and grandpa."

Joe tightened his grip on Christopher's hand and said softly, "No, I never was." He shook his head, "I have just been in the home for as long as I can remember. I have never been anywhere else."

"Oh, this is great, Joe, this is great, you'll love it. I tell you you'll love it. I know I did." Chris pulled Joe closer. He hadn't known that Joe had been in the home for so long. He did know he had been there for some time but to think he could not remember being anywhere else was so sad. He was about to repeat how much Joe would enjoy the train ride when he spotted Mr McGrath standing with some of the other children waiting for them.

Tom McGrath stood quietly with the children, still all excited about the new novel holiday they were going on. They were all lovely children and had been quiet and very obedient since he had picked them all up yesterday morning. Was it only yesterday morning they had set out on their travels? Yes they were good children, but as he watched the two young boys cross over the deck of the boat to join them, he realised that the elder boy, Christopher, had impressed him and earned a place in his heart more than any of the others. Whether it was the way the boy looked after his smaller friend so well and was so alert and attentive to his needs, or whether it was his very gentle way and good manners which appealed to him. It was probably a combination of everything Tom thought, and now he smiled warmly at them as they approached him.

"Right, all together, children, follow me into breakfast, the lady and other gentleman who were with us yesterday won't be with us for the rest of the holiday. It will just be me, so make sure to stay close."

Tom McGrath had been asked on several occasions by the Christian Committee to accompany children on various trips, to hospitals or to schools and even for day trips to the seaside but never on such a trip as this. And certainly not to meet up with other children from the Sisters of Melbourne Home, as he had been told on this occasion. He had been told to accompany them as far as Southampton and then someone else would take charge. This expedition was a very unusual one and he felt a great sense of unease when he thought about it and looked at these delightful children waiting expectantly for their breakfast. They seemed to be looking forward to the train rides, he could hear some of them whispering excitedly about it all. He did wonder where on earth they were going in Southampton, but he supposed there would be plenty of youth hostels for them and there was plenty of water and sand for them to play in.

The arrangement was that he would take the children outside the train station and there they would be met by another minibus and the children would be transferred from him to another carer. Then Tom's job would be done, and he was to return by train and boat, just the same way he had come. Then he must report back to the superiors in the Christian Committee to let them know how everything had gone.

Chapter 10

"To England, for a holiday, Miss Corken? My goodness!" Monica's voice sounded shrill and sharp, even to her own ears, but she had never expected this. She held the public telephone closer to her ear, dimly aware that someone else was now waiting outside to use it. "How long will the children be away for? I need to know that. And where on earth will they be staying?"

Jill Corken recognised the anxiety in Monica Scott's voice and knew she must do what she could to placate her but her own knowledge about this holiday was so limited.

"Mrs Scott, the children will be back home here in Melton Home in a couple of weeks I understand. I was speaking to one of the members of the committee this morning and although unfortunately she did not have much detail about where exactly they were staying, she was able to tell me the duration of their holiday and that they were in England, just as I have told you."

"Thank you, Miss Corken. I shall ring you again of course, I really would like to know where exactly in England my son is. You see, I'd like to write to him."

"Of course, you would, Mrs Scott, perhaps if you ring here in a couple of days' time, I will know more but sometimes the committee members are difficult to contact and also unfortunately Mrs Foster is not back, or she might know more or be able to find out exactly when the children will be back. But I will ring the committee again until I find out."

Jill Corken did not want to say that Mrs Foster had sent in a doctor's certificate stating that she was unwell and would not be able to return to work for a couple of weeks. She did not want Mrs Scott to know that in case she'd be even more distressed. Jill knew herself that she had to find out from the committee where exactly the children were. Monica said her goodbyes and left the phone booth, acknowledging the lady outside the kiosk with an apology for keeping her waiting. On her way back to Circular Road, Monica decided she needed to do some shopping and as tomorrow was Saturday and she did not have Jennie to look after at weekends she would buy herself a paper and a couple of magazines. She would really like to sit out in Edward Wallace's beautiful garden and enjoy the sight and smell of the flowers and shrubs which flourished in it. She was very tired when she arrived back at her apartment and decided to just heat a couple of sausage rolls, she had bought. She had just put them in the oven when she heard Agnes's voice outside her kitchen door saying, "May I come in, Monica?" Just the sound of Agnes's cheerful voice was enough to dispel Monica's sadness. She went over and opened the door to her new friend. "Well, Monica, did you find out any more about your son's holiday? How long are the children away for?"

Monica went over and switched the oven off, she would have the sausage rolls later, and she began to fill the kettle for tea before answering Agnes, "The children, it seems, are away for two weeks so I have to be patient, Agnes." Monica smiled and went on, "I'll make a cup of tea for us and I will tell you what I know." Monica busied herself making the tea and carried it to the table with a couple of currant buns she had bought during her shopping trip. Then she related to Agnes what Jill Corken had told her, "She tells me they are on holiday in England somewhere, she thinks it is Southampton, probably in a youth hostel there but she suggested I call again in the next couple of days. She hopes to know the exact youth hostel then and I hope so too. I would like to write to Christopher."

Monica went on in a more dejected tone, "I just want to see him. I just want him here. I haven't seen him for almost four weeks now. They did not recommend visiting very often you know; it might upset him they said." Monica burst into tears as she tried to convey to Agnes her feelings. Between sobs she went on, "It will be six weeks by the time I see him next." She looked at Agnes, "I should be grateful, I know, that he is having a holiday and it is probably selfish of me to want to have him here with me."

Agnes rose from her chair and reached over and gave Monica a tight hug, "Of course, it isn't selfish, my dear, it is totally natural." Secretly Agnes thought it was shameful that the home had not informed the parents of this holiday. She thought to overlook such a thing was very negligent or else they just couldn't be bothered to do so, probably thinking the parents were quite insignificant in the lives of the children.

"Come and sit on the sofa, Monica." Agnes led her over and sat her down on the comfortably squashy seat. "There that's better than that hard-backed seat." Agnes handed her a cup of tea. "Now drink up, Monica. I will stay a while. As you know, Edward and Jennie are away so I am free for the weekend. I see you got yourself a couple of magazines. Oh, and a newspaper. The Newsletter, my favourite paper, although I only manage to get it sometimes." Agnes lifted the magazines and the Newsletter as she talked. "The magazines were a great idea, Monica, a good bit of escapism for you."

Suddenly, Agnes's eyes were drawn to a picture on the bottom half of the newspaper and, as she opened it out, she realised Monica would not have seen it because of the way the paper had been folded. She sat calm and still while she read the article and then she spoke, "Monica, what you said was the name of the lady, the matron, I mean, in the home? The one who is off sick?"

Monica looked over at Agnes and then at the paper in her hand and some dreadful unease seized her. "Mrs Foster, Agnes. Her name is Mrs Foster. Why? Has she been in an accident?" Monica reached tentatively for the paper. As Agnes still held the paper, she read out a headline ever so quietly, "Eleanor Foster, well-known matron of Melton Home has been found dead in her home off Wesley Street in Lisburn. Although police are investigating, foul play is not suspended. A post-mortem is to be held." Silently, Agnes handed the paper to Monica.

Chapter 11

Jill Corken finished clearing up the dining room after getting the children their lunch time drinks of milk and jam sandwiches, and before putting the kettle on for tea for herself and Lily, the other carer. It was the same routine that had been in place since Jill had come here three years ago. When they had their tea, then they must begin to get the two dormitories clean and tidy for the children's bedtime that evening. Jill was glad she was off duty at six o'clock this evening, she was very tired and missing Mrs Foster so much, she felt the responsibility of the home was just too much for her.

Now her thoughts were interrupted by the telephone ringing in the reception office.

She was surprised to recognise Mr Baird's voice at the other end of the phone. She had begun to think he was never going to return her calls.

"Miss Corken?" He asked brusquely.

"Yes Mr Baird, thank you for returning my calls," Jill replied.

"I need to come over to the home this afternoon to speak with you and other carers who are there." He continued, "I will be there within the half hour to the hour." As an afterthought, he went on, "Will that suit you, Miss Corken?"

"Yes Mr Baird, I do not go off duty until 6pm."

Jill set the phone down and went out of the office to tell Lily Mr Baird was coming, although she was a bit mystified about why he was. Surely, he could have told her over the phone where exactly the children had gone on holiday and when they would be back. He really did not need to come and make it all so formal. Indeed, his formality and sense of occasion on his last visit had made Jill feel very uncomfortable. This time he was coming alone, or so Jill thought, as he did not say anyone would be accompanying him. She checked that the office was clean and tidy and that there were chairs for them if he was going to stay for any length of time. She put out a carafe of water and a glass and then placed the children's register centrally on the desk. No doubt he may need reminding of the names of the children who were away on holiday.

On his arrival and before entering the office, he confirmed with Jill that there were just the two carers on duty this afternoon.

"Yes," Jill said, "just Lily and me. Then there are three girls on at night for extra security and four in the morning to get all the work done."

"I see." Mr Baird hesitated and then closed the office door. Then he went on quickly, "I am afraid I have very bad news for you, which is why I thought it best to come myself."

"Bad news?" Jill stumbled over the words, the children, she thought, and the children on holiday, had they been hurt?

Then Mr Baird's words broke in on her thoughts, "Yes, I am afraid I have bad news. Mrs Foster is dead."

"Mrs Foster? Dead, did you say?" Jill queried. She was shocked and Lily too had turned very pale. "Mrs Foster? What happened? I know she was off sick."

"I am afraid her husband found her dead when he arrived home from his work yesterday evening." He hastened on, "I do not have any details yet, but I know someone will need to act as matron in the meantime. So that will be you, Miss Corken, if you are happy to do so. I will also need you to inform the other carers and cleaners, if you would please."

Jill nodded dumbly, dimly aware of what the man was saying. Mrs Foster was dead, had she really been so ill? And she hadn't known? But Mr Baird was still talking.

"I also need you to write to the parents of the five children, one was an orphan I understand, so it will be their relative. Tell them to come here to see me next Monday at 11am." He pulled his diary from his inside pocket and wrote the details in it as Jill and Lily stood shocked and bewildered at this awful turn of events.

"I am sorry to have such news and you must be very sorry to hear it. Mrs Foster was a nice lady." And Will Baird opened the office door, assuring the girls he would see himself out, and before leaving he reaffirmed, he would be there on the Monday morning.

Chapter 12

As Jill slipped into a seat at the back of the church and looked quietly around her, she was taken aback at the number of people present at Eleanor Foster's funeral. The pews were packed with people of all ages, from elderly through to a couple of children, aged around eight or nine, sitting at the front of the church. Jill hadn't known very much about Mrs Foster's private life, she had been a very reserved woman but, in Jill's opinion was an excellent worker in her job and had loved the children in the home so much. She had been in fact, Jill thought, truly devoted to them, her only concern was trying to ensure that each child who came under her wing was truly cared for.

Now to think she had been taken from such an important role in life and from her husband and family was truly heart-breaking. She knew after the service she must have a word with Mr Foster and offer her condolences even though it was something she was not looking forward to. She was afraid she would break down in tears.

After the cortege had made its way out of the church and mourners were beginning to form a queue to speak to Mr Foster, Jill was quite surprised when he seemed to recognise her, and immediately made his way over to her.

He held out his hand to her and Jill grasped it instantly and was about to speak when he said rather hurriedly, "I need to speak with you, Miss Corken. Please come back to my house after the burial, it is important I speak to you in private."

"Of course, I will come," Jill reassured him, he was obviously upset, but of course he was. "I am just not sure where you live."

"No.12 Sycamore Road, it is not far from the church here."

"I know Sycamore Road; it is just around the corner from this church, isn't it? I will be there." And Jill grasped his hand again.

He seemed somewhat relieved and went over to join the mourners gathering to speak to him.

"Miss Corken, I am so glad to be able to speak to you privately for a few moments." Mr Foster had just led Jill to a corner of his dining room where two chairs sat at quite a distance from those in the rest of the room. "I know we have only met on a few occasions when I came to the home, but I did not know who else to talk to." Sam Foster was unable to continue speaking for a moment or two but he regained his composure and went on, "I need to tell you something which is not widely known, and that is that my wife committed suicide last Tuesday evening. She took an overdose of tablets and mixed them with plenty of alcohol."

His tone held such a despairing note that for a moment, what he had just said did not begin to register with Jill, she was so concerned about the man standing in front of her. Then realisation of his words became imprinted somewhere in her head and she automatically put her hands up to her face.

"Oh God, no," she whispered. "Why, why on earth? Oh dear, I am sorry, I shouldn't ask such a question. I am so sorry."

"I thought you could shed some light on the why, Miss Corken. You see, she left a note, I have it here, no one else has seen it only me until now." And Sam Foster reached into his inside pocket and withdrew a piece of paper which he handed to Jill. Jill looked at him dumbly, the note unopened in her hand.

"Please, please, you must read it," he pleaded and Jill silently scanned the writing she knew so well from the children's registers and reports in the home.

My darling Sam, please forgive me but I cannot live with the knowledge of the welfare of the five children I love and cherish so much. I feel the church committee's intentions are so misguided regarding their welfare. I found something out by sheer chance, and I tried my best to stop it but it was all done and covered up. I thought it was just rumour until Jill Corken rang me and asked me where exactly they had gone on holiday. Then I knew I had been cruelly deceived and had left it too late to do anything about any of it. When I think of the mothers of those darling children and what they will suffer, I find I cannot live with myself anymore.

I love you so much, Sam. Your despairing wife, Eleanor.

Jill read the letter twice, still not fully comprehending what Eleanor Foster had been saying.

"I am sorry, I do not know anything about this." Jill said, "Only that I did ring your wife to find out if she knew where five of the children of Melton Home had gone on holiday." Now Jill remembered how distant and preoccupied Mrs Foster had sounded over the phone. "She did seem shocked, now I think about it. She told me very bluntly she did not know anything about the holiday and reminded me she was off duty because she was sick."

"I want you, Miss Corken, to help me get to the bottom of my wife's distress and unhappiness. Distressed enough to take her own life. Please help me, please." His voice now full of emotion.

"A member of the committee is coming next week to talk to the mothers of the children who are on this holiday. I will try to find out where they are and when they are due back and if all is well. I will call back here and let you know as soon as I know," Jill assured him.

"Oh, thank you, Miss Corken. If you find out anything, I will be forever grateful to you." He went on with a stronger tone of voice, "and if there is anything amiss going on, I need to pursue it."

Chapter 13

Jill organised the staff rota in the Home so that she herself would be on duty when Mr Baird met the mothers of the children who were away on holiday on Monday morning. She had thought about little else since that Wednesday when Mr Foster had shown her the letter, which was so obviously a suicide note, which his wife had left. But no matter how she seemed to look at everything, she could not think what on earth the children's holiday and Mrs Foster's suicide was all about. Surely it was only a holiday, and they would be back soon. But why on earth had Mrs Foster taken her own life?

No matter what reasonable explanation Jill came up with, perhaps Mrs Foster had simply been mentally ill, and it had nothing to do with the children. After all they would be back in a few days, but sometimes when she thought about it, she still harboured a great sense of unease and something akin to fear gripped her. She felt the sooner Monday morning came the better.

Mr Baird arrived early and informed Jill he would use the dining room to talk to the mothers of the children.

"How many are able to attend this morning?"

"Just three, Mr Baird. Two others were not able to come today and would like another date."

"After I have seen the other mothers, I will get the address of the other two from you and write to them." He continued, "I would like you to be with me in the dining room. I intend to talk to them one at a time. So, you will need another carer out in reception to look after the mothers who are waiting." He looked steadily at Jill. "Is there another carer available?"

"Oh yes, I will fetch her now." And Jill crossed the hall and quickly climbed the stairs and after locating Lily in one of the dormitories, explained to her she was needed downstairs.

"Just tell one of the other girls Mr Baird is here and you are needed. They won't mind cleaning the rest of the upstairs, I am sure." Jill went on, "Then join me downstairs and I will explain what Mr Baird wants you to do."

Jill recognised Mrs Scott immediately she opened the door. She was accompanied by an older woman who Mrs Scott introduced to Jill as Agnes, her friend, adding that she would like Agnes to meet Mr Baird. Jill reassured her she was sure that would be alright.

"Agnes, I don't think I needed to have worried so much. Another two mothers are here. The man in charge probably just wants to confirm when they all will be home. Or perhaps the Home would like a donation towards their holiday, and now I have a job again I would be happy enough to give something towards it if they need it."

"That might well be the case, I never thought of them needing money, but they probably do like donations, Monica." Agnes looked around the comfortable clean hallway and its beautiful grand staircase and secretly thought it must take some money to maintain a place like it.

"I meant to say to Miss Corken how sorry I was to hear of Mrs Foster's death, and I do wonder what happened to her. She was quite a young woman, I would have thought still in her forties, it is very sad," Monica said quietly.

Before Agnes had a chance to reply, a tall, rather pompous looking man appeared from what seemed to be the dining room and called Monica's name. Monica rose to her feet and indicated that Agnes do the same. They both entered the room that Mr Baird had indicated and waited expectantly.

"Please take a seat, Mrs Scott." And turning to Agnes asked sharply, "And you are?"

"My name is Agnes Finlay," Agnes said firmly, "Mrs Scott asked me to come with her today because she is a bit apprehensive about being called so formally to the Home. When all she wants is to have her son Christopher back home safely from his holiday."

Mr Baird's whole manner seemed to change, and he was no longer the omissive, pompous man she had thought him to be on first seeing him. Now he seemed to shrink a little, his face became pale, and he smiled weakly at them.

"Of course, of course, please do sit down." And he indicated the seats at the table. Then he began looking through some documents sitting on the table and as Agnes Finlay watched him, she imagined he had a shifty, almost guilty look about him. But then he looked up and that look had gone, and he was just the professional again.

"Yes, Christopher Scott, aged seven years of age. Mother's name, Monica Scott. Currently not working and currently living in a room belonging to a friend. Is that correct?" he asked brusquely.

"That was right." Monica was quick to add but to make him aware of her situation now, "I now have suitable accommodation and I know I also have work, so I am here today to establish when exactly I am able to collect my son."

"To collect him, Mrs Scott. To collect him. But that can't be. You gave permission when you first brought him here that if the opportunity arose, you would make way for his adoption." Will Baird rolled his finger under his collar, as if it was too tight.

Monica was now very alarmed and knew she was bordering on becoming hysterical, "Me? Gave permission for adoption? No, never!" She screamed and clutched Agnes's arm. "No, no."

"I am sorry, here are the papers of proof, you see." And he beckoned Jill Corken who had been standing beside him, so silent and so shocked by what she was hearing.

He tried to hand Jill the papers, a gesture she quite purposely ignored. Then she went over to Monica who now was ashen-faced and had a wild look in her eyes.

"I want my son. Get him back to me soon," she muttered several times, all the time holding tightly to Agnes.

"Deal with this lady please," Will Baird ordered Jill, "I have others waiting to see me."

Jill did not answer him but instead concentrated on Monica and her obvious despair.

"We will sort something out for you, Mrs Scott. I am sure it is not too late." Jill opened the French doors which lead to the side path and garden. "Let's go out this way." Taking Monica's arm from where it was placed around Agnes. "We need some fresh air, I think."

Once outside, Jill showed Monica and Agnes to a garden seat and all three sat down, dumbfounded by what they had just heard. Jill was the first to speak, "I intend to find out what exactly is happening here and more importantly, how your son became adopted without your knowledge, Mrs Scott, or without my knowledge either." Jill was finding it quite difficult to find the right words of comfort. "I will do everything in my power to return Christopher to you, I promise you." And Jill held Monica closely to her, "I will keep in touch, but I do need a phone contact." And she turned to Agnes, "Would you have a telephone number by any chance that I could have in order to keep in contact?"

"Monica and I are both working for the same gentleman, so I am quite sure, given the circumstances, he wouldn't mind me giving it to you." And Agnes withdrew a small notebook from her handbag and writing down Mr Wallace's number on one of the pages, tore it off and handed it to Jill.

"Please Mrs Scott, go home with Agnes here and try not to worry." Jill smiled as reassuringly as she could, although secretly she was worried sick.

She turned to Agnes. "Is it possible for you to stay with Mrs Scott for a time this evening and perhaps a warm drink and an Aspirin at bedtime might help her get some sleep." Jill spoke again to Monica, "Please, please know I will do everything to help you," Jill reiterated, she felt so inadequate in the face of such utter despair and disbelief.

Monica nodded briefly in response, too overcome to speak, but she had to believe that Ms Corken would bring her son back to her. Any other outcome was unthinkable.

Chapter 14

The children seemed to love the train journey down through England, certainly for the most part of the time they sat excitedly looking through the windows at all the sights which flashed past so quickly. They appeared awestruck by the squeal of brakes as the train slowed down coming into the different stations. Tom McGrath was himself a real train lover and to see all the children in his care having such a wonderful time touched him greatly.

For the first time since the start of the journey, he was glad he had been appointed to care for these children. Not for the world would he have missed their obvious delight and enjoyment it gave him such a warm feeling of satisfaction and the happy thought that surely everything would be alright for all of them. And he was going to enjoy watching them tuck into the lunch he had bought earlier from the dining carriage, which he had now securely in the cool bag he had brought for the purpose. He had asked David Gillespie—who seemed to be the eldest boy here, and Christopher Scott who was, he noticed, pointing out different objects to his young charge, Joe Totten—to look after the children until he got them some food. He would be back shortly; he reassured the two boys and they had taken his request seriously and everything was fine when he returned. Then they helped him serve the sausages on sticks and the jam sandwiches and drinks of milk for them all, and afterwards, as a treat, they had chocolate marshmallows.

Tom had really enjoyed his time with these children and just wished he could have been scheduled to look after them during their stay in Southampton but the Christian Committee, in fact Mr Baird himself had been insistent that he would meet a replacement carer when he and the children arrived at Southampton Railway Station.

"Please sir, where will we be going to?" It was Christopher Scott who had approached him with his young prodigy, Joe, at his side. "Where is our holiday? Is the train ride our holiday?"

"Oh no, son," Tom answered in a reassuring way and patted the young boy on the shoulder as he spoke, "No, you are going to a place called Southampton, I am quite sure you have never heard of it, Christopher, or indeed young Joe either."

Christopher shook his head vehemently. "No, sir, I've never heard of it."

"Well there is plenty of water and sand for you all to play in and I'm sure you will be in a good hostel and that will be a nice change for you from the home."

"Are you còming with us, Mr McGrath?" Joe spoke up, he had been quietly listening to all Christopher had been asking. Joe liked Mr McGrath, he had been so kind to them and bought them lovely sausages and marshmallows. And he was so cuddly looking Joe felt he would just love to sit on his knee and cuddle into him. But of course, he would never do that, no one only his granny had ever cuddled him. As far as he knew no one else had ever wanted to cuddle him.

"No Joe, I am just sorry that I am not going with you. I would have loved to go but we have to meet someone else when we arrive in Southampton and then they will stay with you." Tom felt that changing the children over to another carer had not been a good idea, it was not good for the children when they were just getting used to him. Who had actually arranged the changeover, Tom had no idea, he knew Mr Baird had given him his rota but that didn't mean Mr Baird had organised the holiday. Whoever had done it didn't have much of an idea of children's welfare. And why on earth had they changed the carers? When he thought about this children's holiday again, he had a deep feeling of unease and he felt suspicious of the whole thing, but why would he feel like that? He must pull himself together and stop imagining things, he really must.

The train pulled into Southampton Station very promptly, at 6 o'clock and Tom marvelled at how trains always managed to be on time. Now he instructed the children to gather up all their belongings and to stay close to him. They would let most other people get off before they ventured to do so.

Soon the children and their baggage were safely offloaded off the train and everything was accounted for, and the children were standing quietly and obediently beside him on the platform. Quietly Tom told them to follow him, and to Christopher and Joe who were leading the queue he said, "Look out for the car park, I was told it is just across the road."

Sure enough, even as they left the station, they could see the gleam of several cars just across the road facing the station. Tom spotted the cream minibus, the same as the one he had parked at the docks in Belfast and would be returning tomorrow. As he looked at it, he felt an awful sense of unease and emptiness inside him and worst of all he felt these lovely children were not having much of a holiday, they were simply being shunted about. He sincerely hoped that the rest of their time would make up for all the travel and all the moving about from pillar to post. For some reason, he would be very relieved when he heard these kids were safely back in their prospective homes, until then he would have to content himself and bury his uneasy feeling.

Chapter 15

"Please sir, why are we going on another ship?" Christopher asked the man who had collected them from the car park and where they had had to say goodbye to Mr McGrath.

When Mr McGrath had left them in the car park and all the children had watched him make his way back into the station to catch the train back to Liverpool, Christopher had a sudden desire to go after him and tell him to bring Joe and him back with him. But of course, he couldn't do that, they were on holiday and the other man standing in the car park was already organising the children into the minibus.

Now they were standing waiting to get onto another ship and Christopher and Joe had been waiting too, hand in hand when the other boy David, from the other dormitory in Melton Home came over to them and said, "Would you ask that man why we are going on another ship? When we thought, we were going to stay here where there is lots of seaside and sand." The boy repeated what he had just said, "Would you ask him, please? Ask him where we are going."

He sounded quite agitated, and Christopher looked kindly at the boy, he thought he must be the same age as he was.

"Of course, I will ask him, but you come with me, will you?"

"Yes, I will come with you, but you talk to him." The boy looked relieved. "My name is David; I know I haven't seen much of you even though we were in the same home. I was only in Melton Home for a week, you know when they sent me on this holiday. Then you seemed to need to look after this boy here," and he indicated Joe. "And I did not like to come over. But now I think we need to know. Let's go over to him. I just want you to ask him why we are going on another ship. We thought we were staying here where there's plenty of seaside and sand."

"Certainly, I'll ask, but you must come with Joe and me."

"Yes, I'm coming too, but you do the talking."

"My name is Christopher," he said to David, "and this is my friend, Joe." Christopher reiterated, as they approached the person who had brought them here.

Now all three children looked up at this man as they waited for the answer to the question David had seemed so anxious for Christopher to ask. The man, who had only spoken briefly to the children as they boarded the minibus in the car park, now looked sharply at the three boys before him.

"What did you say, boy?" his voice sounded gruff and quite unkind as he spoke.

"Please sir, why have we to go on another ship? We thought there was plenty of seaside and sand here. He said we would be staying here in this place."

"Who told you that then? Huh? Who said that?"

"Mr McGrath thought we were staying here, here in Southampton, I think he called the place," Christopher answered hesitantly.

"Well we are not; we have to go a bit further yet." Jack Newell realised no one had told these children in his care where they were going and where they would end up, and he certainly was not going to tell them, that was for sure. They would know soon enough. Anyway, they would probably be far better off where they were going than they would be in Northern Ireland. Besides, they were from children's homes anyway and more than likely, no one wanted them. So yes, they would be better off where they were going.

Now he added in a warmer manner, "We are going a bit further, you will be on this ship for a day or two, but you will like the place when we get there. The sun always shines where you are going and you will see plenty of beaches." He attempted a smile to endorse what he had just said. "For now, enjoy the ship ride and we will make sure you are safe and well fed."

"Thank you, sir," Christopher said and making sure he had a tight hold of Joe's hand, and that David was behind them he made his way back to where he had been standing watching all the activity on the big ship docked close by. And as he looked at it and then down at Joe, Christopher knew that he did not want to go a bit further, as the man in charge had just told them, he would just like to go back to the Home and see the carers who were always so kind to them.

Above all, he longed to see his mum again, he knew she had been coming to see him soon. If he wasn't there she would be saddened, he knew that because after his daddy died, he was the only person who could help her sadness. When she had cried then, he sat close beside her and hugged her ever so tightly until she stopped crying. But now when he thought about this holiday he was sure that the carers would have let his mum know that he was away. If she knew that and knew they would see each other again very soon, she would be alright. Meantime he intended to help Joe as much as he could, he didn't want Joe to say he too would just like to go back home. He thought if Joe said that it would be sure to make Christopher cry and he must never ever let Joe see him do that or be upset. He would also like to be friends with David and then perhaps together, David and he would be able to make Joe happy and then they would be happy too. Anyway, surely, they would not be too long on this ship but would soon be stopping somewhere nice and in no time at all, they would be on their way back home again.

Chapter 16

"Monica, I have arranged an appointment for you at two o'clock today with my solicitor." Edward Wallace looked at his new employee and was pleased to see she was somewhat calmer this morning. Certainly not in the state she had been in yesterday on her return from Melton Home without her son. She had been totally distraught then, weeping continuously, struggling to speak and was totally incoherent. It was only after repeated reassurances from both Agnes and him that she calmed down a little. And no doubt the fact that Agnes had stayed with her all night had helped tremendously.

Edward had made up his mind he would help Monica Scott all he could. He believed she knew nothing about the adoption and had signed no legal paper to agree to it. But getting to the bottom of what exactly had gone on in the Melton Home would take some time. Meantime, she must try to continue in her new role as best she could. In the coming days, that was going to be of vital importance for her if she were to cope with not knowing anything about her son. He desperately needed her to be fit to look after his young daughter. The idea of having to give Monica Scott notice to quit because of her inability to cope and then to have to advertise for someone new was totally abhorrent to him. He knew he would feel very guilty and saddened by the whole business if that was how things turned out.

"Monica, I do hope you will continue with your governess role here with Jennie, I really need you to do that." Edward's voice was gentle but quite firm. But he did not add that it would help Monica too and might take her mind off the appalling situation she was in. He felt that if he said that it would somehow belittle the trauma she was suffering and that was the very last thing he would want to do. Because the grim reality of what had happened without her knowledge was, in his opinion, monstrous.

"I also intend to speak to my doctor. Hopefully, he will order you something which may help you sleep at night." Edward spoke to her in a firm voice, "You must promise to take them, Monica. Getting some sleep at night will help you feel better the next day but if you agree, I also want Agnes to stay with you at night."

Edward looked over at Agnes for agreement to this idea then added quickly, "I would not want you to be on your own at night at present, Monica, even if it is just for a night or two. So please say yes."

"Agnes, I would love you to stay, you are such a comfort to me, you really are. I don't want to be on my own at the present time."

Monica did not add that if she was alone, she would be likely to imagine the worst and that would be that she would never see Christopher again and she could not bear that.

Then she spoke to Mr Wallace, "Thank you for everything that you have done." Monica went on in a steady tone, "Of course I will take a tablet at night, I would be very glad to. And I would also like you to accompany me to the solicitors, I would not want to go alone." Monica just hoped she would not break down in the solicitor's office and she knew she would be less likely to if Mr Wallace was there. "I am sure he will need some details from me about Christopher, how long he had been in the Melton Home and about the supposed signed adoption papers."

Monica's voice wavered and she paused for a moment and then went on, "As for Jennie, in spite of everything, I will do everything I can to teach all the school subjects she will need for the future and to the best of my ability and I will do my utmost to make her time with me a happy one."

"Good, Monica, that is settled then. I do hope this uncertainty is short-lived." Edward continued, "Now regarding your appointment we will need to leave here around one-thirty. The solicitor's office is in the centre of town so the traffic can be a bit heavy at times. So, Monica, if you come through to my hall around that time, we will be on our way."

The solicitor was an extremely pleasant looking man with a thick mop of curly grey hair and sideburns and deep blue eyes. He looked directly at Monica which gave him an air of openness and honesty and Monica warmed to him immediately. Edward introduced Monica and recapped a little about her situation and Mr Dunn listened attentively, at the same time jotting down notes on a page in front of him. When Edward had finished speaking, Monica opened her handbag and handed Mr Dunn an envelope.

"I brought my son's birth certificate, my marriage certificate and my husband's death certificate for you." Monica went on, "Did the Home think I was an unmarried mother and that I could not or did not wish to look after my son? Nothing is further from the truth, Mr Dunn, I love my son dearly, as he does me and I want him back with me." Monica hesitated for a moment and then taking a deep breath, she went on, "Melton Home knew it was only a very temporary arrangement—they definitely knew that. And they also knew that I had obtained accommodation for him and I and I also had been very fortunate to get employment, thanks to Mr Wallace." And Monica gave Edward a warm smile. "I had even arranged a day and time to come for him. Something terrible went wrong, Mr Dunn, were they always planning to do this to Christopher and I?" Monica knew now she could say nothing more without breaking down and she just shook her head vehemently, her hands clasped tightly together.

"Mrs Scott, leave all this with me. I will be writing to the Melton Home and will demand some answers to this very disturbing situation." Mr Dunn paused and then in a compassionate tone went on, "I will hope for everyone's sake that we will be able to halt this business before it is too late. And I will be in touch as soon as I hear anything, Mrs Scott."

Edward rose from his seat then and Monica stood up too.

"Thank you very much, Mr Dunn, thank you." Edward reiterated his thanks and escorted Monica out of the building and into the car where it was parked outside Mr Dunn's office.

They were silent on the way home, a companionable silence but each thinking of Mr Dunn's last words, that he hoped they would be able to halt this chain of events before it was too late.

Chapter 17

Jill had had a very traumatic day in Melton Home after Mrs Scott and her friend had gone Jill had gone back into the office where Mr Baird was sitting behind the desk with another lady, who she recognised as Ms Marks sitting facing him. Lily stood quietly beside the lady who appeared to be quite apprehensive and distressed. And now as Jill began to concentrate on what Mr Baird was saying, she realised the reason for the lady's distress.

He was simply repeating to her what he had just told Mrs Scott, that her daughter Helen had been adopted and that she had signed papers when her daughter was first admitted. Now the lady concerned was on her feet demanding in a loud voice to see the alleged paper signing concerning her signature. In response, Mr Baird slid an official looking document across to her and at the same time asked Lily to show the lady out. Lily allowed the lady time to look at the paper with her signature on it and proceeded to accompany her out.

Jill went over and quietly said, "I will show Ms Marks out, Lily, could you bring Mr Gillespie in please, thank you." And Jill left the office and when she closed the door, she turned to Ms Marks. "Would you like a cup of tea? I will stay with you and have one with you," Jill said. "We will just have it in the kitchen. Have you anyone waiting for you?" she asked. Josie Marks was weeping openly now, but between her tears, she managed to tell her that her boyfriend was waiting out in the car but said she would need some time before she would even be able to give him an idea about what had happened.

After Jill had given her tea and a biscuit, she walked with her to the car where her boyfriend was waiting patiently. Jill introduced herself as she helped Josie into the car and then she said, "Your girlfriend is very upset, she has some rather distressing news to tell you I am afraid. If you wish to speak with me about anything at any time, please ring me. I will do my best to help you, and as I said my name is Jill Corken. Perhaps you might want to write it down in case you don't remember it."

"Oh Neville, the Home has had Helen adopted, they've just told me so. And I don't see how they can I never, ever agreed to it. Oh, Neville what are we to do? And Ms Corken, I will always remember your kindness to me today," Josie intervened shakily.

"Thank you for that, Miss Marks, I am so sorry for your trouble. Please do keep in touch and let me know how you are."

"Yes, I promise I will do that, but I will need to talk to Neville here and see what he thinks."

"Of course, you must. I must go in now; Mr Baird will wonder where I have got to."

And as a last goodbye Jill turned and made her way back into the house. She found Lily tidying up the office, but of Mr Baird and Mr Gillespie there was no sign.

"Where is Mr Gillespie, Lily?" That was Jill's first concern, had he been told the same thing as Mrs Scott and Ms Marks? "Where is Mr Baird?"

"Oh him." Lily's voice was derisive. "He is away back to Belfast and his religious committee, Jill, I don't know how I am going to go on working here after what has happened here this morning." Lily paused and then spoke in a more respectful voice, "If it wasn't for you, Jill, I would be away today, I really would."

"No please Lily, don't, please don't, I need you here. I take it from what you are saying that Mr Gillespie was told the same thing this morning, that his son has been adopted? Is that right?"

"Yes, it is Jill that would be exactly right, the only difference being that David Gillespie left here dry-eyed, his head held high and threatening to take Mr Baird to court for forging his wife's signature and having their son adopted illegally." Now Lily was smiling for the first time this morning, "He wasn't long in gathering up his belongings and heading off, no doubt, I am sure to get some advice."

"So, you are concerned too, Lily, that these parents never signed any such documents, because I know I am," Jill answered.

"Of course, it is all a fraud but no doubt they will get off with it, a religious institution always does." Lily's voice was scathing again.

"Well, I hope they answer for it, Lily, I know if I am ever called to give evidence, I will tell the truth and say that I do not believe any of them signed any such documents. Unfortunately, we cannot even scrutinise them now because he seems to have taken the relevant papers he had with him this morning, back to headquarters."

"Yes, he couldn't wait to gather it all up after David Gillespie threatened him and he left this office rather quickly."

"Well Lily, I believe that Mrs Foster got an inkling about all this before she died."

In light of all that had gone on here this morning, Jill felt compelled to confide in her friend about their matron, "I hate to tell you this, Lily, but Mrs Foster's husband told me that his wife actually committed suicide." Jill hesitated. "It was an awful shock when Mr Foster told me, I could scarcely believe it, she was so dedicated to her work and loved the children. Then he showed me the note she had left, and it inferred that she could not live with what was going on here and what was going to happen." Jill emphasised, "I think she got wind of these illegal adoptions."

"Oh God! This whole thing gets worse by the minute, Jill, it really does. Unfortunately, we don't even have anyone to complain to because our bosses are the culprits, plus we have no evidence of wrongdoing." Lily now sounded quite despairing.

"Let's go get some tea and a slice of toast in the kitchen. Then we best see to the other children in the place and the other two carers, let them go on a break. But we will say nothing about this morning, Lily, in case it might harm the parents' chances in getting their children back. Do you agree?" Jill asked.

"Oh definitely, I don't really want to talk about it anyway, it is just so awful." Lily's voice sounded so sad. Then when she was sitting in the kitchen having their tea and toast a thought struck Lily.

"What about the other mothers who didn't come this morning, Jill? I wonder when they do come, what they will be told."

"I don't know, and Mr Baird did not suggest sending for them but no doubt we will hear soon enough. It's Amy Matthews and Joe Totten who are still away," Jill confirmed as she looked at the register. "And they are just four years of age, it's time they were back home again. Amy's mother and Joe's grandmother will be in touch asking when they are due back."

Chapter 18

During the next few days, Jill thought a lot about the events that had taken place in the home. She thought a lot about Mrs Foster and her death and wondered what exactly she had found out about the children. She knew she had promised Mr Foster she would let him know if she discovered anything, and she did think the adoptions of the children and the fact that their mothers were kept in the dark was totally illegal. Surely what had happened here in this home must be considered criminal and Jill hoped that Mr Gillespie, who had threatened Mr Baird, would carry out his threat.

Since Mr Baird's visit and Jill and Lily having had to deal with the trauma of watching heartbroken parents listen in disbelief what they were being told about their children, Jill had seriously considered leaving her employment and going to the Christian and telling them exactly why. But jobs such as hers were very hard to come by, with most of the Catholic homes only employing Catholics and most of the Christian Committee Ireland wanting only Protestants, so she was very limited at thirty-four years of age and she needed money to pay her rent and to keep herself in food and clothes. Besides, she loved her work, and she loved the children dearly. She knew they all responded so readily to kindness and compassion, so she felt she must stay here and hope that such a nasty incident never happened again.

She just prayed that the children concerned would have happy lives with their adopted parents. She had to try to put it all to the back of her mind and move forward. One thing she still had to do, was to contact Mr Foster and tell him what had happened and what she believed Mrs Foster must have discovered about the children but could do nothing about. She would ring him later today and arrange to visit him.

Even though Jill had been to Eleanor Foster's home on the day of the funeral she had been too upset to take in any of her surroundings. She had only been thinking of Mrs Foster. But today despite everything she had been through, and her latest information about the adoptions and perhaps the relevance of it all to Mrs Foster, she was able to appreciate the area she was walking in.

The avenue that Mr Foster lived in had an almost village feel to it Jill thought, with the trees lining both sides and extending the whole length of it. Every house Jill passed was of red brick design with well-tended gardens, displaying rows of lovely roses of all colours, lupin and rhododendrons and neatly trimmed hedges. It was a beautiful avenue and Jill certainly hadn't known Mrs Foster had lived here in such a lovely setting with her husband and two young sons. She had rung Mr Foster yesterday morning to say she would like to confide in him, and they arranged she would come this evening around 7.30pm and they could have a cup of coffee together.

It was such a lovely early July evening; the sun was still shining brightly when Jill set off. She had decided to walk because of the good weather but also because the buses were very few and far between in the evenings in Lisburn. Now, as she rang the doorbell of no. 6, she tried to gather her thoughts and remember exactly what Mr Baird had told Mrs Scott and the other parents on that awful morning. She wanted to tell everything, as far as possible, exactly how it had all happened.

"Oh Miss Corken, please do come in." Although Mr Foster had a welcoming smile on his face, there was an aura of deep sadness there too and suddenly Jill wondered if she was doing the right thing in coming here. Would she just be adding to this man's heartache by talking about the children, the Home and the secret adoptions?

"Hello, Mr Foster." Jill hesitated. "Are you sure you are ready to hear what I have to say? Besides, it may not be relevant you know."

"Please, Miss Corken, come in." He extended his hand to hers.

Once again Jill stepped inside the large square hallway with its walls all decorated in warm cream tones. She remembered this space well when she came here on the day of Eleanor Foster's funeral, not least because of its lovely mahogany staircase which was set well back in the hall giving the room a great feeling of spaciousness and elegance.

"This is the sitting room here." Mr Foster opened the door into a room with a large bay window at one end and a beautiful marble fireplace in the centre of the wall opposite. Then Jill realised that she and Mr Foster had been in the dining room on the other side of the hall on the day of Mrs Foster's funeral. She vaguely remembered the dining table laid out with refreshments, but she had only been intent on what Mr Foster had been saying that day and the letter he showed her.

"Have a seat here, I think this is quite a comfortable sofa," Mr Foster said, "My sons are insisting they want to meet you, Miss Corken, and they have offered to make some coffee for us."

"Isn't that lovely, Mr Foster?" Jill felt a warmth inside her, such a lovely greeting from people she scarcely knew. "Please Mr Foster, would you just call me Jill, everyone calls me that. Miss Corken is not very familiar to me." Jill smiled encouragingly.

"Jill it is then, and you must call me Sam. It is so much easier, isn't it?" Sam Foster seemed to relax and then he continued, "I will call the boys down and remind them about the coffee. Then you can tell me what you have found out and we can think about its relevance, is that alright with you, Jill?"

"That is fine, Mr Foster, I mean, Sam. That will be fine." Now Jill felt embarrassed about having asked him to call her by her first name as he had naturally insisted, she must do the same and she felt she was being much too familiar because the man was Eleanor Foster's husband and Mrs Foster had been her superior. But it was too late now to change things, then she heard Mr Foster out in the hall calling his sons and telling them to come and meet Miss Corken. She decided that if Mrs Foster's sons were to be present and during any of the conversation she would, out of respect for them all, still call him Mr Foster. She knew she would be more comfortable doing that.

Mr Foster reappeared in the sitting room and with him were two dark-haired boys who were now looking at her intently.

"This is Miss Corken," Sam began as way of introduction, "Jill, this is Ryan." He indicated the taller of the boys, then turning to the quiet, smaller boy, he added, "This is Andrew. They are making coffee for us now, isn't that so, boys?"

"Yes, Dad," the elder boy said, and Jill was immediately struck by his sober sad demeanour. Both boys went out of the room together and Jill's emotions threatened to overwhelm her as she thought of the loss those two boys had suffered and the manner and tragedy of their mother's death.

"I like to keep them involved, Jill, I don't want them to feel any more isolated than is necessary, they are very young." And Sam shook his head sadly. "Ryan is only twelve, you know, and Andrew is ten, I feel they need all the attention and comfort I can give them." He went on in an emotional voice. "Maybe I am being selfish, but it helps me tremendously too, just to have their company."

Just then the boys appeared, Ryan carrying a tray with cups, saucers and a plate of biscuits. They proceeded to hand out the coffee and biscuits first to Jill and then to their father.

"You must have done this before," Jill felt compelled to say something. "You are very good at it and thank you."

Andrew, the younger boy, smiled shyly and nodded to her, Ryan too smiled over from where he was now standing beside his father.

"Thank you, boys," Sam said. "I will give you a shout when we want you to clear up for us. Miss Corken and I have some papers of importance to discuss."

When the boys had left and even before she had touched her coffee, she came straight to the point, "The last time I spoke to your wife, Sam, I told her that five children from the home had gone on holiday."

Sam nodded silently.

"Well," Jill continued, "they have been gone now for over two weeks and just a few days ago one of the committee members asked me to arrange for two of the mothers and one father of the children to come to the home. Parents of two of the boys and one of the girls." Jill hesitated, scarcely knowing how to continue and the possible implications for Eleanor's death. "When the two mothers and one father came, the committee member concerned was there, and told them their child had been adopted. He showed them documents, although very briefly, that they had supposedly signed agreeing to the adoption. The two mothers were shocked and vehemently denied signing any such papers. As for the father of one of the boys he is threatening to sue the Home."

Sam Foster looked over at Jill in shock and disbelief, "Are you saying they had these children adopted without the parents' knowledge?"

"Exactly, Sam. Two of the mothers were so grief-stricken that they could not speak although I did my best to console them and suggested they may not be too late to get their child back, and as I've said, the man was so angry he threatened to sue the Christian Committee establishment."

"He would be quite entitled to do so, the Christian Committee Staff can't possibly do that, surely they could not possibly forge other people's signatures? And for what purpose, might I add?" Then Sam seemed lost in thought and Jill waited for him to speak again, and she was quite relieved when he said, "I am convinced from Eleanor's letter that she knew something was going to happen to some of the children in the Home. I think her words even suggest she knew exactly what was going to happen and knowing Eleanor she would have tried to put a stop to it all. And then because she failed, she could not live with herself."

Now Sam was on the verge of tears and Jill sought to console him, "I am so sorry, but I did promise you if I found out anything, I would let you know. Drink some of your coffee, Sam. It will help you, you know." Jill's voice was compassionate.

"I do want to know, don't get me wrong, I need to know, but it is just so difficult." Then Sam asked Jill, "You say, three children had been adopted, but what about the other two? Didn't you say five had gone on this holiday? Would they still be on holiday?"

"I don't believe so, nor do I believe there was any holiday. I think all five were adopted three weeks ago." Jill was quite adamant. "No, I don't believe there was a holiday at all."

"Dear God, this is truly terrible. These parents all believed their children were going on a lovely holiday and they would all then return, and they would see them soon. It is very likely they will never see them again." Sam sounded bewildered and helpless. "But surely someone can do something about it? They can't just get away with it, can they?"

"I hope not, Sam, but I am just wanting to hear about the other two children, one boy aged four and a girl aged four, I think they must have been adopted too."

After coffee was finished and Ryan and Andrew had come back to clear up the tray and empty cups, Sam and Jill talked at length about the situation, the legalities of it all and what Sam should do to clarify the cause of Eleanor's unhappiness and suffering. Should he go to the Christian Committee and show them his wife's letter, or would they distort everything about her suicide and belittle her very existence and her role as matron in the Home?

Neither of them could come up with firm answers to any of it and when Jill said she really must go as it was coming up to ten o'clock and beginning to get dark, Sam said firmly, "You are certainly not walking back, my car's right outside the front door, I will just let Ryan know I will be back in ten minutes."

Jill was about to object, but Sam had already gone to tell the boys and besides she was feeling very tired and did not really relish walking back to her flat. Going by car only took five minutes to Jill's place, and during that time they were both quiet, pondering on their evening and what they had achieved.

Jill bid Sam goodnight as she got out of the car and said she would let him know when she heard anything about the other two children and their whereabouts.

"Yes, please Jill, if you would. I am sure you will hear soon."

It would be sometime later before Jill would learn anything about Joe and Amy and exactly what the committee had told the next of kin.

Chapter 19

"No, please, Joe, don't cry, please don't." Christopher hugged Joe tightly to him as they sat together at the long dining table and Christopher tried his best to comfort him. But Joe was quite heartbroken this morning, as indeed Christopher was too. The feeling of distress and isolation had been growing in him for a couple of days and he knew Joe felt the same, but their emotions had come to a head when their new found friend, David, had summoned up the courage to ask Mr Newell when they would be getting off the ship. Usually, David asked Christopher to ask the questions but this morning at breakfast David had just blurted the question out.

Mr Newell was silent for a time, a long time, Christopher thought. When he did reply, he said it would be another three weeks before they would be getting off. But he assured them they would just love where they were going, the sun shone all the year round and there was sand everywhere.

Joe began to cry again and to cry very loudly. Christopher quickly put his arm around him, "What is the matter, Joe? Try to eat your breakfast, your egg is going to get cold." Christopher spoke very gently when Joe continued to sob, his scrambled egg forgotten on his plate. "What is wrong, Joe? You can tell me."

"I want to see my granny. I just want to see my granny, or even Mama Foster would be lovely." The words were strung between sobs. "I want to get off the ship, Christopher, I just want to get off. Why was Mama Foster off sick when we were sent on this holiday? I don't think she would have wanted us to go so far away, do you? Christopher?"

And the young boy leaned heavily on Christopher and was now looking at him with pleading eyes. Christopher was silent for a moment and just kept hugging Joe and rocking him gently and then he spoke, "Mama Foster couldn't help being sick, Joe, but she must have known we would miss her terribly being so long away from the home. It would have been good if she had been able to come with us, Joe, then we would have felt safe and cosy with her. As for my mummy, I'd love to see her too, Joe, but we will, I know we will after we get off the ship and see this other place." Now Christopher's eyes filled with tears, but he knew he dare not cry openly, he mustn't.

Many times during this trip he had thought about matron—Mama Foster as she liked to be called—and even though he had only known her for a short space of time he had become attached to her, she was warm and loving to all the boys and girls. Like Joe, he did not think she would have wanted them to go so far from the home and for so long.

For now, he needed to take his mind off everything and so he began to encourage Joe to take some of the egg with his teaspoon and was relieved that he did eat most of it.

After that, the day passed quietly enough, Christopher and David took turns keeping Joe occupied by reading to him or teaching him to play the card game, Snap. Books and games were given to them by Mr Newell on several occasions and it did help to keep the feelings of some awful fear and dread at bay. But now, this evening, when they had gone back to their cabin, Joe had become even more distressed than he had been in the morning and Christopher too now felt heartbroken. Both for himself and for Joe.

He just wished that David would have been in the same cabin as they were, David always seemed quite jolly and in spite of the fact they had already been on the ship for three weeks and would be on it for another three, he didn't seem to mind. Although he was always wanting to ask questions Christopher knew it was not out of any worry he might have of where they were going. It was just out of interest, nothing more than that. Christopher admired his whole manner towards their journey. David did not seem fearful or worried, indeed he seemed to be quite looking forward to going to this place which Mr Newell had not yet told them the name off. Nor did he seem to miss his mummy. He never spoke of her, unlike Christopher and Joe when often they would talk about rather being home with their mummy or granny than on this huge ship.

Now Christopher, holding tight to young Joe, cried silently too for his mummy. He wondered again, as he did many times, had she been told where he was and where exactly he was going. Christopher had no idea about anything anymore but wondered why it was taking so long and seemed so far away.

For a time sleep evaded Christopher, although Joe thankfully was sleeping very peacefully, his head on Christopher's chest. As he lay listening to the young boy's breathing a thought struck Christopher, when they came to the place of their holiday, he was going to get permission from Mr Newell to write to his mummy and let her know he would be home soon. Indeed, if they could just get a letter to Joe's granny somehow Joe would feel better, Christopher knew. Sure, if they sent it to the Home, they would see that Joe's granny got it. With these last happy thoughts Christopher drifted off to sleep his arm still around Joe and Joe's head still on Christopher's chest.

Chapter 20

"Monica, Mr Dunn rang me this morning to bring me up to date about the children in Melton Home but as you were engrossed with Jennie when I looked into the library earlier, I decided to leave speaking to you until now." Edward looked at his governess sitting quietly in the kitchen with his daughter where they always had lunch.

Edward had been amazed at Monica's fortitude and strength of spirit during the past week when she had first been told of her son's supposed adoption. Whatever agonies and despair she was suffering and he had no doubt she was, she had kept her composure very well indeed during the hours she spent with his daughter. Agnes, who reported back to him on her time spent with Monica, had told Edward on several occasions how Monica truly believed everything would work out for Christopher and her.

But now as Edward spoke to her and Monica looked up, he was saddened by her expression. It was one of abject fear and anguish and she now seemed incapable of hiding her feelings. He noticed too that she had begun to shake. Immediately he went over to her and pulling up a chair alongside hers he held her shaking hands in his until the shaking stopped.

"Monica, my dear." He spoke quickly to reassure her, "It is not bad news. No, not at all." Then he turned to Jennie. "Jennie, darling, I need to speak to Monica for a moment, if you go into the drawing room, I will join you shortly."

"Yes, Dad." Jennie obediently left them.

Then Edward turned back to Monica and continued, "Mr Dunn tells me he has spoken to a lady in the Home, according to him she is acting matron following Mrs Foster's death. She told me she had written to the Christian Committee on his behalf asking for the details and proof of Christopher's adoption. She also gave him the telephone number and the name of the man from the committee who she had written to. So, you see Monica, Mr Dunn is working to do his best. It is slow, I know, but you must continue to hope."

Monica nodded dumbly for a moment, then recovering her composure she said, "I do believe we have a good case, Edward. We must have. I signed no adoption papers."

Edward regarded her with compassion and then said softly, "You have been so strong during the past week, you have refused to let your heartbreak interfere with your care of my daughter and I so appreciate what you are doing in spite of your trauma." His voice was full of emotion and as he regarded her, he vowed he would do everything in his power to make this girl's life somewhat more bearable.

And now she was smiling at him, a slow hesitant smile which told him she was determined to maintain her belief and resolve in a future for her son and herself.

"I would like Agnes and yourself, Monica, to join Jennie and me for a meal on Sunday evening. Would you be happy to do that?" Edward hurried on, "I mean, would you feel you would be able to have Jennie's and mine's company for an hour or so? I understand if you would prefer not to, but it would be a bit of added company for you." Then Edward said, as an afterthought, "I would also like to show my appreciation of Agnes, she has been so flexible in her workload, as indeed she has always been during her years of service for me. She will, of course, be responsible for cooking the meal."

Edward went on, "I do believe Agnes's support for you this week has helped a little. I also believe it enabled you to continue with your work with Jennie and that has been important to me because I know Jennie's learning is somewhat behind even for her young age I think, Monica. You see, Jennie's last governess did not work out for Jennie and me. That is why I really did need you to continue your work, Jennie has suffered enough."

"Edward, I never intend to give up my position, if at all possible, and it is thanks to Agnes's support and wonderful company that I have been able to work, I don't know how I would have managed otherwise." Now Monica was smiling widely and her deep blue eyes were shining, "So, thank you so much, Edward, I will look forward to coming to your home on Sunday and what's more, when Christopher comes back to me, I shall return the invitation and have Agnes and you over for dinner."

"I will look forward to that." Edward said firmly, "And now I will go and spend my usual half hour with Jennie before she returns to you in the library and I will see you on Sunday, around six o'clock, Monica."

"Thank you again Edward, I will come through over to you on Sunday."

After Edward left her and while putting the kettle on to make tea for herself, Monica thought over what he had said about Mr Dunn, the solicitor, and although there had been very little progress in her fight for Christopher, Monica felt that at least Mr Dunn was working on it and the acting matron, who surely must be Miss Corken, had been quite prepared to help them and that thought warmed Monica and she felt that surely she would see Christopher very soon. When she thought of Edward Wallace's invitation to her for Sunday dinner, she found she was quite looking forward to it, It had been so kind of him to extend the invitation to her because she knew Agnes deserved a special treat far more than she did and she felt he was very kind and considerate to her to have thought of it.

Later that evening after Agnes and Monica had had their tea, Agnes said how pleased she was with the invitation.

"Edward has only asked me to join him for dinner since your arrival here, Monica. He only ever asked me to join him for a cup of tea." Agnes smiled at Monica. "You should be very flattered, Monica, to be asked in for a meal. He certainly never asked Jennie's previous governess, I could tell you." Then Agnes hurried on and changed the subject. "Edward certainly feels very angry about what has gone on in Melton Home, he told me so himself. I think he can scarcely believe that anyone connected with the Christian Committee could be responsible for such underhand behaviour."

"Yes, he has been so understanding about it all, Agnes. That is why I must concentrate on Jennie and educate her the best I can and see to her needs. And I find I can deal with it all quite well despite everything else."

"Yes, both Edward and I can see that. Jennie is quite settled and for a child of four seems very keen to learn and even though you have only been here a week you have really hit it off with her."

"I feel very comfortable with her, I must say Agnes. But that is enough about me for the moment, I want to know if I can help on Sunday to make the meal or do the washing up."

"I doubt if Edward would be happy about an arrangement like that, I think you are the special invited guest. Besides, he is used to me doing the cooking and the cleaning up, so you just have to look pretty and enjoy your evening."

Agnes was relieved to see Monica much brighter this evening than she had been on any other evening in the past week, she was certainly showing remarkable spirit and resolve during this traumatic time for her. Agnes was resolved to just continue to pray every night that the boy would be returned to his rightful mother.

Chapter 21

"Lily, Mrs Scott must mean to pursue her search for young Christopher. Her employer's solicitor, who is acting on her behalf, was on the phone enquiring who exactly he could speak to regarding the supposed adoption papers for Christopher Scott." Jill and Lily had just come upstairs to begin their work of checking and tidying the dormitories while the other two carers supervised breakfast. "Mrs Scott was so shocked when Mr Baird showed her the paper with her signature on it. I don't believe for one minute she signed any such thing, but please Lily, don't say anything." Jill was very firm about keeping it between the two of them.

"Well, I am glad to hear that a solicitor is going to become involved, and I hope Mr Gillespie meant what he said when he threatened to take Mr Baird to court for having his son adopted illegally." Lily was emphatic. "And don't worry, Jill, I need this job too much, my Albert can't find work anywhere here, I would be destitute without it, so I will certainly not be repeating anything either in here or outside."

"The only person I have said anything to is Mr Foster but because of his grief and loss over his wife he certainly wouldn't be saying anything anyway. Now I did promise to ring him again if I had any news, so perhaps I should let him know a solicitor is involved. When you say solicitor, you begin to realise the seriousness of this whole thing." Jill said, "Indeed I will ring him later on today and tell him."

Later that day when Jill rang Sam Foster, he suggested she call and see him later. He said if it suited her to come straight from work and he would rustle up something for her to eat. He said it would be his way of thanking her for her help and support during this difficult time. Jill found that as she made her way to Mr Foster's home on Sycamore Drive she was glad he had suggested that they have tea together before she went home. She agreed with him it was a good idea because sometimes when she came home after her day's work in Milton Home, she did not really want to go out again.

"It is the boys' Scout night, so they always have tea early before they go," Sam explained to Jill as he took her coat from her and hung it on the rack in the hall. "So even though it is just the two of us, we will have our tea in the dining room. Eleanor always thought it was very important that we sat down together. She thought of it as an opportunity for good family time." He proceeded to lead the way into the dining room. "So I hope, Jill, that you don't mind, it may seem a bit formal." Sam hesitated. "It is just I do want to keep things as familiar to the boys as possible."

"Of course, I don't mind, and this is lovely," Jill answered warmly, aware Mr Foster sounded quite emotional as he spoke.

Jill looked around the room, the room she had been in the day of Mrs Foster's funeral, the room where Sam Foster had handed her his wife's suicide note. Jill realised she loved the room despite the awful news she had heard that day, it was a very welcoming room with its red velvet curtains and pale golden painted walls.

"This is a room to be used, I think Sam, it has such a warm feel to it, I am not surprised Eleanor liked to use it every day. I do hope you keep up the tradition—but of course you will." Jill waited for a response, hoping she had said something that might bring some measure of comfort to this man in his torment.

Now, as she watched him, he seemed to relax visibly and when he spoke his voice sounded much steadier, "Indeed I do, Jill. I do love this room and as you say it is a warm room so thank you. Now do sit down." He pulled out a chair at the table. "I will be back shortly. I will just put the food on our two plates and bring them in, that is what I have been doing for the boys, so I will just do the same now."

"That sounds good, I am not used to having it served to me you know, I have to do it all myself," Jill said.

Sam made his way into the kitchen which just led off the dining room and he was soon back with a plate of stew for Jill and one for himself.

"I hope you like that, Jill, I am a bit limited in what I can cook but I have been making that particular stew for years."

"Well, it smells lovely." Jill began to eat. She was very hungry as she had had nothing since one o'clock and then only a cheese sandwich.

"It tastes wonderful," then looking at Mr Foster's plate, Jill was embarrassed, her dish was almost empty and his was still half full, "Oh dear, you must think I am very rude." She decided to be frank about it, "I have almost finished eating and you have barely started. But I have had very little all day." She looked at him, a flushed look on her face.

"My dear, I am so happy to see you obviously enjoying my very simple fare. There is more if you would like some." He wanted to put her at ease. "Do you not have lunch provided for you in the home?"

"Well yes, there is bread and usually just cheese, occasionally some ham and of course we have tea making facilities," Jill said. "The provisions come on Monday mornings and there is of course plenty of food for the children, but it is strictly for the children."

"Oh, that sounds quite a meagre diet for you, is it not?" Sam continued.

"Well, I am always very hungry when I get home in the evenings and then of course I have still to cook it." Jill still wanted to explain her rudeness, "So you can guess how quickly I eat then."

"I am just so glad you enjoyed it." And Sam, having just finished his meal, rose and lifted the dishes. "We will have some tea and a slice of cake in the sitting room." He made his way into the kitchen.

Jill waited until he reappeared with a tray carrying tea and cake, and together they went into the sitting room. It was over tea that Jill told him about Mr Edward Wallace's solicitor ringing her earlier in the day about Christopher Scott's supposed adoption.

"I gave him Mr Baird's name and the telephone number for the Christian Committee, and he said he would be in touch at a later date for any information I might have. He told me Monica Scott categorically denies signing any adoption papers and Mr Wallace says she is heartbroken." Jill was able to confirm how much in despair Mrs Scott was. "When she was first told about the adoption, I took her and her friend outside. She was distraught and if her friend had not been present, I would have had to have taken her home that is how bad it was. I know I touched on it the last evening I was here with you. I found the situation difficult to deal with."

"I think I will do nothing at the moment, Jill, until we hear what progress the solicitor makes," Sam said, "and I think you must hear news of the other two children soon. If not, I think you should ring Mr Baird and ask him directly."

"I was thinking of doing just that and if I don't hear anything about Joe and Amy soon, I will speak up and make a complaint, Sam. I just have to."

Chapter 22

Mr Baird looked at the list of names in front of him, one of the lists had some names of children from Baron's Home, The Sisters of Newbourne and the other list from Melton Home in Lisburn. He studied the names on the list from Baron's and noticed that four names there had the word Adoption written and their names had been ticked off, so those children had been dealt with, he reckoned. The Sisters of Newbourne's list indicated that the names of the children concerned had also been ticked off. Not that the process seemed to have represented much of a problem at all.

But then he studied the other list, the one naming the children in Melton Home, where three names there had also the word Adoption written beside them. Only one of these names had been ticked off, where the other two names were listed, brief comments had been written, one stating a solicitor was now involved who wanted a copy of the adoption papers, the other that the father of the little boy named David was threatening them with legal action.

Mr Baird sat down on one of the chairs at the desk and considered the names of the other two children of Melton Home who still had to be dealt with. One, according to the list, was a boy named Joe Totten age four years of age, the other a girl by the name of Amy Mullin ire, age four years of age. There and then, Will Baird decided he would not consider any more adoptions from Melton Home. The project was going to be such a successful one for everyone, the government, the churches and the care homes and they could not afford any more denials about signatures and the like. The more complaints there were from relatives, the more likely it would soon be public knowledge and that was to be avoided at all costs.

He intended—in relation to these other two children—to make everything appear, on paper, very final. It was better that a couple of untruths were told now, it would save considerable fuss later, never mind the risk of solicitors and court proceedings. This way he had just thought of would be entirely free from the threat of any of that publicity. Now, momentarily he thought he ought to discuss his intentions about Joe Totten and Amy Matthews with someone else but decided the less fuss that was made the better the chances of success.

Now he looked through the books until he found the nearest relative of both the children concerned. One was a grandmother, Sara Totten, aged forty-nine with an address in Lisburn, the other was a Mrs Mabel Matthews with an address in Dromore, Co. Down. He found his writing pad and envelopes in the drawer of his desk and proceeded to write to the two relatives explaining the reason for the two children's absence. He then sealed and addressed the envelopes and taking them through to the post out tray in the reception hall he felt very pleased with himself and felt that a great weight had been lifted off his shoulders.

As he headed out of the building towards his car, he knew the next thing he must do was to inform his supervisors about his decision regarding the remaining two children from Melton Home, but he was in no hurry to do so. He would let them know tomorrow that all the children were well on their way to their destination as had been agreed and organised by the top men. He knew he would also have to prepare them for the possibility of legal action being involved. He also decided on the spur of the moment to write to Miss Corken, she was still acting matron at Melton Home, but he had no desire to ring her or explain anything to her. He thought that a phone call might lead to some questioning from her, and he thought a letter could well prevent all of that.

"My goodness Jill, what is it?" Lily was half shouting as she ran towards the reception area where Jill Corken was standing, sobbing loudly and crying out, "It can't be, it can't be!" Lily was beside Jill now and pulling a chair out, half pushed the sobbing Jill into it.

"Please Jill. What is wrong? Please tell me."

In answer, Jill, her arm trembling, pointed to a letter sitting on the occasional table beside them. "Read it, Lily." Her words were barely a whisper.

Lily read the letter and the words written in Mr Baird's handwriting leapt out at her, "It can't be, it isn't possible." She shook her head in disbelief. "Sure they only went on a holiday and now he is telling us that little Joe and Amy are dead. Dead! How on earth can that be, Jill?"

Slowly Jill shook her head, doing her best to regain her composure. "Read on Lily, please. He says he has written to their next of kin to let them know." Jill swallowed hard, "What about wee Joe, how could he be dead, Lily? He was as fit as a fiddle and Amy, well, Amy was a healthy wee girl."

"He says they took an infection in England, and they were buried over there." Lily read the words out loud and then she added, "Let's go into the kitchen, we won't tell the other carers until we get a cup of tea." And Lily gently helped Jill out of the chair and into the kitchen where she immediately set Jill down at the table and went and put the kettle on.

"Lily, it is hard to believe that five of our children left this home to go on holiday but looks like none of them will be coming back, unless Mrs Scott and Mr Gillespie can win their cases." Jill had regained her composure but was still finding it difficult to comprehend the loss of five children from the home and in such a way. "At least Lily, if Mrs Scott and Mr Gillespie don't win their cases, they still can hope that their child will try to trace them but for the relatives of Joe and Amy, that hope is gone forever. They will never see them again."

While Lily had been making some tea and toast for the two of them, she had been deep in thought and now she turned to Jill. "Jill, don't you think it very odd, very odd indeed that five children from here were picked to go on a holiday and that they haven't returned. They haven't returned because we have been told three of them have been adopted and we have been told the other two have died." Lily sounded almost hysterical now.

"What are you trying to say, Lily?" Jill was at a loss as to what Lily was thinking. "Do you believe they are all dead?"

"No, oh no Jill, but you and I agree that the adoption papers were fake and that those mothers never ever signed their child over for adoption."

"I know but Mr Baird must have been confident that those papers looked authentic or maybe, just maybe, with Mrs Scott's solicitor the whole adoption cases will collapse."

"Well Jill, I just can't believe that any of this is happening, I really can't, there is something wrong here. I don't know what it's all about, but you probably think I am rambling now, Jill." Lily paused for breath. "I just can't bear to think that those two lovely, wee children are really gone. I really can't." Lily's voice wobbled as she reached over for her tea, her hands shaking.

"Lily, let's wait and hope that Mrs Scott's solicitor will be successful in returning Christopher to his mother, that is what I am going to hope and pray for, Lily." Jill paused for a moment. "But I know this, I will have to let Mr Foster know about this latest development, that two of the children that Mrs Foster knew were going on holiday have actually died. I don't know how I will tell him this latest development or what bearing it might have on Eleanor's death, I really don't know." Jill was close to despair. "But I could not face him with any more bad news so soon again, I will leave it for a day or so."

Chapter 23

"Monica, after Jennie's lessons are over, would you mind calling over to my drawing room and I'll tell you what Mr Dunn would like to do to help trace Christopher? Or I can call with you, if you prefer."

"Of course, I'll call over to you, Edward. What time would you like me to come?" Monica asked.

"Perhaps we should wait until after Jennie's bedtime, around seven-thirty. I think that might be better than just after her schooling is over. Would that suit you?"

"That will be fine, Edward, I'll come then."

"Right, I'll see you later." Edward made his way out from Monica and his daughter, all the time wondering what her chances of success were at getting her son back.

Monica's predicament had been in Edward's mind constantly since he was first told about it by Agnes. He realised it must be agonising for the girl, not knowing where her son was or who he was with and whether she would ever see him again. Edward knew her situation really occupied his thoughts far too much. She was his last thought when he went to bed at night and his first thought in the morning when he woke. Yet it amazed him how she applied herself during the day so diligently to her work and gave no indication that her trouble occupied her thoughts and yet he knew it must. When he called for Jennie each day at four o'clock. He was always anxious to see how Monica was. And he always knew by her anxious, questioning look that she was hoping for news. News that he didn't have to give her, not until today when Mr Dunn had called him.

He sought Agnes out when he left Monica and found her in the drawing room shining the brassware.

"Agnes, I wanted to bring you up to date about Monica, she is going to call over here tomorrow evening around seven-thirty and I will let her know then what Mr Dunn is doing about this adoption." Edward went on to explain, "He is going to organise a preliminary hearing in court and demand evidence of the adoption. I thought I would let you know, Agnes, as you have been involved with this awful business from the beginning and you have been such a support for Monica." He nodded his head vigorously. "I know if you had not stayed with her at night, I think she would have had a breakdown."

"Maybe it helped a little, Edward, but I believe having to teach Jennie and spend so much time with her has been a real blessing in itself."

"It has helped but now she has to face a court to fight for her son and I am sure that will be a big trial for her." Edward said, "Would you mind staying in her annexe a few more nights, Agnes, just until we see how this all goes for her."

"Certainly Edward, I quite enjoy our evenings together." Agnes confided in him, "Sometimes we listen to the news, sometimes we read the paper and sometimes Monica talks about her husband and what happened to him and of course she talks a lot about Christopher."

"Well let's hope the court sitting will be a short one." Then Edward added, "Tomorrow evening I would like you to bring in some tea and cake around eight o'clock and put a cup on the tray for yourself, Agnes, and we will have it together." And he went on, "Tomorrow morning I must leave early and do a round of my shops. I have neglected to call with any of them for a week, I have just been in touch by telephone and that is not good enough. I know I have excellent managers and hardworking staff in all three premises, and I don't anticipate anything going wrong. But it looks negligent I believe, when the owner of a business doesn't seem to show an interest. And of course," he added, "I can't tell them about Monica and her son, it is imperative we keep that confidential or it might just jeopardise her chances of getting Christopher back and that would be awful."

Agnes listened quietly to what her boss was saying, surprised to hear him being so articulate, he was usually a man of few words. Then she said, smiling as she spoke, "I'd love to join yourself and Monica for tea tomorrow evening, but now I must go and put some dinner on for yourself and Jennie later, I like to cook my meat slowly." She added, "Thank you for the invitation for tea and I look forward to it."

Agnes was glad that Edward Wallace had told her why he was arranging to see Monica because when Monica returned to the annexe she was distressed and agitated about the prospect of going to a court hearing and the real threat of failure. And Agnes remembered what Edward had said about Monica having a breakdown. Seeing her in such despair this evening Agnes felt that it was a possibility and wondered if perhaps she needed Edward's doctor's help again and possibly some medication to calm her. It certainly had worked well in the first week, then Monica had decided she was alright without any sedation. But this evening was proving to be a difficult one until Agnes had the idea of getting hot drinks for them and told Monica this, "I am going across to get some whiskey for the two of us, Monica. I am going to make two hot drinks for you and I. They're probably a better idea than any sleeping tablet, at least the drink is worth trying. So just be patient, Monica, I'll be back in a jiffy."

Monica nodded and said firmly, "I am not going anywhere. And I will take whatever you give me, I have faith in you, Agnes, I really do."

With that reassurance, Agnes quickly left the sitting area and crossed the hall into the dining room and retrieved some whiskey from the side cabinet. She would explain to Edward later, after she had given Monica a hot drink and when she was reassured Monica had settled down.

On her return, she quickly organised the drinks for both of them in Monica's kitchen and when she entered her sitting room, she was relieved to see that at least she had stopped shaking. And even managed to give Agnes a weak smile.

"This is some of Edward's whiskey we are having, but I will tell him we borrowed it and we will replace it."

"I will replace it, you mean, Agnes. Just me." Monica was adamant. "This is my first ever alcoholic drink." She added as she took a sip of the warm drink, "It is rather nice you know, but I wouldn't want to make a habit of it."

"No, and I can't imagine you ever doing such a thing, so let's relax and enjoy it this evening, Monica," Agnes said and then made a sudden decision to tell her friend about Edward's last governess, it would help to distract from the reality of having to attend the court for the hearing. And she would be as factual and truthful as she could be in remembering it all. Now she was glad she had decided to tell it, she didn't really feel she was being gossipy, she was genuine in believing it might help Monica, even on a temporary basis.

She related to Monica how the girl had pestered Edward quite relentlessly. She had, she told Monica, went over to his own private drawing room in the evenings and sat for hours at a time or she would have asked him to come and look at the sink, telling him it was leaking, or perhaps a window or even a door was not shutting properly. Agnes could see by Monica's face that she was appalled at anyone doing that to Edward Wallace, such a private and respectable man as he was.

"It came to a head one night when she entered his bedroom in her nightdress and slippers and proceeded across to his bed. Luckily, Edward was not yet asleep, he quickly got out of bed and led her firmly out of his room."

"What did he do then?" Monica asked ever so quietly.

"He called me, and as my room is just along the landing, I soon sized up the situation and told Edward to lock his door and I soon marched her back to the annexe here. In the morning he gave her an official letter of instant dismissal and asked me to see her off the premises, which I was very happy to do." Agnes went on, "She was a really awful wee madam, Monica. I do know he thinks he has a gem now with you. She did threaten him, saying he had raped her but that was quickly dropped when she got a solicitor's letter. I know Edward has never heard from her again."

"Oh, that is an awful story, Edward only deserves the highest respect. And I hope I give it to him, Agnes."

"Certainly. You do, Monica."

A thought struck Monica. "Is that why, when he advertised for a governess, he described himself as an elderly gentleman, was he wanting to ensure the same thing wouldn't happen again?"

"Oh yes, he told me he was going to do exactly that." Agnes answered, "He thought that if he even reduced the chance somewhat of it ever happening again, it would be something. So now you know the reason for his style of advertising." And Agnes smiled broadly and was rewarded with an honest, open smile back. She was so glad she had told Monica about the previous governess. Because she could see it had had the desired effect of distracting Monica from her troubles. And tonight, Agnes vowed, she would pray more fervently than ever that Christopher Scott would be returned to his mother.

Chapter 24

Jill had promised Mrs Scott she would keep in touch with her and let her know if she heard anything, anything at all, about the other children who had gone on holiday. She really should let her know that little Joe Totten had died during the holiday and was buried over in England. Jill knew that in Monica Scott's fragile state, she would be most distressed to hear that the little boy had died, especially considering Jill had stressed Christopher had been picked to go on the holiday primarily to look after Joe. But still Jill felt it was very important to tell Mrs Scott about the other children's deaths; besides, she was anxious to know how her appeal against her son's adoption was going. She just hoped the solicitor would be successful. She was very grateful that Monica's friend, Agnes, had told her an address to come to if she wanted to come and see her. She had explained briefly to Jill that Monica was employed as a governess to a Mr Wallace, whose residence it was.

Later that evening after Jill had finished her shift for the day, she caught the bus which would take her to Circular Road. Following Agnes's direction, she soon arrived at number 10. The door was opened by Monica's friend, Jill recognised her straight away, and she smiled warmly when she saw Jill standing there.

"Hello," she said warmly. "Have you come to see Monica?"

Jill said, "Yes," and then went on, "I promised Mrs Scott I would call to see her when I had any further news about the holiday." Jill nodded solemnly. "So yes. I have some news."

"Oh, please do come in." Agnes urged, "I have completely forgotten your name, Monica was in such a state that day that I was forced to concentrate on her, so I heard very little. I am sorry."

"I am Jill, Jill Corken," Jill replied as she stepped into the hall.

"I'll lead the way to show you where Monica's place is, we go through the main kitchen, and this is the back hall, and that door leads us to Monica's kitchen." And Agnes indicated the door on the far wall of the large, main kitchen. "Monica has her own sitting room, bedroom and bathroom as well, so it is all very compact for her."

"It sounds lovely," Jill responded and as Agnes led the way through the neat and tidy kitchen, she was surprised that after knocking on another door. It opened to reveal a lovely sitting room. Mrs Scott rose from her seat by the window as she saw Agnes, then seeing Jill, she came across the room to greet her.

"Miss Corken, how kind of you to come." Monica was genuinely pleased to see her. She had thought she would never hear from her again. "Please have a seat." And she indicated the big squashy sofa. "Would you like some tea? I was just about to make myself a cup but was waylaid by looking at my post. Agnes, would you like some too?" And Monica proceeded towards the kitchen.

"Let me make it, Monica. I'll be quicker, I think, and you and Miss Corken have a chat."

Monica was on the edge of objecting but then relented, "Thank you Agnes, there is some fruit cake in the tin, I bought it on my last outing for groceries."

After Agnes disappeared into the kitchen, there was a deep silence between the two women, then Jill decided she really had to tell Mrs Scott what she had come to tell her.

"Mrs Scott, I did promise you I would let you know if I heard anything about the other children who went on holiday." Jill began, "It is thanks to your friend Agnes I am here; she had the foresight to write down this address and here I am." She hesitated, reluctant now to tell her about Joe, perhaps it would only cause her more heartache.

Then Mrs Scott spoke, "Thank you for thinking of me, I have worried and wondered so much since I heard of Chris's alleged adoption. I have been worried about Joe, how he might be, if he doesn't have Christopher whom he depended on so very much."

"Oh, Mrs Scott, that is exactly why I am here." Jill went quiet for a moment—it was important to remain composed. "Little Joe is dead, Mrs Scott. Joe is dead." And Jill felt the tears well up in her eyes, and she struggled not to let Monica Scott see how upset she was.

"What? What did you say?" The words were a whisper. "Dead, did you say? How can that be? Joe was very well. I know he was thin, but he was fit and wiry. I know he was." Monica sounded as though she was rambling on and was shaking uncontrollably.

Jill put out a hand to steady her. "It seems he took an infection on the holiday, and he is buried in England somewhere."

Just then Agnes returned with her tea tray and quietly handed a cup of tea to Jill and sat at the table beside Monica. She passed the cake, insisting they both have some, and then she sat down herself with a cup of tea in her hand.

"You have had more bad news, Monica, is that right?" Monica nodded dumbly and then Jill spoke.

"The little boy that went with Christopher on holiday died when they were away. I thought it was best to let Mrs Scott know in case she wondered about him." Jill said softly, "He was on her mind, as he was the first child she asked me about." And Jill looked over at Mrs Scott who nodded in response.

"Such an awful holiday this is turning out to have been, with two, perhaps three children we know of, adopted and one boy dead, it really seems strange. I think somebody will really have to look at the whole setup, how can children be adopted under such questionable circumstances and then a little boy dies," Agnes said.

"There were two deaths actually, a little girl called Amy also died." Jill, anxious that little Amy Matthew's death too would be acknowledged, rushed to tell Agnes and Mrs Scott about it.

"So," Agnes emphasised, "three adoptions and two deaths during what was meant to be a fortnight's holiday. It beats me."

"There was definitely three supposed adoptions and two deaths, Agnes," Jill confirmed.

"How many actually went from the Melton Home on this holiday?" Agnes asked. "Five in total, three boys and two girls. Two boys and a girl were adopted it seems, and one boy and a girl died. Am I right?"

"Yes," Jill answered quietly.

"So, none of the five who went on holiday have returned to the Home?" Agnes went on.

Jill nodded sadly, her face full of emotion. She glanced over at Mrs Scott and was shocked at the change in her. Her face was ashen, her face full of unshed tears and she seemed so much smaller as she sat listening to Agnes. But when she spoke, she surprised Jill, her voice sounded quite strong.

"I would like to visit Joe's granny, if I knew where to go, perhaps you could give me her address, Miss Corken. I did get to talk to her in the home on a couple of occasions and I knew she was very attached to Joe. And I also know she was injured during the Blitz when Joe's parents were killed." Monica looked over at Jill for approval. "Did you know that is what happened? That is what happened to Joe's parents and because his grandma was so injured, he had to go into the home. Did you know, Jill that Joe was only six months old, and he was the only survivor in the house. He was found in a cot under a small table that had been placed under the stairs. He was unharmed and to think he survived the Blitz only now to die from some infection in a strange town, in a strange country, is so terrible."

Monica pulled her handkerchief from her sleeve and blowing her nose loudly went on, "All over a stupid holiday. A stupid holiday. Look at the heartbreak for us all. I don't know anything more about Christopher either, that was just a preliminary court session. Mr Wallace's solicitor received the supposed signed adoption paper from the Christian Committee. He is sending the documents to a handwriting expert to see if they can establish whether the signatures are forged or not." Monica continued looking at Jill. "And to be honest, I do not know how I will ever pay a solicitor for it all, I really don't." Now her voice just faded away and tears flowed down her face.

"Please, Mrs Scott, try not to give up. If the documents are forged, the courts will soon know. I can get you Joe's granny's address but better still, come with me when I am going. I feel it is my duty to see her, so I'll definitely be going." Jill was very aware, as she sat sipping her tea, that at least Monica Scott still had hope, but for Joe's grandmother, there was none.

Chapter 25

Jill arranged to meet Monica Scott at the bus stop in Lisburn Square on the following Friday afternoon at 2pm. She had a day off from Melton Home and she had decided to see both Joe Totten's grandmother and Amy's mother to offer her condolences. She knew she would not be able to tell them anything more than they already knew, but she did feel that by going in person showed some compassion rather than by sending letters informing them of the children's death. Jill felt Mr Baird had acted in a very cold-hearted way towards Mrs Totten and Ms Matthews, Amy's mother. At least he had had the decency to come in person to tell the other mothers their children had been adopted, why had he not done the same regarding the deaths?

Jill knew she ought to let Mr Foster know the latest developments but just now she could not face giving him anything more to worry about, so she didn't intent contacting him for another day or two. It was enough at present to go and see Joe Totten's grandmother and Amy's mother, they must be so heartbroken.

Monica was already at the bus stop when she arrived. "It is good to see you, Mrs Scott," Jill greeted her. "How are you?"

"I am fine, really I am," Monica replied. "I have to go back to court next week to hear more regarding the false papers, so I am sure everything will work out after that." Now she smiled at Jill. "Would you please call me Monica; I am not used to such formal names."

Jill smiled in return. "Yes of course and no more Miss Corken, I am Jill."

"Oh, good, Jill, and now here comes the bus."

The nursing home was a short bus ride form the town centre. It was quite a cheerful looking, welcoming building built with red brick and had beautiful, white framed windows and it looked spotlessly clean. The door was opened by a carer who was known to both Jill and Monica. Due to the injuries Mrs Totten had received during the Blitz, she had to have a below knee amputation of her right leg, and as a result she was now confined to a wheelchair. This was the same carer who had always accompanied Mrs Totten on her visits to her grandson. It was she who had explained to Jill what had happened to Sara Totten.

"Would it be convenient to visit Mrs Totten?" Jill asked.

"Yes, of course, if you just follow me. Her room is at the end of the corridor, it is at the back of the home, but it looks out onto a fine garden." The carer spoke quietly as she led the way down a long hallway and opened the door at the end, indicating that Jill and Monica proceed into the room. "Mrs Totten, you have a couple of visitors."

Mrs Totten looked up at the two people in front of her and immediately burst into tears. "Joe. My Joe. My Joe." She kept repeating between her sobs.

"This is how she has been for the last few days since she got that awful horrid letter," the carer said as she went over to Mrs Totten and hugging her warmly said, "I will leave you for a while with these nice girls."

"Thank you," Jill said, "do you recognise me, Mrs Totten? I am from Melton Home."

"Of course, I do." And turning to Monica, she said, "Aren't you the other boy's mother? The boy that was always so kind to Joe."

"Yes, I am Christopher's mother," answered Monica. "I wanted to come to offer my condolences to Joe's grandmother."

"That is kind," the carer intervened. "Stay as long as you would like to. I will bring some tea for the three of you."

Monica and Jill stayed for over an hour with Mrs Totten. She was desperate for them to stay with her, their presence seemed to give her some comfort and Jill felt if it helped in any small way to ease her grief, they would sit with her. Monica told her that she hadn't seen Christopher for three weeks before the holiday and now another three had passed. When she was coldly told her son had been adopted. They had shown Monica alleged proof that she had agreed to the adoption. Monica did not know why she decided to tell Mrs Totten about her suffering, but perhaps Mrs Totten might feel they could be some of comfort to one another. Anything that might help this poor woman in her bereavement was alright with her. Seeing her grief at the loss of her grandson made Monica determined to fight to get her boy back. She would get the money from somewhere. If Mr Wallace could pay the solicitor, she could pay him back out of her pay.

Before they left Mrs Totten, they made sure a carer was with her and with promises to come back the following week, they left the home and made their way back to the bus stop.

Chapter 26

Dennis Patterson was just putting the final touches to his findings, before he went to give evidence in court in the afternoon, when his telephone rang. A vicious sounding voice asked if he was speaking to Dennis Patterson, and when Dennis confirmed that it was him, the man said he was the legal representative for the Christian Committee. He needed to know what his findings were regarding the adoption papers for a child by the name of Christopher Scott.

"I am convinced the signature is not a true one of Monica Scott. There are two subtle differences in the adoption paper signatures with others in Christopher Scott's file.

But you must not say that, on no account must you say that. After all, you might be mistaken. Signatures surely are hard to tally, are they not?" The man's voice sounded quite threatening. "The Christian Committee are highly regarded people, some of whom are even high up in British government positions. If you categorically state in court that they are wrong here, you might find, Mr Patterson that a lot of people will turn against you. That is how it would be I'm afraid."

He carried on, relentless now in what he wanted to say, "Whereas, if the opposite were to happen, and you stated the signatures on the adoption papers were a true genuine copy, I am sure you would find the Commission grateful and make sure you have a continuing business." The voice at the other end paused, obviously waiting for a reply, but Dennis was so stunned by the phone call that he was silent for a time.

When he did attempt to make some sort of reply, he was shocked at himself, "I could have got it wrong, I suppose, yes I could have." He hurried on, anxious for this call to be over, "I have a very difficult job and thank you for reminding me how difficult it really is. I intend to agree with Christian Committee. They are held in such high esteem I would not wish to bring disfavour onto them."

"Thank you then." And suddenly, the phone went dead.

Back at his desk, Dennis prepared another document to take with him to court. In this document he stressed that, in his judgement, the signature was genuine, omitting the facts of several letters appearing different from the original signature. He had been so intent on doing a professional job, he had completely overlooked how incriminating such evidence might be and had agreed with the voice on the phone that this must not happen. The Christian Ministers and Committee had such status and influence in Northern Ireland, and he should have considered that when he was doing his piece of work.

"Be quiet!" The magistrate thundered across the court room in Monica's direction as she stood up shouting, "It isn't true! I tell you it isn't true!" Monica stood looking at the magistrate, shaking her head and repeating, "That's not true."

"Please be seated and be quiet, or we will have to remove you from this courtroom."

Monica felt the firm, strong arm of Edward Wallace gripping her hand and gently saying to her, "Yes, Monica, sit down." She obeyed him, the whole while gripping his hand tightly. When she sat down in her seat, Edward released his hand from hers and then encircled her tightly with his arm. Monica, now with a comforting arm around her, was somehow able to block out some of the last words she had just heard from the magistrate.

"This court has been informed of the handwriting report by the analysis expert that the signature on the adoption papers is genuine and matches Mrs Scott's original signature. Her son Christopher has been legally adopted and Mrs Scott gave consent to the adoption. The law forbids anyone trying to trace or make any contact with this child." The magistrate looked across the room at Monica, his face expressionless, as she sat with Edward on one side of her and Mr Dunn on the other. "This court is now in recess." With that the magistrate stood up and proceeded out of the court.

Wearily, Edward helped Monica out of her seat, followed closely by Mr Dunn. When they left the courtroom and came out into the fresh air, Edward's first concern was for Monica. "Will you be alright with Mr Dunn, Monica, I will go and get the car, so you don't have to walk. You have had an awful shock," he said, and looking at her appearance, her ashen face and the bewildered, frightened look in her eyes, he longed to get her home. Home to Agnes as soon as possible, Agnes would know what to do.

"No, please, Edward, I want to walk to the car. I don't want to wait here—I can't stand to be here a minute longer."

"That's fine, Monica, Mr Dunn and I will each take an arm, we'll be at the car in a jiffy."

Dennis Patterson watched as the beautiful dark-haired woman, whom he had noticed earlier in the courtroom and indeed realised with a sinking heart who she must be, being helped down the steps of the courthouse by two men. He wanted to call out to her and tell her he had made a mistake. He wanted to tell her he could help her, but he knew it was hopeless. It was all too late and besides, he remembered again about the phone call he had received earlier that morning, reminding him of the position and influence the church had in the community and how badly people needed their work. Now today, the Christian Committee had achieved the outcome they wanted. But Dennis Patterson knew that Mrs Scott's heart-breaking appearance and anguished look would stay with him for a long time to come.

Chapter 27

"Agnes, I don't know how Monica has managed to go to Jennie as usual these last few days, it is all quite amazing. When I ask her how she is, she insists she is coping alright with everything." Edward was sitting down to his dinner and had not yet asked Agnes to fetch Jennie, because he was anxious to know what Agnes thought, she was so astute. "How have you found Monica in the evenings, Agnes, when you go through to the annexe?"

"Like you, Edward, I am pleased she seems to be coping, she has this resolve about her." Agnes said, "She tells me she intends to ask Mr Dunn to get her another handwriting expert and see what happens." Agnes hesitated but thought it wiser to let Edward know what Monica's intentions were. "She says she wants you to take something out of her pay each week for Mr Dunn so he can continue to help her." Agnes was concerned. "But my concern would be, what if she fails again, Edward, what then?"

"I know, Agnes, and according to Mr Dunn, the handwriting analyst is a real expert and knows forgeries when he sees them. But there is one thing worrying Mr Dunn, he tells me he rang Dennis Patterson in the morning of the court to find out what he believed to be the truth, and Dennis told him he had found discrepancies in the signatures, but then to hear him say in court there were no differences was a shock to Albert Dunn. Albert rang him that same evening, and Dennis Patterson told him he had been looking at other signatures and had made a mistake, but I know it still puzzles Albert."

"But if that is the case, perhaps Monica is right to think about getting another expert," Agnes replied.

"I'll need to speak with Monica and see what she really wishes to do. She hasn't said anything to me since we came back that last day, she did say she wanted to keep on working if I would have her, and of course I said yes. I would not dream of any other alternative." Edward went on, "Yes, I will talk to her. Now I will go now and get Jennie for dinner."

"I will wait for your return, and I'll serve you your meal, then I will go to Monica for the evening and stay the night as I have been doing."

"I think your presence is so important to her, Agnes, she looks to you. I know she does. And," Edward added, "If you can find a way to let her know, very subtly, that I do not intent to take any money out of her pay, I'll be sorting the solicitor's fees out. So, I will leave that with you, Agnes, but there is no hurry, keeping Monica well is our main priority, I think." Those last words were said as he left Agnes and went to fetch his daughter.

Monica did not know how she was able to function at all following the court's findings. What she did know was that, if it had not been for the need to get up each morning, go through to Edward's house and begin her day of teaching Jennie her English and arithmetic, supervise her drawings and play time, she surely would have had a breakdown. Then there was Agnes, her dear friend Agnes. She had been her support each evening when she had finished work for the day. She was always there for Monica, comforting her in her moments of utter grief, listening to her during her angry outbursts about the court and the registered magistrate's summary. She made her tea in the evenings, stayed with her at night, and in the mornings helped her prepare for the day ahead.

And always, there was Edward Wallace in the background, with his quiet and understanding ways, assuring her that if she wished him to be in touch with the solicitor at any time he would do so. What on earth would she had done if she had not been fortunate enough to come here? This house and the people in it were her salvation, and she would always be eternally grateful to them, and to the fate that had brought her here. She intended to dedicate herself to young Jennie's welfare, and at the same time do everything possible to find Christopher. She could only look forward to the thought that she would see him again. During the last few days, she had tried to tell herself that her grief could be nothing compared to Joe's grandmother's grief. At least Monica knew she had hope whereas Mrs Totten had none.

Chapter 28

"If you wish to let the children disembark at this port we are shortly coming into, for an hour or two, they must be supervised at all times. They must never leave the side of those who are responsible for them."

The ship's captain had arranged a meeting with all the passengers on the upper deck this morning.

"This is Port Said. It is a seaport in Egypt, and we will be arriving there very shortly. We must refuel here, and we must get food and other provisions, so we will be docking here overnight." The captain said, "But anyone who goes into the port must report back by five o'clock this evening, is that clear? It gives everyone the chance to see the place and will no doubt relieve some of the boredom of just sailing the seas." Again, he emphasised the importance of never letting the children out of the carer's sight. Then he said, "If you decide to leave the ship, a register will be here." He pointed to a table in front of him. "We ask you to sign it on your way out, we need to account for all of you returning safely."

The boys, standing quietly beside Mr Newell who had been looking after them, could hardly believe their ears.

"We are going to be getting off here, isn't that wonderful," David said. "I am so bored on this ship, there is never anything to do all day long."

"Yes, we can get off, or we can stay on the ship, that man said." Christopher wasn't so sure. "I don't know whether I want to get off or not, it might be a bit scary, and for Joe too, you know." These last few words were said in a whisper, and Chris tightened his hold on Joe's hand as he spoke. Christopher looked across at the port they were slowly sailing into, and it seemed to him that all the bright lights shining in the place were meant to dazzle and confuse him, even more than he already was. There seemed to be ships and buildings everywhere, and Christopher couldn't understand why the captain had told them they would only be here for a short time.

But was this not where they would be staying? But where were they going? No matter when David asked Mr Newell when they would be arriving at their holiday place, he just told them brusquely they would have to wait and see. Christopher knew they had been on this ship a long time and when he asked David he said 'yes' it had been weeks because he had been counting them. He was glad that Joe really didn't seem to have any idea of time, or how long they had been on the ship. Nowadays, Joe just seemed content enough, when he had Christopher and David beside him. He still talked about his granny from time to time, talking about when he would see her again, he would tell her all about the big ship and all the people on it.

Christopher had gone along with David's wishes to go and see the place they had only been off the ship a short time and had entered one of several streets stretching in front of them. Now though, Joe told Christopher he was scared and wanted to go back to the boat.

"I don't like it here, Christopher. All these people, they are scary."

"Joe, you just hold on to me and David and we will stay close to Mr Newell, the people are alright, you know. They are just dressed differently from us." Christopher wasn't scared exactly, but he found the street they were walking down so unlike any at home. He felt confused and taken aback by all the bright colours of the shops and the clothes that the people wore. They were beautiful people, Christopher thought, just like his mummy was, with her dark hair and skin that tanned so easily. He had noticed the women's hair, always held in place by very bright jewellery. As for the men, they wore tight, smooth suits, waistcoats, and strange-looking hats on their heads. It was all so different from how his daddy had dressed.

Now Mr Newell was speaking to them, "These people we are all seeing here are Egyptians, boys, and this country is called Egypt. You would never have heard of it, but as you grow up you will hear the names of lots of countries in the world. And this is just one of them." Then he added, "There isn't much for you here boys, so I think we will make our way back to the ship."

Christopher turned to Joe. "Joe, we are going back, did you hear that? We are going back to the ship." Then he spoke to Mr Newell, "Thank you sir, we would rather go back." The he looked at Joe. "Joe is getting a bit anxious, so he will be glad to go."

"I'd rather go back too," David said.

They turned and walked back past the brightly coloured shops, past the women in their beautiful costumes and the men and their proud bearings. Later that evening the boys talked a lot about what they had seen, and they wondered at the vast difference in the place they had just visited and their home, and the quiet nondescript town that was Lisburn. Back on board the ship, the days slipped past, and David and Christopher rarely mentioned when they might be finishing the trip, nor where they may be going to. Mr Newell had become much closer to them, and he let the two girls who had also come from Melton Home, to come to the dormitory they were in to play with them and stay for some parts of the day. The food was good, and Mr Newell always made sure they got their fair share of everything.

Then a storm came. The captain had called everyone together on board to tell them that the weather was changing, and it seemed as though a storm might be coming. He advised everyone to go to their dormitories or cabins at the first signs of this happening and to stay there. He emphasised the danger if anyone stayed on deck, that area was strictly out of bounds, he stressed to everyone. He also said that everyone should lie as flat as possible and keep a towel handy in case they might be sick.

Afterwards, Christopher did not know how he and Joe would have managed without David that night. Throughout the duration of the storm David was not sick at all but Christopher and Joseph were violently so, time after time after time. So much so that Christopher was simply retching constantly with nothing more in his stomach to bring up. The noise in their dormitory was frightening, people being sick, moaning and crying in pain and despair, and all the time trying to take the advice from their captain to lie flat and still. It was Dave who held Joe, soothed him and cleaned him up each time he was sick. Christopher could not have done anything to help, he felt so violently ill himself all night.

Then morning came, the storm abated, the ship steadied, the dormitory became quieter, and people began to realise the storm had passed, and thanked God for it. Later, when Joe and Christopher began to feel somewhat better, David fetched a basin with water and his own towel from his bag. Then he took the soiled pyjamas from Joe, washed him all over and laid him back in his bed. He fetched water for Christopher who managed to change his clothes and wash himself before sinking back into his bed again, exhausted. David lay beside Joe, and before long all three were asleep, all thought of food forgotten.

Chapter 29

"We will shortly be arriving at a place called Australia," Mr Newell said. He had gathered the children from Melton Home, Baron's Home and the Sisters of Newbourne, here on deck this morning. "It is in Australia that we will be staying for a time. Some of you will be going to different houses, and by that, I mean the girls will be going to a different house to the boys. We will be met by someone when we come off the ship, and they will take you to the houses you will be staying in."

David, Christopher and Joe stood together silently, listening to what Mr Newell was saying. Then David turned to Christopher and remarked quietly, "I don't really care anymore where we are going, as long as the three of us are going to be together, that is all I want."

"I don't care either, David, as long as we are going to get off this ship. I couldn't face another one of those awful storms nor do I think Joe could either." Christopher turned to Joe. "What do you think, Joe? Will you be glad to get off?"

"Yes, Christopher." Joe turned to David. "David, didn't Mr Newell definitely say the boys would all be together? Didn't he?"

"Yes, he said the boys will go to one house and the girls to another, so we will be together, Joe, don't worry," David reassured him.

Christopher put his arm around Joe's shoulder. "We three will still be together and that's the main thing, isn't it?" Christopher wanted to reinforce David's words; he knew Joe well enough to know he would be worried they might be separated.

Now, Mr Newell was telling them all to go to the dining hall for lunch. After that, they would be docking at a place called Freemantle, a port in Australia.

The port of Freemantle was a busy one, the noise and bustle of activity made it hard for the boys to carry on any conversation. The sun beat down relentlessly while they waited with Mr Newell for somebody to meet them and take them to the house they were going to. The girls from Melton Home and Sisters of

Newbourne had already been over to the boys. They wanted to say their goodbyes and a bus, it seemed, was waiting to take them to their home. The boys were disappointed to see the girls heading off but reassured each other they would be going back home again soon. Then hopefully they would all be on the same ship, so they would meet again.

Soon after the girls had gone, a man approached Mr Newell and announced their bus was waiting, and they all needed to follow him to the car park. Mr Newell said a brief goodbye as the children left him. There were fifteen boys on the bus, and they were grateful that they all seemed to be going to the same place. But the journey seemed endless and was quite awful.

They soon left the busy part of Freemantle and were travelling through sparse, desert-like conditions. Here, grass and trees were burnt to a cinder by the strong sun and looked as if they had also suffered from some very strong winds. The bus full of boys was unduly quiet, they were all tired, but that was not the only reason for their silence, some of them were very apprehensive. They had begun to realise, because of the length of time they were on the ship, that this was no holiday they were on. They had all been deliberately brought here to this sun scorched country, every one of them. But why? And what for? And where were the girls being taken to?

Although Christopher and David had never voiced any of their fears to one another during their time on the ship, the dread had lain between them for some time. Now, on what they realised was probably the last leg of their journey, they simply huddled together with Joe between them, who blessedly, had no real concept of the depth of their feelings of apprehension. Indeed, the two older boys were grateful for Joe's presence, it helped relieve their minds from the fear of the unknown which lay ahead for them all. The boys had rarely spoken of their mothers recently or now of his grandmother indeed during the last couple of weeks, all their anxieties and apprehension had been taken up with the idea that this trip was certainly no holiday.

Now, as they travelled through this alien place, Christopher wondered had his mother been told they weren't really on a holiday and that they were quite far away, in a faraway country. Christopher just carried this dull ache in his heart for her and felt it must be the same for Joe and David. He felt sometimes now that they were so far away, he would never see her again. Then, at other times he did try to believe his mother would search for him until she found him. It was at these times that Christopher felt he must do whatever was asked of him, from whoever had arranged all this, and he would accept wherever they were going.

Chapter 30

"I was telling Edward that I was going to visit Mrs Totten with you this evening, Jill, and he said he was glad to hear we were keeping contact. He always seems really interested in her welfare."

Monica and Jill had arranged to meet up and return to see Joe's grandmother again. It was now into the month of July, and it was three weeks since they had seen her, and both women were determined they wanted to keep contact with her. She had been so utterly heartbroken at the loss of her grandson on their last visit, and Monica and Jill felt, in some way, they were helpful and of some comfort to her.

"Edward said if I wanted to arrange to bring her to the annexe some evening or on a weekend afternoon, to do so. In fact, he has told me repeatedly that the annexe is my home, and I can have any visitors I like," Monica said. "So perhaps today when I call, we can arrange to collect her when you would be free, Jill, and you could come too, that is, if you would like to," Monica hastened to add.

"I would love to, Monica, and you will certainly need help with her you know, but we will arrange something," Jill answered, "and today we will spend a bit of time with her." Jill hesitated. "Have you had any further news about Christopher?" She knew it was a sensitive question but did not want to sound callous and uncaring by not enquiring about Monica's son.

"Well, my first attempt to prove the adoption was fraudulent has failed, so Edward is going to speak to the solicitor to see what he suggests is the best way forward." Monica's voice wavered and cracked. "I must have hope, Jill, I really must. Unlike poor Mrs Totten, who has no hope now. I know it was a fake signature on those papers so surely the truth will come out at the end. It must do, it has to." Monica shook her head now and turned away to look out the bus window and Jill realised she did not want her to see any loss of control.

She squeezed Monica's arm lightly and said, "Of course it will, truth will pay, I pray that it will, Monica."

Sara Totten seemed to need to talk about that awful time during the Blitz and Monica and Jill stayed for a couple of hours in the Home with her. They had brought her a couple of magazines and did read some interesting snippets to her, but then they realised she just wanted to talk about the Blitz and how she had saved Joe. They listened at length to her talking about her beloved grandson, about how the Blitz had killed her parents, and robbed her of her ability to walk properly. She cried a lot of the time they were with her, and they did their best to comfort her. Monica told her the next time they called they were going to bring her to Monica's apartment for tea and cakes, and to see where Monica lived. At that, Mrs Totten seemed to become more alive and interested than she had been since they started calling to see her.

"Mr Dunn has found another handwriting analyst, Monica, and he is going to apply to have the adoption papers back with him to enable him to let this expert have a look." Edward had called in to Jennie's class as Monica and her were just finishing for the day. "He does say, Monica, it will take a few days to have them back on his desk, and he will contact me as soon as he has something concrete to work on," Edward informed her, and then looking at her with some concern, he continued, "How are you? Do you find being with Jennie too much for you? Would you like to have some time off?" He thought the girl had lost a lot of weight.

"Oh no, please Edward, I am much better working. I could not bear to sit about," Monica said and then added, "Are you happy for me to be with Jennie? I try not to think about anything other than her when I am working."

"Jennie seems to love you, Monica. She seems to me to be learning very fast and she talks about you a lot. I know she feels very close to you and yes, I am very happy for you to be with her, now does that answer your question?"

Monica nodded and gave him one of her rare smiles. "Thank you, Edward. I must organise myself and have you and Agnes for dinner soon, you have all been so kind to me. I would like to show my appreciation."

"I need to take Jennie to see her grandmother in Enniskillen this weekend. But I insist that dinner will be in my place, and I will sort it out with Agnes and let you know, and," he smiled, "I want to ensure you are eating plenty of good food, even though you may not have much of an interest in it at present."

"I will do my best, Edward, I really will. I do know I have lost some interest in food, and yet I also know how important it is to eat well. So, I do force myself to have nourishing food and Agnes makes sure I do too." Monica felt it was important her employer knew she was looking after herself. She felt it was essential if she was to continue to live and work here. She had nowhere else to go, and it was imperative she would have a good home and a job when Christopher came back to her. She knew that, despite everything, it was the knowledge of her security here, and how totally blessed she was in obtaining a job here and with it, a home. This drove her to get up each morning and prepare for the day ahead. It was that knowledge that helped her sleep at night and gave her such hope of finding her darling son.

Edward arranged with Agnes that the three of them would dine together on the Friday of the weekend after they had been to Enniskillen. On the Saturday morning he had a phone call from Mr Dunn, his solicitor, to tell him that the Christian Committee had eventually responded to his request for Christopher Scott's adoption paper. They informed him that they had been so long in replying to his request because they had had a thorough search for the papers, but they seemed to have been lost in the system.

Jill knew she must go back and see Mr Foster and tell him of the latest development regarding the Melton Home children and their holiday. The fact that two of the children had died from an infection while they were away on the holiday, and although Jill felt it might add to his distress, she believed it could not have any bearing on Mrs Foster's death as the children died after her suicide. Jill failed to see any connection at all between the tragedies, but she had promised to keep him informed about anything to do with the children concerned, so she had to be true to her word. She rang him from the Home in the afternoon and said she would like to call with him after work if that suited him.

"Of course, Jill, at what time might I expect you?" Sam Foster replied.

"I am going to have some tea here with Lily, just to keep her company, so I should be around at seven o'clock, if that is alright."

"Yes, of course, seven o'clock is lovely. I was going to suggest I would make dinner for us, but we will do that another time hopefully."

Jill thanked him for his offer and reaffirmed she would be with him around seven.

"Jill, I don't know what to make of everything you have told me." Sam Foster was shocked to hear that two of the children had died from an infection while on holiday. "It must have been devastating for the parents to be told such terrible news. I do feel for them, I know what it is like to lose a loved one so suddenly." He gave a sigh. "And their deaths only make Eleanor's death even more of a mystery. They can't have any bearing on her suicide, but I still think the holiday had something to do with it. But exactly what, I do not know."

Jill thought Sam sounded so close to despair and automatically she reached over and held his arm. He placed his other hand on hers and held it tightly. Then in a dejected manner, he removed it.

"I know, Sam, I don't think so either," she said softly. "But I still find it hard to accept that out of the five children who said goodbye to me that morning, none of them are coming back. Three have been adopted and two died."

"It does seem very odd, Jill, perhaps all five were lined up for adoption and two died before that could happen."

"Yes, that is probably right, but Amy and Joe were so well that I cannot believe they are gone." Jill went on, "Regarding the adoptions, we can only hope they are well treated, have good homes, and will have a good life with whoever they are with." Then Jill remembered Christopher. "Christopher Scott's mother is querying the adoption papers and their validity, so we will see what comes out of that and I will keep you informed. I hope to meet up with Mrs Scott soon and hopefully she will know more then."

Jill stayed with Sam Foster that evening until his sons returned home, he seemed glad of her company. Tonight, he appeared more dejected and defeated than he had been on their last visit, so she felt compelled to stay with him. Then, of course, as he had done on her last visit, he insisted on driving her home as it was getting late.

Chapter 31

Preoccupied, Edward replaced the receiver into its base, while at the same time trying to digest the impact of the call he had just received from his solicitor. Was Monica's fight to prove that the adoption papers were fraudulent over? Was there no other way for her to fight on? How on earth would she take this latest news? Would she crumble now with the weight of the loss of her son? Edward began to pace the floor of his study, distraught now, at the thought of what Monica was going to hear and the loss she was going to have to live with. He thought back now to what exactly Mr Dunn had said, he had been very straight with him, there was no doubt about it. In his most professional way, he had told him that Christopher's adoption papers were lost.

"That is what they are saying, Edward, but I don't believe a word of it. It is all a cover-up, I think," then Albert Dunn hurried on, "I never said that you know. I will deny I ever said that." His voice was forceful now. "The Christian Committee have said that the papers have been lost and that is it I am afraid." He went on, "We have no proof of anything, and I wouldn't want Mrs Scott to try to fight on. It would cost too much, and she has no hope against a stronger force than she is." He sounded apologetic. "That is my belief, Edward, and my advice, It is a dreadful business for her and for you too, as her employer, I mean."

"Thank you, Albert, I appreciate everything you have done for Monica, and I shall settle up with you soon," Edward answered, his voice weary. "But I must think of the best way to break this awful news to her, and I am lost at the moment."

"I know. I know, Edward," Albert said with sympathy. "I want to say I won't be sending any bill your way, or Mrs Scott's way, not this time, Edward."

Edward was touched by this generous gesture and in shaky tones thanked him for everything and told him he would let him know how Monica was. Now, as he thought of the kindest way to tell Monica, he was glad she and Agnes had joined him for a meal last night. Monica seemed to have decided to dress up and

Edward thought she had looked so much better. They had had a quiet reflective time together and all three were optimistic about the future. He had to tell her this morning, she was entitled to know and needed to know, as soon as possible. He would seek Agnes out and ask her to take Jennie for a walk in the garden. And instead of Monica coming here, it might be too formal for such news, he would go to the annexe and tell her in her own, more familiar surroundings.

So here he was at her annexe, and he could hear her coming to open the door in response to his knock. Seeing her initial look of surprise at him being there, to be quickly followed by a look of fear and apprehension, he automatically folded her in his arms, led her gently into her living room and they sat down together on the sofa.

He still held her firmly as she said quietly, "I was not expecting you. You have news for me, have you?"

Edward tightened his grip on her and said gravely, "Yes I have, Monica."

Her head came up and she looked directly at him. "Tell me, please."

"Mr Dunn rang me to say Christopher's adoption papers have been lost, according to the Christian Committee but Mr Dunn thinks it is a setup and one we have no hope of getting to the bottom of."

There, Edward thought, *I have told her just as Albert Dunn really wanted me to.*

Now Monica sat in the circle of Edward's arm, frozen and unaware of where she was, or who was supporting her.

"Is he saying I have no chance of getting Christopher back? Is he saying that?" Now she was trembling all over and Edward steadied his arms around her. "Please. I must know."

"I am so sorry, Monica. He says he believes there never were any valid papers for any of the children, but we can't prove a thing in a court of law."

Monica seemed to shrivel up in his arms and sink closer into his body for some reassurance.

"What we can do, Monica, is to keep avenues of enquiries open. Maybe, just maybe, we could find out who adopted him and where he is. As the law stands, I know you are not really allowed to make contact even if you did know where he was. But I think Christopher will contact you, you know, I am sure he will." Edward was rewarded with a slight nod of her head and her hand gripped his tightly. He knew in that moment she looked on him as her lifeline and her support, and for him that would do for now.

He had just realised this morning, as she leaned into him, that he wished for something much more than that. But he knew that, for now and for some time to come, he could never intrude on her terrible grief for the loss of her son. It would be unseemly and disrespectful of him to try, at this time, to be anything more than a good friend.

Monica began to regain a level of composure, and now conscious she was resting against Edward's side, with his arm protectively around her, she remembered he was her employer. She was also just remembering what Agnes had told her about the previous governess and how she had thrown herself at him. Now she cringed at the very idea that Edward would ever need to become wary of her, and that he might ever think she would make up to him in any way.

In normal circumstances, she would never be the least familiar with him, but this morning was certainly not a normal morning for her, now through her tears, she removed herself from the security of his arms, and thanked him for his understanding and the comfort he had given her at such a time. She straightened up and regarded Edward steadily. "I have to hope, I have to try to trace him, but I promise I will do my utmost for your daughter, Edward, through it all. That is, if you are happy for me to stay?" She managed to keep her voice firm and continued to look at him steadily.

Edward just wanted to draw her into his arms and continue to comfort her, but he sensed she was intent on putting on a brave face, so he just said very warmly, "As I said when this arduous, shocking experience started, Monica, you would always have a job here as long as Jennie needed you, and that still stands." And then he added, "I will send Agnes in to you, you will need someone for a while and some tea perhaps, I will call back later this evening." Edward began to make his way to the door.

Then Monica rose from her seat and placed her hand gently on his arm. "Thank you for your kindness and understanding here with me, I appreciate it so much."

Edward nodded and smiled encouragingly, and as he left her, he was thankful that she had no idea of the depth of his feelings, she thought he was just being kind and that was good.

Chapter 32

Swandon Home lay in deep, wild countryside approximately forty-nine miles, and over an hour's drive, from the city of Perth in Western Australia. It was no longer a children's home, but a new Catholic student college. The approach to it was most unwelcoming and frighteningly eerie with its bare track bordered by grass, trees and hedges burnt black and dry by fierce sun and wind, and by utter neglect. The whole roadway and surrounding area had a creepy, uncomfortable feeling, and when the road widened out into a large square courtyard where a huge elegant, stone building with a red tiled roof sat surrounded by other properties in such a state of disrepair that the feeling of unease intensified.

To Christopher, Joe and David and the rest of the children on the bus they were in awe of, and alarmed at, what they were seeing. They wondered if this was where they were going to be staying, or would they still be expected to travel to yet another place.

As the bus pulled up in front of dark, wooden doors, they were quickly opened, and two men in dark clothing came down the steps and made their way over to the bus. It was then that the boys were all told to vacate the bus in an orderly fashion and wait to hear from the two men approaching them, where they would be going.

"Make sure you have all your belongings with you when you are getting off," one of them said. "This is where you will be staying." When the driver was assured that all the children were safely off the bus and had all their belongings with them, he started up the engine, did a circle round the courtyard and disappeared down the roadway he had just driven up. In subdued silence the children stood stricken as the bus and its driver disappeared in a cloud of yellow dust. They were now standing in a strange, fearful looking place with two complete strangers. Strangers who were, without a doubt, as they slowly walked past them, surveying them up and down. When they had finished their inspection one of them spoke.

"You have been sent here to a lovely country where the sun always shines and there is plenty of good food. And this is your home now," he indicated the building behind him. "This is a children's home, and you are in Australia. It is a very, very long way from where you have come from. You will get good food here and clean clothes when you need them." The man paused and regarded them all. "I am Father Brady, and this is Father Kelly. He wants to talk to you." With that, a huge man, who seemed to dwarf the first man, came forward until he was very close to them.

"I am Father Kelly. My colleague has told you all you have a home here. And will get good food and a bed. But I want to say you have to work hard here in return for what you get." His voice rose. "Do you understand? The rules must be obeyed here by every one of you. If they are not, you must be punished. Is that clear?"

Father Kelly looked at the subdued children in front of him "I said, is that clear? Answer me. Please."

"Yes Sir," came the quiet, muted response from some of the children, some others simply nodding their heads.

"You will be starting work here, not tomorrow, but the next day, to help build more houses out here. You will all need to be up and ready for work by six-thirty in the morning. You will have had breakfast before you start the day." He looked them over. "Is that clear?"

Once again some of the children said a quiet yes and others just nodded.

"Now you will follow Father Brady and I, and we will show you the dormitories, washrooms and where you will eat during your stay here."

With that the two priests turned towards the house with its red tiled roof and as the children prepared to follow them, one of the men led the way and the other man went to the back of the group to shepherd them in.

Joe, Christopher and David kept to the centre of the group and stayed close together as they entered the building. Then they were all silently led upstairs and shown a huge room with endless rows of beds in it. Christopher thought he had never seen so many beds in one place but was immediately grateful that that was the case. The three of them were unlikely to be separated from one another and Christopher, who had always been taught to say a quiet thanks to God, did so now when he saw the dormitory they would be sleeping in. He believed that things here in this place were not going to be easy. He had felt it when the priests had spoken to them earlier and he feared for Joe.

He felt that David and he would probably manage, but Joe was different. And Christopher believed that Joe must realise by now that he would not be going home for some time. For quite a few days now, nothing had been said about going home to Lisburn, but Christopher knew it could not be far from his friend's thoughts. Now they were here in this place surely Joe's desire to contact his grandmother would become very strong, as David's must be to contact his mother. As indeed was Christopher's.

Did his mother know now, he wondered, that this was no holiday he had been sent on? Christopher knew with certainty they had all been sent here to work. He had read about kidnappings, and he knew now, without a shadow of doubt, that they had been brought here against their will and against their mummies' will. They had been kidnapped. There never was going to be any holiday.

Chapter 33

Jill was not really looking forward to meeting Monica this Saturday afternoon. Monica had telephoned her two days ago asking if she would like to visit Joe's grandmother with her, with a view to asking Mrs Totten to come to tea at Monica's apartment. Initially Jill had not recognised Monica's voice, it was so shrill and sharp. Tentatively, Jill asked her if she had heard anything more from the solicitors and the forged adoption papers. Monica, in a sombre voice, said 'yes' she had, but would tell her all about it when she saw her.

Now, as Jill watched her newfound friend walk towards her, she was struck anew by her beauty. On first meeting Monica, Jill had certainly thought her very attractive, but she had lost weight since Jill had last seen her, and that seemed to emphasise her grace and elegance and the perfect bone structure of her face. She smiled at Jill as she approached but Jill could sense that her smile hid some inner agony. And instinctively, Jill knew she was not going to hear any good news about Christopher Scott.

Jill greeted Monica warmly but did not broach the subject of Christopher until they were seated comfortably on the bus. Not wanting Monica to think she had forgotten about her trauma or that, indeed, she did not care, she placed her hand in Monica's as it lay in her lap and said softly "Do tell me about Christopher, have you any news at all?"

"Yes, I have, Jill." Monica returned her grasp. "Edward Wallace's solicitor, Mr Dunn, tells us that he requested the adoption papers in order to send them to a second analysis expert, but the Christian Committee informed him that Christopher's adoption papers have been lost in the system." Monica's head was bowed as she started to speak, then she straightened up, and in a firmer voice continued, "Mr Dunn assures us that the whole thing is a cover-up, but unfortunately we have no proof of any forgery or fraud."

Monica added, "He did tell me that I could try to trace who adopted Christopher and where he might be. He did warn me that I might not have any success, but it is the only hope we have." Then she looked directly at Jill. "Have you any ideas at all, Jill? About any of it?"

Jill shook her head sadly. "Our Mr Baird took all the papers away with him on the two occasions he came to see me, firstly about the supposed holiday and secondly to let you know about the adoptions." Jill felt the need to stress her ignorance of everything to Monica. "The whole episode came out of the blue—I was even unaware of the supposed holiday. But if I hear any whimpers at all from anywhere, about what went on, I'll let you know post-haste, Monica," Jill said reassuringly. Then went on, "I have not told Sam Foster anything about the two children dying, and now Christopher's lost adoption papers simply add to the whole mystery and the callousness of everything. I think he will find it all difficult to take in. But I do intend to tell him everything, Monica. He may remember something that Eleanor said or did, you just never know."

"Thank you, Jill. Meantime, it is essential I keep my job with Edward Wallace. It is vital I do that. I want to live here in Lisburn in case Christopher ever comes looking for me." Monica's eyes filled with tears, and she gave a great sigh, then in an effort to change the subject she said, "Let's encourage Mrs Totten to come to visit me next week. You are off duty; didn't you tell me when I rang you?"

"Yes, Monica, I'm off all next weekend—the first one for some time. I'll look forward to coming with Mrs Totten," Jill said warmly, then noticing their bus was almost at their stop she added, "Let's go, Monica, this is our stop."

Later that evening when Monica was back in her apartment, she thought of her afternoon with Joe Totten's grandmother, and realised that she had had even greater empathy for her today than she had had on her previous visit. She accepted it was because of the so-called lost adoption papers and her agony of despair about it. She was starting to believe that her Christopher was lost to her, just as surely as Joe was lost to his grandmother.

Before Monica made any final arrangements to have Mrs Totten and Jill to visit, she sought Edward out one evening, and asked his permission to have them visit her apartment.

"Of course, Monica, as I've said, you don't have to ask my permission, the apartment is your home, and you must have your friends around any time you want." Edward smiled warmly.

"It is the lady from the old people's home who lost her grandson, and Jill Corken who works in the children's home Christopher was in," Monica said. "I have known Joe's grandmother for some time, but just recently befriended Jill."

"The lady in the home, is she mobile?" Edward asked her.

"She has a wheelchair provided for any outings she goes on. Besides, it is only a short bus ride from the home to here."

"Monica, I must insist that I collect your friends by car and bring them here." Edward was adamant. "You can't start hauling a wheelchair about on a bus and try to help Joe's grandma as well. I insist on doing this."

"My goodness, Edward that is so kind of you, I never dreamt of you doing such a thing." Once again, Monica was taken aback by her employer's thoughtfulness.

"If you were injured, you would be of no use to anybody," Edward said, but he smiled as he spoke which helped relieve the seriousness of his words. Words he was using to cover his true reason, simply wanting to accompany her.

"I never thought of that, Edward. And of course, that might happen. So, thank you for thinking of that. I'll ring Jill and let her know we'll collect her at the Melton Home and then collect Mrs Totten at the old people's home, and…" Monica added, "I am so grateful to you. You have been so kind to me." She added in a timid tone of voice, "Your kindness has made everything so much more bearable for me, and I do want you to know that."

"It is so easy for me to be kind, Monica. But it is you who has the burden of loss to face every morning and to think about every night." His voice was heavy with emotion for her. "Your stoical approach to your care and education of Jennie is truly remarkable in your circumstances."

"Thanks again, Edward. Jennie is simply a joy and inspiration for me," Monica stressed. "She is also good company and gives me very little time to think about myself and to dwell on all my trauma."

"I'm glad to hear you say that, Monica. Children can be invaluable to us all, as I myself know only too well." Then, on a lighter note, Edward went on, "Ring your friend and let her know I shall do all the driving next Saturday and I look forward to meeting your friends."

Chapter 34

Monica was initially quite embarrassed at Edward's insistence to collect her friends and bring them back to the annexe. He was, after all, her employer and she felt she was imposing on his good will. But as they drove along, he seemed so relaxed that Monica too, began to feel very comfortable beside him. And later his friendly, easy manner as he helped Mrs Totten into the back seat and put her wheelchair into the car boot, the women too, began to feel more and more at ease. On their arrival at the apartment he insisted on wheeling Mrs Totten into Monica's sitting room even though Jill assured him she was more than capable of doing it. He said his goodbyes to them and confirmed he would be back around five o'clock to take them home.

Monica was pleased at how well she coped with everything that afternoon. Initially they talked about Christopher and Joe which did distress all three women. Then Jill began to divert the conversation to Monica's role with Jennie, insisting she was very interested to know what exactly she did. Monica was keen to relate to her friends how much she enjoyed her job.

"I am teaching Jennie at elementary level at present, I do know that Mr Wallace is keen for Jennie to attend a grammar school when she reaches that age, so I do strive to give her the best grounding I can," Monica said with enthusiasm. "Jennie is a pleasure to teach, she is so keen to learn. Our mornings are spent doing English and arithmetic and the afternoons are spent doing knitting and sewing. We also have gardening and painting sessions, so all in all, Jennie and I have a very full, busy day." Monica smiled warmly at her friends, talking about her work with Jennie was always a pleasure to her.

Later they had tea with egg sandwiches which Monica had made earlier, and sponge cake she had bought from the local bakery all too soon it was five o'clock and Edward appeared to take Jill and Mrs Totten home.

"I would like you to come with me, Monica, I'm sure I know where to go but another trip out will do you good."

"Of course, I'm coming too, Edward. I need to report back to the staff that Mrs Totten is safely back with them."

The trip back was a quick one because there were few cars on the road on Saturday evenings and Edward soon found the road, and the flat where he had picked Jill up earlier. Edward and Monica were silent for a time as they travelled back towards home, when Edward spoke, it was to enquire about Mrs Totten.

"What happened to Mrs Totten's leg, Monica? Was she in an accident?"

"No, not an accident. She was severely wounded when the Nazis bombed Dee Street and Joe's parents were both killed in it," Monica answered, then added quietly, "As were mine."

"Oh, how awful for you. I didn't know, Monica. I am so sorry."

"You weren't to know, Edward. It is seven years ago now, I know, but the horror of it all never leaves you. I was told they were both killed instantly." Monica hesitated, unsure whether to open her heart any more to this man who had been so kind to her. Then she went on, "Christopher was left without any grandparents—my husband, Thomas's parents, who were quite elderly, died when Christopher was only three years old. They lived in Cork, so Thomas and I saw very little of them, as you can imagine."

Suddenly, Monica decided to tell the whole story to her employer, "When my husband was killed by a speeding car, Christopher and I were left on our own with very little savings. That is why I had to put him temporarily in a home when our money ran out and I could not get a job. Then our landlord served an eviction notice on us." Monica sighed and looked at Edward. "So here I am." Monica felt a great sense of relief that Edward had the full picture of her background.

"I did not realise you had been through so much," Edward said with deep feeling. "No wonder you are so desperate about your son. If you wish at any time to take a few days off, please do, Monica. I can take time to look after Jennie— well, Agnes and I together can do it." And briefly, Edward placed his hand over Monica's as they lay in her lap.

Monica broke in, "Oh, no, please, as I've said, Jennie is my lifeline and I feel so much better when I'm with her." Now she sounded very distressed.

"That's fine, Monica. That's fine, my dear. It was only a thought." He did his best to appease her. Then he changed the subject. "So, Joe's parents were both killed in the Blitz and his grandmother was injured—how awful. Mrs Totten looks very young to be so crippled. She looks to me to be just in her fifties."

"Yes, I think so too, Edward, she can't be much more, I think," Monica replied.

"I suppose when I heard it was Joe's grandmother, I was expecting someone very elderly. How wrong can you be?" Edward said, then he brought the conversation back to Mrs Totten's injury. "Did anyone ever consider a prosthesis—an artificial limb for her?"

"Not that I am aware of. Mrs Totten never mentioned anything to me about such help for her. Probably she would be expected to pay for it. I do know that priority for such treatments were scheduled for anyone in the army who had been injured. And that is, I suppose, how it should be," Monica replied, suddenly conscious how much she had taken Mrs Totten's injury for granted. It had never entered her head that there might be some help available out there. Now she was wondering what Edward's train of thought was regarding Mrs Totten.

"Do you think Mrs Totten would mind if I had a word with some of the staff in the Home about the possibility of her being fitted with one? I would be prepared to pay for it. I hate to see such a young woman so incapacitated. And I do feel so sorry for her having lost her son and daughter-in-law and now Joe. But I believe if she could walk unaided it would make a difference to her life, and perhaps help her cope with her loss." Edward added, "I know they have made great advances with artificial limbs because of the demand for them for the wounded military."

For a moment, Monica was speechless as she listened to Edward's concerns for someone he had only just met and how prepared he was to help her.

"You are so generous, Edward. And so kind and thoughtful."

"I haven't done anything yet, Monica, so let's wait and see if we can." And Edward played down her praise for him. "I wonder if you would come with me when I go to speak to someone in the Home. They know you, Monica, whereas I'm a stranger to them."

"I would love to come. If you let me know when you are likely to be free, I'll arrange a meeting in the Home around that."

"I'll leave it with you. And Agnes will be very happy to look after Jennie for us when we do go."

As Edward drove into his driveway, although the journey had been a short one, he realised he had enjoyed his time with Monica and was already looking forward to her sitting in the car with him very soon.

Chapter 35

Jill thought a lot about Monica and Mrs Totten in the days following their visit to Monica's apartment. It was so difficult to believe that they were having to deal with so much grief—the death of young Joe and the illegal adoption of Christopher. Indeed, the images of the five children as they left the Melton Home that morning to go on holiday rarely left her mind, and the whole situation weighed heavily on her as she went about her duties. She had indeed, started to think there was something odd about everything. The three adoptions, the two deaths and then the missing adoption papers.

Jill had not discussed her thoughts about the children with anyone, but she had promised Sam Foster that she would be in touch if she had anything new to tell him. Not that she thought for one minute any of the latest information bore any relevance to Mrs Foster's death, and she doubted if Sam would be able to throw any light on any of it. She wondered if she was doing the right thing by keeping him informed but she had promised him, so she would walk over tonight after work. It wasn't far and hopefully she would find him at home, but she would make sure she had something to eat here in the Home before she left.

Now, sitting facing Sam Foster in his comfortable sitting room, Jill watched him as he tried to make sense of what she had just told him.

"You're telling me, Jill that out of the five children who went on holiday, this man Baird told three of the mothers their children had been adopted and had to tell another two their children had died." Sam spoke slowly, considering what he had just heard. "And you also tell me, Jill, that Christopher Scott's adoption papers have been lost. What about the other two adoptions? What happened there?"

"Well, Sam, one of the mothers, a very young unmarried girl, was very upset. I took her outside to where her boyfriend, Neville, was waiting for her. He said he would look after her. I haven't heard anything since." Jill paused for a moment. "Perhaps her family thought it was the best option for the little girl. I don't know." And Jill shook her head sadly. "The third parent, a father, was so angry and threatened Mr Baird with legal action, but again, I have heard nothing more. He probably doesn't have any money to go to court." Jill paused again. "That's it. Sam, that's all I know."

"This is very hard for you, Jill. Five children being taken to go on holiday and then to learn what happened when they were on holiday. You know, I don't think it adds up, and in Eleanor's letter, she insists she was deceived, and her words lead me to believe that she knew something was going to happen to the children."

"You think, Sam, Eleanor got wind that something was going on but the powers that be denied it. Is that what you think?"

"Well, it looks like it," Sam replied. "I believe adoptions without parental consent were planned for all five children, but unfortunately two of them died suddenly."

Jill nodded silently and Sam continued, "Eleanor must have heard something about the Christian Committee planning adoptions without parental consent. I know that would have broken her heart."

"In my wildest dreams I could never imagine the Christian Committee doing anything illegal, especially not illegal adoptions. It is certainly not the image I or any of the general public would have of them." Jill was finding the whole business hard to understand.

"I know, Jill, and perhaps I'm wrong, but I doubt it. Perhaps I should speak to my solicitor and see what he thinks," Sam said.

"We have no proof without the adoption papers. It will be a futile fight, I think," Jill answered him.

"I think you're right, but I'll see what the law says." Then Sam added, "I've been informed that Eleanor's inquest will not happen for another three months so perhaps we will know something more by then."

"I hope so, Sam. If Eleanor was deceived, that is bad enough, but if Management knew she suspected something but was just expected to carry on as usual. Well, that's just scandalous," Jill remarked angrily. "I know I have been deceived, but it was too late for me to do anything about it all. Besides, I thought it was a genuine holiday for the children whereas Eleanor knew something more than that, but it was out of her hands to do anything about it."

"Well, let's just hope and pray that we'll get to the bottom of things, not only for Eleanor's sake but also for everyone else's sake."

Jill nodded briefly, too overcome to say anything more about anything much and Sam, seeing her so downcast, quickly offered to drive her home in his car.

Chapter 36

When one of Mrs Totten's carers first told her that she would soon be going to the outpatient's department in the local hospital to be assessed to have an artificial limb fitted, Sara could not believe it. It was something she had longed for, and dreamt about, after her initial recovery from the nightmare of the Blitz. A horrific night which had claimed the lives of her beloved husband, her son and his wife and left her disabled. It was for her darling grandson Joe's sake, she had so longed to be more mobile and able to look after him, and she knew an artificial limb might be the answer. And to think she was being offered one now when her darling Joe was dead, it was so bittersweet and so very difficult to reconcile to.

The carer had told her that a very kind donor had offered the money for the prosthesis, but he did not wish Mrs Totten to know who he was. Sara cried many tears in the coming days, tears for her grandson, who would have been so delighted for her and would have enjoyed seeing her mobile again. She cried tears in abundance for the kindness of her unknown benefactor who had sought to give her help with her affliction. Sara had not experienced such kindness since the Blitz had visited Belfast and its people. That cruel, awful time still haunted her, and she knew it always would. She believed she would always have nightmares about the gruesome sights the Nazis left behind in their trail of destruction.

So many people had lost their lives, others had much worse injuries than she had, and because of this she was one of the lucky ones. She was always reminded that she had just lost her leg below the knee while there were those who had been left limbless, paralysed, or disfigured beyond recognition. Yes, it was sad she had lost her husband, son, and her daughter-in-law on that dreadful night when their whole street had been demolished and scarcely a wall left standing. People sought to comfort her by saying how lucky she was to still be here and to have her grandson.

As for the actual night of the Blitz, Sara knew she would never forget it. The flash of the enemy's flares of light as they illuminated the whole sky, the rumble of the German aircraft and then the burr and whizzing sound of the bombs as they began to rain down on Dee Street. At the very first sound of the siren her daughter—in—law, Eliza, had been so quick to act, she had placed Joe, in his little cot, under a table which sat under the stairs and they themselves, lay down under a table in the kitchen, at a loss as to where else to go. After one bomb—which seemed to land right outside their front door—Sara got up from where she was lying and raced to where Joe lay, cocooned and sleeping soundly, in his cot under the stairs. In desperation, Sara positioned herself over the cot to try to give him some added protection.

After that, all she remembered was the awful shriek of another bomb, so much closer this time, and the whole house began to shake. Then the terrifying sounds of splintering wood and crushing brick seem to reverberate everywhere.

Sara had been told a couple of nights after her admission to hospital that she had lost her husband, son and daughter-in-law, but that her grandson had survived the air raid and she needed to be strong for his sake. His survival, the staff told her time and again, was down to her having protected him so well. She was still lying guarding him when the all clear had gone and the search for survivors was taking place. Sara was informed that Joe had gone to a children's home as he was now an orphan and of course, at present, Sara would be unable to look after him. She was assured that the Melton Home was renowned for its caring attitude and that the matron there, a Mrs Foster, was responsible for its excellent reputation. Sara was accepting of the fact that Joe had to go into a home, she herself was being advised it was the best course for her too because of her amputation.

After Sara had been told by the surgeon about the necessity of having to have an amputation, she had brought up the subject of being fitted with an artificial limb. But the ward sister had very gently explained that soldiers injured in battle were being given top priority for artificial limbs. In the case of civilians needing one they had to make a generous contribution. So, Sara had to accept the fact that, like Joe, she too must go into a care home. She insisted she wished to go to one in Lisburn because that was where Joe was staying. It would be easier to organise visits if they were both in the one town. Besides, the Homes were at breaking point with so many people now maimed and injured for life and the Belfast Homes in particular, were already overcrowded and understaffed.

118

To think that when she was first told about the nursing home, she had dreaded going and felt she had suffered so much heartache, grief, and loss, that she could not stand it if the place was a disaster. But she had been so very fortunate in her choice, from the outset the staff had been lovely—so caring and kind—that Sara had settled in very quickly. The food was good, the place was kept spotlessly clean, and the staff made a point of taking her out round the grounds in a wheelchair when the weather permitted. They had even organised her to visit Joe in the children's home from time to time, and on learning of her grandson's death had been so attentive and caring.

Now today, her friends, Monica and Jill, were coming to visit her, and she could not wait to tell them about her unknown benefactor and what he was prepared to do for her.

Chapter 37

Many times Monica longed to tell Sara that it was Edward who had been her secret benefactor in paying for her artificial limb, but she knew she must never do that. She must respect her employer's wishes and never, ever say anything about it. This was very difficult to do but because her respect for Edward was increasing by the day, she remained tight lipped about it.

On the afternoon that Sara was having her prosthesis fitted for the first time, she asked Monica and Jill to please come and give her all their encouragement. For some reason, although she was very excited about the whole thing, she was also very apprehensive. Indeed, she had become so used to hopping around her bed and being pushed around in a wheelchair she believed she might never get used to such a thing as an artificial limb. Now, as she waited anxiously with her friends for the carers to come to her, she told them shakily that "she might never be able to use it and…" she added, "to think that some kind person has spent a lot of money on me." Sara burst into tears.

Immediately, Monica was by her side and hugging her close said, "Of course it will take a lot of getting used to, but you'll get there, Besides," Monica said firmly, "as you've just said, we have to remember the benefactor who will, no doubt be enquiring from time to time how you are getting on. So, believe me, Sara, we must make sure you master the use of it," Monica said very decisively and then aware she had spoken rather sharply—she had been thinking of Edward and his disappointment if Sara would be unable to use it—she hugged Sara again and fetching a tissue from the bedside table gently dried Sara's eyes for her.

Monica also knew that Sara's tears were not only about anxiety over the limb but also for her darling grandson. Monica knew Joe would have been encouraging his grandma all the way. But now Joe was dead, and Sara just had Monica and Jill for support and Monica vowed she would do all in her power to help Sara.

When Monica returned to her apartment later that evening, she sought Edward out almost immediately, and thanked him for giving her free time to go to see Sara.

"Monica, I wanted you to be with Mrs Totten today. I'm sure it is all very daunting for her, and sad too for her, after losing her grandson," Edward answered when Monica thanked him.

"Yes, actually it was, but I thought she managed rather well with the prosthesis," Monica told him. "It might take a little bit of time, but I don't really foresee any problem. And…" Monica added, "She's very determined."

"Good," Edward replied. "Now, what about you, Monica, how have you been? Have you eaten anything this evening yet?"

"I'm alright, I'm just waiting all the time to hear something from someone. I don't even know who anymore, just to tell me Christopher is coming back." Monica was determined not to cry but the whole afternoon and evening seemed to have been so emotional. "I'm going to go shortly and make myself something to eat."

"Please join us, Monica. You do really look too tired to begin cooking, and as you know, Agnes always makes plenty for Jennie and me." Then he said encouragingly, "Indeed, I would like Agnes to join us as well. I'll seek her out shortly." He looked questioningly at Monica.

"I would really like that, Edward, thank you." The thought of having to go and make herself something to eat was not something Monica relished doing this evening. It would probably help her take her mind off things if she was sitting talking with Edward, Agnes and young Jennie. Would it help take her mind off the wild thoughts she had about Christopher, and indeed all five of the children who had left Melton Home to go on such a surprise holiday?

Chapter 38

November 1948

Jill had mixed feelings about meeting Sam Foster for a meal in The Gables, one of Lisburn's renowned restaurants. She had known that Eleanor's inquest was being held earlier in the day and when Sam had telephoned her, he said he would like to see her, and tell her how everything had gone. He said he would like to eat out if she would care to join him, explaining the two boys had gone to Kilkeel for the weekend to stay at his sister's home. There and then Jill said she would love to, she was sincere about that, and she did wonder how he was, and how everything had gone at the inquest.

The mystery of Eleanor's suicide remained a source of deep hurt and concern for Jill, nor was she anywhere nearer seeing any link between her death and the five children who went on holiday, but never returned to the Melton Home. She had searched all the files in the offices of the home hoping to unearth something, anything at all which might help to throw some light on who had instigated the so-called adoptions. Through all her doubts and worries, Jill was sure of one thing that the adoptions had been carried out illegally. No one had signed any paper agreeing to such a thing, but how would anyone ever prove any of it? The Home contained not one scrap of evidence about any of the children who had left that morning in June for a holiday, except that their names were still in the register. They were still recorded there, a constant reminder to Jill of their absence.

Jill was so very aware too, that Mr Foster was anxious to be kept informed of everything that happened, so Jill had always kept him up to date. But Jill did wonder many times if it might have been better had she never told him quite as much. Would he have been better to have been left in the dark? But it was too late to think like that now, so Jill could only hope that the inquest might give some explanation for the suicide and bring Sam Foster some peace.

The Gables restaurant was situated in the centre of Lisburn and although Jill knew it well, it was just a short walk from her flat, she had never been in it. She couldn't remember the last time she had been in a restaurant, she had to be content with her own home cooking. She simply could not afford to eat out. As she pushed open the door, she spotted Sam immediately, he seemed to be studying the menu. He looked up at the sound of the door chime and smiled warmly at Jill as she approached him. Then he stood up and pulled out a chair for her. "It's good to see you, Jill, especially after today's ordeal."

"It must have been so difficult for you." Jill was at a loss for words. What could you say to someone who had just attended his wife's inquest?

Sam nodded briefly, then went on, "I think if we order our meal first and then, while we're waiting for it, I'll tell you all about it." He lifted the menu and held it out to Jill. "I'm quite hungry, I did not feel like eating all day, so I hope to enjoy this. I think I'll have the sole, Jill. I don't want any starter, but you feel free to order something if you want to."

"No, no, Sam. If I have a starter it would surely put me off my dinner, and I am looking forward to that." Jill went on, "I'll have the sole too, Sam. Thank you."

After the waitress had taken their order and placed a carafe of water on the table and while Sam was pouring Jill some into her glass, he began to tell her about his day.

"The coroner was most sympathetic and understanding today, I must say," Sam began. "However, he did say that judging by the contents of Eleanor's letter, she must have known something about the children's adoptions and was upset about it. The coroner also stated that Eleanor must have surmised that the parents of the children were not going to be informed in advance of what was happening. It must have weighed heavily on Mrs Foster's mind that they were in ignorance about it all.

"However, the coroner stressed, in the strongest possible terms, that although the relatives did not know when the adoptions were taking place, they had signed the papers approving of their child being adopted, so any suggestion they might be illegal was rubbish—it just wouldn't have happened." Now Sam's voice was shaking but he managed to continue, "He said that knowing the adoptions were going to happen must have given Eleanor undue stress, and he must return a verdict that she committed suicide while the balance of her mind was disturbed."

Jill looked across at this man who had been through so much, and his face wore such a haunted expression that Jill felt compelled to get up from her chair and put her arms round his shoulders in an effort to give him some comfort. Gratefully, Sam lifted his head and attempted a smile and then grasped her hand where it lay on his shoulder.

"I'm sorry, so very sorry." Jill could not think of anything to say, then she noticed the waitress heading their way. "Here's our food now, Sam, so let's do our best to eat it and enjoy it." Jill released her hand and returned to her seat. After the waitress had served them and they both agreed they were enjoying their meal, Jill told him about her search for some clues in the offices in Melton Home.

"There is not one clue or any chart in the Home relating to the children. Only their names and date of their admission to the Home is recorded in the register. No one has filled in anything about where they've gone or what happened to them, especially Joe and Amy who died. Surely Mr Baird should have filled in the date of their death, and as I am only a carer it would not be my place to do so. Besides I don't know the exact dates of their death. There are just blank spaces, spaces which are supposed to be filled in if they get a job or go to another home or die. But these are just spaces nobody can be bothered to fill in."

Jill hesitated, then went on, "It looks as if nobody cared what happened to them. The next time Mr Baird calls, he hasn't visited for some time, but just gives us a brief phone call, I'll be asking him to please fill in those blank spaces."

Sam listened to what Jill was telling him and thought Mr Baird was, at the least, a careless man who paid no attention to detail, and at the worst a most uncaring, cold individual. Eleanor had always said she could not warm to him but blamed herself for their lack of rapport. But now he realised that Eleanor had probably been right about him, she had always been a good judge of character.

After all the sad conversation they had had, Jill and Sam were surprised they had enjoyed each other's company. And the restaurant Sam had chosen had turned out to be excellent. The food was delicious and the staff very attentive and they promised each other they would repeat the experience. Before leaving Jill, Sam begged her to keep in touch with him. She was, he insisted, a comfort to him at this time in his life. Jill assured him she would, and she believed that, in time, something about the children would unfold, she was sure of it. "Meanwhile," and she smiled warmly at Sam as she spoke, "we will definitely come back to The Gables."

Chapter 39

"We've been kidnapped, haven't we, Christopher?" Joe asked Christopher in a voice which was little more than a whisper. "We were never going on any holiday, sure we weren't?"

"It certainly looks like that, Joe. I think—just like you—that there was never going to be a holiday," Christopher answered quietly as he helped David and Joe shovel broken stones and debris, which they themselves had produced after knocking down old existing walls earlier, into waiting wheelbarrows.

They had been summoned to get up at six o'clock this morning and the big priest, who they had met yesterday, hovered menacingly over them as they washed and dressed. Then they were all directed into the dining room which Father Brady had shown them the previous evening. To Christopher, there seemed to be boys everywhere in that room, certainly far more than there seemed to have been on their ship or any of the buses they had been on. As he waited in the queue for his breakfast, he reckoned that some of these boys must have already been living here, they seemed so used to the routine. Suddenly, one of the boys behind him spoke to him quietly, "You're just new here, aren't you? You must have come yesterday evening."

Christopher turned around and saw a tall fair-haired boy looking at him. "We did." Christopher indicated David and Joe and some of the other boys who had travelled here with them.

"Well, take my advice and quite simply obey every order and I mean, every order you're given, and you'll be alright." He gave Christopher a rueful smile. "If you don't—well, things can be pretty bad. I'm here six months now and I do everything I'm told to do. I live for the day I'll be back in Belfast and believe me, I will. I intend to sometime go home, live with my uncle again and work in Belfast."

Christopher was in awe of what this boy was saying. "Were you told you were going on holiday too?" he asked him.

"Oh, aye, that's what they tell you. But what they tell your mum and dad I have no idea. I don't think anybody knows what they were told, I doubt if they were told what happened to us or where we are," he said, with a slight shrug of his shoulders.

"You, boy, hurry along there." Christopher realised that the burly priest was speaking to him and approaching him. Quietly, he encouraged Joe to move forward, and Dave and he followed quietly. Christopher was determined he would remember and act always on the advice of the boy he had just spoken to.

After they had breakfasted on thin, bitter porridge and stale bread dipped in equally bitter oil, they were all ushered outside and shown crumbling walls, picks, shovels and wheelbarrows and told to start demolishing the decayed structures. Every boy who had been in the dining room was soon bending low with either a pickaxe or a shovel in hand, intent on doing the work they had just been ordered to do.

"Joe, you keep with Dave and me and just do your best, we'll do the heavy stuff, and you do the clearing up."

"Thanks, Christopher. I will do the clearing up, but I intent to do my share of the heavier stuff too, you know," Joe replied. "I'm fit than I look. And when I heard that boy talking to you at breakfast time about going home to see his uncle, well, I intend to get home too, some day to see my grannie. And just thinking about that will be sure to keep me going in this awful place."

Christopher and David were really taken aback by what Joe had just said. Shy Joe, who always said so little and seemed so fearful. The two boys looked at one another, and then it was David who spoke first, "That's the spirit, Joe, but if you do ever feel the need to take it a bit easy, be sure to say, and Christopher and I will keep the work going between us.

"Thanks, Dave." Joe's voice was very firm. "But I intend to pull my weight and I intend to get out of here."

And that is how it was that day, and the next, and the next. The life of the three boys became an endless round of hammering, lifting masses of broken stones and boulders into skips, dust and debris into wheelbarrows. And all the time the intense heat of the Australian sun beat down on them and on all the other boys who had been brought to Swandon under similar circumstances. And as they worked and sweated, to build new properties for Swandon, all of them thought about home and families. And all of them vowed that one day they would leave this awful place, and then they would see their mummies and daddies again.

They had only been there three days when they witnessed one of the older boys getting beaten by one of the priests. The boy concerned was from one of the groups from the other dormitories. Christopher had only seen them fleetingly across the dining hall and landing and had never spoken to any of them. He first realised something was terribly wrong when he heard the all-too-familiar, raucous voice of Father Kelly shouting out a name. And a young boy stepped out from where he had been working.

Immediately, Father Kelly removed a thick, leather belt with a huge buckle on it, from around his waist and approaching the young boy immediately began beating him mercilessly, all the time shouting obscenities and warnings at him. All the other boys who had been concentrating on their work, stopped what they were doing, and frozen now with fear, could only stare at the horrific scene in front of them. Then the all-too-familiar voice again, "Get back to work, the lot of you, if you don't want the same treatment. And just to remind you all, you don't come in here late for breakfast or to this job here." And with that, he walked away, belt in hand, towards the house.

The boy, who had been beaten, lay curled up on the ground, his screams now subsided and only the odd whimper could be heard, but somehow the boy's silence was even more frightening and concerning than any of his screams had been. As Christopher looked at him, he could see blood pouring from his legs and body, and he began to worry who might be going to help this boy. Just as he turned to Dave to voice his concerns, three of the boys ran over to their friend lying on the ground, and very gently began to help him up and support him across the forecourt and back into the house. Christopher turned to Dave "I'm sure they'll get into trouble for helping him, by the look of Father Kelly, don't you think so, Dave?"

"I would think so, but what else could they do, they had to help him. They couldn't leave him lying there," Dave replied. "But I think we better pull ourselves together and get back to knocking down walls. We can't be seen to be shirking."

Christopher realised how wise David was, they really had to stay out of trouble at all costs. But just the same, Christopher kept watching for the boys who had helped their friend return to their work. As they drew near, he signalled for one of them to stop. Then he said, "Will you not get into trouble for helping your friend?"

"Oh, dear no, you'll soon learn. 'Our father', as we call him, loses his temper mighty quickly and then doesn't care who picks up the pieces. And then he'll act as if none of it ever happened," one of the other boys remarked. "And you can't complain here, you know, there's nobody to complain to. So, we all just stick together as best we can and when we can. And we will expect all you new ones to do the same, and we'll help you and your friends all we can."

He smiled warmly at Christopher. "It takes very, very little to set him off, you know." He paused and then went on, "Just keep low and quiet, sometimes it does help to avoid trouble. And he does not seem to notice you so much."

With that the boy made to go on but Christopher forestalled him, "How long have you been here? And is it easy to remember how long it is?"

The boy, with a rough edge to his voice, answered, "I'm here three years now, brought from England three very long years ago. And how do I remember that? When I was first brought to this awful place here, I started checking off every day that passed, and I still do. You boys should do the same, start counting the days, the months and possibly years."

Chapter 40

November 1956

It would soon be Christmas again, Monica thought as she looked at her diary, checking some notes she had made regarding Jennie's progress in her schoolwork. She had told Edward she would let him know what his daughter's work was like and if she was capable of the standard required for grammar school. Monica had no doubt that Jennie was an excellent candidate for grammar school, and she had been working so hard these last few months she deserved to be accepted. The entrance examination for Friend's School was always in February and Monica and Jennie had set their sights on Jennie successfully passing it, and they had been working towards such a goal.

Monica knew Edward was keen for his daughter to go to grammar school, he rated grammar school education as a great steppingstone to future success. Although Monica was determined to do all she could to help Jennie succeed, she knew Jennie's entry to grammar school meant Monica's role as teacher and governess here must come to an end. She must leave this comfortable, secure apartment which had been such a haven for her during the last eight years. It was here she had cried endlessly for her lost son, here she had prayed incessantly to God to help her find him, but her prayers had all gone unanswered. She had had to try to cope with the knowledge that Christopher had other parents now, and another family.

Then there was Agnes, she knew she must leave Agnes too. Agnes, who had been like a mother to her, and whose support and understanding had been invaluable. Without Agnes Monica believed she would have had a nervous breakdown and would have been unable to be of any service to Edward and Jennie. Because of her dear friend's unfailing loyalty to her, Monica had, despite her grief, helped to bring out the best in Jennie. The young girl was clever and confident, she was diligent and painstaking in all aspects of her work and Monica was secretly proud of her pupil.

But Monica also knew Edward's influence had been of prime importance in moulding Jennie's character and giving her such an interest in her education. His quiet, firm manner coupled with his open affection and unconditional love for her had given Jennie a most charming but modest personality. Indeed, as well as her despair in leaving Agnes, every time Monica thought of leaving both per pupil and her employer, she was secretly heartbroken. They had both, in their own personal way, brought security and comfort to her life and in her darkest moments, when everything seemed hopeless, the knowledge that they were close by, and so willing to support her was a source of joy to her.

Now it was only four weeks to Christmas, and she had no doubt this would be her last one here with Edward, Jennie and Agnes. She had spent the last seven Christmases here in their company, and now she hoped and believed that dear, kind Edward would wait until the New Year before talking to her and terminating her employment. Meantime she had put her name down with the Housing Executive for a flat in Lisburn. She must stay here in Lisburn town in case Christopher came looking for her. If she moved to some other town, he would not know how to trace her. She had also been looking for some suitable employment but had not seen anything so far that appealed to her.

Even though Monica was unhappy about what the future might hold for her, she was determined to enjoy this last Christmas here with Edward, Jennie and Agnes. No doubt they would do what they had been doing every Christmas, and that involved so much preparation of both the house and doing all the shopping with them that the whole atmosphere ensured that everyone, including herself, were in good Christmas spirits. Edward always had his parents stay over on Christmas Eve through until after Boxing Day.

On Christmas morning, they all walked to Lisburn Cathedral for the early morning Christmas service, and on their return home Monica insisted on helping Agnes as best she could in the kitchen. Agnes was always so well organised she would have most of the meal ready, so Monica insisted she would do most of the clearing up. The presents, which were all placed under the tree on Christmas Eve, were opened after dinner, and on the first Christmas Monica spent with Edward, she told him she had bought a present for her son and intended to do so every year. Edward had put his arm round her shoulder and said quietly, "You must bring Christopher's present in here and put it under the tree too. You will feel he is closer to you I believe, Monica."

Monica was taken aback at Edward's level of understanding for her loss. She had half expected him to say, 'You shouldn't do that—it will only get your hopes up.' But he had empathised with her and despite everything that had happened, Monica felt her heartache ease that first Christmas without Christopher, and she knew it was her friends here who had helped so much.

Now today, with so much to do before this special Christmas and Monica wanting it to be especially memorable, she wanted to buy presents they might all remember her by. Then of course, there was Christopher's birthday on the 28th of this month and she always put a photograph of him in the daily newspaper, something she had been doing for over seven years, since he had been taken from her. With the photograph, she always put her usual plea that if anyone recognised him or knew anything about his whereabouts to telephone the number listed. She also explained that he was no longer the boy of eight he had been in the picture but would now be a teenager of almost sixteen.

During those seven years, never a day went past without her thinking of him and praying that his adoptive parents were good to him, and that she would see him again. She had bought him a present and a birthday card—as she had done every year—and the present was then very carefully wrapped, and the card attached to it, before placing it in the small wardrobe in her bedroom. The wardrobe which had been meant for Christopher's clothes.

Despite all Monica's promises to herself, she found that the closer it was getting to Christmas, the more she began to wonder how on earth she was going to cope with everything—all the celebrations and the warmth and kindness of everyone—knowing she would soon be leaving them all. Knowing too, that she would have to face yet another Christmas without Christopher because he was with another family now. She had kept herself very busy helping Agnes decorate the house and the annexe.

Edward and Jennie had gone to Enniskillen to stay overnight with Edward's parents before bringing them back to his home to spend Christmas with them, so there was just Agnes and her. As Monica put the finishing touches to the decorations in her annexe—Agnes had always insisted Monica must decorate her apartment, assuring her it would be sure to make her feel better and to think how much Christopher would have loved it, she made a spur of the minute decision to ask Sara Totten to come and spend Christmas with her. She could just cook dinner for the two of them in her apartment. She would explain to Edward she had thought to ask Sara to come to her as she always had Christmas in the Home.

She believed she could cope better with everything this Christmas if she was removed from Edward and his family's celebrations.

"Monica, I won't hear of you spending Christmas in the apartment with only Sara for company. You must ask her to come to my place and join us for dinner just as you have done since you came into my employment," Edward was insistent.

Monica now realised that Edward extending his invitation to Sara was not something she had even considered. Now, despite her reservations about spending Christmas with Edward and his family, she was inordinately pleased he had extended the invitation to Sara. "Oh, Edward, Sara will really love that, I know she will, and I appreciate you extending the invitation to her." Edward never ceased to amaze her, Monica thought, as she thanked him. "I mean to call her tomorrow and let her know what's happening, she will be thrilled, I do know that."

"She manages the prosthesis well, doesn't she?" Edward asked Monica.

"Oh, yes, the wheelchair is very much a thing of the past. She is so independent and gets off and on buses herself and refuses a helping hand."

"I'm so glad I did what I did. I do feel for Sara Totten, I must say. Left without any near relatives. And her a young woman with such a disability. Her renewed ability over time must be of great comfort to her and is all the thank you I need."

"She's always asking me if I know who her benefactor was, but I have never said, Edward, even though I'm very tempted to tell her."

In reply to Monica, Edward just smiled broadly at her. Then Monica went on, "I am also going to ask Sara to stay over on Christmas night. It would give her a bit of company. It is a difficult time of the year." Monica knew Edward would probably wonder why she was doing this this particular Christmas when there had been others equally difficult.

But now he just said, "As I have told you before, the apartment is yours and you are free to have anyone you wish to stay, Monica." Edward did feel sad to think Monica had not asked Sara Totten on previous Christmases and did wonder why she had only thought to do it this year.

Monica nodded in response, then added, "I know you have stressed to me about feeling free to bring friends here, but I do like to keep you informed. My apartment is, after all, under your roof."

132

"Yes, I suppose it is good to know about these things." Edward seemed about to say something else but decided not to. He just nodded his head as she thanked him again and made her way back to her sitting room.

Chapter 41

Monica arranged to meet Jill on the day before Christmas Eve in order to do some shopping. Originally, it had just been to do some last-minute shopping together but then, out of the blue, Edward had asked her to go for a meal with him to the Conway Hotel later this evening, He said he wanted to show his appreciation and to thank her for all the love and attention she had given his daughter during the years she had been with them. Although Monica saw it as a sign of a very final thank you, she was determined to look her best despite her agony at leaving them all soon.

She phoned Jill and told her she needed to buy something decent to wear as Edward had asked her to accompany him for a meal to one of the most upmarket hotels in the area. Monica knew she just did not have anything suitable in her wardrobe, any clothes in there were just serviceable. She had bought very few clothes for herself since Christopher had gone, apart from the essentials in looking professional in her role as teacher. She had nothing even remotely suitable for an evening out in such a lovely hotel.

Jill was waiting outside the coffee shop which they both liked and used when in town, and Jill wished Monica a blessed Christmas as she had done for the past number of years and Monica returned her greeting warmly. She always felt it was a perfect word for this time of year.

"Jill, let's go in and grab a quick cup of coffee, then I need you to help me pick a dress." Monica went on to tell her again about Edward's invitation.

"Of course, I'll help, I just love shopping for clothes, not that I can afford to very much, so I'll just love this." Jill smiled broadly as they entered the coffee shop. "We'll get our coffee, then I have something to tell you before we go shopping, but it won't take long."

Monica was immediately intrigued—had Jill some news of Christopher and the other children? Monica was always on the alert, hoping for news from perhaps Mr Dunn or from the Melton Home. After all, the three children who had been adopted illegally, were now teenagers and in a couple of years would perhaps, be able to try to make contact, if they knew how to, with their blood relatives.

Jill immediately realised she had raised Monica's hopes and was anxious to set things right. "No, Monica, it is not anything to do with the Melton Home, but it is to do with another home in Antrim." Jill was anxious that Monica might see the same connection to the Melton Home, as she had. "I met a girl I used to know in Belfast last week—in fact, she worked for a short time in Melton Home, then she went to work in another home in Antrim, the Sisters of Newbourne I believe she said it was. But…" Jill emphasised her next words, "she said she had left the Home because she didn't like how some of the children, and indeed the parents, were treated. She told me," Jill went on, "eight children from the Home had been taken for a supposed holiday, but they never returned to the home because they were all adopted, without any parental consent.

"So, Monica, these supposed adoptions don't seem to have just happened in Melton Home, it has happened in another Home as well." Jill's voice was at fever pitch now that she was able to talk and tell someone what she had discovered. Especially being able to give Monica some news, whether it would help her ongoing sense of loss Jill did not know. But at least Monica knew there was other parents who had suffered just as she had.

Monica had been sitting quietly, her coffee untouched as Jill told her everything. When she spoke, her voice was little more than a whisper, "Poor mums, poor dads, and indeed poor grandmothers. Why, oh why, Jill, is this happening? Why is someone doing this? First the Christian Committee and now it is the Sisters of Newbourne doing it. Where's the link, Jill? There must be one somewhere." Monica shook her head in despair, then she spoke forcefully as an idea struck her. "I'll ask Edward if he could ask Mr Dunn, his solicitor, to try and investigate this home in Antrim and see what he comes up with. Do you have any idea when the eight children from this Home were sent on holiday, Jill? Is it some years ago? Around the same time as Christopher's supposed holiday?"

"According to my friend who worked in the Sisters of Newbourne Home, it happened three years ago and she left shortly after it all happened. She has been working in a shoe shop, she told me, for the last nine months. But she did also tell me, that one of the other staff in the Home told her that it was not the first time it had happened, it had happened before."

Jill reached over and held Monica tightly. "I agree with you, Monica, I think someone needs to ask a few questions at this Home, we have never had much success with the Christian Committee because they made sure they covered their tracks. But maybe someone can find out something for us, Monica. It might well be worth it. So, I'll leave that to you, in the meantime, you and I have some shopping to do. So, let's get started. We do need to find you something, just a little bit glamorous, to wear tonight." Jill smiled at Monica, anxious to raise her spirits. "Fancy going for dinner to the most expensive hotel for miles around, and with one of the richest men around here."

Monica smiled back at Jill, and suddenly she was looking forward to doing some shopping and to her evening out with Edward, despite her firm belief it was his way of saying goodbye to her. But he was always so kind and considerate to her that she knew tonight would be no exception.

Jill's voice broke in on her thoughts, "I haven't told Mr Foster anything about it, Monica. I don't know how relevant it would be to him regarding Eleanor's death but then I did promise him I would always keep him up to date with anything I heard, however trivial it might seem to be. Actually, he has asked me for Christmas dinner at his home so I will see him then after I finish my shift at work."

"That's lovely, Jill. I had originally asked Sara to my apartment on Christmas Day, at least that was my intention, but Edward insists she and I must join him in his home. So, I didn't want to impose on him, or I would have asked you along too. But I knew you would understand."

"Certainly, I understand, Monica," Jill said, then went on, "I haven't heard from Sam for some time, and I didn't contact him—something I feel guilty about. So, I am glad he has contacted me. To tell you the truth, I did wonder how he was, but I did feel a bit awkward about being in touch, because I had nothing new to tell him. So, I'm glad to hear from him and when I see him, I will tell him about the other Home." Jill rose from her chair. "That's enough about me, let's get going and get you dressed up for this evening."

Chapter 42

Monica studied her appearance in the long mirror in her bedroom. She knew she was looking better than she had done in the last couple of years, and that was simply because of the dress she had purchased in the afternoon. It was the very first dress she had tried on, and it was Jill who had discovered it hanging on a rail at the back of Menary's shop. The dress was a pale blue colour with long sleeves and a heart-shaped neckline, the material was fine jersey and Monica knew it was a very flattering fit. But it was the blue, sparkling, buckled belt which lifted the dress from being a fine, tasteful one to a breath taking, stunning one. Monica simply loved it and Jill just kept clapping her hands in delight. At ten pounds, it was much more than Monica had intended to spend and said so to Jill.

"I do not want to see you walk out of here without that dress, Monica," Jill almost shouted the words. "If you don't pay for it, I will. You told me yourself this would be the first evening out you have had since Christopher disappeared and just think what the lad would say if he saw you in it."

Monica always appreciated Jill's open way of talking about Christopher, and although it often brought tears to her eyes, as it was doing now, she still loved her friend for it. Jill was not going to ever forget about Christopher, Monica knew. That was what Jill was always subtly telling her.

"Oh yes Jill, I will, I must buy it." And Monica turned to the sales assistant, who was standing discreetly a little way from them, and began to count out the ten pounds as she spoke. Soon the two girls left the shop with Monica carrying a bag with the precious dress in it.

Now looking at herself in her room, she knew the dress was well worth the money and would be wearable for a long time to come. And the grey stole she had had for some time would be perfect with it. She just hoped Edward would not think her overdressed when he saw her, but sure, it was Christmas, and she would tell him that.

She also intended to stress to him how Jennie had been her salvation in the last few years. If she had not had all the work with his daughter, and having responsibility for her education, and constantly observing her development, she would have gone under. Yes, she really needed to let her employer know how much being here had helped her come to terms with her loss. Yes, it was time she learnt to be a bit more articulate, and she must say these things before she left her employment. She felt it was important that he knew that, because Edward was always telling her the wonderful job she had done and was still doing with Jennie.

Well, tonight Monica vowed she would do most of the talking, there would after all just be the two of them. Usually, there was also Agnes and Jennie around the table, so she ought to have a better chance to thank him for giving her the position in the first place, and all he had done to help her since.

When she entered Edward's hall, he was waiting and he moved forward to greet her, "Monica, you look really lovely tonight." Edward's voice, as he regarded her, sounded quite strained, Monica thought. Perhaps he was not looking forward to telling her that soon, he must terminate her employment.

"Thank you, Edward, I treated myself to this dress today. A Christmas treat and a 'cheer me up', I think. Do you like it?"

"It is beautiful," Edward answered and taking her arm, helped escort her out of the house and to his car, where he settled her comfortably in the front passenger seat. As they drove along the Belfast Road, Monica thought Edward seemed preoccupied and somewhat on edge, and in order to break the silence, she decided to ask after Jennie, "How has Jennie been enjoying her holiday with her grandparents?"

"She tells me she has been having a lovely time. She rings me every evening, telling me all about her day. But I go for her in the morning to my parent's place, and I will bring my parents back here for Christmas as I always do on Christmas Eve. So, I will see her then Monica, and she will be wanting to see you, you know. She always asks about you"

"I look forward to seeing her. I have missed her, Edward, very much indeed. She has been such a lifeline for me," Monica said softly.

Edward placed his hand lightly on hers, where they lay clasped in her lap.

"I know, Monica, I know you have helped one another so much in the last few years. Jennie never mentions her mother now, not at all." Edward paused and then went on, "I never did tell you anything about Jennie's mother, but I would like to; that is, if you would like to hear it." Edward turned the car into the car park of the hotel and was silent as he looked for a parking space. "I will tell you about it over dinner, Monica." And he parked the car deftly into a space convenient to the entrance.

"Monica, wait," Edward said as she was about to open the car door, "allow me to open it and escort you in properly."

Monica withdrew her hand from the handle and allowed Edward to open the door and help her out. As she stood there, gathering her bag and gloves together, he helped arrange her shawl around her shoulders. Then he offered her his arm and they walked across the forecourt together into the hotel. Edward was recognised by the staff immediately, and they were shown to a table in the corner of the restaurant.

"Such a lovely room," Monica remarked. "All decorated for Christmas and with such taste, don't you think, Edward?" Monica still had the impression Edward was preoccupied, perhaps it was just because it was Christmas, and no doubt Edward had his own memories of previous Christmases before his wife left him. Probably what Edward had to tell her about her position was also on his mind. She knew it was all very difficult for him, he was, by nature, such a kind man and would have no desire to hurt anyone. Regarding Edward's wife, however, Monica was glad Agnes had told her very briefly one evening, when she was staying with her after Christopher's disappearance, that she had gone to America with her lover.

Thinking of this, Monica spoke in a very gentle manner now, "Thank you for bringing me to such a wonderful place, Edward, it is really lovely. You do so much for me, and Jennie is just a treasure to me, she really is." Monica wanted to say so much about his kindness to her, but he did not seem to be listening to her, he was so preoccupied.

Then he spoke, "What would you like to drink, Monica?"

"I would like some orange with ice, if I may."

"That sounds good, I might have the same." The waiter, who was hovering nearby, seemed on cue to come over with the menus and asked them what they would like. After they ordered their meal and were sipping their orange in relative silence, Edward suddenly leaned across the table and caught her hand tightly where it lay.

"Monica, may I ask you something? Something pretty serious?" Certainly, Edward was very anxious.

"Of course, Edward, of course."

"Monica, would you marry me please?" he said in a half whisper.

Monica was speechless as she looked over at this man who had helped her so much, through all her very darkest days. And who now, she realised as she stared at him, she loved so very much. Love that she had never been able to recognise, or acknowledge to herself, because of her profound grief and heartache over her son. But now she gripped his hand tightly and smiled broadly at him. She knew Christopher would love this dear man too, and he would be so very happy for her.

"Oh yes please, Edward. I will, I will indeed."

With that, Edward rose from his seat and, pulling her to her feet, kissed her. As they stood there, they became aware of the waiter biding his time to serve them their meal. Edward turned to him and said excitedly, "This young lady has just agreed to marry me!"

The waiter beamed at them both as they pulled apart and sat down to their meals. The waiter gave them all his attention, spreading their napkins and pouring some water for them. Then he left them to enjoy their dinner, only to return with a large bottle of champagne and champagne glasses, assuring them as he poured some, that it was all on the house, a free gift from the manager to celebrate such a wonderful occasion. As they sipped the champagne, Edward told the waiter to share some of it with the two couples sitting just over from them.

Later, as they drove home, Edward insisted they shop the very next day, Christmas Eve, for a ring. He wanted their engagement to be official at Christmas.

"Monica, I have to tell you this, from the first day I interviewed you and you answered me in open your personal credentials, I think I fell in love with you then. And since then, I have waited patiently but did not wish to intrude on your grief too soon. I thought it would seem as if I had no regard for what you were going through when the opposite is true."

Monica put her hand warmly on his arm as he drove slowly back home and said lovingly, "I could never have thought you had no regard, Edward that is one thing I was always very aware of, your empathy and sensitivity to my trauma and loss." Monica hesitated. "It would so complete my happiness if Christopher was here to celebrate with us. But you never know, someday soon my advertisement in the paper may be answered."

Chapter 43

"It's just so terrible that we're still here, in this awful place, eight years we're here. Can you really believe it, Christopher? Eight years, and what have we done? We've built walls, helped put in windows, helped put on roofs. And what have we got for all our hard work? Good beatings and hidings, that's what we've got. And, for most of the time, horrid, inedible food. You and me, Christopher, we're eighteen and Joe, you're what, fourteen, aren't you? I hope you've been counting too."

"Yes, I made sure Joe counted every day just as we did, David," Christopher assured him. "I know the three of us here have been subject to some awful beatings over the years, but with help from one another, we have survived them." Christopher hesitated, then went on quietly, "From what I have gathered from other boys, David, is if you aren't picked out for a good thrashing, then you are picked out to be taken from your bed and taken to some of the priests' rooms. There you would be the subject of a series of fondling and assault, as some of the other boys quite openly told me about."

David nodded thoughtfully. "I know, Christopher, they say if you are one of the ones taken from your bed, nobody will ever hit you. It seems to be either one or the other—I don't know if that's true or not." He continued hesitantly, "Or maybe it's because they have plenty of choice, the three of us always stick together and as much as possible we keep up in this corner in the evenings. We're not as noticeable..." David's voice tailed off, the thought of what some boys told him they had to endure both nauseated and terrified him.

He believed if they ever took young Joe away from his bed some evening, that he himself would personally seek out the priest responsible and kill him. Yes, he could watch Christopher and Joe getting beatings, it was not easy, but he could not bear to think of them being taken to any of the priests' beds. The first time one of the other boys told him, ever so quietly, what he had endured, David did not want to believe any of it. But when he looked at the boy's ashen face and looked into his lifeless, soulless, eyes, he knew with certainty the boy was telling the truth.

"Sometimes in the papers that sit about here, I've seen advertisements from farmers looking for workers. It seems they are always looking for lorry drivers, some are looking for help on their farm, and yet others are looking for building labourers."

Christopher broke in on David's train of thought, "You know, we could do any of that kind of work, couldn't we, Dave?"

"No doubt, but how do we know where to go to talk to these people who are looking help? We can't even see any other building from here, or any sign of any life or activity. To tell you the truth, Christopher, I imagine we are very far from other people. We live in a wilderness here, you know."

"I know that alright." Christopher nodded somewhat downheartedly. "I don't mean to look for work right now. I want to wait until all three of us are ready to find it. I think somehow we'll be successful and get work, something will turn up." Christopher was anxious to keep looking forward. "And, they have let other boys get jobs and go elsewhere, so let's hope we'll be able to do the same."

"We'll just have to keep working hard and I intend to try to learn everything you teach me, Christopher." Joe had been listening quietly to the other two boys and now he smiled broadly at them. "I think too, we'll get out of here and we'll keep watching for the people in their big cars coming here and get a hold of the newspapers they bring with them."

To Christopher's ears, Joe sounded somewhat anxious, and Christopher immediately reached over and put an arm round him. In a firm voice, he said, "We've stuck this now together for eight years, Joe, and I don't intend to go anywhere without you. I never have since we left the home and I don't intend to without your agreement."

Joe smiled broadly at Christopher. "Thank you, Christopher," and he turned to David, "thank you too, David. I might be younger than either of you, but it is only by a couple of years—that's not much. After all, as you say we have put up with eight years of this awful place." Then Joe added wistfully, "I would just love to know where my grandma is." And his eyes filled with tears. "Do you think she might still be alive, Christopher?"

"I believe she is, Joe. Just as I believe that my mum is, and David's dad, too." Christopher turned to his friend and David nodded hopefully.

Shortly after they had become friends, David had told Christopher why he had been in the Melton Home. He told Christopher that his mother had left them and shortly after that his father had started to drink a lot. He drank so much he had become very ill, and David had had to fetch the doctor for him. His dad was taken into hospital and then the doctor arranged for David to go into the home, on a temporary basis, until his father was discharged from hospital. As soon as his father got out of hospital, he began to make arrangements to bring David home.

On his last visit, he told him that everything was organised for him to be brought home the following week and he would be back for him then. During this time the home informed him just the evening before, he would be going on a holiday first before he went home. And here he was with other children who had been told the same.

The day David had told Christopher his story, he had cried throughout the telling of it. He worried, he told Christopher, that his father would start drinking again when he discovered his son was away somewhere. He wondered what the people in the home would have told his dad. Now today, Christopher wondered how much longer it would be before they saw their loved ones again. They all prayed constantly that they would see them soon Joe prayed his grandma would live to be very old, David that his father had never touched drink again and Christopher to feel his mother's arms around him.

Nobody worked on Christmas Day in Swandon Children's Home. That is, they did not do any building work, hauling heavy concrete blocks, or knocking down stubborn walls with a sledgehammer. It was a day to be free of the thick dust that always clogged the workers' throats, noses and eyes. Instead, they would attend the chapel in the morning and again in the evening and between these sessions they were sent to scrub the walls, windows and floors of the dormitories and landings in the home. Christopher, Joe and David agreed with each other that it was the best day of the year despite all the indoor scrubbing and cleaning.

In truth, on their first Christmas in the place, they had not expected any let up on the outside labour, which they did day and daily, month on month, for the rest of the year. And for breakfast, instead of getting the thin gruel they were so accustomed to, they all had a sausage each with bread which had been dipped in some lard like substance. It looked unappetising but the children in Swandon were very thankful for the change of food. They all found it quite edible. As for going to chapel, Christopher liked going to it and he knew Joe and David did too.

This was now their eighth Christmas here. And they always made the most of their time in the chapel, praying to God that they would not have many more Christmases here, and he would help them get back home. Not that Christopher did not pray often elsewhere, indeed he did, every night without fail. But Christmas was such a special time of the year, and Christopher thought about his mother more than ever and prayed that she was well. But above all, he prayed earnestly she was not too sad that he wasn't with her. He felt that by praying to God so constantly, eventually He would help them get back home. In the chapel he felt so much closer to God, and he believed God was listening to him, whereas lying in his bed at night in the stark, cold dormitory, sometimes he seemed to be very far off from heaven.

Now, as they made their way back from the chapel, Joe remarked to him, "There's your other friend, Brian. Isn't that his name?"

Christopher looked back and there was Brian waving at him and shouting 'Happy Christmas.' Christopher waved back and gestured to Joe and David to do the same.

"Hello Brian, I always think of what you advised me more than seven years ago, to take count of everyday and so I do, and thank you for that advice. I think if I hadn't have started to count when I did, I would have no idea either what time of year it is, or even what year it is." Christopher rushed on, "I know I always say the same thing every time I see you, but I always want to thank you again, Brian."

"Well, it works for me, Christopher, and I try to tell others to do the same thing."

Christopher nodded and then went on, "I am sure we will see you here tomorrow as usual. Did you have to scrub your dormitory today?"

"Oh yes, just the same as last Christmas, but sure it is better than what we do out here."

"It certainly is, Brian, but no doubt I will see you from afar tomorrow, still doing the same dusty, dirty, hard work."

"I am sure you will, but just keep marking off the days and I'll know I have another comrade here." And with that, Brian turned and made his way back to his other friends and Christopher re-joined Joe and David. Then they quietly entered the house and made their way to their dormitory. Once they were back into their sleeping quarters, David and Joe sat quietly on Christopher's bed, and watched and waited, while Christopher pulled out a book of the New Testament and some pens and paper. Then Christopher started to call out a word and spell it out while David, Joe and Christopher himself wrote it down on some of the paper.

This was their school now, here in secret in their dormitory, since David and Christopher had discovered soon after their arrival that there was no such thing as school, in this isolated, lawless and forsaken place. So, they were determined to try and teach themselves something, anything which might help them, if they ever managed to escape from Swandon. They were also determined to teach Joe how to read and write, and to learn to recognise words. Christopher had taken the Testament, which he kept under his pillow, from the chapel some time ago. He had known then it would not be missed because there was so many lying about.

Then, during the week, the three of them would keep an eye out for any newspapers left lying around. And if they got the chance, they would hide the paper under their vest or shirt, then get it quickly to one of their beds. Although Christopher was happy enough with what they were learning in reading and writing, arithmetic was harder because there weren't any books on it. They just concentrated on counting sticks and bricks during their working day, and then from what they remembered from their counting, David was the one who would plan small sums, then jot them down for the three of them to count.

But above all, they counted their days, months and years in the place, referring always either to the calendar which hung in the dining hall or the one in the great hallway. But they were always careful not to seem interested. They knew only too well, that very quickly, they could be accused of shirking their work, and suffer a cruel beating as a result of it. However, there were never any beatings on Christmas Day, something all the children in Swandon were so thankful for.

On this Christmas night, after the three boys had done a good bit of reading and writing, and some sums, they were very tired and climbed into bed exhausted. But Christopher found he could not get to sleep he was thinking so much of his mother and what she might be doing. He thought about her all the time but tonight, for some reason, he felt her presence stronger than ever. As he went over the work they had done tonight, he promised himself that he would do his very best to learn. He wanted, above anything, to make his mum proud of him when he next saw her.

Chapter 44

Monica wakened early on Christmas Eve morning and her first thought was that she had had a lovely dream that Edward proposed to her. Then as she became fully awake, she jumped up quickly realising it was true, it was no dream. She hugged herself tightly as she sat on the side of her bed, her mind a turmoil of emotions. Was she really going to marry Edward? It was all so sudden, and Monica was still trying to come to terms with the shock of his proposal and her own realisation that she really loved this man. She wasn't just grateful to him for all he had done for her, she wasn't just full of respect for his generosity and sensitivity to others. No, she knew now she had gradually fallen in love with him, and she wanted to become his wife.

Now, as she sat in her bedroom, she thought of Christopher. She yearned for him that morning and the tears flowed freely because he was not here to know Edward Wallace, and she was acutely aware her son would not know anything about her marriage. Wherever he was, and whoever had adopted him, was still unknown. It was just as if Christopher had vanished off the face of the earth. She realised now, now that Edward had proposed to her that her grief for Christopher had overshadowed her love for Edward. But was she doing the right thing in agreeing to marry him? Could she really make Edward happy, or would the weight of her grief and the enormity of her loss always interfere with their future happiness? Would it cast a long shadow over it?

Well, their future was very important to her, and Monica was resolved to discuss this with Edward this morning. He was coming to her apartment for coffee, then he wanted her to come with him to collect Jennie and to meet his parents, when he would then tell them his news.

Now, Edward listened intently while Monica told him her concern about her inability to accept the loss of Christopher, and that she would continue to grieve for him all her life unless they found out where he was and who had adopted him. They were sitting side by side on the sofa, and when Monica looked at

Edward in such a beseeching hopeful way, Edward immediately drew her to him and hugging her fiercely said, "Of course, Monica, you are going to grieve for Christopher always. I am fully aware of that, and I would not wish you to feel any different. You must remember that I had only just met you when you learnt of Christopher's disappearance, so I have been with you every step of the way."

He kissed her gently on the forehead and went on, "Not that I would presume to understand the enormity of your feelings, no one could, unless they have been through such an experience themselves. I also think darling, that your experience of tragedy and torment, is different from other losses. You were lied to time and time again, and accused and convicted, I might say, of agreeing to have your son adopted." Edward held her close, "But it is this Monica sitting here, who has been through so much, and with such fortitude, that I love and wish to marry. And our future will include grieving and searching and hoping to find Christopher. Besides, Monica, I feel almost as if he is my son, I have been so involved in any dealings we have had."

"Oh Edward, I do love you." Monica was too tongue-tied to say anything more.

"And Monica, at our wedding service, we will include prayers for Christopher, and at the reception we will speak of him, I want to do this, that is," he said, "If you agree?"

"Oh Edward, how wonderful that will be." Monica hugged and kissed him.

"We best be on our way," Edward remarked, "because in the afternoon, when we return home with Jennie and my parents, I would like to go into town and help you pick an engagement ring, as I suggested last night."

Monica rose to her feet, her eyes shining and such a happy look on her face, Edward noticed, as she spoke, "Edward, I would love to go shopping with you. I was there yesterday with Jill, and now today, I will be with you. Two of my favourite people, and I can't wait to tell Jill. I know she will be so happy for me. I think sometimes she despaired for me. I was such a torment ringing her so often to find out if she had heard anything about any of the children."

Then suddenly, Monica remembered what Jill had told her about the other home in Antrim and related to Edward about it all. About the eight children who had not come back to the children's home. "I forgot to tell you last night, Edward, but I am sure you understand why."

"So illegal adoptions are still going on in other places? Well, after Christmas we will establish if we can, what home it was, and perhaps if Albert Dunn can find out anything about what exactly is going on," Edward said. "We might just find out something, Monica. In the meantime, we will have a lovely Christmas, enjoy our love for each other and still leave room to think about Christopher."

Chapter 45

"Miss Corken, I'm going to need to talk to this carer who worked with you in Melton Home, and I believe she also worked in the Sisters of Newbourne Home in Antrim. Monica tells me your friend told you eight children in the Home she worked in were sent on holiday, but never returned to the Home. Did she tell you when this happened?"

When Edward told Mr Dunn about the eight children going on holiday from the Sisters of Newbourne Home and being given up for adoption without the parents' consent, his solicitor was interested in trying to investigate the situation. Unfortunately, he had been laid low with influenza and pneumonia just after Christmas and when he returned to his office, he had to deal with quite a backlog of problems, consultations and queries from different people. It was only when he had caught up on his work that he asked Edward to arrange this meeting with Monica and her friend.

"Do you have any means of contacting your friend?" He asked the girl Monica had brought with her.

"Yes, I do, Mr Dunn." Jill proceeded to open her handbag and withdrew a slip of paper which she handed over to him. "I'm sorry, she did not tell me when this happened. I suppose I thought it must have happened quite some time ago, perhaps when Christopher was adopted, but of course that can't be, because Alice told me she left the Sisters of Newbourne Home soon after the incident took place. She is working in the shoe shop almost three years now, I know she told me that. That's her name and the telephone number of the shop she is working in."

Jill was so thankful now that she had taken time to get a contact number for Alice. "We exchanged telephone numbers at the last minute of meeting each other. I suddenly thought it would be nice to meet up with Alice again, that's all I thought about, really." Now Jill felt she could well have slipped up very badly and have no means of getting in touch with Alice. It might turn out to be so important to have the contact. She felt guilty now that she had not taken the time, when she met Alice, to find out what she knew about the supposed adoptions. She did feel better when Mr Dunn next spoke, she felt reassured she had contributed something to this most horrible of events.

"It is wonderful to have this number, Miss Corken," Mr Dunn said as he copied the name and number into his diary before reaching the slip of paper back to Jill. "I just hope," he added thoughtfully, "your friend will remember some of the children's names to enable me to follow this up. Perhaps she might even have some of the mothers' details, but maybe that is too much to hope for."

Albert Dunn smiled openly at the two women in front of him. "If I do find there have been more illegal adoptions, I would begin to think that this idea is not coming from any religious order, but from someone or some organisation higher up the ladder. But we'll wait and see how I get on, and I'll let you know if I find out anything." Then he added, "I'm just so sorry it has taken me quite a few months to arrange this meeting, but I'm sure Edward told you about my illness, Monica."

"But, of course, Mr Dunn," Monica was quick to reassure him. "It's so kind of you to show such an interest in this whole business, any leads at all that we get are very welcome. So, I thank you so much for your help."

Monica and Jill thanked him again and left his office, heartened by his optimism and attitude.

Albert Dunn arranged to meet Alice Warring in a coffee shop in Royal Avenue which he knew was not far from the shoe shop she worked in. He was aware he was a total stranger to her, but when he mentioned Jill Corken by name and outlined briefly his occupation and why he wished to meet her, she seemed quite enthusiastic to meet. He described his appearance to her and then, as an afterthought told her he would place his hat on the table in front of him as a means of identifying himself. When she entered the coffee shop, he recognised her immediately from Jill's description of her, and he signalled her to join him. As she reached his table, he stood up and extended his hand to her in greeting.

"Would you like some coffee and scones while we discuss why exactly I wanted to talk to you, Alice?" Albert said as he pulled out a chair for the girl. "I know I told you it was about the children who were adopted from the Home you worked in, but I would like to tell you a bit more about what I know."

Alice nodded in response to what Albert was saying, then added eagerly, "I would love coffee and a scone, please," and Albert realised that coffee and scones might be a rare treat for a young girl of her age.

While they were enjoying their coffee, Albert explained briefly what exactly he was trying to find out, and he touched briefly on Monica's situation. "This lady's son was sent on holiday more than eight years ago from Melton Home. He never returned because he was adopted—adopted without his mother's consent, I might add," Albert said. "But that is some time ago, there may not be any connection between the events."

"I am in my present job three years now and I left the Sisters of Newbourne Home just before that, so it is three years since those children went on their supposed holiday. But" Alice spoke in a scathing voice, "I did hear a rumour in the Home just before I left. That it wasn't the first time it had happened, that it had been done before. I mean it might have been just a rumour I heard that children were taken away on a supposed holiday some time before, but really it was for illegal adoptions."

Alice was now wondering how true that rumour might really be and was there a possible link between the two Homes. But it was too late for her to learn anything about it all. She had moved on from that awful time when she had done her best to support disbelieving, distraught parents. Parents for whom she felt so inadequate and so hopeless to be able to help in the face of their loss and grief.

"I certainly think this Home, and the events that have happened in it, are worthy of some investigation. But I would really like to speak to some of the mothers or fathers first, to try to find out exactly how it all happened to them," Albert said.

"Yes, you did explain briefly on the telephone that it would be beneficial if you would obtain some of the names of the families who were affected by this. I have a note here of four of the children's names, their Christian name and their surname. I'm sorry I don't have any Christian names of parents or addresses.

"This is great, Alice. I should be able to discover something from some of the names and thank you for taking the time to meet with me. I really appreciate it," Albert replied.

"Oh, Mr Dunn, there is one address now I recall, just as we speak. I remember so well because the mother was so young. It was Leopold Street and, as I said, the mum is just a young girl. Leopold Street is just around the corner from the Home, so it will be easy for you to find."

"Thank you so much, you have helped make my job so much easier, Alice." Albert rewarded her with a broad smile. They left the coffee shop together; Alice returned to her work and Albert made his way back to his office, keen to begin his research straight away.

Leopold Street lies off the Crumlin Road in North Belfast. The street consisted of small terraces of houses with access to the back of the properties from the street. Leopold Street had not been a casualty of the Nazi Blitz in 1941 because of its position, and the houses had always been kept in good order by the residents.

Albert Dunn had never frequented this area of Belfast before, but he had found the street, and the house he was looking for quickly. To see the name of the street written on a wall as he entered confirmed he was indeed in Leopold Street. Now armed with this information, all Albert had to do was call with the family who lived in number five. He knew he would be faced with a very daunting task, if the child concerned had indeed been adopted without her parents' consent. He just hoped they would be agreeable to talking to him.

In response to his ringing the bell, the door was quickly opened by a tall, quite formidable looking woman, with short grey hair and deep grey eyes. Albert decided to speak quickly and decisively as to why he was there. He stressed he was conducting an enquiry with young mothers, regarding illegal adoptions being carried out in some children's homes.

"You better come in," the woman said, as she furtively looked up and down the street before opening the door wide to let him in.

As Albert entered the house into a room which led directly from the front door, a figure came forward from the shadows beside the fireplace, and he realised it was a young girl. A young girl, who looked to be around twenty years of age, and who had the appearance of someone who had been ill. Her dark hair hung lank around her head, her face was colourless and devoid, Albert thought, of any expression. He knew, instinctively, he was looking at the mother of the child, Ruth Smart, who had been adopted illegally.

"Isobel, this gentleman says he is a solicitor, and he is investigating illegal adoptions from children's homes," the tall, grey-haired woman said.

The girl replied immediately, "Adoptions, who sent you here?"

Albert hastened to say again, "I am a solicitor." He pulled out his identity card from his inside pocket. "I am investigating the possibility of an illegal adoption of a little boy, and in so doing I was told about other adoptions happening in another home." Albert waited expectantly for either of the women to reply, and then he realised they were both crying, tears running down their face.

"I'm so very sorry." Albert was lost for words in the face of the obvious distress of the two women. The grey-haired lady recovered herself quickly and taking a huge handkerchief out of her apron pocket, she spoke, "Please take a seat." Peering at the card Albert had handed to her, she repeated, "Mr Dunn, please take a seat."

"Thank you," Albert said, as he took one of the armchairs sitting against the wall, just over from the fire.

Albert realised she was more receptive of his presence now, and as she continued to speak, her tone was much gentler. "I'm Mrs Smart and this is my daughter, Isobel." Indicating the young girl. "Isobel has been in hospital with pneumonia and is just home two days ago, it is her third bout in as many years." Mrs Smart looked lovingly at her daughter as she began to explain, "Isobel has a little girl of four years of age, Ruth is her name, and when Isobel was ill and had to go into hospital, I had to put Ruth into a children's home—just on a temporary basis, you know.

"I work from nine in the morning until six in the evening in the Linen Mill just up the road from here, I could not take time off, you see, I would have just lost my job, and mine is the only income that comes in here. My husband died five years ago." Mrs Smart sat very quietly now, as her daughter Isobel sat sobbing beside her. "I'm so sorry, it's all so very unreal, so unbelievable, but it did happen."

Albert waited patiently now for Mrs Smart to continue, and to tell him in some detail what exactly had happened, even though he believed he already knew. It was obvious now to him that Mrs Smart was having trouble putting into words what exactly had happened to her granddaughter, Ruth. Her next words confirmed to Albert how reluctant Mrs Smart was to talk about or relive the reality, and the circumstances, of what had happened to her granddaughter.

"I can scarcely believe that you are who you say you are, but if you can help Isobel and myself in any way, we will be forever grateful to you." Mrs Smart's tears began to flow again.

Albert sat silently for a few minutes until Mrs Smart had recovered her composure, but it was Isobel who next spoke to him, "When I was discharged from hospital—I was in it for almost three weeks—Mum and I went to collect

Ruth at the children's home. We were told she had been adopted by people who could give her a better home than I ever could." The girl spoke quickly, now anxious, Albert felt, to let him know her story before she broke down again and was unable to tell him.

"They showed me some papers I'm supposed to have signed, when I first brought Ruth to them, agreeing to the adoption. I signed no such papers. I was already in hospital that same day, it was Mum who took Ruth to the Home and explained the situation to the carers, who were so very helpful to her."

"Yes, the carers were so professional on that day," Mrs Smart said. "They were so professional. But when we went to collect Ruth and bring her home, there was no sign of the carers. There were a couple of nuns there and a very officious looking man. It was the man who did all the talking. He did not even tell us his name, so we have no idea who he was. That's all we know. We are both totally heartbroken, we just want, we need to get Ruth back. Here, with us. So please, please help us, Mr Dunn."

"I will do all I can, but it might prove difficult to follow up." Albert did not want to give these two women any false hopes and felt he must be truthful with them. "Do you happen to know of any other children in the Home that it happened to?"

"Yes, of course. I'm sorry, we're so wrapped up in our loss of Ruth that we forget there were others there who were coming through the same thing." Mrs Smart said, "The parents concerned told Isobel and me that the children were told they were going on holiday, but they never returned to the Home. They too, were told they had signed adoption papers. But neither Isobel nor I have any idea who the mothers or fathers concerned were, simply because Ruth was only in the place a short time and, because of my working day, I was only able to visit her very briefly. So, I never met any of them until the day we all learnt what had been done to the children and to us."

As Albert listened to the two women, he began to realise that here in Northern Ireland, two different children's homes had been involved, he fervently believed, in placing children for adoption without obtaining any parents' consent. He was beginning to believe that, with the knowledge he had, it was not a religious order who was making such unprecedented and cruel decisions, but someone much higher up in authority.

With many repeated assurances that he intended to try to help Mrs Smart and her daughter, and that he would keep in touch, he left them, he knew, in better spirits than they had been in when he first met them earlier in the day. And that thought weighed on his conscience. What if he could find nothing of value for them? What if barriers had been put in place to prevent someone like him from making any kind of discovery? He knew he was faced with a very daunting task, but he would do his best for Isobel and Mrs Smart.

There was one thing he was very thankful for, and that was that he had not disclosed to either of the women how long Monica's son had been gone from her. And he was very glad neither of them had thought to ask him. He knew if he had told them that it was some years ago since Christopher Scott had been illegally adopted, they would have been in despair at the prospect of all those years without little Ruth.

On the way back to his car Albert Dunn thought a lot about the house he had just left and the mother and daughter who lived there. When he had first rang the doorbell he had been, even with all his years of experience, uncertain and somewhat apprehensive about how to broach his subject to whoever opened the door to him. Even when Mrs Smart invited him in, he felt ill equipped to ask some of the questions which he knew he must. But now, after an hour in the company of these two women, he felt so motivated and strong that he was resolved to do his utmost for them.

The young Isobel had shown courage and resilience as she had talked to him, but Mrs Smart had portrayed such a true and abiding love for her daughter she had left Albert feeling the highest respect for her. Not for one second, she told him, had she ever considered that her daughter, because she was pregnant, must go into one of those mother and baby homes. She loved Isobel, she told Albert, and her place was here with her mother. And they had been so happy when Ruth had come into their lives.

That from this, she said through her tears to lose her granddaughter through some illegal adoption scam, was just sheer heartbreak for them both. And if Mr Dunn could just get Ruth back safely to them they would be eternally grateful to him and would find some way to pay him. Before leaving, he assured them money was not an issue, and he promised he would be in touch regarding any progress he made.

Chapter 46

"What day can we expect these British officials to visit and check us out? Has anyone confirmed anything about any of it yet?" Father Brady sounded quite anxious as he talked to his fellow priest, placing his chair nearer the table. Sitting down now, he began to eat his bowl of stew while looking expectantly at Father Kelly sitting across from him.

"Actually, I received a telephone call from their top man this morning to say they hoped to be here tomorrow—Wednesday—around two o'clock," Father Kelly replied casually.

"Oh, as soon as that," Father Brady said sharply, "as soon as that."

Father Kelly thought for a moment and then answered him, "Look, these officials have twenty-six institutions to inspect and, it seems, only a few days to do it all in. So, I'm hoping they don't intend spending too much time checking out things. Besides we were always meant to be checked over once a month, since we started to get these children from other places, but that never happened here, not ever. So, we have escaped very easily, and I have no doubt it is because we are so remote from any town or indeed from anybody." His tone was reassuring. "I thought we should just have a few of the older boys working outside, just light work, nothing very heavy, mind you. We want it to look as if they are just tidying up outside. And I thought the other boys could be sent to spend some time in our reading room."

On hearing this, Father Brady looked quite shocked with his colleague, and said with some degree of surprise in his voice, "Our library? But none of the inmates here have ever been allowed in the library. They're sure to think it very strange indeed, are they not?"

"Look, Father," Father Kelly addressed his colleague in an exasperated tone. "It doesn't matter what any of those boys think. We have had such short notice of this inspection that this is the best idea I can come up with. Certainly, we can't have them all outside, nor can they be seen to be doing heavy work. So, I intend to tell the officials that our reading room is where the boys all have lessons."

Father Brady was silent for a moment as he considered what Father Kelly had said, and then he had to say he thought it was a very good idea.

The next morning, when Christopher, David and Joe were summoned with some other boys to Father Kelly's office, they went in fear and trepidation, and were convinced that some of them had been identified as miscreants and were due another beating. They were astounded by what the priest proceeded to tell them.

"You will work outside for a couple of hours in the early part of this morning, then you will go to the washroom and wash and change your clothes. In the afternoon, you will be given the privilege of spending some time in our reading room. You must be very quiet in the room, and then sometime after three o'clock three men will come into the room and may ask some of you a few questions."

Father Kelly had been speaking in soft, measured tones, a tone which was usually a precursor to his thundering, threatening one. This time was no exception, his expression began to change, and he looked as if he was indeed going to pinpoint someone to beat up. His voice now echoed loudly and menacingly around the room. "You will only speak to these men when and if they address you directly and you must answer 'Yes' if you are asked if you are well cared for here. Which you are, as you well know. You must tell them you are very happy here. We don't want to hear of any complaints, sure we don't?" He paused and glared down at the boys watching him silently, and now his voice sounded even more menacing. "Is that clear?"

The boys all nodded and said 'Yes' quite emphatically, just relieved they were not called to join the queue to get yet another beating. Instead, wonder of wonders, above all things, they were going to spend time in the priests' reading room. And Christopher, for one, was excited that they would have excess to some worthwhile books. He had no doubt about that.

"We are expected to write a report on the condition of the homes we have visited. You will receive a copy of my report, and recommendations we will make to improve the standard of care here for the children who are already here, and for others who may be sent to you in the future. However, there are a couple of things I would like to draw your attention to today." Mr Lawson looked steadily at Father Kelly as he spoke. He had just finished his inspection of the home and neither he nor his colleagues were impressed.

"We must insist that in the younger boys' dormitory more attention needs to be paid to the careful drying and fumigation of the mattresses and under the beds. Cleaning and fumigation must be carried out on a very regular basis." Jim Lawson was going to ask just how often cleaning of the young boys' dormitory was done but decided against it. Really, the upstairs dormitories told him all he needed to know. The whole place just reeked of negligence and a sheer lack of love for any of the children who lived here. "I would also like to address the situation with some of the older boys in your care. The members of the committee are always interested to hear when some of the children obtain gainful employment." Jim Lawson told the priest, "They need to be encouraged to become independent and become valuable members in the community. What age are your eldest boys?"

"Around eighteen, I think," Father Kelly answered.

"Well, I believe I can help you find work for some of them." Jim Lawson proceeded to open his briefcase and taking a page out of one of his files, he handed it to Father Kelly. "One of the other homes gave me a list of farmers and landowners who are always looking for help with their stock and crops. The other homes we have visited do send their older boys on to work." Jim Lawson indicated some names and addresses on the page and went on, "I strongly advise you to seek these landowners out, and if some of the boys here are taken up for employment, it will leave you room for some new children in the future."

"Yes, that's true, it would." Father Kelly brightened up at the thought of some new faces and bodies coming here to Swandon. "No farmer or landowner ever approached us looking for help, which is odd, don't you think?" Father Kelly felt the need to defend his lack of knowledge about work for older boys.

"Farmers and landowners may not know of Swandon's existence here, you are really so remote, miles from anywhere."

Father Kelly thought for a moment that he detected criticism from this man Lawson. Perhaps he thought no one should ever have considered having a children's home miles from anywhere, and seemingly somewhat inaccessible to people. But the inspector was probably just being factual because they were, indeed, miles from anywhere.

Now he gratefully took the page from Mr Lawson and reassured him he would do his best to get some of the older children work. "They have been here long enough in the home I think," he said reassuringly to all three British officials who it seems had completed their tours of inspection of the children's homes.

In truth, now that the seed had been planted to get rid of some of the older boys, he intended to work on doing exactly that as soon as possible.

The British officials did deliver a report on their findings in the 26 institutions they inspected, and their report was a critical one. They identified a gross lack of childcare and a serious lack of hygiene and cleanliness. They also expressed concern that the children were living in extremely remote, rural areas.

There was no mention of physical or sexual abuse in the report. But later children would testify they were terrified of criticising the Brothers in any way. They knew they would receive the most life threatening beatings. Nevertheless, even though physical or sexual abuse was not reported a cover-up of the report began. Some members of the governing board urged that it would not be published, as did the Director of the Orient Line.

In 1959, the Commonwealth Relations officer sent a secret telegram to the UK High Commissioner in Australia, stating they did not want to withhold approval for more children to be sent. So, more children were continued to be sent until into the 1960s. One child aged three, Ruth Smart, was one of a group sent during the latter part of the Child Migration Scheme.

Chapter 47

Father Kelly stood silently at the top of the room studying the six youths standing before him, and secretly he knew he would be glad to see them leave the place. He didn't know why he hadn't thought of it before, but thanks to the visit by the British officials, he now had the opportunity to get rid of them. The truth was their whole appearance had held no appeal for him since they first arrived here. He did quite enjoy beating them with his belt, but the sight of one or other of them lying on the ground, bruised or bleeding, made him nauseated, and the thought of touching them or holding them filled him with revulsion. They were so bony and scrawny looking as they lay there curled up, writhing in pain. There were other boys in the home he would never beat, he couldn't bear to see their perfect skin marked in any way. He just held those boys and caressed them— they were a delight to hold and fondle.

Now today, he would be able, having found work for these youths standing here, to rid the place of them and prepare the home and himself for the arrival of another lot of boys. He understood they would be coming at the end of the week.

"You will be collected here by farmers and landowners in three days' time and offered employment by them. Each employer needs two of you, and you will be given accommodation and food." Father Kelly was silent for a moment as he studied them, then went on, "You will not do any more outside work in the next three days, but you will scrub your beds and lockers, clean the windows and wash the floors of the dormitory before you go." He paused for a second, then went on, "That is all, you may go."

Stunned and speechless, the boys looked at one another as they silently left the room. Never in their wildest dreams had any of them expected this.

Brian was the first to speak, "In the time I've been here before you came, I never heard of six boys being given leave to go and work. There were, of course, one or two older ones who did get work, how they got it, I don't know. But the British officials must have thought it was time quite a few of us found work, and

I'm sure it's just the start of others going. We all are starting to grow up, you know, boys. And we can't stay here forever."

"I can scarcely believe this is happening. Do you think it is genuine?" Joe had a very worried look on his face.

"I just don't know, Joe," Christopher answered truthfully. "But we don't have any choice only to go along with it." He turned to David. "What do you think, David?"

"Like you, Christopher, I want to believe it is true. But it seems to be too good to be true that we are finally getting out of this awful place. It just seems so easy after all these years."

David sounded so worried that Christopher felt the need to reassure him, even though he felt anything but secure himself about everything. "David, we must try not to worry. I believe those British officials had a lot to do with it. After all, it was the British who sent us over here all those years ago. We were just dumped here, nobody cared," Christopher stressed. "I have thought about what they did to us so many, many times. But I knew there was nothing we could do about it. The British government stuck us out here, far from civilisation. So maybe, just maybe, they have decided to do something about it, do something for us."

Christopher was determined to be optimistic about this change in their circumstances. "At least we'll know in three days' time, and we have plenty of work to keep us occupied in the meantime."

David nodded, looking somewhat happier now, and then he added, "I wonder what Brian and his friends think of it all. I was glad to see him in the library this morning. If it is genuine, he needs to get away from here even more than we do. He has been here a couple of years before us, Christopher."

"That's right, David, and if we get the chance in the next couple of days to talk to him, we'll find out what he thinks. But we must not make problems for ourselves where there may not be any."

The driver of the mini cab taking the boys to their new destination was so pleasant and helpful that all six of them were stunned by his kindness. He had explained in detail how he was to deliver them to three different farmsteads with two boys going to each place. He reassured them that although it was about forty or fifty miles between each homestead that counted for nothing in Australia, and once they were settled in, they would find ways of keeping in touch with one another.

It had been a busy morning in the home after the boys had been told their transport would be arriving at nine-thirty am to take them to their destination. After breakfast they were ordered to take all their bed clothes to the laundry room and put them into the huge washing machine. Then it was back to their dormitory to fumigate their bed and floors before going to the library to collect any papers relating to their circumstances during their time in Swandon. And if they were lucky perhaps get their birth certificate. Then it was out to sit on the verandas with their holdalls containing their meagre possessions.

Before leaving, Chris made the excuse of going to the toilet, he wanted to seek out Father Brady, and he was fortunate enough to meet him in the corridor. He begged the priest to promise him that if anyone ever came looking for Joe, David or him at any time, Father Brady would let them know where the boys had gone.

Christopher and Joe were nominated by the other boys to go to the first farmstead that they arrived at. They were the two youngest in the group, Brian insisted, and the other four boys would know exactly where to find them and how to keep in touch. And that first stop would serve as their base for meeting up and keeping in contact. According to their driver, they had been driving for over an hour when he announced they were about to enter the driveway of the first farm. All six boys in their excitement to see anything, a new stretch of land, something they had not witnessed in the last twelve years and longer, in their lives, began to get up out of their seat.

Immediately, the driver reprimanded them, stressing just how likely they were to cause an accident. He assured them he would let them all out to have a look around, so that they might envisage where the first two boys would be. As the minicab drew to a halt in a large square courtyard, Joe and Christopher just looked at one another, scarcely believing the scene in front of them. The house the driver was stopping in front of was a long brightly coloured cream painted building with numerous windows, and beautiful flowery curtains shielding them from the sun. The front door with its ornate windows at each side was painted a beautiful sea blue colour.

As all six boys tumbled out of the car, the door of the house was opened by a small dark-haired woman who had a very welcoming smile on her face. Christopher reached over to Joe and grasped his hand tightly as he whispered, "This looks ok, doesn't it, Joe?"

In response, Joe just nodded, speechless at what he was seeing. The whole place was lovely, but to see a woman smiling so warmly in greeting was just remarkable. He, nor any of the other boys, had seen a woman in twelve years and here was one now, who just reminded Joe of his grandmother. It was all so overpowering that Joe knew he was close to crying but had to make a conscious effort to control his feelings.

Chapter 48

The two oldest boys, who were not very well known to Brian and David, were happy to go to the third and last farmstead of their travels. They assured their two co-workers that they were enjoying the drive looking around them, wondering where they might be. So, David and Brian were left off at the second farmstead.

The house the driver drove up to was an L-shaped building, with numerous out houses with corrugated roofs dotted around it. This house appeared to be the family home. The whole area looked a much busier place, David thought, than the first farm had seemed to be. There were huddles of cows in the field, and close by there were dozens of goats in another field and they were very inquisitive as the mini cab drew to a halt, looking seriously at the cab, and the boys stepping down from it. In yet another field, sheep grazed happily, undisturbed by anything that might be happening.

David and Brian were welcomed to the farm by a man whom David would have put his age as being in his forties, and by a young boy who looked to be about sixteen years of age. The older man introduced himself as Colin Ward, owner of the farm. "And this is my son, Roy. He helps us on the farm, but he is still at school, he needs his education as well, you know." Then Colin Ward addressed the driver as he consulted the page he had in his hand, "Which of the six boys have we here?"

The driver was quick to introduce David and Brian, thankful now he had had plenty of time, and had thought to find out the boys' names as they drove along their journey. He exchanged a few pleasantries with the farmer, and then said he must be on his way and said his goodbyes. Colin Ward then turned to David and Brian. "If you just bring your bags, I will show you the accommodation and set a few ground rules for the duration of your stay." Then, indicating that the boys follow him and his son, he led the way along the side of the house until they arrived at the L-shaped part of the property.

As he opened the door leading into the area, Colin Ward spoke, "This is the accommodation for the two of you, if you just follow me, I will show you around." He smiled encouragingly at them as he entered a small hallway which led into a fair-sized living room with easy chairs, a sofa, and a dining table with chairs placed around it in a comfortable way. "This is your living room and dining area; you will eat breakfast and lunch here, but your evening meal will be taken in the family part of the house, which is accessed through this door here."

Colin Ward opened one of two doors situated in the back wall of the bungalow. "This corridor here leads to our dining room and our evening meal is at six o'clock. You will stop work at five o'clock, and wash and change your clothes before you join us. You have a fridge here which my wife will replenish every day with food for your breakfast and lunch."

Colin then indicated the other door. "That door leads to your bedroom and bathroom. You will start work at eight am each morning and, as I said, finish at five. You will have alternate Sundays off, which you will switch between the two of you." Colin Ward hesitated and looked at the boys. "Do you have any questions you would like to ask me?"

David and Brian shook their heads and then David said, "I think we understand the routine, sir, thank you."

"There is one other thing; although my wife will leave food out for you daily, and will clean the place once a week, you must clear up everywhere as you go along. You must keep your kitchen and bathroom tidy, and you must remember that it is vital to keep the curtains closed while you are away, as the house will be extremely hot for you if you don't." Colin Ward looked at his watch. "I will leave you both to unpack. It is five o'clock now, so we will see you at six for our family dinner in the dining room. We will discuss what your pay will be when you have been with us for a week. Is that acceptable to you? That is the way I have always worked."

"Of course, Mr Ward, that is fine," Brian was quick to say. Later, after David and Brian had unpacked and stowed away the few belongings that they had with them, they sat down on the beds in the room Mr Ward had indicated was their bedroom. They were both very deep in thought as they sat there. David was the first to speak, "This is some spot we have been brought to, isn't it, Brian?"

"It is, indeed, David. We have decent beds and bedding to sleep in for the first time in years, and whatever hardship or hard work we undergo here, at least we will be able to sleep well," Brian commented.

David looked around the bedroom before he spoke again, "It is also good we have our own beds, wardrobes, and a decent toilet and bathroom, and the living room, well, it is just lovely. I know we are still uncertain about everything, how we will be treated during our working day, but I think if we work hard for this man, we will be alright."

"I think so too, David, but I am glad to hear you say it. Now we better make our way through to Mr Ward's dining room for our tea."

Christopher and Joe did not have anything like the quarters David and Brian had. They just had a bedroom with two single beds in it, but it was a spacious room, and the family bathroom was just across the corridor. Mr and Mrs Moore had no family, so the two boys soon found themselves becoming part of the household, sitting for all their meals with their boss and his wife. Mr Moore had given them a few guidelines on their arrival, what his expectations from them where, and in return he and his wife would treat them well. He explained he was considered by many other farmers to be one of the poor ones because his farmstead was quite small with just fifty acres. But he stressed to his two new workers, it had always been enough for him and his wife, Mabel.

"We are not getting any younger, lads, so that's why we put our names down for wanting to employ some young people looking for work," Mr Moore told them. "This is the first time we have had anyone come to work for us, so it is a new experience for us. But we did benefit from some advice from the government, some officials did come out and explain the routine, and how we should give you good accommodation and meals, and if we did that, your pay would be minimal." Mr Moore looked at Christopher and Joe. "How do you feel about that?"

"Sir, we will go along with what you wish. Isn't that right, Joe?" Christopher turned to Joe.

"Oh, definitely, Mr Moore, we don't know anything about what pay we would be due. We know nothing about that sort of thing. You see, Mr Moore, we have been in a children's home and although we worked very hard, we never were paid, but we never expected to be paid because we were living there," Joe said.

Christopher added, "To be truthful, Mr Moore, we don't really expect you to pay us if we are going to get our food here."

Tom Moore looked at the two boys standing before him and was quite shocked at their naiveté. He was also shocked at the knowledge they had never been paid by anyone, even though they had been working for years. Now, they were telling him so directly they didn't really expect to be paid. He was so glad these boys had been sent to him, and not to some other callous farmer who, on hearing what this young man had just said, would not have been paying them anything. But Tom Moore knew his conscience would not let him treat anyone badly, and he decided there and then he would give them one pound fifty a week each.

Later that evening, after their first tea with Mr and Mrs Moore, and when they were in their bedroom, Christopher told Joe he had a really good feeling about the place. "I think we are going to be happy here, Joe, and I am glad I was not tempted to say anything about the home and I never will, Joe."

"That's a good idea, Christopher, I never will either, it is all in the past after all." And even as Joe said the words, he still found it hard to believe they had left 'that awful place', as he called it when talking to Christopher.

"I am glad we both agree about this, Joe, I would not want Mr and Mrs Moore to think we were in the habit of complaining about things. They might think if we were to do it about one place, we might just do it about others, and they seem really kind, so we will keep quiet about Swandon and how awful it really was for us."

It would be some time before the extent of the ill treatment and abuse of the children in Swandon Children's Home, and other homes in Australia, came to light. When questioned years later as to why none of the children complained or reported the ill treatment to anyone, they were unanimous in saying they had no one to complain to, and even if they had, they did not think they would be believed by some others. When interviewed in later years, simply said they were too terrified by the beatings they got regularly at the hands of the priests, and thought if they said anything, the beatings would be even more severe.

The other two boys out of the six, who were sent to farms from Swandon kept limited contact with the other four boys. This was no doubt due to the distance their farm was to the others—one hundred and twenty kilometres. Their workload was such that they had little time for relaxation, and this was due to the large herds of cattle and sheep on the farm, which had over two hundred acres. Then, of course, these two boys had never known Chris and David or Joe well. They had only become close to Brian since their years in Swandon but like many friendships, their contact with Brian soon became infrequent due to all the constrictions of their placements and workload until eventually communication ceased.

Chapter 49

"You don't need to show such desperation when you are working here. It is very hot, and a good steady pace when you are clearing out the milking parlours will be much healthier for you." Thomas Moore could see that his new employees were very vigorous and intent, almost frantic, he thought, on anything they were doing on the farm. "Is that how you always worked in the children's home you were in?"

"Yes Mr Moore, there was always a lot to do and we were working to a strict timeframe," Christopher answered. "Certain jobs had to be completed within certain times, maybe hours or sometimes on large jobs it was so many days." As he spoke, he did his best to be quite truthful but without including the serious, ominous threat of beatings they would get if a certain job was not completed within the timeframe.

Thomas Moore nodded and smiled at Joe and Chris, "Well, just keep at an even pace here, you are not working to any great time schedule."

He was somewhat reassured by Christopher's answer but could not clear his head of the nagging doubts that these young boys had been seriously overworked, and by the look of them, seriously underfed as well.

"I am glad to see you have on the long sleeved tops my wife laid out for you, it is important you don't get burnt. This sun is so strong and then you would be in agony. And when you go out around the fields, as we will be doing to repair fences and such, please wear the hats that my wife gave you."

"Thank you, Mr Moore, we like the shirts and the hats very much, so thank you," Joe joined in. He had been listening intently to what his boss was saying about their work, and he could scarcely believe that anyone would be so kind to them. Why, no one had even spoke to them so caringly since they arrived in Australia.

For David and Brian, in the much larger farmstead, their boss, Mr Ward, kept everything on a very professional level. He was very much the boss and they were the workers. At the end of their first week, they were told their pay would be two pounds a week. Like Christopher and Joe, Brian and David were delighted with this, now earning their very first money. Indeed, they were very happy with it, it was more than they had expected. After all, they had their own quarters and Mrs Ward was an excellent cook and she made sure they had a nourishing dinner every night. She also kept their fridge well stocked with whatever they might need for their breakfast and lunch.

Besides, they loved their work, milking the cows and the goats in the morning, checking the sheep in the fields, and checking fences were safe for all the animals. The work was, however, never ending. Just a constant round of chores, and the huge expanse of the farm remained daunting to both David and Brian for some time. They were always glad of Roy's help after school, even though they found him to be a rather quiet, even somewhat dour lad. He seemed to have little to say but just worked silently beside them until everything was cleared up for the evening. So, David and Brian were very surprised when, as they sat round the dining room table having dinner one evening, he asked them if they would be interested in enrolling at night school in September.

"It is because at the end of June, I will be finished with day school that is in a couple of weeks. I am signing up to do maths and commerce at night school and I wondered if you would like to do it too?" He looked across with an expectant look on his face at David and Brian sitting across from him. "Dad will be taking and collecting me, so if you are interested, we could go together."

David was the first to speak, "Why, that would be wonderful, Roy … Mr Ward!" He looked across at his employer. "That is, if you do not need us here? I am sure I speak for Brian here too, Mr Ward, isn't that right, Brian?"

"Yes, very much so, we would love to be given the chance to have some education and thank you, Roy, for thinking of us."

Brian now smiled over at the young man who was trying to give them the opportunity to learn.

"As long as all the milking is done and the animals are fed, have clean beds and are safe, I'd be happy to give you a lift with Roy. Now, the school is in Perth city, which is quite a distance from us, so it will take up your entire evening once a week." Colin Ward hesitated, and he was silent for a moment and seemed lost in thought, when he spoke, he surprised David and Brian once again, and "I will pay for your fee for night school on one condition, that you will both attend very regularly and give the class your best attention. I believe a good education is essential nowadays, not that I had the opportunity. I am however self-taught and if you do not attend the class regularly, I will not hesitate to deduct the school fees from your pay."

"I promise you, sir, we do not intend to waste a minute of our time in school, we have had no chance of an education in the past number of years, so we are just delighted to be getting the opportunity now, thanks to your son and yourself." David was overwhelmed by this offer from his employee, he knew Brian too was very appreciative, he added quickly, "I know I speak for Brian also, Mr Ward, we are overwhelmed by your thoughtfulness."

"Well, that is that then," Colin Ward said gruffly, embarrassed now by these two young men's gratitude to him. He had, in fact, been wondering how he might help them on in the world. They were such good workers and deserved to succeed, and now this opportunity had presented itself, and the two boys had grasped it, which was at least a good start.

"Oh, Joe, this is a letter from David, and Brian too, of course." Christopher indicated the letter in his hand which had just been brought to him by Mrs Moore. "Imagine a letter for us, isn't it wonderful, our very first letter." Christopher's face was glowing with the joy of contact with someone outside of Joe's and his small boundaries. "You read it, Joe; it is actually addressed to you as well as me." Christopher handed the letter over to Joe, then he went on, "I am so glad that day we left the house that David thought to ask Mr Moore the address of this place here, because it is just so wonderful Brian and he have made contact with us."

"They seem to like where they are, Christopher," Joe remarked as he read the letter. "But listen to this, their boss is starting to drive them to night school in September and because his son is going to go anyway, he has offered David and Brian the chance to go too." Joe looked up at Christopher who was standing waiting to hear all the news from his friends whom he had not seen or heard from for the last four months until now. "But that is not all, Christopher, David thinks we should enrol as well and find some way to get there. David reckons that we are only half the distance from the school compared to them."

Christopher reached over for the letter. "Let's read this, it sounds very interesting." And as Christopher read the much appreciated words written by his friends, he was overwhelmed by the knowledge that not only were they well away from Swandon but that they might, just might, be able with some help, to get some education.

172

"I am going to show this letter to Mr and Mrs Moore and see if they can give us any idea on how we would get to this school, if we would be eligible and how much the enrolment would cost." Christopher hugged the letter to him as he thought how wonderful it would be if he would be able to attend this night school and see David and Brian at the same time.

Mr and Mrs Moore were somewhat taken aback when Christopher and Joe talked to them about the night school, they seemed quite naïve about the importance of education, and Christopher realised that schooling had not featured highly in their lives. However, they were most agreeable to giving the boys any time off they might need. Mr Moore said he would take them on their first evening, but he intended to ask Colin Ward which road he travelled on to the night school because, he told Christopher, he probably passed the Moore's homestead on his way to leaving the other boys off. This proved to be the case and Colin Ward would call once a week at the Moore farmstead in his jeep and Chris and Joe squeezed in beside Brian, David and the young Roy Ward boy. It was a tight fit, but no one minded that one little bit.

So began a new phase in these five boys' lives. A phase which without doubt improved their standing in Australian society. But all the schooling and learning they got did nothing to ease the knowledge that they did not really belong here. They had no family, they had never known love since they had arrived in Australia all those years ago, and for Christopher and Joe, this knowledge made them even more determined to earn decent money and try to find their way back home. Indeed, the kinder Mrs Moore was to them the more Christopher pined for his own mother, and trying to make his way home was becoming an obsession with him.

Chapter 50

Monica and Edward were married in the Presbyterian church in the centre of Lisburn. It was a beautiful sunny day and Monica wore the blue dress she had worn on the night Edward had proposed. With Jill's help she had found a small pillbox hat in the millinery department of Acheson's. Her shoes were also blue, with a hint of silver across the straps. She carried a very simple posy of white freesia, with pink and blue coloured roses. It was Agnes who accompanied her up the aisle to hand her over to Edward.

There was nothing anywhere in a magazine or paper that Monica had read that said it was not appropriate for a woman to do such a thing. Jill was her bridesmaid and looked demure in a knee-length cream silk dress, and Jennie was flower girl, looking delightful in a cream silk dress with blue flowers in her hair. And she had carried out her duties to perfection.

The only guests that Monica had was Sara, Joe's grandmother, and Lily, Jill's friend, who had been so delighted to get the invitation. Edward's mother and father were present, as was his brother, who was best man, and his wife, having flown in from England the day before. Mr Dunn and his wife were also there.

The afternoon reception was in the hotel where Edward had proposed. William, Edward's brother, made a short speech as Edward had requested, and then Edward rose to thank everyone for their presence at their wedding, and for all their help and support. He asked the small group of people to raise a toast for Christopher, that he was well and happy, and that soon he might be reunited with his mother. Monica listened to this man who was now her husband and was filled with love for him and optimism for Christopher and the future. She was determined not to cry today, she had to believe that Christopher would be alright, besides it was much too wonderful a day to spoil it with tears.

After the meal, Edward invited everyone back to his home, something Monica was very happy about, she had not had a chance to speak to anyone and wanted to know what everyone had thought of the service. And she was keen to talk to Jill and Mr Foster and was glad Jill had asked if he might have an invitation.

Once everyone was back in the house, Monica removed her hat and placed her bouquet and Jennie's in a bowl of water, she would take them to the cemetery tomorrow, to her first husband's and her parents' grave.

"Jill, thank you for your help this morning, that is the first time anyone has spent so long on my hair, I can tell you." Monica smiled at her friend, who was now sitting beside Sam Foster and Monica thought they both looked very much at ease with one another. She was anxious to welcome Sam Foster, as she knew he had suffered so much regarding these illegal adoptions and losing his wife in the tragic way he had. "It is lovely to see you with us today, Mr Foster, and I hope you have enjoyed it."

"Please, call me Sam, and yes, it was all lovely. The minister's prayers for Christopher were very poignant, as were Mr Wallace's toast for him at the meal."

"I am so glad you liked them, Sam. Edward has been wonderful about Christopher, you know," Monica said quietly.

"I realised that when I heard him speaking, he must be a great comfort to you, there has been so much suffering, such unnecessary suffering, over all this," Sam spoke quite harshly. "Jill introduced me to Sara outside the church and she is, I believe, the grandmother whose grandson died on the holiday the children were sent on."

"Yes, she is, Jill, and I do try to support her as much as possible, and she has agreed to stay the night at my apartment, rather than go back to the home." Monica looked over at Sara, who was talking animatedly to Agnes. "Sara has an artificial limb now and that has transformed her life. She is broken hearted about her grandson, but she copes very well."

Just as Monica spoke, Edward joined them and Monica introduced him to Sam Foster, Monica had told Edward just recently about the circumstances surrounding his wife's death. Edward greeted him warmly, and then he offered him a drink. "Would you like some wine, Sam, or a whiskey perhaps?"

"A glass of wine would be lovely, Jill and I came by taxi, and we had a glass of wine at the hotel, just to celebrate your happiness."

"Well, I am sure you would like another, Jill?"

"Yes, please, and then I will go and ask Sara and Lily to join us over here."

Monica spent some time with her friends, but she made sure she followed Edwards's example of sitting down with everyone and talking to them. Mr and Mrs Wallace seemed very happy spending their evening mostly with Jennie, and after a warm exchange between them, Mrs Wallace told Monica she looked stunning, and that her dress was perfect. Monica appreciated her new mother in law's obvious approval of her and found Edward's parents a very endearing couple. She talked to Edward's brother and his wife whom Monica had never met until today, simply because they lived in England. They only came to Northern Ireland on occasions, to visit William's parents and sometimes Edward would have been able to go to see them while they were at their parents' home. They both agreed it was lovely to be here today, and to be a part of all the excitement and happiness.

Then, on approaching Mr Dunn, he greeted her very warmly, and introduced her to his wife, a small plump woman with the most beautiful blue eyes that Monica had ever seen, and which seemed to light up her whole face. It was she who referred to Christopher first.

"The prayers for your son during your wedding service were so very touching, Monica, as was the toast for him at the reception. Your husband means to keep his name to the forefront for as long as it takes to find him, I thought it was all so lovely," Mrs Dunn said with feeling. "And as for Albert, he intends to try to do the same."

"I know Mr Dunn has done all in his power and I am indebted to him, as Edward has stressed to him on many occasions." Monica smiled gratefully at Mrs Dunn.

"I believe, Monica, we will trace him sooner or later, or he will contact us," Mrs Dunn assured her. "You do know about the other family Albert visited whose little girl seems to have been in actually adopted, don't you?"

"Yes, Edward told me all about it. It is just so cruel what was done to us and our children. And why, I'll never understand," Monica said sadly. "But I must keep hoping, I really must." Then she added, "I must re-join Edward now and help Agnes serve some supper."

Jill phoned her a couple of weeks later and asked to meet her for coffee in their usual café because she had something to tell her, and later over coffee Jill told her Sam Foster, and she were getting married in a registry office in three months' time and she would like Monica to be a witness at the ceremony. She hadn't told Monica sooner because she wanted Monica to get used to being married herself, without Jill telling her all about her and Sam's plans. They had also wanted to leave a reasonable time after Eleanor's death had passed, as a mark of respect for such a lovely woman who had been destroyed by people in high places. People who were supposed to be above reproach.

Chapter 51

"Christopher, I need to talk to you about night school," Joe said to Christopher as they were preparing for bed. They were always extremely tired after the hour-long journey to the school, then the two hours of concentrated study, then the journey back to the farm, and all of this on top of a hard day's work in the fields with the animals. Christopher was immediately alerted when Joe spoke, he had always been sensitive to Joe's feelings and frame of mind. Now he felt guilty that he must have missed something, and all because he was so taken up with the interesting subject of maths, book-keeping and commerce—all the work they were doing in night class.

"What is it, Joe, do you not like night school? What's the problem?" he added.

"I'm not really interested in the subjects we're doing, Christopher," Joe spoke hesitantly. "I feel stupid and uncomfortable." He was reluctant to complain, but after five weeks of attending the courses, he knew he had very limited interest in commerce or any related topics.

"Aw Joe, I am so sorry." Christopher was quite shocked. Joe had given no indication at all that he was struggling with the subjects. "What do you think we can do about it? Can we change class, do you think? After all, it is only five weeks since we started, what do you think, Joe?"

"I would like to change, yes, I would, Christopher, but you mustn't do it, definitely not. You, like Brian and David, are excelling at commerce." Joe paused, then added, "I do know that English and Art classes run on the same evening as the commerce one, so maybe I would be allowed to transfer over. I am certainly going to see what I can do about it when we go next week."

"That seems like a good idea, Joe. It certainly sounds a very interesting course for you and," Christopher stressed, "I am just so sorry, I railroaded you into this."

"Christopher, you did no such thing, I was as keen as you were to go, I just didn't know I have no flair for maths whereas you do have. I do think I may have a flair for English or Artwork, I know I like it, so let's hope."

"Do you realise, Joe, that if you enrol in a different class, I know it's only for a couple of hours, this will be the first time since we came here that we have been separated."

"I know that alright, Christopher, I think it is high time I got used to not having your such valuable company all the time." Joe smiled. "After all, Christopher, you may meet a nice girl here and decide to spend quite a lot of your time with her, so then I would have to do without."

"It's unlikely I will meet anyone here, Joe; besides, we have a pact to make our way back home, so we mustn't forget that."

"I never do, and that is still my aim in getting an education here, Christopher, make some money and leave here."

The headmaster was very agreeable to changing Joe's programme when Joe approached him. He also told him, on this occasion, he would waive any transfer fee involved. Mr Reid was very aware that the four boys who had recently enrolled in commerce were migrants, and he could scarcely believe they were only coming to the school now. He knew that at least three of them were aged around twenty-two, and the youngest was probably eighteen. Whoever had been responsible for these boys' welfare and education had been most negligent. He felt the least he could do to help was to cooperate with this young man and help him find some subject or subjects which would be of interest to him.

Chapter 52

"Christopher, can you remember much about that last morning when we left the children's home? I have been wrecking my brain trying to remember something, anything. All I remember is all of us getting into a bus. I remember you and me going, and I think there was a couple of small girls, am I right?" Joe sounded breathless when he spoke. They were on their way home in Mr Ward's jeep and they were a bit crushed sitting so closely together, but Christopher thought their cramped conditions had nothing to do with Joe's breathlessness.

"Well, I do remember a bit about it, Joe, in fact I've never forgotten it. The excitement of thinking we were going on holiday, only to discover that really, we had been kidnapped."

"Do you remember who, along with you and me, and David of course, was on the bus?"

"I remember there was six of us I think, five of us organised to go from the home, two girls and three boys and then of course, the driver. I remember too, that the bus was empty when we got on it, we were the first ones to be collected." Christopher looked at Joe, puzzled at Joe bringing up the conversation, so totally out of the blue. "Why Joe, what made you think of that day? You were only four years of age, so I am sure you don't remember much about it."

"I know I only have some fleeting memories, Christopher, but I remember the kind man on the train journey giving us sausages and marshmallows. I do also remember the five of us getting onto the empty bus, and then the two girls being directed by the driver, I think, to sit in front of us." Joe hesitated for a moment, then added quickly, "I remember one of the girl's names, it was Amy I think, the other one I should remember but I just can't grasp it. You are asking me, Christopher, what made me think of that morning. Well," Joe hesitated again, anxious not to be thought over imaginative, "there is a girl in the English and Art class who is a bit familiar looking, she really is, Christopher, and her name is Amy."

"Really Joe, you think she might be a bit familiar looking, but after all it is fourteen years since we saw her, and she must have changed considerably in that time, don't you agree?"

"I knew you would say that, Christopher, but I can't shake off the feeling that I did know her from somewhere."

"Have you spoken to her at all, Joe?"

"No, I haven't, but next week when class is over, I would like to point her out to you, and see what you think," Joe said. "I mean, you were eight, so your memory of that day would be much clearer than mine."

"Well, that sounds like a good idea, Joe, and perhaps during class next week you may get a chance to talk to her, wouldn't it be wonderful it if really was her?" Christopher felt he needed to go along with Joe here, not that he thought for one moment that Joe could remember anything much about that day, it was so long ago. To try to recall events from fifteen years ago would not be easy for anyone, never mind a boy who had only been four years old at the time. Never mind how all the unhappiness, the fear and the physical pain endured during the last years must have impacted so much on their brains and their memories.

The following Tuesday evening after class was finished, Christopher, David and Brian were waiting outside the college for Joe when they saw him coming down the steps with a young girl beside him. As he regarded the young girl, who was quite shyly approaching him, Christopher wondered how on earth they would know if this girl was indeed Amy. He only had a vague recollection of the two girls from the home, who were sent with them on the holiday.

On that morning, he did recall Miss Corken helping the five of them onto the bus which was waiting for them. Waiting to take them away from the children's home, away from their families and friends, and from their country. If he had only known then that they were never coming back to the home, he would have paid more attention to everything. He did remember Amy, and the other girl sitting side by side on the bus, and when other girls joined later, they sat on one side of the bus and the boys on the other. He was ashamed to think that was all he could remember.

Now as Joe and the girl drew nearer, she began to roll her sleeve cuffs back where it had creased down over her wrist and hand, then she extended her hand in greeting, still shy, but now smiling at him. It was as Christopher extended his hand out to her that he saw the mark on her wrist, and immediately his mind travelled back to the morning he was in the queue for breakfast behind Amy. As she reached for her porridge, he saw the mark, a small mark on her wrist the shape of an apple, here he was seeing it again, and now he recognised it as a very delicate birthmark. All those years ago, he had no idea what it was, but unbelievably he had remembered it. Now he smiled happily at the girl facing him.

"Hello again, Amy, it has been a long time since we saw you."

Chapter 53

"We must ask Mr Moore if he would be kind enough to give us a lift into Perth on the occasional Saturday afternoon. We know he and Mrs Moore go to visit her elderly brother sometimes. I'm sure he won't mind, that is, if we have all the work done."

Joe and Christopher were in bed, and Christopher was about to put the light out when Joe spoke. "What do you think, Christopher?"

"Well, we certainly didn't have much time to talk to Amy tonight. We still know little or nothing about how her life here has been," Christopher replied. "But that's how it's going to be at night school because we are dependent on a lift each week, and understandably Mr Ward is keen to get back home. It is a long drive for him every week, and we are so fortunate in getting a lift because he is bringing Roy anyway. We can't very well hang about talking to others and expect him to wait. I think your idea of asking them when they are next going to Perth is a good one." Christopher paused, then went on, "Then next week at college we can arrange to meet Amy somewhere for a cup of tea and a bun. I look forward to finding out how things have been for her here in Australia and tell her all about ourselves."

The following week at night school, Joe was able to arrange for Christopher and himself to meet up with Amy on the following Saturday afternoon in the little teashop on the other side of the street from the school. It was all thanks to Mr and Mrs Moore who were more than happy to give them both a couple of hours off work to enable them to travel with Mr Moore, who was going into Perth anyway. In return for their time off on the Saturday, Christopher and Joe insisted on working for a couple of hours on the Sunday. "It was," they insisted, "the least they could do in return for Mr and Mrs Moore's kindness."

"I'm beginning to realise, Amy, that there is not a great deal of difference in the treatment inflicted on all the children in the Home you were sent to, and the one Joe and I found ourselves in." Christopher said. He and Joe had been listening avidly to all Amy was telling them about her experiences. Amy was much more open and graphic, when describing the beatings some of the children got, than Christopher and Joe were about the traumatic incidents they had witnessed, and suffered, in Swandon. What shocked Christopher most, as he listened to Amy, that it was nuns who had carried out the beatings in the Home she was in. Christopher had never thought any woman would ever be capable of, or would have any desire, to beat any child.

"Amy, Christopher and I have tried our best to remember the name of the other girl who boarded the bus with you at the Melton Home, and I'm ashamed to say neither of us can remember it," Joe said. "Do you know what happened to her? Was she with you in the same Home?"

"I'm not surprised you can't remember, Joe. If you hadn't had a vague recollection of knowing me from somewhere, we would not be meeting up like this today. I had no idea I had ever met you before in my life. Christopher and you were total strangers to me. I think it's a bit of a miracle, really," Amy answered. "The girl with me that day, that was Helen Marks and yes, Helen and I were both sent to the same Home. At times Helen was a bit of a rebel, and did get a few beatings, but like me, she survived them all and now works in a similar post to myself. We do keep close contact even though she now has a boyfriend."

"Maybe you could bring her with you some Saturday afternoon, that is, if she is interested. Maybe she is well settled here and doesn't remember anything about her past," Christopher said.

"Unlike me, she has some memories, she does say they are vague, but she remembers a woman's warm hugs. She believes it was her mother," Amy replied. "I'll make contact and bring her along some Saturday soon."

Christopher and Joe were heartened to hear that very soon, they might meet up with someone else from their homeland, and they spend the next hour with Amy hearing how, like themselves, British officials had called at their Home and told the nuns that work must be found for some of the girls there. Amy knew she had been fortunate to be sent to a beautiful house in the suburbs of Perth to help with housework and look after an elderly lady. The house was just a short walk to the college, and she had enrolled herself the same week as Joe and Christopher had. Little did she realise she would meet someone who would remember her as a young child. She had no recollection of the dark-haired youths, but there was some fleeting memory of being on a bus somewhere with small boys a bit like them.

In spite of realising they had all been together in Melton Home, very little else fitted into place, but Amy hoped that perhaps it was the beginning of starting to feel she wasn't such a nobody, as she had believed she was all these years. But just like Christopher and Joe, her aspirations were, first and foremost, to try and get back home no matter how long it took or what changes they would surely find there when they did get back.

Chapter 54

Monica sat alone with her thoughts, her coffee cup in her hand, on the terrace looking at the beautiful rose bushes and lilies which flourished so well under the care and supervision of John, the gardener. She was looking at them, but their appearance wasn't registering much with her this morning, her mind was so full of mixed emotions. She had been sick again this morning, she had now missed two periods, and she recognised the sickness as the same as when she was expecting Christopher.

Christopher, who was now gone from her over fourteen years, he would be twenty-two years old this year. He should be here with Edward and her, and hear everything about their coming baby, his brother or sister. He should be here to join in the joy and happiness that Edward and she would have. Her son should be here. And as she thought about him, she was glad Edward had taken Jennie shopping this morning. She felt she needed the solitude to think and rejoice in her pregnancy, but knowing it was tinged with sadness because of Christopher's absence from her life.

She knew before she ever told Edward that he would be delighted. Monica had talked and wondered about her difficulty in conceiving, after all they were married for almost six years now. But Edward, in his quiet and supportive way, had assured her there was plenty of time. In the meantime, they must appreciate each other, and enjoy their time with Jennie. And now of course he had been proved right, and as she thought about him, she made a vow that she would be the best mother to her child as she could possibly be.

Later that day, after Monica had told Edward the wonderful news, the two of them sought out Jennie and Agnes and told them about the baby. Agnes was delighted for them, and it was an excited Jennie who raced across the room, and hugged and kissed Monica and Edward in turns, while at the same time jumping up and down beside them. As Monica sat there in Edward's arms with his daughter beside her, she felt a certain peace steal into her heart for the first time since her son had gone from her life. She knew she was blessed by a wonderful caring husband, and a beautiful eighteen-year-old stepdaughter who was attending the local grammar school but would soon go to university. They were delighted with Jennie's progress in both her schoolwork and her social behaviour.

Monica knew too that Edward was very proud of his daughter and appreciated Monica's influence in her life. Jennie was now head girl in her year at school and had told her father for some time, she had ambitions to become a doctor, a career which her father had every intention of encouraging her in. But Monica knew that every step Jennie took in her progress to prepare her for her worthwhile career, she, Monica, felt the hurt of knowing nothing about Christopher's progress in life. She knew it was distasteful of her to imagine any comparisons between Jennie and Christopher, and even though she knew it gave her no credit, something in her continued to wonder and try to compare. She did hope that with the birth of her new baby, she could escape these unworthy thoughts and her baby would help her focus on her whole new family more graciously.

"Is it today you are going to see Jill?" Edward remarked as he sat at the breakfast table spreading butter onto a thick slice of toast.

"Yes, I am calling at her house and then we intend to catch the bus to go and see Sara. She is expecting us later," Monica replied then added, "Sara is in a great way to try living independently again, her artificial limb has made such a vast difference to her. She now helps other women in the home who are more disabled or older than Sara. She says she has put her name down in the housing association for a flat. She is so determined about this."

"What does the home think of this idea? And the couple of times she stayed over here with you, how do you think she managed?"

"The staff in the home are very supportive of her idea, Edward. Certainly, on the occasions she stayed here with me in the annexe, she was trying to do things for me," Monica said, "so I think she would be fine living independently."

"Well then, let's get things moving for her. What is wrong with letting her have the annexe, after all, it is unused now. I did contemplate giving it to my parents, but it would be too small for them. Besides father told me earlier this week that they have bought a piece of land just around the corner from us. It is on the Antrim Road before the bridge. They want to come nearer to us to live,

Monica, and they want to build a bungalow. So do offer the annexe to Sara please, my love."

In answer, Monica pushed her chair back and went to the side of the table to hug Edward passionately. "Edward, how do you think of all the kind things you do, I just don't know. I would never have thought of such a thing. It is such a lovely idea on your part." She kissed him again. "I love you so much."

Edward returned her hug. "Let me know when she wants to come, and we will get it spruced up for her. That is, if she wants to come, she may not, you know Monica, there is that I suppose." Edward sounded disappointed.

"I think she'll be delighted, and I intend to tell her today as soon as I see her."

"Monica, I feel so fortunate that I am in a good sound, strong, financial business position and can offer to help Sara. That is how I feel, I feel blessed that the line of business I chose has been so rewarding, and now I feel doubly blessed that I have you with me at all times in my life. I also have the pleasure of getting to know your friends, and I am very happy to help them."

Chapter 55

"Agnes, I think the baby is coming. I had to come back to bed this morning the pain in my back was so severe, and now I have started to have some cramps." Monica tried to sit up straight in the bed, but a pain gripped her, and she put her arms around her body to try to ease it.

Agnes came forward to the side of the bed. "Oh Monica, but the baby isn't due yet, sure it isn't?" Agnes paused, waiting for confirmation that that was the case.

"No, it isn't due yet. I am supposed to have about another three weeks, but I do know it is happening now, Agnes."

Agnes looking at her, her hair dank with sweat, and beads of perspiration on her upper lip and forehead, knew that, yes, Monica's baby must be coming. "Yes Monica, I do believe you are right, but there is no point in ringing Edward just yet, he will be in that meeting in Enniskillen at the moment." Agnes looked at the clock on Monica's bedside table. "It is only ten o'clock, Monica. So, we will leave that idea at present, but I will ring the hospital and ask for an ambulance. I will only be away from you for a minute or two, and then when I come back, I'll give you a little wash. And perhaps you would feel better if I helped you change out of your clothes and put on a nightdress."

Agnes, reassuring Monica that she would only be away for a short time, went downstairs to ring the hospital. When they heard the details, they reassured Agnes an ambulance would be with them shortly, and somewhat relieved, Agnes made her way back upstairs.

"I have a small case packed, Agnes, for the occasion," Monica informed her quickly, when Agnes told her the ambulance was on its way. "It is in the bottom of my wardrobe, I packed it sometime ago, just to be sure." Monica caught her breath on her last couple of words as another pain gripped her. Agnes held her as firmly as she could, and when the pain had passed, she went to the chest of drawers to look for a nightdress. "You will find one in the third drawer," she directed Agnes.

Soon Agnes had Monica out of her clothes and into a cool cotton nightdress, just as they heard the ambulance pull up in the driveway.

"I will come with you in the ambulance, but I need to nip across to the annexe just to let Sara know what is happening, she will be wondering." And Agnes left the bedroom, went downstairs, directed the ambulance driver upstairs, and then hurried across to the annexe to tell Sara that Monica was in labour and on her way to the hospital.

"Mr Wallace, you have a daughter, a beautiful baby daughter." The nurse who had just left Monica, smiled a happy smile at him.

"Is everything alright, is my wife alright?" Edward asked, panic in his voice.

"Everything is fine, your wife is tired, but all is well. You can go in now."

"I had to drive from Enniskillen, you see," Edward explained to her as he walked with her, "the baby is early, isn't she?"

"Yes, of course," the nurse reassured him, "but everything is fine."

Edward began to rush forward to go into Monica, but then he hesitated, and remembering his manners, he thanked the nurse profusely for all her kindness. On entering the ward and seeing Monica propped up on a pillow, very pale and weary looking, with their new baby in her arms, he was overcome with emotion. Unable to speak for a moment, he made his way to the bed and enveloped his new daughter and his wife in his arms.

"Darling, she is beautiful, she really is, as you are, my love."

Monica smiled happily up at Edward and said quietly, "I would like to call her Faith, Edward. What do you think of that name?"

"How lovely," was all Edward could whisper as he held them both close to him, "and I think we should put a good announcement of her birth in the newspaper and appeal for help in finding her brother with photographs of Faith and of Christopher. You never know, love; it might jog someone's memory."

In reply, Monica gave Edward a loving smile and cuddled in close to him. She needed him now, more than ever, her heart was such a whirlwind of mixed emotions. She was feeling elated at her present happiness, and yet the loss of her son was always with her, and no less so than today. As she held her new-born daughter in her arms, she could only hope her son was well and happy and that sometime soon she would see him again.

Chapter 56

"A friend of mine has a second-hand car for sale, if either of you young men are interested."

Joe and Christopher were having their evening meal with Mr, and Mrs Moore when Mr Moore addressed them. "I think he's looking around two hundred dollars for it. What do you think, boys?" Mr Moore regarded them as he spoke. "It would mean you could go into Perth any time you wanted to. You would be independent. Think about it, maybe you could afford to buy it between you and if you need to borrow any money, I'll lend it to you, and you can pay me back. I can take something out of your wages every week. But you would need to let me know tomorrow. Somebody's going to snap it up, it's a good car, I would recommend it. And," Mr Moore continued, "you have plenty of scope here, around the house, to practice your driving before you go near any roads."

"What do you think, Joe, about us buying this car between us?" Christopher and Joe were in their bedroom, preparing for bed. They had thanked Mr Moore very much for thinking of them and told him they would think about the car but, Christopher emphasised, Joe and he needed to talk about it seriously. They needed to make sure they could afford it.

"Well, it's like this, Christopher, I couldn't afford to buy it myself. I have managed to save about sixty dollars, and that's about it, I'm afraid," Joe said.

"I have something the same in a bag, in that drawer over there." Christopher indicated the chest of drawers sitting below the bedroom window. "I've been saving as much as I can to try to raise my fare back home, but that is going to take such a long time. Meanwhile, we do have to become more independent, Joe, or we'll not get very far with our careers. We'll just be stuck here, Joe, and although the Moores are so very kind, we need to try to move on. So, I think we must let Mr Moore know in the morning that we want to buy it between us."

"We must buy this car, even if it's just to save Mr Moore from taking us into Perth on Saturday. I do believe that sometimes he goes on a Saturday just to suit us," Christopher said.

"I agree with all you're saying, Christopher. After all, there is no other form of transport around here and, as you say, we can't go on indefinitely looking for lifts from people."

"We'll still try to save something out of our pay each week, Joe, for our airfare back home. That's all I want."

Christopher knew so well how kind Mr and Mrs Moore had been to them since they had come to work for them almost two years ago. Although he did appreciate it and did his best to show it, his heart still yearned for his mother and home. He knew if the chance of going home arose—unlikely as that chance was—he would be prepared to leave all this, and people's kindness to him, just to go home.

The car, after a thorough inspection, was bought by the two boys, and they did make good use of it. Between going to see Amy most Saturday afternoons, or just going for a drive to familiarise themselves with the surrounding farms and roads. Then a couple of months after Joe and Christopher had first started to meet Amy on a Saturday, Christopher knew that Joe was becoming very fond of the girl. He decided then he would encourage Joe to go alone, and Christopher could have the car on his own on one of the weeknights.

Indeed, initially Christopher had found himself being attracted to Amy, she was a beautiful girl, but Christopher had no desire for any romantic involvement with anyone. Not while he was so set on getting back home. Besides, he would never wish to cause Joe any further unhappiness than what he had already suffered. He felt well rewarded when about six weeks later, Joe told him Amy and he were going to meet one evening in the week, as well as Saturday afternoon. It was then that Joe told Christopher that he really loved Amy, but he intended to take things slowly with her. He did not want to rush her; they were so young. Secretly, Joe believed she had feelings for him, and he cherished those thoughts of her.

Christopher was so glad, when Joe told him all this, that he had decided to step back from the initial Saturday afternoon meeting with Joe and Amy.

On the evenings that Christopher took the car out, although it was an hour's drive there and an hour's drive back from Mr and Mrs Moore's house, he visited David and Brian. He had found the place easily enough on his first attempt, by simply following Mr Moore's directions. David and Brian always made him most welcome in their own private annexe. Christopher thought his two friends had a wonderful set up with their own sitting room, kitchen, bedroom, and bathroom, but he did not envy them with all they had. He was more than happy with the accommodation Joe and he had with Mr and Mrs Moore, they were very comfortable and well looked after.

From time to time, they met up with Helen Marks, who related all her heart-breaking experiences in the Home to them. She told it all to them in a most matter of fact manner, with little sign of the distress she must have endured. When Christopher remarked how much he admired her stoic manner, she replied, "I made up my mind early on that those horrible nuns would never break me, and they never did. I developed a resistance, I think, to all their nasty words and beatings," Helen told them. "Now, hopefully, it is all in the past and I have a comfortable place to live, a job that earns me reasonable money and," she smiled openly now, "a nice boyfriend."

"Do you feel fairly settled here then, Helen?" Christopher asked her.

Helen was silent for a moment, and when she spoke, Christopher realised there was considerable emotion in her voice.

"Do you mean, if I had the choice between staying here or going home, what would I do? Like yourselves, Christopher and Joe, I still yearn for my vaguely remembered home, some roots, but most of all I yearn for my mother." Now her voice held a certain force. "Like yourselves, I want to be with my mother. I can remember her hugging me, you know. No one, not one person, ever hugged me since, until now, until I met my boyfriend, he hugs me closely, but still, he's not my mother."

There was a profound silence after Helen talked to them, and Christopher empathised with her feelings, at the same time he felt real admiration for her, and her stoic manner.

Joe and Christopher's life took on a certain routine, working hard during the day. Going to night class once a week, Joe meeting Amy every Wednesday night and Saturday afternoon, and Christopher going to David and Brian routinely too. Sometimes if all the work was done, Joe would accompany Christopher on his visits to see them. The time drifted by, and Christopher passed his examinations in book-keeping and commerce. Joe too, did well by gaining his certificates in English and Art. Meanwhile, Amy was awarded best student of the year while simultaneously obtaining a distinction in her English Language examinations.

Then a couple of weeks later the headmaster of the technical college offered her a part-time position, helping teach some of the students, provided she enrolled into the teacher training college.

Chapter 57

Tom McGrath was deep in thought as he inserted the key into the front door of his father's bungalow. Well, he corrected himself, really it was his parents' bungalow. This had been his parents' home, and indeed his, until he left when he married Eva thirty years ago. Then his mother's sudden death fifteen years ago had left his father so alone and bereft, that he and Eva had spent the last number of years trying to persuade him to live with them. However, one bitterly cold January day, when there was three or four inches of snow on the ground, he had told Tom that he would like to take Eva and he up on their offer of him coming to live with them.

"Dad, that is wonderful news, but just be sure it is what you want and not because Eva and I have spent too long talking about it," Tom replied to his father's blunt statement. "Why the change of heart, dad, after all this time?"

"I just feel it is time for me to get some help, and I feel lonelier and colder in the winter. I mean to say, look at the ground out there. It's far too slippery, too risky for me, I'm afraid. So, because I can't go out, I do get very lonely."

"Well, I am delighted, and I know Eva will be too." Tom smiled encouragingly at his father. "We will have to get this place on the market, Dad. In the meantime, Eva and I will organise the space we have downstairs for you."

Now today, three months later, he was entering the family home, which was going to be his last time in it. The property had sold quite quickly, much to Tom's surprise, and he had spent the last few days clearing and cleaning the house. Today he had only the built-in wardrobes in the spare room to clean out and that would be him finished, ready to take the keys to the estate agent.

When he opened the wardrobe doors in the small spare room, he was shocked to see the number of books, magazines, and newspapers his dad had collected. He had never thought of his father as someone who hoarded anything much, but his wardrobe indicated that Mr McGrath senior liked to gather up some things—at the least—reading material. Well, he would bring all of it down to the living room and sit down on an easy chair, a chair Tom intended bringing home with him today. It had been his mother's chair, and this morning Tom had attached his trailer to the car in order to bring the chair to his home. It would be perfect at the window of the sitting room he had organised for his father.

Now, Tom settled down in the chair and began, firstly, to consider which books he should keep for his father. His father was such an avid reader that Tom would have no doubt he would have read both the books and magazines some time ago, but still, he would bring them back for him. He must have kept them for a reason. The newspapers, however, were a different matter. Tom could think of no reason as to why his father would have hoarded those. He began to leaf through them in a half-hearted manner, and soon discovered the bundles consisted mainly of Belfast Telegraphs, newsletters, and the local Lisburn newspapers.

Tom felt ashamed that he had never shown a decent interest in his father's favourite pastime, reading. He hadn't even known he bought the Lisburn Star, but there was the evidence in front of him. He himself had always considered it a paper with little news but plenty of advertisements. Intrigued now as to why his father bought it on a weekly basis, Tom began to flick through two or three of the pages.

Suddenly, his eye was drawn to a picture of a young baby, and underneath it a picture of a young boy. The baby was a beautiful child, but it was the young boy's image that was haunting him, it was somehow so familiar to him, but he had no idea whatsoever why it should be. He turned over two or three more pages, but still wondering, he went back to the page with the photograph in it. It was then that he noticed there was a phone number, and a short paragraph obviously relating to the insertion. He began to read the words and when he read the words, 'Mellow Home' he immediately looked at the image of the young boy again and, despite the years, his memory came flooding back.

He remembered Christopher Scott so very well now, he had left such an impression on Tom regarding his manners and, more importantly, his caring attitude towards the young boy with him, who obviously depended on Christopher Scott for so much. He read the article avidly now, as he began to realise, with disbelief, that this boy, Christopher Scott, whose photograph was in front of him, had not returned from that holiday to Southampton. The holiday that Tom had taken him and some other boys and girls on. According to the article Tom was now reading, the children had been adopted. What age would they all be now? Tom wondered as he looked at the date on the newspaper. The paper was two years old, so if his memory served him right, it was now about fifteen years since he had travelled with those lovely children to Southampton.

Chapter 58

"I think it would be best, Mr McGrath, if you could see your way to come and meet me in person." Edward was cautious, listening to the voice on the other end of the phone. He had over time, especially over the last two years, since Christopher's photograph had first started to appear in the local newspaper, learnt to be quite sceptical. They had had so many supposed sightings of Christopher and wrong information that he was becoming convinced that his thought of putting his picture in the paper on a regular basis, had not been such a good idea. However, the man on the other end of the phone was adamant that he recognised the boy and could give Mr Wallace some information about him. Mr McGrath did stress that it might not lead them very far, but he felt he should tell Mr Wallace what he knew.

"I agree with you, sir, that I should meet you in person and give you the details as I remember them." Tom McGrath was now warming to the idea of meeting this boy's mother and stepfather to tell them, especially Mrs Wallace, what he knew. That evening, after discovering young Christopher Scott's photograph, he had locked his father's door for the last time, he thought a lot about the bereft mother and her sorrow. And he knew the last thing he would want to do, would be to raise any parents' hopes, only to destroy them. But then, Tom decided that he had the certainly of taking the children to Southampton all those years ago. He must share this information with the parents, who were still searching for their son fifteen years later.

"Thank you, Mr McGrath, for coming to see my wife and myself, I do hope you will be able to help us." Edward had invited Mr McGrath to call at his home in order to tell Monica and him what he knew. He thought a home environment would be more informal than waiting for each other in a coffee shop. Besides, it was better for Monica to be in her own home if this man had any information. However, he felt a certain reticence emanate from this man, a reluctance even perhaps, just to talk.

So, he was not surprised to hear him saying, as he sat opposite Monica and himself, "To be honest, Mr Wallace, initially I felt in a bit of a quandary about coming to meet you and Mrs Wallace." And Tom smiled over at Monica as she sat listening intently. "I don't want to get your hopes up," Tom said quietly, "I am sure that has happened to you a few times, so I am anxious just to reiterate to you what I know, and what exactly I remember." Tom paused. "It is so many years ago, as my records show."

With these words, Monica leaned forward eagerly. "That is exactly right, it is just over fifteen years since I last saw my son, please tell us what you know."

"Yes of course I shall, Mrs Wallace. I was employed by Christian Committee as a social worker, after the war ended in 1945 until 1952 when I left to join the health service. During my time with the Christian Committee, I was required to visit children's homes, and children who had been hospitalised due to the war. I was also involved with rehoming adults whose homes had been obliterated during the war years.

"As part of my remit, I would collect children from children's homes and take them to the seaside for a few hours and deliver them back a few hours later to the care of the staff in the home. On this occasion, I was told to collect five children from Melton Home in Lisburn at 6am, then eight from the Sisters of Newbourne in Belfast and four from Baron's Home also in Belfast. I was informed I would be taking all the children to Southampton via the ferry from Belfast to Liverpool, and then by train to Southampton. Here, I would meet the driver of a mini cab with a registration number which I was quoted and took note of. I was given the assurance this driver was taking them to a youth hostel for their holidays. So, after having left them with him, I must say I was disappointed I had to say my goodbyes to them in a car park."

Tom hesitated for a moment, as he watched Mrs Wallace, he hoped it was not too distressing for her to listen to what he had to say. He could see she was resolved to be strong, so he continued, "I did become quite attached to some of the children on the train journey down to the South of England, but I have to say your son's whole gentle manner and his caring thoughtful way with his younger companion was lovely to see Mrs Wallace, really lovely." Tom finished speaking, but when he saw the couple facing him waiting so expectantly, he said hopefully, "I am sorry, that is all I know. I am so sorry." He was beginning to think he should not have come after all because really, what had he told them, only that the children were going to enjoy a holiday in Southampton.

It was Mr Wallace who spoke first, "I think your information may prove to be very helpful, that is, if the youth hostel concerned is still functioning. I would like to send someone there to ask some questions discreetly. So, thank you, Mr McGrath, for all this."

Tom just nodded his head quietly and then added, "I did try to trace the driver who I met in the car park, and I did see all the children board the minibus. I felt if I found him and if I spoke to him, he could tell me where exactly he left them all, and if he had been going to stay with them." Tom paused. "I am sorry to say I have had no success in tracing him. You see," Tom said somewhat guiltily, "I never asked the man his name that day, not that I can recall. I was just so anxious to know where the children were going, and if they would be alright. He was most reassuring, and he told me they used the people who would be looking after them quite often. To be honest, I can remember having a great sense of relief at his words, because I felt it was a long trip for young boys and girls to go on. Something they were not at all used to."

Edward and Monica had been listening intently to every word Tom had said. Now, they sat silently contemplating and wondering what it all meant, and how on earth illegal adoptions had come up in such a setup.

Then Edward spoke, "I intend to pursue this information you have given me, Mr McGrath, and I will be looking for help to do so. Are you in a position to assist me in any way?" Edward looked directly at him. "I will pay you well for your time."

Chapter 59

Tom was preoccupied as he packed his small overnight bag that he had not used for some time. Since his father had come to live with Eva and him, they had little interest in holidays. Somehow their days were more occupied than they had previously been, and Tom knew it was all down to having his father's company in his home. Tom and Eva found John McGrath to be a simple joy to have in their home and before his father retired for the night Tom always joined him for an hour or so for a chat or do a crossword puzzle together.

Now, as he folded three shirts before placing them in a bag along with a pair of shoes, underwear, and soap bag, he thought a lot about the place he was going to, Southampton. Southampton, where he had left the children all those years ago. What he hoped to achieve after all this time, he had no idea, but Edward Wallace and Mrs Wallace wanted him to go to trace back and find anything that might be of any help in tracing Christopher.

Well, at least he was going to have company. Mr Wallace had told him he was sending his solicitor, Albert Dunn with him. He told Tom Mr Dunn seemed to have a deep interest in the illegal adoptions which seem to have been happening in some children's homes throughout the province. On the day before the departure by ferry to Liverpool, Mr Wallace had given Mr Dunn and himself five hundred pounds each to cover their expenses.

"That money is for your expenses only, Mr McGrath," Edward stressed. "I will pay you separately for your work and dedication, as I will with Albert."

The ferry trip across from Belfast to Stranraer only took about two hours and was uneventful. Then they caught the overnight train to London that was a long wakeful night for them. After they had eaten a fairly adequate meal in the ship's canteen, they both retired to the cabin where the bunk beds were.

"I have a notebook, Tom and I have just taken a note of when the train left Stranraer, the price of our meal and where we ate." Albert Dunn looked over at his companion. "I want to be meticulous in all our travel, Tom. It is important that we remember two children from Melton Home died and I wonder how they were on the train journey. I suppose we will never know that now, but if Joe Totten had been sick, I am sure Christopher Scott would have known and said to you, Tom."

"As I said before, Albert, I don't recall all that much about most of the other children, but I do remember how attentive and thoughtful Christopher was to Joe. There was no sign of the young boy being unwell, I am pretty sure of that. I have discovered that illegal adoptions were going on with the nuns at Newbourne Home and going on much more recently than Christopher Scott. Although I tried to help one mother and grandmother, I had made contact with, I am afraid I found out nothing. I just seemed to hit a brick wall," Albert said, somewhat wearily. The truth was, sometimes he thought of Ruth's mother and grandmother's distress and sorrow. He felt he had let both down, then he forced himself to concentrate on the other boys.

"At least we know with certainty Tom that they were in Southampton; it is solely thanks to you noticing the photo in the newspaper." Now, as Albert talked on, he was beginning to feel somewhat more optimistic about their project than he had been at the beginning. After all, if Tom found a lead in Southampton, no matter how tenuous it might be, it might help not only Christopher Scott but perhaps the Smart family too. He encouraged Ruth's mother to put Ruth's photo in the local paper, but so far there had been no response.

The hotel Tom had chosen for him and Albert to stay in was not over-the-top in Southampton but a more modest one. Tom and Albert were anxious not to waste Edward Wallace's money and, secondly, Tom thought perhaps a more basic hotel would know more about the youth hostels in Southampton. They had a good hearty breakfast with sausage, bacon and egg with a strong hot pot of tea and both agreed as they sat planning their day at the table Tom had chosen well regarding their three or four days stay in Southampton.

"Our first enquiry has to be regarding car hire here," Tom said. "These youth hostels might be out of town, and we do not want to weary ourselves, what do you think?"

"Most certainly, Tom, that is our first priority," Albert agreed.

A member of staff behind the reception desk was very helpful and soon had a hire car organised for them. The hire car representative met them in the foyer to sign them up with the car they suggested to the receptionist.

"Thank you for all your help," Tom said. "I wonder if you could tell us where the youth hostels are around here and how many there are." Tom asked her.

Albert and he arranged that Tom would ask the necessary questions wherever they were and Albert, who was well used to record-keeping, would do all the note-taking during their enquiries.

The receptionist slowly shook her head as she spoke, "I am sorry, I have only moved to Southampton a short time ago, but I was lucky enough to get this job." Then she smiled at them. "I do know someone who works in here and has lived here all her life, so she will hopefully be able to help you." She began to move from behind her desk. "If you wait here, I will see if she is free to talk to you." And with that the girl made her way towards the dining room.

She returned a few minutes later accompanied by the waitress who had served their breakfast a short time ago.

"This is Sylvia, Mr McGrath." The receptionist introduced the waitress to both men. "She has lived in Southampton all her life and knows it very well."

As Tom extended his hand in greeting to her, he realised she was in her forties. A perfect age, he thought to remember the last fifteen or sixteen years in Southampton. Later in the hotel car park sitting in their hire car Tom and Albert discussed what they had just been told by Sylvia, the waitress.

"I have the three youth hostels and their addresses all written down, Tom," Albert said. "Sylvia said there was one in the town centre, the other two lay a little way outside the city." He looked at Tom. "I suggest we go to the one in the centre of town firstly and then the other two. Sylvia said one lies to the east of Southampton and the other to the west. As you know, she did insist we would find the addresses she gave us by just following all the road signs."

"I totally agree, we will go to the town one first, Albert, even though I think it unlikely to have been used for holiday places for children. Surely, they would be sent to one of the others, which according to Sylvia, are situated close to the coast."

"I agree, Tom, but we need to get it over and done with."

Some three hours later, Tom and Albert were heading back down the Christchurch Road into Southampton. They had learnt a lot from both the youth hostel in Southampton city centre and the one they had just left on Christchurch Road. They had been told from the manager from both the hostels that they had never accepted children as young as the ones that Tom McGrath was talking about and secondly, they never organised holidays. Both managers were keen to explain that it was casual bookings and drop in travellers, most of them just anxious for a bed for the night before moving on to the next stage of their journey.

"We must look for somewhere to have lunch," Albert said as they drove along. "I will watch for any signs for ale houses or restaurants along the way."

"Turn in here, Tom," Albert said as he sported a sign indicating food served daily and a wide entrance leading to a car park and an interesting looking and typical looking old English public house and restaurant.

"This looks good, Albert, and despite a very disappointing couple of hours, it has not affected my appetite."

"I am very hungry too," Tom said.

"Good," Albert said as he opened the car door, "let's go inside then."

Over a lunch of tea with chicken salad sandwiches, the two men discussed their morning and their disappointment in not realising a youth hostel's position within the community.

"I might have known better." Tom felt rather foolish that he hadn't thought about youth hostels in any detail, but they had taken the suggestion from the Melton Home that was where the children had gone. No doubt the girl in charge thought it most likely because of the cheap rate for rooms in a hostel.

"Will we pursue the one on the Fountain Fairhaven Road, what do you think, Albert?"

"Well, as we are already heading that direction, we may as well finish off our enquiries, I am expecting to be told the same thing here, you know," Albert replied.

"I think so too, so we need to think about our next step," Tom said. "And that is a worry, a worry for me." He went on, "I was the one who brought them all here all those years ago. We need to know, Albert, where they've gone to."

"Let's hope something turns up. We must have hope." Albert's heart went out to Tom McGrath. He knew Tom felt guilty that he had never established exactly who the man was who was waiting in the car park to take the children, but Albert understood Tom McGrath had just been following instructions.

Later, as they drove back to the hotel Tom asked Albert to drive to the car park beside the town station. Albert did so and when they arrived Tom asked him to park the car and there, he got out to stretch his legs for a moment. When they were walking around the car park Tom spoke and his voice had a note of desperation, "This is where I left them, in this very car park with a man in a minibus, just as I had been directed to do, Albert." Tom turned to Albert and gripped his arm, "But where did they go to? Where, oh where are they?"

"Did you find the youth hostels without too much trouble yesterday?" Sylvia asked Tom as she served them their coffee and toast.

"Yes, your directions were very good indeed, Sylvia," Tom answered, "but they were unable to help us in any way. It is a bit of a long story, you know."

"If I knew more about what exactly you are looking for accommodation wise, I might be able to help you," Sylvia said.

Up until now, Tom had been reluctant to discuss the children with anyone, preferring to wait for some proof of their whereabouts. But now he found himself telling the waitress, who was serving him, the whole story.

Sylvia sat in stunned silence when Tom had finished then, in a voice no more than a whisper, she said, "The docks, you must find out from the docks. Find out when the next ship is due in. Lots of children from here have been sent from Southampton to foreign countries over the years." Sylvia looked at the two men, her face a mixture of horror and disbelief. "I believe the children that you are looking for have been sent to another country. If you ever tried to mention anything about how awful it was for these children, you were always told to be quiet, they were going away for a better life."

Chapter 60

"I think, Tom, that we'll have to ring Edward Wallace and get his advice before we do anything else," Albert said quietly as he took a seat beside Tom in the foyer of the hotel. They had left Sylvia a short time ago at reception and had assured her that if they had any questions at all they would come back to her.

She had answered them in a most reassuring manner. "I may not be able to help you with the children you are looking for, Mr McGrath, but I do know that hundreds of children were shipped abroad and if I can help you find out anything more I will." Tom and Albert, both stunned into silence, had managed to assure Sylvia they would indeed come to her for help.

"I think so, Albert," Tom answered soberly, his mind full of troubled thoughts. "I know that Sylvia said to go to the docks and ask a few questions there. She suggested that we should enquire when the next liner was due in and ask a few questions to the workers on board."

Albert paused, considering what Tom had said. "Yes, I think that Mr Wallace needs to be informed of this development in our search. I think it will be grave news that we are giving him, but we have to do it. Let's go to our room and call him from there." Albert said with a sad tinge to his voice. "How will we ever know where all those children have gone? We must share the information with the Wallace family."

"Yes, I am afraid this news we have now about the children from Melton Home may well be the reality of what happened to them. I'll ring and speak to Edward, Tom." Albert felt it was best he spoke to Edward rather than Tom as he had known him for a lifetime, and he did not want Tom to be the bearer of such bad news.

Albert was glad it was Edward himself who answered the phone call and he relayed the information they had learnt earlier to him. He was finding it very difficult to tell his friend such news, but he knew he must. After telling him about the liners which had left Southampton port on a regular basis, and always packed with children, he decided he must tell everything they had learnt from Sylvia, including the different destinations they may have gone to.

"Yes, Sylvia said that as far as she knew the children had been shipped out to different countries. Australia and Canada were mentioned, but she also thought some went to Africa." Albert felt this was the most difficult part of their conversation. If it had only been one Continent they had been sent to, it would have made things easier for their search, but it seemed to be several countries they had been assigned to. How could they ever trace them? How could they?

Edward listened intently to all Albert was telling him, he knew this news was important to Monica and himself, and indeed too many mothers and fathers whose children had been taken from them, as he realised the enormity of what Albert Dunn was telling him. Telling him hundreds of children had been sent away.

"Thank you, Albert, for your prompt phone call to give me this information," Edward said. "I would like a word with Tom if I may."

Albert turned to Tom and said, "Edward would like a word with you." He held the phone out to Tom.

"I wonder if Miss Corken gave you a list of the children's names when you collected them on that morning from Melton Home." Edward asked.

"Yes, I was given a list of all the children when they boarded the minibus, Edward," Tom answered. "I handed the list over to the driver I met up with in the car park in Southampton."

"Well, at least they had identities of a sort," Edward said, "I intend to list the names of the five children who left Melton Home and try my best to trace them through the government of those countries you think took them in." Edward was already trying to formulate a plan in his head to trace the children. "In the meantime, Tom, if Albert and you go back to the docks, you may be able to find out when the next ship is due and let me know if you learn anything."

The following morning, as suggested by Edward, after breakfast Tom and Albert established, they could book their room in the hotel for another couple of nights, which they did. Then they made their way to the docks area scarcely knowing why they were doing so, or what they hoped to establish, but if Edward thought they might learn something about the children it could be beneficial to visit them. As Tom was parking the car, Albert spotted a small coffee shop situated in a block of houses overlooking the dock area.

"Maybe we should have a cup of coffee here, Tom?" Albert indicated the coffee shop. "You never know what the owners may have witnessed over the years and perhaps they may know something about the ships and their activities."

"Good idea, Albert, surely somebody about here, apart from Sylvia, has witnessed something of importance to us."

The main area of the dining shop had obviously once been the living room of this terraced house. The brick fireplace was still in place with its shiny brass fender, brush and coal tongs. Although it was quite dark and shadowy, a great feeling of warmth and homeliness emanated into the room. Even though it was still early in the morning most of the tables were occupied, and Tom and Albert made their way to a table situated beside the window which gave a clear view of the docks. They discussed what they should have to drink and if they should order scones in case, they needed to linger for a time to find out any useful information. Just as they had decided on coffee and scones a grey-haired lady around fifty years of age approached their table and with a smile asked them what they would like to order.

Tom promptly returned her smile and ordered two coffees and scones and the two men settled back and waited for her return. "She seems to be the only one serving, Albert," Tom remarked quietly. "So, we will have to wait for the right moment when the waitress is not busy to have any conversation at all with her.

"Well, Edward did say to take our time and try to find out as much as possible," Albert said. "He didn't say anything about what he was going to do but no doubt he will have to tell Monica that it is possible her son was sent abroad."

"That will be heart-breaking for her, it will be awful for them both," Tom said with feeling. "He will do anything he possibly can to trace Christopher and the others who left Melton Home that morning."

"Do you think he means to contact the Christian Committee?" Albert asked.

"I don't know." Tom felt pessimistic when he thought of Edward Wallace contacting Christian Committee. He didn't think he would learn much from them. Because, the other Homes he now believed some authority, or someone higher up, was involved in this whole business. He had mentioned that to Edward and Monica on his first visit to them.

"The waitress doesn't seem to be just as busy at the moment, Tom," Albert observed, "maybe we ought to ask her for another coffee. It might give you the opportunity to talk about some of the children."

"Good idea." Tom beckoned to the woman who was now cleaning some tables and whom Tom believed to be the actual owner of the coffee shop.

When she brought the second coffees to the table, Tom asked if she could spare a moment as he would like to ask a couple of questions about the ships that sailed from the docks with children on board.

"My husband is the one to ask, he has worked on those docks there for thirty-five years." The woman nodded her head towards the dock area as she replied, "I will go and fetch him for you. He is off work today, so he is having a late breakfast in the back room. His name is John Brown, and I am Mrs Linda Brown." With a smile she made her way out of the dining room to return a couple of minutes later accompanied by a tall, thin, but very fit-looking man. As Tom and Albert watched, John Brown immediately pulled a chair over beside theirs and proceeded to sit down on it. Tom realised this man was very keen to talk about his job and the environment he worked in. Tom hoped and prayed that meant that when they told their reasons for being here in Southampton he would be able to tell them what had really happened to the children Sylvia had told them something about.

Chapter 61

"Mrs Logan, it is such a lovely morning for a walk, don't you think?" Amy addressed the elderly lady as she wrapped a warm rug around her knees. She was responsible for Mrs Logan's welfare four days a week until her daughter returned from her work around 2.30pm. "We are going to the park today. I have arranged to meet my friend Helen; she also hopes to bring the lady she is looking after."

"Oh, you mean Mrs Irwin, that's great." Mrs Logan smiled happily. "I like Mrs Irwin, we always reminisce about old times when we meet with you and your friend Helen. We don't meet up enough I think."

"I agree, Mrs Logan," Amy replied, "but somehow the days just seem to fly by. I am kept quite busy, I suppose."

"Of course you are, my dear. Don't mind me, dear, I'm very happy really but a little extra outing every now and again would be wonderful."

"I will mention it to your daughter and see what she thinks; if I can cut down on one or two of my chores, I could take you out more often," Amy remarked thoughtfully, all the time thinking she would like nothing better than to go for more walks and forget about the drudgery of housework. Amy felt she had now spent years cleaning cupboards, toilets, washing bed linen, mopping floors and sometimes although Mrs Logan's home was beautiful, and Mrs Logan herself was a lovely person as was her daughter and husband, the hum drum side of her employment made her restless and dissatisfied. She knew deep down that she did really want to become a teacher but how she could ever hope to attain this she had no idea but at least studying literature at college was a start.

She really loved her English sessions and was able to dabble with the arts side of things as well. When she first started to work for Mrs Logan, she had no idea what she wanted to do with her life but gradually seeing all the books in Mrs Logan's house, never mind the books her daughter brought home from the school library, Amy had developed a great love for English literature.

Amy had tried her best to encourage Helen Marks to join her in enrolling in the English classes, but Helen was adamant that she had no intention of doing so and Amy sensed Helen had little ambition to achieve much. She always stressed to Amy she had achieved a lot in her life by surviving the torture she had endured at the hands of the nuns in the children's home. Amy was saddened to realise that Helen's experiences had indeed deprived her of any desire to succeed in life. The only time she showed any interest in her future was when she told Amy she intended to marry her boyfriend who was about ten years older than her and held a good position as an engineer in the local council.

Now as she approached the bench that Helen was sitting on with Mrs Irwin, Amy knew that despite all their different views about education they were still close friends. Their experiences in the children's home had developed a bond between them and they felt easy in each other's company, they often talked and wondered if they would ever feel content in Australia or would they always yearn for home. She had already confided in Helen about her feelings for Joe, even though she had known him for such a short period of time. Helen was always keen to listen how Joe and Amy's romance was developing because they knew they may have to settle in Australia they had such a forlorn hope that they would ever see their homes or their mothers again.

Amy told Helen Joe had said he could remember his grandmother so well, but he had been in Australia for so long, she might be dead. Amy felt very sad when Joe brought up the subject of his grandmother and her possible death, she knew it was a real possibility that he was right.

"I do try to reassure him, Helen but I'm sure she is a very old lady by now, so it's very difficult for us."

"It must be, Amy," Helen answered, "because our mothers are so much younger I suppose, so we have more hope, but then you never know. It's just so terrible we were all brought here, that we're still here, no way of getting back home and worst of all, knowing nothing about our families." And now, Helen was sounding quite angry. "And do you know something Amy? Nobody really cares how we are, or how we really feel."

Amy just nodded dumbly; she knew Helen was right.

Chapter 62

As Connor Brown was pulling his chair closer to the table Tom and Albert were seated at, Tom decided that he would come straight to the point on what their purpose in coming to Southampton was and why they were anxious to talk to someone who could tell them about the ships that sailed from these docks.

"Can you tell me, Mr Brown, is it true that a considerable number of children were shipped out of Southampton to other countries?"

Without any hesitation, Connor replied, "Of course it's true, it was common knowledge you know, lots of people around here knew all about it." He paused and then emphasised, "It was no secret, at least around here it wasn't and why are you asking me now, it started quite some time ago and it doesn't happen at all now. Why are you interested?" he repeated.

"I am asking, Mr Brown, because some fifteen years ago, I brought children here from children's homes in Northern Ireland for a supposed holiday, but they never returned to the homes and the parents and relatives were told they had been adopted," Tom said. "They certainly do not seem to have been in any youth hostel all these years ago."

"Yes, there were children from Northern Ireland, Scotland, Wales and England children's homes sent abroad," Connor Brown said gently. "I witnessed most of it happening myself. They were sent to different countries. I won't say definitely that is what happened to the children you are looking for, but it is quite likely."

There was silence at the table as all three men thought soberly about what had been said, then Albert spoke, "Can you tell us what country or countries they were sent to, do you know?"

"Yes, the favourite countries seemed to be Australia and Canada and then New Zealand and South Africa as well. It was all done in an orderly manner I have to say. Lists were handed in to the man who seemed to oversee everything by whoever had brought the children to the docks."

On hearing this, Tom was quick to remark that he had given a list over to a man in the car park beside the station. "I regret I never got his name, I knew nothing about him, nothing whatsoever. I just did what my superiors told me to do. Give the children into his care and give him the lists of the names. Who would he have been working for, the shipping company?" Tom asked.

"They were keen on this project, they employed men to collect the children at certain places and they were well paid for their trips, I believe. So yes, the shipping company would have been paying him," Connor answered.

Connor warmed to the subject of the shipping companies. "I believe they never wanted to stop transporting children from here, they were getting so well paid for it all, but it did end." He managed a smile despite the sombre nature of the subject. "I listened well to all of it over the years while I went quietly about my work as an overseer at the desks, berths and dining halls."

"How do you think we might be able to trace these children?" Tom asked hopefully.

"I am sorry, I have no idea. I do know that the lists were given to the purser on the ships, so I am sure they had to be handed over as a means of identification in whatever country the children would end up in," Connor Brown replied. "But," he continued in a serious tone, "I think it would be quite a job to trace any of them now. You are talking here about hundreds of children that is what I witnessed personally over the years. I am sorry to seem so pessimistic, but I think I am simply being realistic."

"We do appreciate your frankness, Mr Brown; we have no choice but to try to pursue this," Albert replied firmly.

"Would you like some more coffee?" Connor offered.

"Thank you, but we must be getting back, and we need to pay for our coffee and scones."

"No, your coffee is on the house as a mark of respect. To the good work you are trying to do."

"Thank you so very much, Mr Brown, both for the coffee and all your help. If we need any more information, is it alright if we can contact you again?"

"Of course it is, I am often here seven days a week," Connor replied.

After saying their goodbyes, the two men left the coffee shop and made their way to the car; they didn't say anything until they were in the car then Albert said, "It is our priority to let Edward and Monica know what we have been told."

Chapter 63

Edward sat quietly in his study, stunned by the news Albert and Tom had given him over the telephone. He felt it was totally incomprehensible to think that small children had been sent from this country to some foreign country and from what Mr Brown had told Albert and Tom, it had been going on for some years. Who were all the children who had been sent? He suspected they couldn't all have been orphans because he believed, although it was the last thing he wanted to know, that Christopher had been one of those children. Why else was he brought to Southampton and why was there no trace of him ever having stayed anywhere? He was beginning to believe that indeed Christopher was one of those children Mr Brown had seen, and perhaps talked to, as he was being shipped abroad. How could he tell Monica all this? He was at a loss as to how he could do so, but tell her he must, he thought wearily, as he rose out of his chair and went to seek her out.

"Please Edward, how can such a thing have happened to Christopher? He was not an orphan and Ms Corken in the home knew I was coming back to collect him." Monica was almost hysterical as she spoke. "How could anyone do such a thing and who was responsible for doing it, Edward? Why, Edward? Why would they do it?" Monica's voice was in turmoil as she struggled to comprehend what Edward was telling her.

"Yes, love, we need to try and find out who was responsible. Above all we need to try to find out what country Christopher has been sent to, and what happened to Joe and the others," Edward said as calmly as he could. "We need to contact Jill and ask her to come over and we will tell her this latest news. How would you feel about ringing Jill?"

"Definitely, I really need to talk to Jill and of course she needs to know what Albert and Mr McGrath have found out." Monica made an effort to steady herself, after all, Jill was present on the morning the children left the Home. "She will, I'm sure, be as stunned and shocked as I am to hear this news." Then

Monica remembered Sara. "We must let Sara know what has been happening, even though Joe would not have been one of the children to be deported."

"Yes, I remember about Sara, but I wanted to give you time to digest what I have told you," Edward replied. "I will go now and fetch her from the annex for you."

"I think I'll ring Jill first, and when she comes around, we will be all together when you go over it again."

"I am really finding it difficult to grasp, Monica. You are saying lots of children, from children's homes have been shipped out of Southampton to foreign countries." Jill's voice sounded breathless and held a note of disbelief. "Who would do such a thing?"

"With your help Jill, that's what I want to try to find out." It was Edward who spoke. "I want to talk to someone in charge at the Christian Committee and I wonder if you could give me a couple of names of staff, Jill, and perhaps you would be present too, to fill in the spaces for me?" Edward looked over at Sara Totten. He was very aware that she was sitting silently in a chair beside Monica, with a deeply distressed look on her face. "I am so sorry to say we have no news of your grandson, Joseph, we are still in the dark as to when or where he died and the little girl too, we were unable to establish anything there."

Sara just nodded dumbly. Like Monica and Jill, she too was unable to comprehend the enormity and the implications of what they had been told. She was very bewildered by it all. Did it mean Christopher had not been adopted, but simply sent abroad to a foreign country? If that was the case, he might be able to be traced, which was what Edward was talking about. It was all very bittersweet for Sara because whatever plans were made it could not include Joe, her darling grandson, because he was dead.

Chapter 64

The next morning, Edward was up very early and after making himself a hot cup of coffee, he went to his office and closed the door firmly, then settled down beside his telephone to make a few critically important phone calls. He could only hope that one of the calls he was about to make might tell him something, anything. He had chosen to prioritise Australia first in his search for some answers for Monica that was on the advice of Tom.

Monica had just washed and dressed Faith, had given her breakfast, and put the kettle on to make herself a coffee when the kitchen door opened, and Agnes' warm calm voice greeted her. "It is such a lovely morning, I thought we could take Faith for a walk, it would pass a bit of time, don't you think?"

"It's a lovely idea, I'll just make coffee for us first and then we can leave," Monica answered as she proceeded to spoon coffee into the cups, which she had set on the table earlier.

Later as Agnes and Monica, with Faith comfortably strapped into her pushchair, began their walk, Monica was deep in thought and preoccupied and could only think of how Edward was progressing with his telephone calls. It was a quieter walk than usual, but it was not an uncomfortable silence between them, as Agnes knew as Monica was thankful for her presence today. Monica was grateful for Agnes' calm approach and unquestionably understood what she was coming through and comforted her so much. On the return from their walk Monica was so disappointed to see Edward's study door still firmly closed, which meant, to her unhappy frame of mind, that he was still trying to make some worthwhile contacts.

"I think we should just keep Faith in her pram in the kitchen," Agnes said; the little girl had fallen asleep on the way back home and Agnes knew if she moved her, she would surely awaken.

Monica did not answer Agnes but instead began to pace up and down the kitchen with her head in her hands and repeating over and over again "Christopher, darling, where are you?" She began to shake.

Gently Agnes led her back over to the seat at the window and said, "I'm going to make tea, Monica, and then we'll talk, but please try to be patient, I'm sure this search is going to take some time." Agnes held her close for a time before going over to switch the kettle on.

"I'm sorry, Agnes, for my hysterical outburst, but to be truthful, the thought of Christopher being illegally adopted was one thing, but to be shipped out of this country just like a piece of wood or material does not bear thinking about." Monica's voice was rising as she continued to talk.

Agnes held her firmly and set a cup of tea on the table in front of her. Gradually, Monica stopped shaking and became silent and still, which to Agnes' ears was almost as moving as her words had been. To Agnes' relief, she began to sip her tea and spoke quietly, "You are right, Agnes, this will take some time and effort and I'll have to have patience and behave reasonably. I intend to, especially for Edward's sake, who is trying so hard to find some evidence."

"Yes indeed," Agnes said firmly. "And now I'm going to make some sandwiches, you must eat something, and I shall bring some to Edward with a cup of tea."

Chapter 65

Edward remained quietly in his study for some time after he had finished his calls, he was finding it very difficult to accept the news he had received. As he sat there on that warm September afternoon, he knew he had to be direct with Monica about the information. When he entered the sitting room, he was surprised and somewhat relieved to find Monica sitting quietly and composed, alone at the window. He went over to her at once and drawing a chair over, sat beside her, and immediately drew her close to him.

"I have news about Christopher, my love, I've spent today talking to both the British and Australian governments. I have to tell you that Christopher, along with other children, was shipped to Australia, and the government has notification of the date of his arrival." Edward pressed her slim body closer to him. "At the moment, this is all I know."

Monica began to make agonising moans while clinging to Edward, but he added hastily, "I've been told by those in high authority that they will be able to find out more very soon. It would seem, my love, the Australians have endless lists of children who were shipped to them over many years." Edward stopped for a moment and considered Monica lying close to him. "Are you up to hearing all this, this evening?"

Edward was relieved that his wife's cries had softened considerably, and she was listening intently to what he was saying. "The people I have spoken with today made no secret of the fact that they had accepted thousands of children from Britain into their country, and simply because of the volume of it all, it will take some time to go through the names." Edward paused. "The fact that I have the date and the year of Christopher's disappearance will be a wonderful help to start, I was assured of that and the last gentleman I spoke with today was optimistic that Christopher would be traced. He stressed the government would be meticulous with keeping records. So please, love, we must keep hoping that somehow, we will trace him."

Somehow, Monica managed to pull herself out of her pit of despair and, on hearing the news about Australia, a land she scarcely knew existed, the name now seemed to be printed indelibly on her mind. She believed it to be thousands and thousands of miles away and even if they did find Christopher, how would anyone manage to go to see him. "Edward, my love, you have had a very trying day, I don't want to add to it and I'm sorry I was so upset but I feel much stronger now." Monica moved closer into the comfort of her husband's arms. "Please tell me all you know."

"Of course, I'll tell you what I've learnt, my dear, and what I have learnt today does not portray either the British or Australian governments in a good light." Edward paused, choosing his words carefully. "The British government began shipping children to many countries, as far back as 1938. Negotiations between Australia and Britain began with a Christian brother who was sent by Australia to the UK to bring back boys. In 1946, a migration scheme was made in Australia, and it was decided they would rely on religious organisations to promote child migration."

Monica was quick to speak as Edward took a breath. "Edward, did you get any sort of explanations as to why it happened?"

"Yes indeed. It seems the Australian government was very unpopulated, and they felt threatened from their neighbours, especially the Asian forces and wanted a predominately white population. As for the UK, after the Second World War, the children's homes were overcrowded with orphans and children of single mothers and that's when the two governments jointly began their scheme," Edward explained.

"So they just took other people's children and did whatever they wished with them?" Monica's voice was raised in anger. "The whole thing is so unbelievable, so criminal."

"I certainly agree but I was very careful with what I said, love, I did not want to jeopardise my investigation in any way. Now Monica, I'm going to ask Agnes to fetch the two girls and some tea and biscuits, and we will have an evening meal a little later, and we need to tell Agnes the latest news."

When they were all together later that evening and heard the new information, Agnes was very encouraging. "I think you must have worked so very hard today to learn so much about what has actually been going on." Agnes sounded in awe of her employer. "To be told so much and so openly, indicates your skill, Edward, in getting information, and I'm sure you will learn a lot more about Christopher and hopefully his friends and their whereabouts."

"Thank you, Agnes, for all your support, and although I only gave Christopher's details, I have not forgotten the other children." Monica smiled lovingly at her husband. Agnes nodded sagely as she rose from her chair. "Could you put Faith to bed please tonight, Agnes, and then join us for the evening meal? Ask Sara if she would like to join us, so we can update her on our progress as well."

Chapter 66

The next morning, Edward and Monica rose at their usual time even though they had talked together for some time when they went to bed. They had talked about the news from yesterday at length and what Edward intended to do to try and trace Christopher. Monica felt incapable of going down that road with her thoughts but instead moved closer and held Edward tightly until she fell asleep. Now, this morning after breakfast, she got Faith ready for nursery school which she took her to three days a week.

Jennie was usually the first to leave as she caught an earlier bus than Monica and Faith did as she travelled to Belfast to university, whereas Faith's nursery was near Lisburn. After leaving Faith with her favourite teacher, Monica made her way back to the bus stop. She had thought she might walk home alone with her thoughts and emotions, but decided she would prefer to catch the bus. Knowing Edward was under the same roof as she was seemed to hearten and inspire her.

Meanwhile, Edward had quite an eventful morning with more interesting phone calls than he had had the day before. Because of what he had just learnt he decided to ring Jill and ask her if it was possible to come to his house around eleven o'clock, he explained he had something of vital importance to tell her and Monica. He thought it best they were together when he told them what he had learnt. Monica was surprised to see Edward at the table with a cup of coffee in his hand. It was obvious to her that he had learnt something more during her absence this morning. He seemed particularly sombre.

"What is it?" Monica almost whispered as she sat down beside him.

Edward immediately turned towards her and in a reassuring voice said, "Everything is certainly alright, but I did ring Jill and ask her to come around. What I have learnt this morning is of interest to both of you." Just as he spoke, the doorbell rang and Agnes stepped into the hall to greet Jill, then led her to the kitchen to join the others.

"Hello, Jill, thank you for coming so promptly." Edward greeted her, then he turned to Agnes. "Perhaps you would kindly bring some tea for the three of us and yourself in about twenty minutes' time."

"Yes Edward, I will do that," said Agnes.

"Let's go into the sitting room and then between us we can think of what to do." Jill was wondering what he was talking about so very mysteriously. When they were seated comfortably, Edward began to speak. "This morning I decided to get the names of all five children of Melton Home who left for a supposed holiday. I also gave Ruth Smart's name to them and her date of disappearance from the Sisters of Newbourne Home."

Edward, lost for words, looked over to Monica and Jill but they waited patiently for him to continue. "One of the staff in charge of Migration for Australia confirmed to me that all the names I had told them did arrive in Perth, Western Australia, all these years ago and they were all well." He took a deep breath. "The boys went to a Children's' home in Swandon and the girls went to a nuns' home called Goodwood."

"That means that Joe Totten and Amy Matthews may be alive and well, living in Australia," Edward said. Both Monica and Jill were shocked and in disbelief with this new information.

Jill spoke, "This must be a mistake. I received letters from Will Baird telling me of the two deaths and their nearest relatives were told the same. I saw the letters myself."

"The government were absolutely adamant that both of the children had arrived in Australia. I believe there have been so many lies about the children and the adoptions that I believe being told Joe and Amy dying and being buried in England is a part of those lies and the easiest way to explain a child's disappearance. This would lead to a finality to not lead to any more questions." Edward who was usually so calm was becoming more and more outraged as he spoke.

"If this is true," he looked at the two women in turn, "it would be the most evil act of all, relatives condemned to a lifetime of grieving." And now his voice sounded very sad, and Monica knew he was thinking of Sara and Amy's mother who was so unaware of any of this.

Chapter 67

"Edward and I really appreciate your decision to go with Albert and Mr McGrath, Jill. It is very kind of you to try to help me once again." Monica smiled gratefully at her friend, then went on, "Are you sure Sam doesn't mind you going? You could be away for some time, Jill."

"Sam has been very encouraging here. And he wants to play an active role here while we are away," Jill answered. "He would like to be the one to go and speak to the parents when the children are found, and then sort out the communication side of things. So, Monica, you must not worry about me going to Australia. Sam and I know it is some distance away, so we both expect that I will be away for some time. But our priority when we do get there, is to try to locate the Children's Home where the boys were supposedly sent to."

"Edward has been advised by a senior member of the Australian government that the children Edward had named had been quite easily traced because, the official stressed, they had always kept very stringent records. The name of the Children's is Swandon, and the official also named a girls' home by the name of Goodwood. So that is probably where the girls from here were sent to." Monica sounded so hopeful, Jill thought, as she gave Jill the details as she knew them.

Edward wasted no time in asking both Albert, his solicitor, and Tom McGrath, if they could see their way to being available to take the journey to Australia. Edward knew Monica had no real desire to go while so much uncertainty and possible disappointment lay over everything. Besides, she could not possibly take Faith on such a long, arduous trip at her age. And she would never, ever leave her in anyone else's care. After much discussion between Edward and herself, as to who they should ask to go with Albert and Tom, Monica suggested Jill. They knew they wanted someone who could be of assistance with the young people they hoped to meet.

Still, Monica had been reluctant to do this, she felt it would be such an arduous journey for her friend. She had, after all, never been out of Northern

Ireland, and it would be in the company of two men she scarcely knew. But on the other hand, Jill was the ideal person to go. She had changed so little over the years that Christopher might even have a vague recollection of her. But most of all, perhaps she might recognise something in the lad who was Joe Totten in Australia, compared to the Joe Totten from Northern Ireland.

Now today, Monica had asked Jill to her home, mostly just for reassurance that Jill was truly happy about going on such a long journey and for such a reason. Also, she did not want her to simply feel obliged to do this. Jill assured Monica quite strongly that it was what she really wanted to do. She had her own memories and thoughts, she said about the whole scam and how she could vividly recall the morning she saw the children off, little realising that they would never be back in Melton Home. Over the years, those memories had always been with her, throughout her life; never mind the horrific news that two of the children had died.

"Do you think, Jill, we are making the right decision in not telling Sara that Joe might still be alive?" Monica asked her.

"I think so, Monica. I think it's better if we say nothing at this stage," Jill replied. "It would be cruel to build up her hopes only to shatter them if we discovered that the registration of Joe's entry into Australia was just another pack of lies told by some untrustworthy Australian official. We have already had that experience here, Monica over adoptions and deaths, so let's just wait until we have verification, one way or the other." Jill's voice sounded quite fierce as she spoke.

"I agree with you, Jill. It's just, sometimes, when I'm with her I feel guilty that I have this knowledge and can't share it with her. Even though she has a right to know about it."

"It is a dilemma for you, I know, Monica, but this search will soon be over, and we will find Christopher well and indeed, hopefully, Joe."

"Again, Edward's good sense prevailed here. He said quite firmly that we needed to bide our time until we knew for certain Joe was alive. Only for him I probably would have forged ahead and told Sara everything," Monica said.

"Sam did as Edward suggested and did eventually manage to trace Amy's mother. He had a bit of difficulty and that is because she is now married. Mrs Faircliff is her married name, and she still lives in Lisburn—in Wallace Avenue—Sam says," Jill told Monica. "So, he will be able to contact her promptly when we learn more. I am confident that I will recognise something, even some small thing, about Joe and Christopher. It would just be so wonderful." Jill's voice held such hope, and even joy, at her own words.

Monica was somewhat taken aback at Jill's optimism, secretly she was not so sure that Jill would know them. After all, they were no longer children, but fully grown adults and must have changed considerably. But perhaps they might remember Jill because she had really changed so little over the years.

"Jill, please, please make sure you keep in touch constantly with Edward and me. You know we will both be on tenterhooks the whole time you are away from us. You see I can't believe this is really happening Jill. That dear friends of mine are travelling to a foreign country to locate my son, and then bring him home to Edward and me. It feels like a dream, Jill, it really does."

"Yes, it is hard to take in, Monica. But it must be true because I have my case packed, my passport ready and the airline ticket from Edward safely stowed in my handbag. This day next week Tom, Albert and I will be in the air. Regarding keeping in touch, that is one sure thing I intend doing. I mean to try my best to be in touch every day, whether I have news or not," Jill reassured her.

Monica nodded her head quickly. "I am filled with wonderful expectations, but I am fearful too."

"That's to be expected. I think we are all rather fearful, but we'll see it through, Monica, and I am optimistic of a happy ending."

"Jill, you are just wonderful and I do hope you have a wonderful flight. Now let's go into the kitchen and have some lunch."

Chapter 68

The morning of Tom, Albert and Jill's flight to Australia—the first leg of which was from Aldergrove Airport to London Heathrow—was on 26th June 1963, exactly fifteen years since Tom had driven the minibus from Lisburn to Belfast docks with fifteen children, who were going on holiday. A holiday which never happened. Instead, those same children were exported to a foreign country—Australia—which was 12,000 miles away. For what reason this happened to the children no one knew, but for those concerned with it all now, they did know it had caused considerable heartache, and questions, as to the reason it had ever happened. Questions which Tom, Albert and Jill hoped to find some answers to when they finally traced the lost children.

Edward had insisted on driving the three of them to the airport himself on the morning of their departure, even though Albert had suggested his son would do it. But Edward felt very strongly that he must see this through. He felt he needed to keep control of everything as much as he possibly could, even though he knew that in Australia, he would have no such control. He would be just dependent on communication from Jill, Tom and Albert. He had specifically asked Albert to be sure he rang him every evening as it would be morning in Northern Ireland. He had specifically asked Albert because he knew he was a stickler for time and always had been. And Albert had duly promised he would indeed ring every evening.

Edward had made sure he booked three seats in the first-class area of the aeroplane. After all, his three friends were giving up precious time with their own families to go on a journey, the likes of which none of them had been on before. Edward felt very strongly that he really should be one of the ones to be going but he could not possibly leave Monica at such a time in her life. He really needed to be with her.

He had also booked a good hotel for the three of them in the centre of Perth in Western Australia for three weeks. Regarding the flight back home he had no

226

booked it yet. Everything was so uncertain. How long it might take to trace any of the children they had no idea. They would no doubt, have moved on from the children's homes by now. They were certainly past the age of being eligible to be in one. And how many of the children would wish to come back home? Some of them would surely have developed close friendships over there and probably had a decent job which they would not want to leave. It was all very uncertain, so for now, Edward had left the flights back home open.

Now, after saying his goodbyes to his friends, wishing them a safe flight and urging them to ring him as soon as possible, he watched as the plane glided along the runway, then lifted and slowly disappeared into the clouds.

Since he had first discovered the extent of the British government's migration of children from their home country, Edward had had many sleepless nights. Then he was shocked when he learnt that Sara's grandson might well be alive and living in Australia. A grandson she had been told had died while on a holiday the British government had sent him on, certainly, they had been told the name and date of birth were identical. But then Sara had received an official letter to say her grandson was dead, a letter she still had to this day.

Edward thought it was all rather suspect and wondered if the Australian government were any more trustworthy than the British government were. How could this boy, who had gone to live in Swandon Home, be the same boy who Sara believed to be dead? Was this just another one of some official's lies just as the alleged adoptions had been? Or had Sara Totten and Amy's mother been told lies all those years ago? And if so, why? Edward had all these unanswered questions running continuously through his head, yet he knew the importance of being patient until hopefully, Jill met this Joe Totten in Australia.

The flight to Australia was not something Tom or Albert or Jill had ever expected to experience in their lifetime. The two men were totally enthralled about everything and peered excitedly out of the windows at the scenery, the clouds and the brightness of everything around them. They listened and remarked on every noise the engines made, and to any comment the pilot made.

However, Jill was quite the opposite, and although she acknowledged she was involved in an experience of her lifetime, she was very uneasy when the plane seemed to drop down a little bit, or if it made some different noise. But the stewardess seemed to be keyed into people's fears, and was always very quick to reassure her, both about the noises and the plane dipping a little. Having been helped so much by the stewardess and then after enjoying a delicious meal, Jill fell fast asleep, she only wakened when the pilot announced they would shortly be landing at an airport named Tehran for refuelling purposes. So, no passengers would disembark here.

Some of Albert's colleagues in his work had told him the flight to Australia would seem quite endless and advised him to take an interesting book with him to pass the time. But Albert thought it would be rude to sit beside Tom and Jill with his nose in a book. So, he decided to bring a deck of cards. The three of them played innocent games of 'sevens' and 'snap', which they surprised themselves by really enjoying. And certainly, it all helped pass the time.

Later, as the sky darkened and the pilot was flying through the night, the stewardess came around with a hot drink and some lovely biscuits. Then, reassuring them they could call on her at any time, she switched off the overhead lights. The three of them slept soundly, only wakening to the noise and bustle of the steward and stewardess bringing breakfast to them. Then they were told by the pilot that they would shortly be landing at an airport by the name of Karachi. Here they could disembark and go into Karachi airport, but they must be back within two hours in order to continue their flight.

To Jill, who had never ventured further from Belfast, Karachi airport shopping area was an exotic cave of treasures, with everything from jewellery to ladies' dresses and underwear, all so stylish, sophisticated and all so very expensive. All away beyond her reach. Tom and Albert too, were amazed at the quality and finish of all the men's wear and the attention that had obviously been paid to the last detail. And then, of course, the prices.

"We'll have a lot to tell our families when we return," Albert remarked as they made their way back to the departure gate. "And we haven't even arrived in Australia yet. But let's hope that merchandise there will be more accessible to us and not outside our price range.

"I know," Tom agreed, "and we can't go back to our families empty-handed after such a trip and our long absence."

Jill was silent, just listening to the two men. All she wanted to bring back from Australia were the children who had been exported so cruelly and so callously to a foreign country.

"We will shortly be arriving at Perth airport. Please ensure your seatbelt is securely fastened, your hand luggage is stowed safely under your seat, and your seat is in the upright position." The voice if the stewardess carried clearly through the cabin, and even as Jill heaved a sigh of relief that the plane was safely out of the clouds, she felt a huge jolt as the plane's wheels touched the ground. She slowly released her tight grip from the arms of the seat, at the same time thinking that flying, as a means of transport, was not for her.

Perhaps if Sam, her darling husband, had been with her she would have felt much more at ease, and felt safer. Not that Tom and Albert had neglected her in any way, on the contrary, they had gone out of their way to try to ensure she was comfortable and less fearful of every noise and bump. But still, they weren't Sam, her dear husband who she missed so much. Now, as the passengers began to move forward to the exit door and the steps down, she simply said a prayer of thanks for their safe arrival in this country so very far from home.

"After we finish our dinner and get organised with all our belongings, I will ring Edward," Albert remarked, as he looked over at the clock in the dining room of the hotel Edward had chosen for his, Tom's and Jill's stay in Australia. The clock on the wall told him the time was seven p.m. in Australia. "It must be around midday with Edward. I believe we are seven hours ahead here. Am I right, Tom?" Albert asked.

"Yes, that's right, Albert. It is midday in Lisburn," Tom replied. "I must change my watch, I'm afraid of getting confused with the time, and I think it's important that we have the right time when we are here. But also, when we do ring Edward that we remember we are seven hours ahead of the time in Northern Ireland."

"I feel really tired, and Monica did tell me that she had read that the time change does make travellers feel weary. So, I'm glad I'll be going to bed shortly. But at the same time, I just want to sit here and enjoy the surroundings. I have enjoyed my dinner so much and am looking forward to going back to such a beautiful bedroom. The hotel is fantastic, isn't it?" Jill remarked to her friends.

"Yes, Edward has been very kind," Albert answered. "He has spared no expense in his search for Christopher. At times, I am just staggered at the lengths he is prepared to go to."

"I think that helps motivate us all to do our best to help him. Don't you think so?" Tom asked.

"There's no doubt about that. And that's why I'm looking forward to going with you early in the morning to hire a car for the duration of our stay here. Most of all, I'm looking forward to finding Swandon Home and Goodwood girls children's home too."

"Just a word of caution, Tom, Albert. The children will all be adults now. And having worked in a children's home for so long, I know that when the children reach the age of sixteen to eighteen years of age, they are encouraged to move on in the world."

"If that's the case, Jill, let's hope the homes have all kept decent records and will tell us where Christopher and the others have gone. And hopefully clear up the mystery of little Joe and Amy," Tom said.

"Let's hope so, Tom, but I'm sitting here chatting and I really want to go and ring my husband. I said I would ring him around midday—his time—and it will soon be one o'clock. An hour later." And Jill rose from her seat and then hesitated. "I want to thank you both, Tom and Albert, for all your kindness to me since we started out on this journey. You have both been very kind."

Both men acknowledged her thanks, stating they would be retiring for bed shortly. Then Tom added that he believed tomorrow would prove to be an interesting beginning to their stay in Australia.

When Jill reached the comfort of her room, she decided to undress before ringing Sam. She thought it was the most marvellous thing that she could ring him from the sanctity of her hotel bedroom. She was experiencing such novel things already, and she had only been away from home for a few days. Sam, she knew, would be delighted to hear that she was ringing him from the privacy and comfort of her bedroom. And of course, she would have to tell him about the flight, about her fear during it, and that flying just wasn't for her.

"Oh, Sam, I miss you so much." Immediately, on hearing her husband's calm voice, Jill burst into tears. And through her tears she managed to stutter, "I just wish you could have been on that endless flight with me, I really do. Flying is just not for me."

"Well, Jill darling, if it's any consolation, I miss you terribly too. As do Ryan and Andrew. And the main thing is, love, you have arrived in Australia safely."

"Do the boys miss me? Well, that's lovely." And at the mention of her two stepsons, Jill brightened up. "Have you had time, or have you had any success in finding out anything about Amy Martin's mother and David Gillespie's father?' Jill asked Sam. "And then, of course, we need to know about Helen Marks parents as well. It's quite a lot to ask of you, love, to try and trace them. Amy's mother is going to be the most difficult to deal with, if the Amy Martin in Goodwood Girls' Home is the same Amy Martin who left Melton Home fifteen years ago. And whose mother I had to try to console when she got the letter saying the little girl had died while on holiday."

"I managed to find the addresses of David Gillespie's and Helen Marks' relatives. Easily enough. Amy's mother's whereabouts were more difficult, simply because she got married and her name now is Mrs Faircliff. But thankfully, I did discover she is still living locally. I have not made any moves to contact any of them until I hear from you, and how your search is going at your end of things."

"You have been busy, Sam, since I left home five days ago," Jill said, with enthusiasm. "Tom and Albert will be delighted to hear you have had so much success in such a short period of time. Now, I intend to ring you every evening after we have had dinner. Albert has arranged with Edward that he will ring him each evening too. So, just remember, love, to be around your telephone around midday every day."

After a few more acknowledgements of their love and numerous, repeated assurances to keep in touch, Jill replaced the receiver. Then she crawled into bed, sleep finally overcoming her.

Chapter 69

The next morning, after a good night's sleep and a lovely breakfast, Jill, Tom and Albert set off for Swandon Home, at nine-thirty a.m. in the hired car Albert had organised to be ready and waiting for them at the hotel. They had been advised by the car salesman, after they told him they were trying to find Swandon, to find the highway which headed north.

"Just follow the Great Northern Highway through Chittering Valley," he directed them, then added, "The journey to Swandon is around an hour and a half, and when the sun comes out fully, it will become very hot. So do make sure you have plenty of water with you. You will really need it. It can become very hot indeed here."

Tom had been nominated by the other two to do the driving and later, he especially, was very grateful for the salesman's advice. He did remember also that he had told them parts of the highway were arid and burnt deep copper with the heat of the sun. And Tom marvelled that any country could have such a high level of heat to do such damage.

Jill and Albert too, were very surprised, as Tom drove along, as they left the suburban area of Perth and began to enter a more desolate, isolated highway. "The whole of the roadside looks so scorched," Jill remarked. "The place must have an enormous amount of sunshine to do all this." She looked out at the blackened roadsides. "It's a pity they can't spare some for the climate we have in Northern Ireland. We certainly get more than our share of rain."

"The salesman back at the hotel told us that once we drove into the more scorched part of the highway to look out for very large, stone pillars with equally massive, ornate, iron gates." Even as Albert spoke, he saw a huge, rather ostentatious entrance and immediately directed Tom to turn in. The gates the salesman had described so well were closed, but Tom quickly got out of the car and opened them.

They drove a short distance and noticed another set of gates just ahead of them which again Tom deftly got out and opened.

"This appears to be all farmland," Tom said, as he gazed in awe at the expanse of land and pasture which lay ahead of them and all around them as they travelled along. "I wonder who owns it all."

"It certainly seems to stretch so endlessly, doesn't it?" Albert too was taken aback by what he was seeing.

Then all three were silent as Jill pointed wordlessly to a monument, a huge monument of Jesus which stood looking over the land. Then it was Albert who asked Tom to slow down as he, in turn, indicated large stone monuments, and there was no doubt, Albert told Jill and Tom, they were the Stations of the Cross, marking Jesus' walk to his crucifixion.

Jill felt totally taken aback by what Albert had just told Tom and her, and by the look on Tom's face, he too, was in the dark about what his colleague was talking about. She suddenly felt ashamed of her ignorance—a total lack of knowledge—regarding beliefs that other people held which were different from her own. She decided, there and then, that she wanted to hear more about these monuments they had come upon. "Can you tell us anything about these, Albert?" Jill asked him.

"Not much, to be honest, Jill. They are regarded as sacred stones by the Roman Catholic Church and each one represents each stop Christ took on his way to his crucifixion," Albert replied. "You do tend to find them in large religious sites such as this one. Because, no doubt, they do take up considerable room."

"I think it is a very touching gesture," Jill said. "And I'm so glad to learn about them today. I shall be telling Sam about them, although he may well have heard of them."

"I, for one, am humbled when I hear you say what they represent, It makes me feel closer to God, whether it is because of the statue and the monuments or just the sheer vastness of the whole place, I don't know. It does make me realise there is a God." Tom proceeded over to the monuments and touched them one by one. And at the same time, his eyes always swung around to the vastness of the earth stretching before them.

In silence and in awe of what they had seen, they drove on over the rough track still cutting through the fields. Then just as they seemed to leave the rough, scorched areas behind them, Albert exclaimed, "My goodness, well, if this is

Swandon Children's Home, it bears little resemblance to any children's homes I've seen." Then he went on, in an apologetic tone of voice, "Sorry about my outburst there, but I've never seen such an impressive building."

Jill strained her head from the back of the car to see what Albert was talking about, and was amazed to see the most magnificent, red brick building come into view as Albert drove onto a smooth, clean courtyard. The place was so beautiful with its ornate windows, numerous porches and balconies and its stunning bell tower—it all looked so unique that it took Jill's breath away. She was so mesmerised by it all, it was such a contrast to the rough, scorched terrain they had travelled for the last few miles, that this was just a mirage to her. As for Tom, he just kept shaking his head in disbelief and then said to Albert, "Let's get parked up and see if the inside of the place is as impressive as the outside."

Tom duly parked the car in one of the available parks at the front of the building and made their way to the grand imposing doors approached by a flight of steps, all decorated with ornate, multi-coloured tiles. Tom rang the bell, and the door was opened almost immediately by a tall, heavy man dressed in shorts and a short—sleeved shirt. A clerical collar was around his neck.

"We would like to speak to the person in charge here, if we may?" Albert asked the man, who appeared to be standing rather threateningly in front of them.

"Step inside please," was the gruff response. "What is your mission here?"

It was Albert who answered in a firm, pleasant voice, "We are trying to trace three boys who were sent here, to this home, about fifteen years ago." Albert paused for a moment and then added, "We were told they had been sent here, to this Home, and we would like confirmation of that. Also, where they might have gone when they left here."

"Follow me." Again, that abrupt, gruff response, as the priest made his way down a long, elaborately decorated hallway which opened out into a beautiful room. This room was bright and airy, and its walls were lined with books, with big and small volumes packed neatly into the shelves. Beautiful mahogany desks with matching chairs were placed around the room. This room was certainly Swandon's library.

The priest walked over to one of the desks close to the entrance door and lifted a rather heavy, dilapidated book from the side of the desk, looked at Albert and still in the same unwelcoming voice said, "What were their names please?"

Albert immediately produced the list of the three children's names and dates of birth from his wallet and showed them to the man standing in front of him

Tom and Jill, meanwhile, watched on in silence, hopeful that this register the priest was now looking through, would tell them where Christopher, David and Helen were. And even by some wonderful stroke of luck, tell them whether Joe and Amy were alive or dead.

"Yes. The names are here alright, but we have no record of where they went to when they left here."

Lost for words, Jill, Albert and Tom just looked at one another. Then Jill spoke, "You mean to say you have no record of where these boys went to?" Jill's voice held contempt.

"They probably went to some farmers to work or something like that," he said in a most dismissive way as he closed the register he had been looking at, with a finality that was not lost on the three friends.

Slowly, they made their way out of the library and were approaching the steps when a priest Jill had noticed sitting over from them in the library came running towards them, saying, "I can help you. I promised Christopher that if anyone ever came looking for him to let them know where he and his friends had gone. I know where they've gone."

Chapter 70

"I'm at a bit of a loose end this evening, Christopher, and I was wondering if you would like to take a drive to see David and Brian. Amy has been given extra hours in her teaching role, so she is busy tonight," Joe remarked to Christopher as they headed back to their room. They had just had a lovely meal of lamb stew followed by sponge cake, all made by Mrs Moore, which they had appreciated very much. And they had told her so, before leaving the table and saying their goodbyes.

"I was meaning to go some evening this week anyway, Joe. So, certainly we'll go tonight. I'm always glad of the company in the car, you know," was Christopher's quick response. "It's a good hour's drive to Brian and David's place, so it can be a bit of a lonely journey. We'll start out shortly and I'll drive most of the way. After all, you've been stuck behind the wheel of a tractor most of the day."

"That's true, but I enjoyed every minute of it, as I always do."

"I know that alright, Joe, you jump at the chance every time," Christopher said jokingly.

Soon they were on their way to meet up with their friends who, they acknowledged, they did not see enough of. But it was the distance that was always rather daunting and the rough terrain they must drive through. During this drive however, Joe did a lot of talking—mostly about Amy and their strong relationship, but still Christopher managed to concentrate on his driving, and the time passed quite quickly.

"You seem really proud of how well Amy is doing at the college and her aspirations to become an English teacher," Christopher said, after Joe had gone to great lengths to tell him all about Amy's progress at the teacher training college and her work in the technical college as well. "It is lovely to see you so proud of her. Some lads might resent their girlfriend's success, I believe. It's good to see you so humble."

"Of course I'm proud of her, Christopher, and I help her all I can, you know."

"And," Christopher went on, "you and I will soon have interviews over and we'll know soon after if we have been successful. So, let's hope we'll do equally well, you with your choice of graphic design and me with my book-keeping and commerce."

"Well, we'll have to do our best at interview. Because it's all we can look forward to. We don't have much hope of getting out of this country, and going home, anytime soon. We might as well try to forge some sort of career." Joe was doing his best to be optimistic.

"If we are successful in getting these jobs, Joe, we'll be leaving the Moore's farmstead, a place that has been home to us for more than three years and leaving a couple who have done their best to be adoptive parents to us." Christopher's voice sounded quite sombre as he talked.

"I know," was Joe's quiet response.

After that the two young men drove on in silence until they reached the farm where David and Brian lived and worked.

David and Brian were always interested to hear how Christopher and Joe's education sessions in the technical college were going and they were delighted to hear of their success in their exams and that they had upcoming job interviews. But David and Brian were keen to stress that neither of them were interested in doing any more education sessions in night school. They were both very content with the work they were doing, and they felt they had learnt some basic information during their nights in the college. All four young men spoke often of the kindness and generosity of Mr Ward for taking them on such a journey every week to help them learn. They spoke highly of Roy too, who had been the one to suggest they might wish to accompany him on his evenings to night school.

"Christopher, we both love the work we are doing here. Ploughing the fields, sowing seeds, keeping all the animals safe and happy mean so much to me. And I know I speak for Brian too, here." David looked at his friend, who nodded emphatically.

"Probably the role we would both aspire to being, would be good farm managers. But," David added wistfully, "Our ideal would be doing what we do here, only doing it back home."

"That's all Christopher and I want too, and we still continue to save what we can. But it's a drop in the ocean towards it all," Joe replied.

"Look, before we get too melancholy, let's play a good game of cards. Mrs Ward lent us a deck this evening and showed us a couple of games over the weekend, and they are very enjoyable."

For the next hour, the four young men had an enjoyable time with each other before Christopher and Joe had to begin their hour drive back to the Moore's farmstead. They played several card games and chatted generally about a few things, but it seemed an unspoken agreement between them not to speak of their memories of their horrific times in Swandon, it seemed much better to let them remain buried.

Meanwhile, Amy was devoting her time to teaching English Language and English Literature to the students, who were attending evening classes in the college. She loved teaching these subjects and really appreciated the opportunity Mr Reid, the headmaster, had offered her. And then, of course, he had also given her the once in a lifetime chance of becoming a fully qualified teacher, by getting her enrolled in the teacher training college. Her position with Mrs Logan was one that Amy knew she must address very soon.

At present she was looking after her at the weekend so that she might attend the training college during the week. She knew that in order to pass all her examinations she would need to do a lot of studying and was going to need the weekends to do it. She knew she would have to give up her present employment and of course that meant giving up the room she was currently renting from Mrs Logan's daughter. It also of course meant she would no longer have close contact with her dear companion, and she would be so sad about that. But she did need a career, it didn't matter if it was in Australia or, by some wonderful miracle, in Northern Ireland. This opportunity Mr Reid had given her, was much too good to miss.

She was very thankful he had also given her the extra hours because she would need the money to pay for rent, as with Mrs Reid her rent for the room had been included in her salary for looking after Mrs Logan. She didn't know what she would have done without Joe's constant support and advice. Although he agreed with her that they both wanted to go home, he felt they needed to take every opportunity that arose here in Australia.

Amy had arranged to meet Helen Marks after college, for a cup of tea in their favourite café. This evening Helen insisted on paying for their tea and buns as treat for her friend. She kept saying throughout the evening how very please she was at Amy's success and showed not one hint of envy or resentment at he friend's achievement. She was adamant however, when Amy tried to encourage her to go to night college, that she was not remotely interested in furthering any learning.

She was very happy looking after her elderly companion and it gave her more scope to spend time with her boyfriend. He was, she told Amy, her support here in Australia, and she felt that when the right time came, she would probably marry him. She believed being married would giving her some sense of belonging, a feeling she had never felt here, in this country. This place was certainly not her home, but she felt just as Amy and Joe did, that their hopes of ever getting back there was just a distant dream. No one was ever going to come for them now, they had just been forgotten about, and that was that.

It didn't matter how much Christopher said he prayed. It didn't matter how much any one of them still cried at night for someone to come, it was never going to happen, and they all had to get on with living here and live with their faint, blurred memories, and with their unhappiness and loss.

Chapter 71

"We were very fortunate just now," Tom said, and his voice held a note, almost of wonder, as he spoke. "After the rather rude reception and uncivil manner of that first big priest, I thought we were going to walk away from here with no idea where the boys were."

"I know, so did I." Albert sounded as surprised as Tom did. "That younger priest must have overheard what we were saying to his superior and the dismissive way he answered us. I think it has to be good news. Doesn't it, Jill?" Albert turned toward Jill and added companionably, "Don't you agree?"

"It's just wonderful, I think. And even though the priest didn't know which of the boys went to which farm, at least we know there are three farms involved in our search and it gives us something to work on." Jill smiled happily, thinking of the initial rude welcome they had received and how despondency had crept into her mind so quickly. Only to be lifted by that younger priest who smiled so happily and said words they were desperate to hear. Jill knew she would never forget those few moments when he walked towards them with a smile and a few words which meant so much. Jill went on, "He said there were six who left the Home together and although he did not have all their names, he did have Christopher's."

"Yes, it's all good news," Tom said. "It's just wonderful that Christopher told the young priest that if anyone came looking for him to let them know where they were." Tom paused and then in an angry voice, went on, "It's hard to believe that big man had no intention of helping us, for whatever reason." And Tom shook his head, at a loss for words. "My worry would be what sort of a Home it must be when someone in authority behaves in such a way."

As they headed back to the car to make their plans for the next day, Jill and Albert pondered on Tom's last words and they were thinking about the impressive building they had just left. How could such a Home have, as its very first reception, such a person as the discourteous priest they had encountered?

And even though the younger priest had been so helpful, all three of them were left with a feeling of real unease.

That evening they went to bed early having decided to have an early breakfast and head off to continue their search. They wanted to have most of the driving done before the Australian sun rose in the sky and started to bear relentlessly down on them. They would like to be at their destination before that happened. But unlike The Northern Ireland sunshine, which remained behind clouds for most of the day, they had quickly discovered that that was never going to happen here, in this country.

"It's such a pity we're having to retrace our steps this morning, and drive right past Swandon, but it wouldn't have been a good idea to go on and try to find anywhere yesterday evening. Not knowing our way about and that it starts to get dark quite early here, I think we did the right thing in heading back to the hotel and starting out afresh this morning," Albert remarked as they drove along, he did feel responsible for the decision to abandon their search yesterday.

"Definitely. It was the right thing," Jill answered him, and Tom nodded his head vigorously.

Satisfied, Albert continued his journey along the same route they had taken yesterday. Tom, as navigator was given the job, once they had passed Swandon, to look out for pleasing looking houses and farmsteads which might fit the descriptions the young priest had given them. They seemed to come on the ornate entrance to Swandon much sooner than they had yesterday, but when Jill looked at her watch they had been on the road for an hour and a half. All three companions were quiet for a time, after they passed the Home, and then Jill spoke, "I'm sorry to say that the older priest left more of a memory of our visit to Swandon than the younger one has. He was just so rude and quite horrible. And I believe the young priest did not want to be seen talking to us at all, never mind giving us all the information we now have."

"I agree, Jill," Tom said sombrely.

"I probably feel it more than either of you," Albert said. "He is a man representing the church I attend, the religion I worship, and I am totally ashamed of such a witness as he is." Albert's voice shook. "We should be trying to concentrate on the kindness of the younger man, and why are we not?"

"Because" Tom intervened very quickly, "the first priest gave such an impression of power and force, that he made us feel afraid. I know I felt somewhat fearful of him."

"Me too," Jill said. "He made me feel really nervous for some unknown reason."

"Yes, I know fear is quite a dominant feeling and we certainly experienced it yesterday," Albert said solemnly, "but surely there should be no room for it in any religion and most of all, in a children's home. I just wonder now, after meeting him, how the children were treated here."

"Indeed, it does not bear thinking about, Albert," Tom replied compassionately, and anxious now to take his friend's mind off the events of yesterday and Albert's sense of shame, he went on, "Do you know what I think. I think when we find the farms and the boys, we will only remember the young priest and how he guided us to them."

Albert brightened considerably at Tom's words and drove happily along the North Road, waiting to hear some shout from Tom or Jill. He seemed to drive for some considerable time, when Tom said, in a self-assured tone of voice, "This might be the place we are looking for. I think you should turn in here."

Chapter 72

"I see some visitors have arrived for Mr and Mrs Moore," Christopher said to Joe as he stood still, trying to shake some of the straw and the thick dust from him, which he inevitably gathered on his clothes when he was cleaning out the animal pens. "I always think its lovely how visitors can arrive here unannounced, at any time, and be made so very welcome here." Then Christopher went on, as he regarded the scene just a little way away from Joe and him. "There you are, Joe. They have just gone in and I'm sure they will be offered lunch by Mrs Moore."

"I am sure they will be," Joe replied, "the visitors will enjoy it because I certainly did today, but then I love Mrs Moore's boiled ham and fried potatoes. She is so hospitable, but then we have no other experience to measure it by except, of course, Swandon Home. And for sure, I believe it was only the 'bigwigs' who were ever entertained in it."

"Mrs Moore has come back out of the house, and now, so has Mr Moore and they are coming this way. The visitors are coming too, Joe, maybe they are wanting to ask us a few questions about some of the animals. There's two men and they have a woman with them." As they drew nearer, Christopher's interest in the people coming towards them increased. "They are middle-aged people, just about Mr and Mrs Moore's own age, I think. I hope it has nothing to do with Swandon and our time in it, Joe." Christopher was becoming concerned as they approached Joe and him.

Then Mr Moore called out to him, "Christopher, Joe, would you like to come down and come into the house, these two gentlemen and lady would like to speak to you both and they think that here, in this field, might not be appropriate."

"Yes, of course, Mr Moore," Christopher said in a most obedient voice, believing now that Joe and he must have done something wrong somewhere. Yet there was no hint of that in Mr Moore's manner towards them. In fact, he seemed to Christopher to have an almost suppressed air of expectancy about him, as if he was waiting, quite impatiently to hear what these visitors had to say.

But as they walked towards the house, Mr Moore did say, "It is not bad news I can assure you, so don't look so worried." Christopher was somewhat baffled by his employer's words as they indicated he knew all about the reason for the visit, but his whole attitude suggested he was waiting, almost with bated breath, to hear why these callers were here.

Mr Moore was very reluctant to say anything more to Christopher and Joe, and that what they were going to hear from his visitors was about to change their lives. It was up to the three people in his home to tell such wonderful news. On entering the Moore's living room, Mrs Moore showed the newcomers to comfortable seats by the window, then, with a smile, said to Christopher and Joe, and indicating two other chairs, she said, "Take those two seats over towards your visitors, Christopher and Joe. Mr Moore and I will go into the kitchen to make some tea for us all, while this lady and two gentlemen tell you why they are here." She smiled happily at them but continued to linger, curious no doubt, Christopher thought, to hear what these strangers had to say.

As Christopher and Joe did as Mrs Moore asked, Christopher noticed that the men seemed to be studying them intently. And he wondered again what wrongdoing Joe and he were going to be accused of doing. Neither Joe or Christopher had time to sit down before one of the men, a tall, grey-haired man with a kind smile came over and spoke directly to Christopher, "Would you mind telling me your name, please?"

"My name is Christopher Scott," Christopher answered, at the same time wondering about the man's accent. It certainly wasn't Australian.

"And you, young man, would you mind telling me yours?"

"Sir, my name is Joe Joe Totten," he replied firmly.

Since Jill, Tom and Albert had first arrived on Australian soil they had rehearsed many times how they might react to hearing those two words 'Joe Totten' being spoken back to them. But nothing could have prepared them for the overwhelming feeling of disbelief and joy at seeing the young man standing before them. Their happiness at tracing Christopher after so many years was so wonderful but could never compare to the realisation that Joe Totten was, after all, not dead. But was very much alive and looked so well and happy.

But Tom and his companions knew how important it was to contain their range of emotions and, at this moment, not to divulge anything untoward. For the young man standing before them, to be told he was on record as being dead and to have been treated with such insignificance and indeed callousness, would take some getting used to. Certainly today, with the news they were about to hear, was certainly not the day to be told anything so distressful.

Jill stood quietly beside her two companions as the young men spoke their names. And as Joe Totten spoke, Jill wondered as she listened, how anyone or any organisation could have deprived any relative or family of this young man's company or love. As she watched him, looking for some sign of the sensitive, loving little boy she had unwittingly sent away from Melton Home to a foreign country some 12,000 miles away, he turned and gave her a somewhat hesitant smile. And Jill knew immediately, and against all the odds, that she was looking at Sara Totten's grandson who everyone had believed to be dead.

"Do sit down," the same gentleman said, as Christopher and Joe stood waiting. And even as he began to speak, Christopher remembered him so clearly now, his kindness to them on the long train journey, then later his reassurances when they were left with some other man in a car park. Suddenly, he began to cry as he listened to the sound of a voice, he thought he had long forgotten, now telling Joe and him that he and his companions were there to bring them home, if that's what they wanted.

It was Joe who turned to his friend and said soothingly, "There now, Christopher. Isn't it the most wonderful news?" Joe's voice shook as he spoke. And then he too, was sobbing and crying while Christopher and he held each other in disbelief.

Tom, Albert and Jill watched the two young men and their happiness and felt honoured that Edward Wallace had given them the privilege of witnessing such naked joy.

Then Joe turned to Jill. "Would it be alright if I hugged you?" he asked her, through his tears.

"Of course, I would love that. I'll come over and hug you both and give you a hug from everyone from Lisburn," Jill said, as she made her way over to them.

The name 'Lisburn' seemed to upset Christopher even more and he began to cry again. Then, between his tears, he said hesitantly, "I want to know about my mum, is she, is she alright?"

"She is very well, Christopher, and has been looking for you all these years. And Jill, turning to Joe, added quickly, "Your grandmother is well too, Joe. I see them both very often."

"I think I remember you," Christopher said excitedly. "You were good to us all in the home. Your name is Miss... Miss... Oh, I can't remember your name." He sounded so disappointed.

"I was Miss Corken then, Christopher. But you haven't seen me for fifteen years, so I'm not surprised you don't remember me."

"I was really scared to ask you about my grandma." Joe smiled broadly at Jill, then turning to Christopher, he reached over and gave him an immense hug and said, "Thank you, Christopher, for looking out for me all these years and helping me believe everything would be alright."

Mrs Moore, who had been watching and listening to all that had been going on, was so overcome that on the pretext of making tea, left the room before she would break down.

"When will we be able to go home?" Christopher asked one of the men sitting quietly beside them. "And what about our other friends from the Home who were brought here, will they be able to go back home too?"

"Are you in close contact with some of them?" Tom asked. "By the way, my name is Tom McGrath, and this is Albert Dunn. But just call us by our first names, it is much easier." Tom smiled warmly at them.

"Thank you, Sir...I mean, Tom, we are in close contact with three or four of them, David, Amy and Helen. And then Brian, but we don't see much of him."

"Do you have their full names?"

"Yes, Helen Marks, Amy Martin and David Gillespie," Joe replied. "But I don't know Brian's other name, but actually he was already in Swandon when we arrived there. Isn't that right, Christopher?"

"Yes, Brian was sent here almost two years before we were. He works with David Gillespie on another farm about an hour's drive from here. Amy and Helen work looking after elderly ladies in Perth, and they live in their relatives' homes. It will be so wonderful for them when they meet you and realise that you have come to take us all home." Christopher's voice shook, his eyes filled with tears and he put his arms around his waist and held himself firmly until he recovered.

"Amy has just started teaching in the technical college in Perth and has enrolled in the training college, so she has to leave her employment with the elderly lady and look for other accommodation. But just think, she does not need to worry about any of that now." Joe intervened in the conversation, anxious to let these caring people know that despite all their hardships over the years, the were still unbent by their experiences, but he was also wanting to sing Amy's praises, as he always did.

"Do you mean to meet up with the others quite soon, sir?" Now Christopher just wanted his friends to be told such good news as soon as possible. News that they were finally going.

Chapter 73

"What do we do next?" Jill asked her two companions as they drove back to their hotel. During the drive, they had discussed, with considerable wonder, their discovery of Joe and Christopher. And then the stark reality that Joe Totten had not died from a fever 'somewhere in England' but had been shipped to Australia with other children some fifteen years ago. After they had confirmation of the other children's names on Edward's list, they had to grasp the fact that Amy Martin, at merely four years old, had also been shipped from Melton Home in Lisburn, Northern Ireland, to here, twelve thousand miles away.

But to add to the horror of such injustice and cruelty, Amy's mother had been told all those years ago that her little daughter was dead. But Tom, Albert and Jill now knew with certainty that Amy was alive and well here, with the other children, in Australia. Later, as they talked at length on their car journey, they agreed that the whole day had been an incredible, unbelievable occasion. And now, after all the uncertainty and fear they had come through, they were experiencing a time of complete, profound happiness.

"Well, our next job of course, is to ring Edward and tell him all about our successful search," Albert said, rubbing his hands in delight as he spoke. "Won't the man be so delighted, and after all his hard work, never mind the expense of us being here, but sure it's just great it has ended the way it has. He'll want to set up a phone call between Christopher and his mum as soon as possible. Then, of course, someone must tell Sara that her grandson is still alive, and Amy's mother the truth too."

Albert paused for a moment then went on, "It's going to be a very difficult task for someone to do. To be told the truth now, after years of grieving for someone you believed to be dead, that their child is alive, will be a very bewildering time for them. It will require great sensitivity on the part of the teller."

"I think so," Jill agreed, "but I have every confidence in Monica and her approach in telling Sara. And," Jill added, "I mean to ring Sam after dinner tonight and ask him to write to the address he has for Amy's mother. You do know, Tom and Albert, that Edward was given the names of the children who had arrived in Australia. Amy and Joe's names were among them. I got Sam to try to trace Amy's mother and he discovered she is married and has family. He was able to find her address, so, I'll ask him to write and let her know he has important information for her." Jill was aware she needed to reassure her colleagues of Sam's awareness of the delicate situation he would be dealing with.

"It's good we have some forward plans for the five children." Tom had been listening quietly to all Jill was saying. "But I think we must also bear in mind the fact that some of them may not want to come back home if they have managed to establish themselves in good jobs here. I think we need to consider that as a possibility, remote as we might think it is."

"I suppose so," Jill replied reluctantly. She did not want anything at this moment to mar their happiness at today's achievement.

Meanwhile, Albert was thinking about Ruth Smart and how much he appreciated Edward at being able to trace the little girl to a children's home just outside Perth. Goodwood Children's Home for Girls was the name of her home and he intended to make contact there as soon as possible. And they had had such success today so surely it would continue for them.

Christopher and Joe returned to their work in a state of euphoria and with assurances from the kind man who had come to find them only about an hour ago, that he would let Christopher's mother and Joe's grandma know of their discovery. Tom, the man Christopher now remembered well, simply because of his kindness to Joe and him on that long train journey all those years ago, had wanted them to come back to the hotel with them for dinner. From there they could ring Christopher's mother around eight o'clock as it would only be around midday in Northern Ireland.

But Christopher and Joe, ever mindful of the Moore's kindness to them over the last few years, and the fact that they had noticed recently that their employers were having difficulty with some chores around the farm, insisted they would drive over the next day, have dinner with them and then make the oh so wonderful phone calls.

Despite all the excitement at the news they had received, the chores were finished in good time just as they always were. And soon they were sitting down to dinner with Mr and Mrs Moore as usual. But the time with them was rather subdued after all the initial elation of the day. Now Christopher and Joe were preparing themselves for going back home to Northern Ireland, yet they were so sorry to be leaving Mr and Mrs Moore who had been so very kind to them during their employment. They were also very aware that, although their employers would both be very happy to see Christopher and Joe united with their families, they would of course, be wondering how on earth they were going to manage the farm. Christopher sought to reassure them.

"We will be here for two or three weeks yet, Mr Moore. Tom, Albert and Jill have still to go to David, Brian, Amy and Helen and let them know someone is here to take them home. Also, Mrs Foster says they need to find out where their relatives are living and let them know their children have been traced." Christopher nodded reassuringly. "So, yes, it will take time for everything to be completed, so we'll be working for you for two or three weeks yet."

"Of course, you will, and I'm really glad to hear it." Mr Moore smiled gratefully.

"I also know that there must be lots of boys in Swandon Home, who would just love to work here," Joe said encouragingly.

"Yes, I did wonder about that, and I intend to apply but I will go in person, even though I understand it is quite a drive, but you will come with me. Won't you, dear?" Mr Moore turned to his wife.

"Certainly, we usually go most places together, and I'm very interested in this particular place, we know so little about it," Mrs Moore replied.

Later Christopher and Joe made their way down to their bedroom to prepare to retire for the night. Here Christopher made his way over to his bed and sat down and Joe joined him. Without any words being spoken and away from their responsibilities involved in an everyday living and having had to control their true emotions during the last few hours, they simply began to hug one another tightly and laughed and cried by turns, for some time, over the news they had received.

The next day, they worked extremely hard on the Moore farmstead. It was a beautiful day, and the pigs, sheep and cattle seemed to be even more cooperative than usual, when they were being moved around in order to clean their pens. And the two Collie dogs, who Joe and he had become so attached to over time were it seemed to Christopher, even more loving than usual. And Christopher felt a pang of regret that he was leaving this beautiful sun kissed place, the beautiful animals, the peace and quietness of the place. But most of all, leaving Mr and

Mrs Moore, who had treated them as if they were their own sons. Over their morning coffee break, he confided in Joe how he felt.

"But that's exactly how I'm feeling this morning," Joe confirmed his own feeling to Christopher. "And although most of the years we've been here have been ghastly and horrible, somehow these last three years have help wipe out the horror of Swandon. And I'm sure we won't remember much about Northern Ireland. It will all be very strange to us, as I'm sure people will find us to be strangers to them. After all, we were only children then, Christopher, and look at us now." And Joe stood up and spread his arms wide.

"Do you know, Joe, I never thought much about how we might have changed. I only ever thought of seeing my mother," Christopher answered. "That's all has been in my mind."

"I just know that Northern Ireland is where my grandmother is, and it's where I want to be. With Amy too, of course. She and I have talked so often about how wonderful it would be to go back but sure we thought it highly unlikely. So, I hope Mr McGrath and his friends soon let her know that she can come home." Joe's voice shook with emotion as he spoke.

"What about Helen Marks, she'll probably be told when Amy is. She seems quite settled here with her boyfriend. Although I imagine we all, without exception, will want to go home."

By five o'clock, even though it was a bit early, all the animals were snugly in their pens and all their tools and equipment were safely put away. Only then did Christopher and Joe feel confident to get ready to go to meet their newfound friends in a beautiful hotel in the centre of Perth, somewhere the young two men had never set foot in in their lives.

Afterwards, if anyone had asked Christopher or Joe how they had enjoyed their very first dinner in such a posh hotel, they would have difficulty in answering them. They did remember that they cleared their plates, but otherwise the time passed in a bit of a haze for them both. They could only think of the phone call Albert Dunn would shortly be making on their behalf to Northern Ireland.

Then, just before eight p.m., as they were all about to make their way to Albert Dunn's room, Jill put an arm around Joe's shoulders and said, "Before you ring your grandma, I need to tell you something quite important. I also want to stress it is not about your grandma, she is very well indeed. It is something that was said about you. Let's sit here." And Jill indicated a seat in the foyer before saying in a steady voice, "There is only one way to say this, Joe," and she looked directly at the young man. "You need to know that your grandma was told when you left Northern Ireland fifteen years ago—she was told by letter that you were dead."

For a moment or two, a great silence lay between them and then Joe said in a compelling voice, "But I am alive, Miss Corken. I am alive. Does my gran know this? Does she?"

"Yes, Joe, she knows. She was told earlier by Tom that it was a big mistake. That you are alive and well and just wanted to come home. Isn't that true?"

"Yes, it's very true and now I just want to hear her voice and convince her I am very much alive and want and need to see her again."

Jill studied the young man before her and marvelled at his remarkable calmness and his capacity for forgiveness. Forgiveness, no doubt, that was determined by his happiness that he now knew his grandmother was still alive, coupled with his compelling urge to go back home.

In Tom's hotel room, Christopher took the telephone from Albert's outstretched hand and in a shaky voice said, "Hallo, hallo. Mum."

Monica, listening at the other end of the line for the sound of her young son's voice, was stunned when it was the voice of a young man who spoke to her. She could scarcely speak then, only managing to say in a voice heavy with emotion, "My son, my son." Before becoming totally overcome with crying. Crying tears of joy for the wonder of these moments she had waited so long for, and tears of utter sadness for all the lost years of his absence from her.

Christopher, on hearing his mother's voice, a voice he remembered so well and which he had longed to hear to comfort him during some of the most awful of times in Swandon broke down completely. It was Edward, his stepfather who then said, in a calm, comforting voice, "We shall ring back later."

The second phone call was more successful for both mother and son. This time, the knowledge that they would soon be together again was all that mattered.

Chapter 74

"Isn't it great news that Mr Foster, our Miss Corken's husband, was able to trace David's father so quickly?" Joe and Christopher were on their way back from the hotel, where they had stayed the night and enjoyed a wonderful breakfast before leaving. They had left early, in order to try to start their tasks at the same time as they usually did. They needed to reassure Mr and Mrs Moore that they had no intention of shirking their duties with them, despite the unbelievable changes ahead for them.

"It's good of Tom McGrath and Albert and Jill to ask us to come with them this evening to the farm where David and Brian are. Albert says that's why they hired a pickup truck in case they needed lots of room for the young people they hoped to trace.

"I'm sure David will find it all almost impossible to believe, as we did, I know, like ourselves, he was reconciled to be here, in Australia, for the rest of his life," Christopher replied. "And he had himself convinced that his father would have drunk himself to death long ago, he really had."

"Maybe he still drinks, Christopher, for, according to David, it is a difficult enough thing to stop."

"Well, no doubt he'll find out soon, Tom McGrath has organised a telephone call from his hotel room to Mr Gillespie's home, just as he did for us. And of course, we have another wonderful call to look forward to this evening from Mum and your grandma, Joe," Christopher said "I intend to be stronger this evening. I really do, I know I need to be, so I can enjoy talking to my mum and indeed, my stepfather who organised all this. I would like to be steady enough to be able to thank him for all he has done. Not that we can ever do that, Joe, thank him enough. But I intend to try."

"We'll be fine tonight, just wait and see, Christopher," Joe said. "I want to try and find out how on earth my gran managed for the last fifteen years. I specially want to find out how she ended up with your mum, Christopher. It's just so wonderful. It's all like a miracle, the whole thing."

Later that evening, David told them all he was very happy to learn from his father that he had never touched alcohol since David had been taken from Melton Home. Brian, who had been sitting quietly listening to them all, said he had something to tell them all.

"I want to thank Mr McGrath, Mr Dunn and Mrs Foster and especially Mr Wallace for their very kind offer to arrange for me to go back with everyone else to Northern Ireland. It is such a generous offer particularly as I was not one of the children from the Melton Home. However, I have decided to stay here in Australia. Both my parents were killed in the Blitz, and I have no close, living relatives in Northern Ireland. My uncle, who was my legal guardian, died a short time before I was sent here. I was then put in a home in Belfast and was sent directly from that home to here."

Brian paused for a moment, and everyone looked and waited in silence, hoping for some further information. Then Brian went on, this time with a smile on his face. "I have also met a lovely, lovely girl here, she is Mrs Ward's niece, and we have been going out together for about six months, wouldn't that be about right, David?"

David nodded. "I think so, Brian."

"Besides, I absolutely love the work I'm doing here. I love the people who employ me, they have been so kind to David and myself during the last three years. Even if I did find a living relative back home, they would be like strangers to me and could never match the love and care Mr and Mrs Ward have shown us. I also love the animals, and I love the climate. My ambition is really to become a land manager in some big farmstead. I'm sorry, but just recently I have become quite settled here, and I now have friendships who I hope for many."

Brian looked at everyone, hoping for understanding regarding his situation. "Had anyone asked me a year ago, I would have jumped at the chance to return to Northern Ireland, but not now." Brian's voice began to shake, and now he turned to David. "I hope you especially understand, we've been great friends and work colleagues, David, and I'll never forget you. Besides, once I know you address I intend to write often and even, some day to come and visit you. And that's the truth."

Brian struggled to speak for a moment, while he tried to recover his composure. "As for Christopher and Joe, I've always looked forward to the evening visits and enjoyed their company. But you are all going back to some certainty in your lives, but I'm not, most definitely not." Brian smiled now at David. "And you've just learnt that your father has never touched alcohol since you were sent away. I think that is so wonderful. How many men would have been able to do that, I wonder? Very few, I think. I believe the most of them would have done the opposite and turned to drink."

Brian's voice was stronger now. "Yes, I think, for me it is right that I stay in Australia. But I want to thank you so much for including me in your project. I appreciate your kindness and thoughtfulness so very much." And Brian nodded and smiled at Jill, Tom and Albert as they sat quietly listening to him.

"When do you hope to contact Amy and Helen?" Joe asked Tom, as they sat waiting in Tom's bedroom for Christopher and Joe could then talk to his grandma.

This was now their third evening coming to the hotel for their precious phone calls, and the two young men had decided they must cut the calls down to two nights a week. Firstly, they did not want to continue to leave their work with Mr and Mrs Moore early every evening, even though Mr Moore had been adamant it was fine to do so. But even so, Christopher and Joe felt they were being paid for a couple of hours when they weren't even there.

Then of course, it was the price of telephone calls from Australia to Northern Ireland. Having studied commerce and business studies at the technical college, Christopher was very aware of the cost of anything overseas. He had spoken to Albert about it, having learnt that Albert was his mum's and stepfather's solicitor, but Albert reassured him that the costs were well covered by Mr Wallace.

"You see, Tom," Joe continued, "I see Amy every Saturday evening and, as this is Wednesday, I wondered if you had any plans to meet up with Helen and her before this."

"We were hoping to, Joe, but Jill's husband has written to Amy's mother, he did find an address for her—hopefully it is the right one—but he hasn't heard anything back just yet, Joe," Tom replied, in a reassuring voice. "These things do take some time, but if we don't hear anything before Saturday, we'll decide what to do before you see her. I'm sure you would find it almost impossible to be with her and not say anything about anything."

"Oh, please, Sir, don't ask me to do that. I must share such joy as soon as I see her." Joe sounded very distressed.

Tom quickly put his arm around the young man's shoulder. "Of course, we would not expect you to do such a thing and I'm sure Mr Foster will have heard of Amy's mother by then."

However, Jill's husband rang her on Friday evening to say he had had no answer to his letter, but he now intended to try to meet up with her next week and tell her personally that her daughter had been found. He also told Jill that she was now married, and her married name was Faircliff, but, he stressed, he had already known that, and had written to her in her married name.

On hearing this news, everyone agreed that Joe must tell Amy the good news. And, most importantly, Jill should be the one to go personally with Joe to let her know that someone was already trying to trace her mother during the coming week, to let her know that Amy had been found. Everyone agreed that the girl needed to be told that her mother had been told, by letter fifteen years ago, that her daughter was dead. And now she was going to find out, after grieving for her loss for years, that that wasn't so, that her daughter was alive and living in Australia.

Chapter 75

Sam Foster felt uneasy as he left his house, and as he closed the front door firmly, he was lost in thought. He knew that what he was going to do this morning was, at the least, irregular, and at worst, immoral. But he had promised Jill he would do his very best to contact Amy's mother, and having written to her on two separate occasions, and received no reply, he was going to try his best to arrange some way of meeting her. He had gone to the address he had been given by the registry office and it confirmed he had written to the correct house. It was a beautiful red brick mid-terrace house that Amy's mother must live in. It was in a quiet street, close to the town centre and within walking distance of Wallace Park.

He was at a loss to know why his letters had been unanswered, but perhaps the family were away on holiday. But this morning he was going to park his car a little way from the house and watch carefully for anyone leaving or arriving at it. He must, at all costs, find an inconspicuous spot to park his car without it raising anyone's suspicions.

As Sam sat there in his car and the minutes seem to creep by, he began to feel more and more like a criminal. In fact, he began to wonder if indeed it was a crime to spy on innocent people. He knew that if it hadn't been for Jill, and her imploring requests to him from Australia, he knew he would never have entertained such action. But Jill had been so adamant that they needed to know whether Mrs Faircliff, who Sam had traced, was indeed Amy's mother. If that was so, could a telephone call be arranged between mother and daughter.

So here he was, sitting alone in his car since before seven a.m. watching and waiting, and he was so thankful now to see the front door open of number 14 Wallace Avenue and a tall, rather distinguished looking man step out on to the pavement. He was immaculately dressed, and looked every inch the businessman, and Sam knew he must be Amy's stepfather. Sam began to consult the notes he had brought with him this morning and according to the Marriage

257

Registrar, he would now be fifty years old. He had married Susan Martin ten years ago and they now had two sons aged seven and nine years of age.

As Sam watched, Mr Faircliff approached a blue saloon car, unlocked the driver's door and efficiently and deftly started the engine, then quickly drove off and disappeared from Sam's view. The fact that Mr Faircliff left the house alone indicated to Sam that his sons probably walked to Brownlee School, which was just a short distance from their home. His patience was rewarded some ten minutes later when the door opened and Mrs Faircliff appeared with her two sons and pulling the front door behind her and checking it was closed properly, the three of them proceeded down the street in the direction of Brownlee School. Now all Sam could do was hope she would come straight back after leaving the two boys. He knew he must speak to her this morning and let her know he was the sender of the two letters, letters which were so very important, and he needed to know if she had ever received them.

He was somewhat encouraged when, around fifteen minutes later he spotted her returning home, and rather than stopping her in the street he decided he must go to her house, it would be the best place to speak to her. He watched her enter her home and then, after waiting a few minutes, he approached her front door and rang the bell, and as he waited, he knew he could only hope that she was on her own in the house. At least it was reassuring to know that her husband was not there, because Sam believed that the man did not know anything about his wife's past. It was something he had wondered about during the last couple of weeks, when he had received no reply from Mrs Faircliff to the letters he had written to her. The door was opened almost immediately after his ring.

"Mrs Faircliff?" he asked.

The woman before him nodded her head quickly and said, "I know who you are. Step inside please, Mr Fisher." She opened the door wider for him as she continued, "I know who you are," she repeated, and opening a door on the left in the hall said, "We can talk in here."

Sam, puzzled by what she had just said, followed her silently into a large sitting room comfortably furnished with two large armchairs and a cosy looking sofa.

"Please," she said, "take a seat. I know you because you married Miss Corken, and Miss Corken looked after my Amy for a time." And suddenly, she sat down and began to cry. "She came to see me after I got the letter telling me Amy was dead. She was so kind, so kind to me then. Yes," she said through her tears, and tried to pull herself together and addressed Sam again, who sat quietly facing her, patiently waiting. "Yes, I got your letters, Mr Foster but," she hesitated, then went on. "My husband knows nothing about my pregnancy nor about Amy and," she stressed, "if he did know about me having a liaison with an American soldier, he would not want to have anything to do with me."

Sam was shocked at the bluntness of her words, and now her voice seemed weighed down with anxiety. "What have you to tell me, Mr Foster? Have you found out where Amy died? Have you found her grave?"

Sam Foster was lost for words, the fact that she knew who he was, and the difficult words of truth she must have felt compelled to tell him about her husband and his feelings towards the GIs who had been stationed here. Then the questions she had just asked him about Amy's death had stunned him into a lengthy silence. But without waiting for any answer to her questions, she hurried on, appearing to be impatient to talk to him. "I thought it better if I did not answer your letters. I was lucky to rescue them before my husband saw them, he would have been very curious because I never get letters from anyone, you see.

"I opened the first one in private when I read that the Melton Home wished to speak to me about some news they had had about Amy, I knew not to let my husband see it. I thought that by replying I would only encourage more correspondence, but of course you wrote again." Mrs Faircliff paused and looked earnestly at Sam. "If my husband knew anything about me and an American soldier, I would have to leave home. He hates them, really hates them and I have two sons to think about and cherish, Mr Foster."

She went on in a much softer tone, "I feel so guilty, guilty about my past, about Amy, about putting her in a Home." She hesitated, "And now I feel guilty about speaking about my husband." Then she said soberly, "You've traced Amy, haven't you?"

Before Sam could reply, her words continued to spill out and she was now talking quickly, she seemed so anxious to explain everything. "My American fiancé was killed, you know, that's the truth. But my husband would hate me if he knew anything about my relationship, never mind discovering I had Amy."

Sam realised that the lady in front of him was very distressed and her distress was overwhelming her, but he knew he must tell her exactly what he had come to tell her.

"I do promise not to send you any more correspondence, Mrs Faircliff, but I have other news for you which I must tell you this morning. The reason I have been so keen to be in touch with you, is because, fifteen years ago, you were given wrong information about your daughter, Amy. Amy is not dead but is alive and living in Australia."

Chapter 76

"Jill, I am so glad to hear your calm comforting voice, I can tell you. This morning I was with Amy Martin's mother for two and a half hours, doing my best to support and comfort her." Sam paused, and then went on." I thought one o'clock would never come around, even though I had only a little over an hour to wait before I rang you. I longed for you to be here with me, you would have known what to say. You could have hugged her and supported her much better than I did today. But I was in an awkward position and could do very little only listen to what she was trying to say through her floods of tears."

Sam thought for a moment, and then went on, "She is distraught and so very bewildered at the thought that her daughter is alive, after being told such an unbelievable, horrific lie that she was dead. And now apparently, she cannot make any attempt to see her daughter. According to her, her husband would disown her if she did."

"Did you go to the house as you said you intended to do? Was her husband away? I know you were worried about him coming back home, if he did go out, and find you there, Sam." Jill had been very worried when Sam had told her that he meant to watch Mrs Faircliff's house from early morning. He could so easily have been reported to the police for acting suspiciously, but listening to him now, she knew that, at least, he had been able to see and speak to Amy's mother safely. But now, from what Sam was telling her, Mrs Faircliff was so distressed that Sam had found it difficult to leave her.

"She did become a lot calmer when I said I could arrange for Amy to be available at a particular hotel around two o'clock in the afternoon on Monday, that would be around eight o'clock in the evening where you are, wouldn't it, Jill? She did show some delight on hearing this, Jill, and stressed that her husband would not be home then."

"That's wonderful, Sam," Jill replied. "It will be good for Mrs Faircliff to have some contact with her daughter initially, and it gives us a day or two to meet up with Amy and tell her who we are and why we are here. Do you think Mrs Faircliff will decide to unburden herself to her husband?"

"I really could not answer that question, love. She seems quite terrified at the thought of letting him know," Sam said. "I'm at a total loss to know what she might intend doing. In the meantime, I'm just so glad she has agreed to the phone call but," he stressed again, "she is really petrified of her husband finding out. I'm not exaggerating, believe me."

"Of course, I believe you, love, and I know you have had a truly awful time today and I wish I could have been there with you. I feel very guilty about it all, dear."

"When do you think you might be back home?" Sam asked her.

"Albert is talking about booking flights in a couple of weeks' time, and, so far," Jill told him, "three of the young men who came here as small boys have said they wish to return home. That's Joe, Christopher and David Gillespie. The boy called Brian Smith has decided to stay here, because he has no close relatives in Northern Ireland that he knows, and also he says he has met a girl he loves and wishes to marry her.

"But of course, we can't book seats until we let Helen and Amy know what has been happening, and then we have the task of telling Amy that her mother had been told she was dead all those years ago. And her mother had a letter confirming this, a letter she showed me when I too was informed and went to visit her to offer my condolences. But I will leave it to Joe to tell Amy that he too, was recorded as being dead. His grandma got a letter too, to say Joe was dead.

"So, you will need to stress to Amy the huge shock it is for her mother to learn that her daughter is, after all, alive and living in Australia." Jill hesitated "But it is wonderful Sam that despite the emotional state Mrs Faircliff was in you were able to arrange a phone call between Amy and her."

"I feel much better now that I have talked to you, love, and I just hope that Mrs Faircliff makes that call. She was very confident that her husband wouldn't be there at that time of the day, so we'll just have to wait and see. She is so torn and disbelieving, so shocked by the corrupt, despicable business. That has all left her very confused, never mind her belief about her husband's attitude. A belief which, let's face it, she could very well be mistaken about. If she told him he might be quite forgiving about it, but I can't see her taking that risk, Jill."

Then Sam added, "Talking of how shocked Mrs Faircliff is, aren't we all shocked by the utmost callousness of a government shipping young children from this lovely country of ours to a foreign one?"

"I know. Albert and Tom are still trying to come to terms with it all. Since speaking to the skipper on the ship, they have found everything very difficult to believe. I think Albert has told Edward quite a bit about it all and I think Edward means to make it public knowledge when he has some of the children safely back in Northern Ireland. Initially, all he wanted was to see the five children who had gone from Melton Home safely back, but now I think he intends to do much more," Jill told him. "Now, I better hang up shortly, this phone call must be costing quite a bit of money." Jill had just realised Sam and her had been talking for some time. "And Edward insists on paying all expenses, you know."

"Of course, love. I get carried away when I am talking to you, I miss you so much," Sam answered. "I will be thinking of you until our next telephone call."

"When Amy and her mother are reconciled, we will all be happy, and Helen Marks and her mother as well," Jill said. Then wistfully saying their goodbyes, they each replaced the receiver, thinking of the conversation they had just had and all their hopes for, not only the children of Melton Home, but for all the others who had been taken so wantonly from their homeland.

When Amy and Joe met up for their date on the Saturday evening, they were both very excited, they had such a lot to talk about. Jill and Tom had visited Helen and Amy on the Friday afternoon and told them they had traced the girls' mothers, who were both alive and well. When she learnt that her mother had been told all those years ago that her daughter was dead, Amy was very distressed and at a loss to understand why her mother had been told such an awful thing.

Jill did her best to console her, and then decided that she must tell the girl that Joe's grandma was told the same thing about him. And Jill reassured her, Joe intended to tell her all about it when he saw her the following evening. Now, here she was with Joe, avidly discussing home and how much they were looking forward to seeing their mothers.

Chapter 77

After Sam Foster left her, Anna Faircliff spent some time sitting in the same chair she had been sitting in when she had heard that her darling daughter, Amy, who she had grieved so despairingly for, was indeed alive, and living in Australia, a country she had only vaguely heard off but knew absolutely nothing about. And now it was too late to rejoice in this knowledge. Amy had been a beautiful, blonde haired, engaging child, when Anna had, on her family's insistence, put her in a children's home. Anna had had to find a job, as her father had taken ill with bronchitis and was no longer able to work. And someone had to try and bring in some money.

During that uncertain time, Anna did not know how she would have managed without her dear brother, Jim. It was Jim who had stepped in and tried his best to provide the money to support his parents, Amy and Anna, and of course, himself. Unfortunately, his pay did not stretch far enough, and Anna could see he was having a constant struggle to try and make ends meet. It was then Anna placed her beautiful little girl in Melton Home, a home she had made quite a few enquiries about and was very reassured by the reputation it had.

During that awful time, Jim was a tower of strength to her, accompanying her on her visits to see Amy. He tried to reassure Anna that there was nothing to worry about when the little girl had been sent with some others, for a holiday in England. But when she received the letter telling her that Amy had died suddenly in England and had been buried there, Anna knew she would never forget the pain of the loss of her little daughter.

But Amy was now nineteen years of age, she was a grown-up, not the lovely little girl she had loved so unconditionally. This girl was a stranger to her now, someone she knew nothing about. Anna did not know her likes and dislikes could she be a loving daughter to her again, and could Anna be a loving mother to her again?

Then she remembered the day Amy was born and how delighted Gerald had been when he saw the baby in his fiancé's arms. She recalled how delighted he had been when she told him she was pregnant, and he had insisted on going immediately to Anna's minister to organise a date for their wedding. It would be a quiet affair with only the minister and her family present.

Gerald had come to Northern Ireland as one of a contingent of troops from America on 26 January 1942. They were always referred to by the locals as 'GIs'. They would be trained in Northern Ireland and then sent to South Africa to fight the Germans. Anna and Gerald had almost two years together but before he could finalise any plans for their wedding, he was informed his contingent would leave in a week's time.

But Gerald never came home. It was an army friend of his who came to the house and told her that he and two others, had been shot dead while holding fort and awaiting the arrival of reinforcements. Gerald's friend told Anna that they were totally outnumbered by the Germans who invaded them. He also told Anna that Gerald and the other soldiers would be recommended for their bravery in staying at their post.

In that moment, Anna realised that all her hopes and dreams had been washed away with her tears. The reality was that she was an unmarried mother, with a child born to a GI from America. And Anna knew what that meant, having listened to other's whispers and asides, to have a child when you were still single, was the utmost sin before God, but to have one to a GI was shame indeed on you. She had just committed a cardinal sin, and she would never now be one of the GI brides preparing to leave Northern Ireland for American shores. She would never have got through the desolate months that followed the news of Gerald's death without the help of her parents and brothers.

And most of all, having to care for a new baby, who did manage, at times, to ease the awful grieving Anna had been coming through. Her parents had loved Gerald and found him to be a gentle, loving man and when Anna told them of her pregnancy they were, despite all the gossip surrounding them, delighted for Anna and Gerald. Through it all they did their best to protect her from the senseless, boorish talk which seemed to cling to the GIs and their relationships with girls, during their stay in Northern Ireland.

Anna met Arthur Faircliff when he came to work as a manager in the department store called Goodrich's where she had been working for two years. He had originally been employed in the sister store in County Fermanagh. His transfer to Belfast meant it was good promotion for him. He was only working in his new position for six weeks when he asked Anna out to the cinema. She gladly accepted his invitation as she seldom went anywhere after her day's work. Besides, she also found him quite an attractive man, he was tall and slim with an attractive face, with deep brown eyes and a wide smile. He was also, the first man to show any interest in her since she had been going out with Gerald.

They were married a year later, a year in which Anna remained silent about her love for Gerald or the loss of her little girl. Initially she did not speak of it because she still found it all too heart-breaking, but then it became impossible for here to open her heart to Arthur. On one of their evenings out, and shortly after their engagement, somehow the conversation came round about the Americans' stay in Northern Ireland, Anna was deeply shocked to hear how derogatory and scathing about the Americans her fiancé was, so much so that she wondered if he had had any personal experience of wrongdoing on their part, but that did not seem to be the case.

He just went on to say that he would not want anything to do with any girl who had had a relationship with any of them. As for the girls who had married one of them and gone to America, he reckoned they would be sure to regret it. The girls who actually had had a baby with one of them well, they were just disgusting. They were trollops.

Anna spent many sleepless nights after that particular evening and contemplated breaking off her engagement but felt she could not let Arthur down because in many ways he was a thoughtful, loving fiancé. Her parents and her brother Jim were delighted that she was being given another chance of happiness after all the suffering she had endured.

Now here Anna was, married for almost nine years with two sons aged seven and five, and she had just learnt that the daughter she had been told fifteen years ago was dead, was alive and living in Australia. A daughter whom her husband had never known anything about, and she wondered how on earth she was ever going to tell him. And soon she would be making a phone call across, she had been told by Mr Foster, hundreds of miles. She would soon be speaking to Am her daughter, but it would not be the excited voice of her four-year-old child but the voice of a stranger.

Chapter 78

"Oh, my darling, what's wrong? What on earth's the matter?" Joe had rushed over to Amy when he saw how she looked when she had finished the telephone call from her mother. She was shaking and she seemed unaware of him standing beside her. Her face was white and tears flowed unchecked down her cheeks.

"Darling, come over here and sit down and try to tell me what has happened." Joe held her tenderly as he guided her over to one of the sofas in the corner of Tom's bedroom. Amy's mother had arranged to ring at one o'clock British time, which was eight o'clock Australian and she had done so, very promptly. Helen's mother was the next relative expected to ring around eight-thirty p.m. Joe just held his girlfriend quietly as she struggled to regain some composure.

Then with a ravaged look on her face, she turned to Joe and in a voice barely audible said, "My mother doesn't seem to want me to come home, certainly not at the moment, and perhaps never." And in a despairing gesture, she put her hands out and gripped Joe tightly. And Joe could see by the terrible look on her face she wanted him to deny what she had just told him.

Joe watched Amy quietly for a moment, conscious that Helen must appear shortly to wait for her mother's phone call. Knowing Amy would not want her friend to see her so distressed, he suggested they leave Tom's bedroom and return to the hotel foyer. When they reached the foyer, Joe continued to hold her gently and then suggested quietly that they take a walk outside. Once outside, he quickly guided her to a garden seat and then spoke as calmly as he could, "Whatever has happened, love? What exactly did your mother say to you? It was her who talked to you, wasn't it?"

Joe was at a loss as to what was going on, and to see Amy so obviously unhappy when everything should be so bright and hopeful for them both, was very distressing for him. And somewhere inside him, he felt a huge heavy, choking feeling begin to form. Then as he held her quietly, she gradually became more composed and said, "My mother got married about nine years ago and I think she said she has two boys, so I have half-brothers and I did say that to her. She says this has all been such a shock to her—discovering that I am alive—and she says she needs time to come to terms with it and," here Amy's voice broke again, "she says her husband knows nothing about me and because my mother thought I was dead she thought it best never to tell him."

"But surely, she means to tell him now about you? Doesn't she?" Joe asked her.

Amy did not answer Joe immediately and Joe realised she was going over the phone call, and when she spoke, Joe thought her voice was quite fearful. "She just said, Joe, that she was afraid to tell him after all this time. It seems as if she was living a false life with him."

"Yes, it does look that way." Joe was really shocked at this piece of news. "Why would she not have told him, Amy? Why not?"

"She told me that my father was an American GI, who was one of many who came to Northern Ireland during the war. They had their wedding all arranged when he was sent to South Africa, and he was killed out there."

"So, Amy, there is no shame attached to their story. They were going to be married, and then he was killed. It's a very sad story."

"But…" Amy stressed, "It seems her husband never liked the American GIs, which was the main reason my mother never told him anything. She said she just felt that she couldn't." Amy looked directly at Joe, and she looked brighter now, more spirited. "She was quite open and honest with me, Joe, and I did feel a bond there somewhere. I do remember her, you know, I remember her holding me lovingly on her knee. So, when I think of that, I'm sure she will want to see me, but not immediately and," and Amy sighed heavily as she spoke, "I have to be content with that."

"Unfortunately, Jill and Allan and Tom keep saying that they must get back home very soon, especially as Mr Wallace wants Christopher safely back with his mum as soon as possible.

"I know, love, but I can't go back to Northern Ireland until my mother is ready to see me, and certainly that is how it is at the present time. So, I must stay here, I have no one else only her to go home to."

"Amy, please say you will come with me when I am going. We have planned our whole future together, surely that counts for a lot with you?"

"Certainly, it does, it really does, darling. You must believe that. But you will be going back to celebrate with your grandmother, Christopher with hi mother, stepfather and stepsister, And I…" Amy began to sob again, and Joe quietly held her until her tears ceased. "And I," she said quickly, "I have no one to go back home to, no one."

"It's all going to work out for you," Joe said firmly. "Your mother's sure to want to see you and love you. She has had a great shock, that's for sure. You have been grieving for years for your mother and that was only because you had been taken from her. But your mother, well, she has been grieving for your death. After all, that was what she had been told. So, it is indeed, some shock for her to be told after all this time that you are alive. And that she was told the most appalling lies. You have to agree with that, Amy."

"Yes, perhaps I'm being selfish, Joe. I'll have to be patient and wait until she comes round, as I'm sure she will."

When Joe then suggested they go back into the hotel and join the others, Amy agreed and asked Joe to tell Jill Foster how things were between her and her mother. Amy felt that perhaps she could help, in some way, to see if Amy's mother would like her daughter back home with her. In the meantime, she must be honest with her friend Helen and tell her of her dilemma. She did wonder if Helen meant to go home to Northern Ireland or would she stay in Australia with her wealthy boyfriend.

Chapter 79

"This whole business is awful for both you and your mother, Amy, it really is. At least you had never been told your mother was dead, and so, just as I did, you always dreamt of meeting up with her again. Then, for your mother to believe for the past fifteen years that you were dead, and now to learn that that simply isn't true is so cruel and unbelievable and must be such a shock for her."

Helen had arranged to meet Amy during their lunch hour in the little café they often frequented and where they had shared so many happy or troubled stories. "I know my mother is stunned and outraged at discovering I was never adopted at all but was simply shipped out to a foreign country. But it certainly is not as contemptible or despicable as what your mother was told."

Helen was doing her best to comfort Amy who was very distressed at times, and at other times, very angry about everything. "I believe that given time to come to terms with everything, your mother will certainly want to welcome you home." Helen hesitated, reluctant to remind Amy that their time here in Australia to decide whether to stay or go, was limited, simply because Mr Wallace naturally enough, was anxious that his stepson would soon be reunited with his mother. "Mr Wallace has made the suggestion that he will pay for your flight later on, Amy, when your mother has come to terms with seeing you." Helen ventured, "How do you feel about that?"

Amy nodded dumbly for a moment and then said, "I know, Helen. Mr Wallace is so kind and generous and if I don't go home now with the rest of you I'll certainly be asking him for his help later. I'm sure I'll need it. And I really think that will be how it will be. Because if I do go home now, as I've said, have nowhere to go at present. Joe will be going to live in his grannie's apartment, and she has only one bedroom, and I would have no one only Joe might be able to join."

"Well, you'll have me too, Amy. I can't wait to go. This is the time I've been waiting for so long. To go home."

"Have you really decided to go, Helen?" Amy asked with some surprise. "What about Andy? I thought you were going to marry him, Helen."

"No, no, Amy. If I stayed here, I know Andy and I will get married, but firstly I want to go home." Helen didn't say 'home to my mother.' She was only too conscious of Amy's emotions at present. "Andy says he'll come to Northern Ireland and marry me in my home place. So, we'll see how it all goes, Amy, and," Helen went on, "if you decide to come home with me, I intend to tell my mother about you, Amy, and I know she will immediately offer her home to you. I know she will."

Amy was silent for a moment. She was quite taken aback by Helen's kind offer and her mind was filled with such conflicting thoughts. Helen Marks had been such a close friend to her for the past fifteen years. They had sat side by side at their desks in the children's home, hoping they might be fortunate enough to be taught something. They had slept just feet apart from each other in the same dormitory. They had cried together whenever they were treated badly by the nuns, and they had laughed together in some of their happier times. Amy had always regarded the two of them as two equals because of their shared experiences.

Now here was Helen, overjoyed at the prospect at going home to Ireland, to a mother who was ecstatic that her daughter had been found. A mother, according to Helen, would welcome Amy into her home with open arms. And here was Amy, whose mother had disowned her, which left her with no home to go to. She had no mother, no home. And suddenly Amy was filled with a wild fury and jealousy at how cruelly things had turned out for her, after being sent abroad when she was four years of age.

Now she shook her head vigorously. "I couldn't go, I really couldn't. I can't bear it, I really can't." Now the tears flowed unchecked down her cheeks and began to soak her blouse. Her emotions overwhelmed her, and she turned to Helen. "I could not bear to see your mother's love for you, still there, after all these years. While mine, well, mine has rejected me without a second thought. Her daughter, a mere four years of age when she last saw her." Amy's voice had steadied a bit and now held a cynical note.

Helen supported Amy as they sat together in a secluded corner of the coffee shop and her voice was calm as she spoke. "I can't do anything about any of that, Amy. I can offer you a home, but you must decide fairly quickly if you want it. But please," Helen added, "don't let pride and jealousy get in your way, Amy. I am making this offer because I am your best friend and I love you. And I believe it is the right thing for you to return home with Joe."

"I promise I will let you know in a couple of days' time." Amy rushed on, some passion in her voice. "Thank you so much for your kind offer, Helen. I am overwhelmed. I know we have been such good friends over the years. Now," she added, as she looked at the clock on the wall, "I must get back to college for my next session. I will ring you, Helen."

"Oh, no, please, Amy, you can't do this to us. Is this your final decision? You can't do this. What about me? Our whole future was going to be together. Please, darling, you must come home with us." Joe was distraught, as Amy knew he would be when she told him her final decision was to stay in Australia. She had spent two sleepless, troubled nights but was resolved now to stay in Australia.

During her last two days and nights, she had come to realise it was the best thing to do for everyone's sake. She didn't want anyone to feel they must look out for her. She didn't want to feel like a hanger-on with any of them and she believed that was how it would be. For now, she had Joe to comfort and offer some hope for the future.

"We can write to each other, Joe darling. And I'm sure my mother will soon get over the shock of me being alive and will want me home." Amy desperately wanted to make the blow easier for Joe.

Joe immediately brightened up. "Of course, she will, Amy. After all, you are her daughter. And then, we will make arrangements for your flight home. We'll raise the money, somehow. Because I still intend to fulfil our dream of a future together." And Joe held Amy close as they clung together, in the knowledge that they had an uncertain future.

Even as Amy sat quietly in the circle of Joe's arms, she remembered her mother's abrupt phone call to her. They had been like two strangers talking and Amy felt that was how it would always be. She was taking the coward's way out now with Joe, but if it eased his parting from her, she must go along with it all, instead of telling him the blunt and honest truth.

Two days later, Amy rang Helen. "I am ringing you, Helen, rather than meet up with you to let you know how much I appreciate your offer, but I have decided to stay in Australia and finish my course in the training college. And to continue my work sessions there. I also mean to look after Mrs Logan on a part-time basis so I will still have my room. I cannot come with you to your home, Helen. After fifteen years you and your mother must adjust to each other's values and views. And I would be an intruder in all that, Helen."

Before Helen could reply, Amy added, "I've told Joe and the three people, Jill, Tom and Albert, who travelled thousands of miles to look for us and I do hope they understand. Tom McGrath said that Mr Wallace sent a message that he will pay for my fare when my mother gets over her initial shock. Such generosity, Helen, from someone I've never even met."

"Amy, how is Joe? You can't do this to him. How is he?" Helen sounded distressed.

Amy quickly put in, "He's fine." She did not want to talk about Joe, it was too heart-breaking. Then taking a deep breath, she went on, "I wish you all the best, Helen, and please, please write to me. You know my address, at the college." Amy quietly replaced the receiver.

Chapter 80

Jill, Tom and Albert were somewhat shocked when they learnt Amy, in the meantime, was going to stay in Australia. Tom had spoken to Joe at length about it, as Joe was the one to tell them how things were between Amy and her mother. Jill, especially, was disappointed to hear such news, even though Sam had seemed dubious about Mrs Faircliff and how she would feel about welcoming her daughter into her home. But they all must hope that everything would work out eventually.

Certainly, for Ruth Smart, the little girl that Albert had, for the last number of years kept to the forefront of his mind, things seemed to be working out wonderfully for her. Her mother and grandmother, on hearing from Albert the whole horrendous story around her disappearance and eventually being traced to a children's home in a foreign country, were at first totally shocked and disbelieving. They were constantly on the phone to Albert asking endless questions, some of which he had no answers for.

Then one morning Ruth's grandmother rang him to let him know that she and Ruth's mother, Isabel, would be arriving in a couple of weeks' time in Australia. The Australian government had finally agreed, after serious threat from Mrs Smart about her granddaughter's unexplained disappearance from the children's home in Belfast and her subsequent incarceration in a children's home in Perth, to pay for both her and Ruth's mother flights to Australia and for their accommodation while there.

Mrs Smart explained to Albert over the phone that they both wanted to see for themselves the place Ruth had been forced to live in, away from her mother and grandmother, from she was four years of age until now at twelve years old.

When Albert heard all this, he was captivated, and reckoned it was the first admission of guilt that had been made by either the Australian or British government, or indeed by any authority. He believed the success of all the interchanges which must have gone on between Mrs Smart and the Australian

274

government was solely down to Ruth's grandmother. Mrs Smart told Albert that she and Isabel would be forever grateful for him and his colleague's hard work in finding Ruth. Albert stressed none of it could have happened without Edward Wallace's hard work and financial support. Mrs Smart was delighted to hear that Albert would still be in Australia when they arrived there. She stressed they were looking forward to seeing him again and express their gratitude face to face.

Back in Northern Ireland, as well as being entrusted with the responsibility of finding Mrs Faircliff, Sam Foster had been given the job of trying to trace David Gillespie's father. Jill had given him some background information she remembered about David during his time in Melton Home. She did remember vividly how angry Mr Gillespie had been when he learnt his son had been adopted without his knowledge.

Jill also told Sam that David's parents had split up and as a result his father had started to drink heavily. But then she heard later Mr Gillespie had never touched drink after his son's disappearance. She emphasised to Sam that she could not confirm this, but she had personally witnessed his reaction on the morning he learnt David had been taken away.

Sam soon discovered a telephone number for a Mr Gillespie just outside Lisburn and when he managed to contact him, he simply said he might have some news which would be of interest to him, but he needed to speak to him directly. In reply, Mr Gillespie directed him to a small holding a couple of miles outside Lisburn.

On arriving at the pretty cottage, Sam was immediately struck by how immaculate the place was. All the hedges were neatly trimmed, rose bushes in abundance, were trained to cascade round the front door. The outbuildings, which lay to the side and back of the property were in good repair and had obviously been well looked after. As Sam parked his car, his mood was uplifted by the whole appearance of the place. This home showed no signs of neglect whatsoever and he was immediately assured that the father who had turned to drink after he had put his son into Melton Home all those years ago, bore no resemblance to the man standing before him now.

Mr Gillespie treated him somewhat cautiously when he opened the door, just looking at Sam with an enquiring look on his face. But when Sam told him he had some news of his son, he immediately opened the door wide. "Oh my God, my son, David, he has been in touch. Oh my God." And the tears began to flow down his face. Then he rushed on excitedly, "Don't stand there, please come in."

Mr Gillespie stood back to allow Sam to enter the somewhat small, but delightfully bright hall.

"In here, in here, Mr Foster—Mr Foster, have I got your name right?" he asked Sam, as he indicated a door on the right and showed him into a bright comfortable sitting room.

"My son, you have news of my son, have you?" Mr Gillespie was talking feverishly and rubbing his hands together as he spoke. "Just sit here, Mr Foster," and he indicated an easy chair by the fire. As Sam sat down, Mr Gillespie sat down on the one facing him. "Now, tell me," he said, his eyes bright and shining. "Were the people who adopted him good to him? Does he remember me? Does he want to see me?"

"Yes, Mr Gillespie, David desperately wants to see you," Sam answered quietly then went on in the same even tone, "This will come as a great shock to you, but David was never adopted." Sam paused for a moment to allow the man facing him to realise what he was telling him.

"What do you mean, never adopted? But the authorities told me he was."

"Yes, they did tell you that. I know they did, but that was simply not true." Sam hesitated and then went on, "He was sent to Australia, him and hundreds and hundreds of other children, Mr Gillespie. It was done, I believe, to help populate Australia."

Sam's words were treated in absolute silence for a moment while David Gillespie's father looked at him with a horrified, shocked expression on his face. Then slowly, Sam recounted to him Edward Wallace's search for Christopher and how it had led them to Australia. Because he knew Mr Gillespie was too shocked to take much in, he related the bare facts of the search and then told him his son was waiting to hear from him. Sam then produced the slip of paper with the telephone number and the day and time which had been arranged for father and son to talk—to talk for the first time in fifteen years.

Mr Gillespie steadied himself considerably at the mention of contact with David. "How wonderful, just to hear him will be so wonderful." In spite of all he had just heard about his son's supposed adoption, he was concentrating on being in contact with him. "I'll be able to tell him about this place I have and how hard I worked, hoping every day to hear from him. I'll also tell him I haven't touched alcohol for fifteen years."

Sam, looking discreetly around the delightful cottage and its grounds, so immaculate both inside and out, believed that Mr Gillespie's abstinence from alcohol was true.

Chapter 81

The flight from Perth airport in Western Australian to Heathrow airport in London ought to have been a truly happy one for Christopher and all the others, but instead it was rather a subdued one, their joy marred considerably by the unexpected blow of Amy's absence and everyone's distress and disbelief about it. Everyone's thoughts were with Joe going home to his grandmother without Amy, they did not talk about any of that on the flight.

For the last few days before they boarded the flight, they had all done their best to encourage Amy to come with them, all to no avail. At the same time, they did their best to support Joe during such an uncertain time.

Quite a few of their friends had come to the airport to see them off, including Mr and Mrs Moore, the Wards, and Helen Matthew's boyfriend among them. But Amy did not go, explaining to Joe it would be too traumatic for her to see them all going off to be reunited with their families when she had none.

But if there had been a subdued atmosphere on the flight from Australia to Northern Ireland, there was no evidence of it in Edward Wallace's household that evening. There were, indeed, plenty of tears, but they were tears of joy mingled with expressions of sheer disbelief that mother and son were actually together again. As was Joe and his grandmother Sara, holding each other so tightly and so thankfully that they too were reunited.

Edward himself, with his beautiful daughters, Faith and Jennie, were part of this wonderful, unforgettable time. Christopher and Joe, together with Helen Marks and David Gillespie tried their best to communicate their heartfelt thanks to Mr Wallace for all he had done to ensure their safe arrival back in Northern Ireland. Before David and Helen left that happy home that evening, David to go with Sam Foster to meet his father, and Helen to go home with her mother. They assured Joe and Christopher they would be in touch soon and make some arrangements to meet up with one another.

"Grandma, how lovely this space is, it is just perfect for you!" Joe enthused as he looked around the annexe which was his grandma's home. They had said their goodnights to Christopher and his newfound family and had promised to join them for breakfast in the morning in Edward's dining room.

"Yes, Joe, it is just ideal for me, and it is still ideal for the two of us with its bedroom with the two single beds and wardrobes," Sara replied, as she opened the door to the bedroom. "Tomorrow we will sort out your clothes. I'm also very glad that Monica and Edward decided to tell me you were alive and well when they did, even though it was a huge shock. But it certainly would have been a much greater one had you arrived here unannounced, my love."

Sara shook her head solemnly as she spoke. "Now, as you see, I have your bed and wardrobe ready for you, but there will be no unpacking tonight, just a nice cup of tea for the two of us and then to bed." Sara hesitated, then went on in a calm voice, "There is so much I need to know, but I want you to tell me in your own time, about your experiences and the treatment you received in that home you were in." Sara gave a long sigh and then went on, "I have thanked God so often that Christopher was in your life for the last fifteen years. That must have made an enormous difference to you."

"There is so much I want to know too, Grandma. I want to know all about Edward and his generosity to you, the prosthesis he managed to get for you and of course, this annexe. I need to know everything. I need to know it all." Tears rose in Joe's eyes again as he hugged Sara.

In response, Sara said, "Let's get that tea and then go to bed."

Chapter 82

"Christopher, I really do need to start looking for a job here, and it may not be that easy for me, but I do need one. We have been back here for two weeks now, and I have given most of my meagre savings to my gran to help with food, heat and lighting here. I insisted that I must pay my way and she does appreciate that. So, I need to find work and I don't know how to go about it all." For the first time since his homecoming, Joe sounded quite despondent.

"It's been only two weeks, Joe, and that's not really very long, but I too, need to find a job. My stepdad has been so kind so me, to us all, in fact, and I do not want to prey on his kindness," Christopher said, then went on in a more spirited tone, "I'll speak to him this evening and ask his advice on the best way to look for employment and make the best use of our qualifications. I do hope the Australian qualifications are on par with the ones here. Dad will be able to tell me, I'm sure." Christopher hesitated for a moment, and looked at Joe questioningly. "Any word from Amy yet? It is a bit soon, I suppose."

"Yes, Christopher, it's a bit soon. Before I left, she was looking for a room to stay in, but she intended to eat most of her meals in the college. So, she did say when she was settled in, she would write to me. So, I just must wait until I hear from her. I miss her so much, Christopher, and I did think of going to see her mother, but I might make matters worse. And grandma said not to interfere in any of it and I'm sure she's right. But in the meantime, I must get work and find a house for myself, so that Amy will have somewhere to come home to. That is, if her mother hasn't come to terms with Amy's reappearance in her life."

Joe spoke quite confidently now about his future and Christopher was relieved. He had been half expecting Joe to be miserable about Amy's refusal to come home with everyone else. But instead, he had been calm and confident about their ability to sort their future out together. And Christopher could only admire his oldest friend for that.

As for Christopher himself, no words could ever express his happiness. He was home, home with his dear mother and with a stepfather who had shown him unconditional love, understanding and support since their very first meeting and his stepfather's deep love and devotion to his wife, Christopher's mother, was apparent in everything he did. Now, with two stepsisters to add to the family, Christopher felt truly blessed.

Then of course, there was Agnes. Agnes, as far as Christopher could see, saw to every need the family had. And she did it all so unobtrusively and willingly, that she was a sheer delight to have around the place. But he knew this whole set up could easily become a way of life and no one would want that for him. So, he was determined to find himself a job. He knew he didn't have to worry about getting a house, this was his home here and he did not have a girlfriend to worry about. He would speak to his stepfather this evening and he was confident he would be able to advise him and point him in the right direction.

"My goodness, Christopher, is there no end to your father's thoughtfulness and generosity to me?" Joe shook his head in a very respectful manner as he talked to Christopher. "Did I hear you right? He's actually giving me a job in his advertising department?"

"Of, course, you did hear right, Joe. He wants me to start working in the accounts office of their local branch here in Lisburn. And you will be in the same branch. So now, we both have jobs, Joe." Christopher smiled happily as he talked. "But there are conditions, you know, Joe. If he isn't happy with the quality of our work, he will let us know." Christopher looked steadily at his friend. "Of course, the opposite applies; if we are not happy with something, we must let him know. It all sounds solid enough and good for both of us."

"It certainly does, and if I can ever find a way of repaying your father, I certainly will." Joe put an arm around Christopher and hugged him tight. "It was lucky for me, the day I first met you, Christopher, and I hope I can make you proud of me. I intend to make your father glad he decided to give me a job and I now I'll just love working for him."

Christopher and Joe settled into their employment quickly, and working in an environment where they could make good use of their talents and the flare they had for their particular line of work, was so very rewarding for them both. And to complete Joe's contentment in his homecoming, he was delighted when he got his first letter from Amy. In it she told him she was enjoying both her studies to become a fully-fledged teacher and her evening part-time work. She related to Joe how kind Mr Reid had been to her and how glad she was that she had taken him up on his offer of renting her the spare room in his family home. She did stress to Joe that it was only a temporary measure until she found somewhere else. She certainly did not think it a good idea to stay at the headmaster's home indefinitely.

In her letter, she also said she had written to Helen Marks asking her to try and make contact with Amy's mother and let Amy know if she showed any signs of coming to terms with the knowledge that Amy was alive and well. She emphasised how much she wanted to come home and ended by assuring Joe of her love always.

A few weeks later, Joe received another letter from Amy; she seemed both heartbroken and angry at her mother's insistence in keeping Amy's very existence from her husband. She reiterated her strong feelings for Joe and her wish to be home in Northern Ireland with him, but while her mother was so intent on covering up that she had a daughter, Amy felt she must stay in Australia.

These two letters arrived with Joe over a period of six weeks, letters which he answered straight away, but then all correspondence ceased, and it was a very concerned and unhappy Joe who confided in Christopher. "I don't know what to do, Christopher, I have no one whom I could write to and confide in over there, apart from Mr and Mrs Moore and I really wouldn't want to worry them. I did think of contacting Brian, maybe he could find out something for me—but I don't even have an address I could write to. I know we did tell him we would be in touch, and I have been very remiss, of course."

"So have I, Joe. I do keep meaning to write to Brian, but I never seem to get around to it. I do know Helen has been writing to him and to her boyfriend. So I'm sure she can help."

After meeting up with Helen and fired with the girl's usual optimism, Joe felt much more cheerful about everything. But then, even before Helen could put pen to paper to enquire about Amy's wellbeing, she had a letter from Brian saying that Amy was in police custody. She had been charged with the attempted murder of Mrs Reid, the wife of Perth's technical college headmaster. Brian stressed in his letter he was sorry to break such awful news to her, but he hadn't known who to write to. He just felt someone in Northern Ireland should know. Most of all, her mother needed to know the predicament her daughter was in.

Chapter 83

"Christopher, who is going to tell Amy's mother this awful news, and more importantly, how is she going to be told?"

"I think Sam Foster should be the one to tell her, after all, he was the one who told her that her daughter was alive and well. So, he does know her a little better than the rest of us." Christopher paused, then continued in a more uncertain way. But it would probably be too much to expect of him to tell Amy's mother such news. I mean, it is going to be such a shock to Mrs Faircliff, and Sam might find her reaction very difficult to deal with." Christopher shook his head as he talked.

"I'm sure it would be very difficult for most men," Joe replied, "but if Mrs Foster went with him, the trauma might be more easily dealt with."

"Well, we're on our own regarding this decision, Joe. No one knows about this; only Helen Marks and we and I think we should keep it this way until we speak to Jill and Sam Foster. At such a happy, contented time in their lives, I'm reluctant to give my mother and stepfather anything more to worry about. And perhaps even feel guilty about, that they didn't do more to try and get Amy to come home with them."

"That's how I feel," Joe countered. "My grandma is over the moon that she has me back with her and this news, I think, would really alarm her. So, let's decide now that we'll call with the Fosters later this evening. It's Saturday and you and I usually go out for a walk anyway, so we can first include a visit to the Fosters' house in our walk."

"I don't agree with you at all that we should keep this news about Amy from Monica, Sara and Edward. They have been through so much over a long time and have shared so much since your reunion. And, of course, we all look on Amy as Joe's girlfriend. So, I have no doubt they would wish to share this ordeal with you and support you." Jill looked at the two young men sitting facing her. "How do you think they would feel if they did learn of Amy's trouble, and no one had told them anything about it?"

Jill and Sam had sat in stunned silence when Joe had told them Amy had been charged with attempted murder. How could such a thing be? Amy had seemed so naïve and unconfident when Jill had met her in Australia. Indeed, she had just seemed to be a grown-up version of the four-year-old child she had looked after in Melton Home.

Now Joe was quick and decisive when he spoke, "You are so right, Jill, but we were only trying to protect them from any more trauma.

"I know you were, Joe, but they are all made of much stronger stuff you know." Jill managed a smile.

"I should have thought of that," Christopher joined in the conversation. "I must say it was my idea really, to keep it from them. I see now how wrong I would have been. So, after we leave you, Jill and Sam, we will go straight to their place and tell them. I'll go with Sam in the morning on his undercover mission to Mrs Faircliff and see how it goes. Then we will come and let you know how it went with her."

"Oh, Joe, my darling Joe, I'm so glad you've told me about Amy now, you could not possibly keep something like this from us." Sara sobbed loudly as she held her grandson tightly. "And I'm sure everyone here would agree with that."

On Christopher's request, Monica and Edward had come into Sara's annexe and had sat quietly until now, in her comfortable sitting room trying to digest what they had just heard. Even though Christopher and Joe had said they had something important to tell them, nothing could have prepared them for the news they had just received. Christopher had just told them bluntly that Joe's girlfriend, Amy, had been arrested for the attempted murder of the technical college's lir administor's wife, Mrs Reid. How could this have happened to such a young girl? What on earth must have been going on to lead to this trouble!

Christopher, watching his parents closely, knew he had spoken sharply and quickly but he felt really out of his depth relaying such a message to his loved ones. The stunned silence in the room seemed interminable and, in an effort, to break it, Christopher spoke again, "That's all we know I'm afraid. It was Helen Marks who had a letter from our friend Brian in Australia telling her about it. He intends to write again when he finds out what exactly is going on. We did tell Sam and Jill because we felt her mother should be informed as soon as possible and that Sam was the one to do it as he seems to know her movements fairly well."

It was Monica who spoke next, and she moved closer to Edward as she did so. "I'm glad you decided to tell us too. Although we never met Amy, we feel we were getting to know her because of what Joe told us about her." She did not say anything about how he had talked about their future together, because surely that must be thrown into disarray now. Instead in a most steady, comforting tone of voice, she went on, "I know I speak for Edward too, but if there is anything, anything at all we can do to help, please do not hesitate to ask us."

Edward spoke only to confirm Monica's words. He would have liked to offer to pay for young Joe's fare back to Australia, but something held him back. After all, they had no idea of the story behind Amy's arrest. So, he felt it was much wiser to keep his own counsel in the meantime.

The following morning, Jill and Sam set off for the avenue the Faircliffs lived in. It was the first time Jill had accompanied Sam on his visits to the avenue, as she had been in Australia trying to help locate Joe and Christopher. Ever since everyone's return and the knowledge that Amy was still in Australia, Sam still made a point of going to the avenue to check that life and routine of the Faircliffs appeared unchanged, even after the shock Mrs Faircliff had received about her daughter. He had done this in case he might be called upon to contact Mrs Faircliff again. This morning he was very glad he had done so because there was now a real sense of urgency to do this, so serious Amy's trouble seemed to be.

"I'm so glad I discreetly continued to come round here from time to time, Jill, just to check everything seemed to be as usual."

"So, we wait until Mr Faircliff comes out of the house and drives off, presumably to his work. Then shortly after, Mrs Faircliff will appear with the children to walk with them to school. When she is coming back, you go and talk to her. Isn't that how you managed to talk to her initially, Sam?"

"Yes, Jill, and she brought me into their house that morning," Sam said.

"Well, it certainly seems a better idea than standing talking in the street."

"Right, Jill, this is their avenue right here." Sam deftly turned the car into the street. "Oh, Mr Faircliff's car is away, we must have missed him leaving, Jill." Sam appeared to be at something of a loss. "We'll have to watch for Mrs Faircliff coming out with the children and then wait patiently for her return. Then we'll go and speak to her. She wanted me to go into the house the last time I met her, so she might do the same today. We'll just have to wait and see."

Just as he finished speaking, he spied Mrs Faircliff and her sons leave the house and begin their walk along the pavement. "Here they come, but because we're parked behind the lorry, they can't see us. She will, I hope, be back in fifteen minutes' time. When we see her reappear at the street corner, it gives us time to walk to meet her and she will be close to her home."

"I'm not entirely happy, Sam, about giving Mrs Faircliff such news in the street. I think it would be better if you told her we had some news for her. But perhaps we should give it to her in her own home," Jill suggested. "You must remember how dreadfully upset she was the last time you met with her, and I think she might be far worse this time."

"I've been thinking about all that too, Jill. So, let's hope she agrees to us coming into her home. We certainly don't want a whole scene on the street. But no matter about anything, tell her we must, because after all, Amy is her daughter."

Just as Sam spoke, he saw Mrs Faircliff reappear round the corner and he said quickly to Jill, "Let's go now and meet her. She may not recognise you from all those years ago, but she'll certainly remember me."

As Jill and Sam approached Mrs Faircliff, they saw her beginning to shake and she became very pale and frightened looking. On seeing her this way, Sam quickened his step towards her and urged Jill to do the same.

"Hello, Mrs Faircliff, could my wife and I have a word with you?" Sam said in as calm a voice as he could muster. "It is very important and perhaps we could do it in the privacy of your own home, as we did the last time, I spoke to you."

"It's about Amy, isn't it? Just tell me what it is please, then you can be on your way," Mrs Faircliff spoke in a great rush and kept looking over to the door of the house. "Just tell me. I can't bring you in. My husband is at home today, so you must tell me here. Right now, what is it?" Her voice was shrill and demanding.

Sam was speechless as he realised the implications for her if her husband saw her talking to two strangers and how distressed she seemed to be. But tell her he must. "Your daughter has been arrested in Australia for attempted murder."

Mrs Faircliff let out a scream, and if Jill had not been there to catch her and support her, she would have fallen on the pavement. Just as Jill was steadying her, both Sam and she knew, by the sound of running footsteps and a loud voice demanding to know what was going on, that Mr Faircliff had joined them.

Chapter 84

"My name is Helen Marks and I understand Joe Totten lives here. I would like to speak to him, it is very important."

"I'm sorry," Agnes replied, "you have missed him, he has gone to work a short time ago. But perhaps I can help you or someone else here might be able to." Agnes was anxious to help the young lady standing before her. She seemed quite apprehensive about something or other and because Agnes had been told, when the children had been brought back to Northern Ireland, who they were, Agnes knew exactly who the girl was.

"I can get a message sent over to Joe, if that would be all right with you."

"Certainly, that would be great," Helen replied, and Agnes could almost feel the excitement emanating from the girl.

"Come on in then, please, Helen, and I'll fetch some notepaper and a pen for you." And as she spoke, Agnes indicated that Helen step into the hall and then, as she opened the door to the sitting room, she nodded towards a plush armchair over by the bay window.

"Have a seat, Helen, and I'll be back in a jiffy."

"There is really no need to write anything down. Anyone involved with Amy is going to know soon anyway." Now Agnes was surprised to see the girl smiling broadly. "I need to let you know that Mrs Faircliff is flying out to Australia on the next available flight and her husband has asked me to accompany her. He intends to pay for both her fare and mine." She looked excitedly at Agnes. "So that's the message, that's all I know."

"Well, well, well," Agnes responded, "It might not sound much, but knowing the circumstances for Mrs Faircliff and Amy, I would say it tells us quite a lot."

"I think so too," was Helen's warm response. "Mrs Faircliff called round to see me yesterday afternoon. She knows Amy and I have been good friends for years. She told me briefly yesterday morning that her husband had just found out about Amy's existence and the trouble the girl was now in. Mrs Faircliff said he immediately insisted she must go to be with her daughter at this terrible time, but he insisted someone must accompany her and Mrs Faircliff said she would like me to. So that's it, that's all I know, really."

"Well, Helen, despite all Amy's trouble, I think this is good news. Firstly, Amy will now have her mother's support at such a terrible time and secondly, I believe they will be reconciled. How things will pan out for Mr and Mrs Faircliff, well, only time will tell."

"I think so too. So, I'll leave you now and hope to hear from Mrs Faircliff. I'll keep in touch with Joe, and Christopher too, of course. And thank you so much, Agnes, thank you. I'll leave you to deliver the message."

"I'm going to ring Joe's boss, Mr Wallace, as soon as you leave, Helen. So please don't worry on that score. It will be done, post-haste."

With another thank you and a final goodbye, Helen left and Agnes went into the dining room to ring Edward and let him know the latest development in this dilemma.

"I certainly think Helen Marks is the ideal person to go to Australia with Mrs Faircliff. She and Amy have been such good friends for years and Helen will be good support for her," Monica said. "I think she is a better choice than Joe because we don't know why Amy is accused of such a serious charge. We are completely in the dark and certainly if Helen Marks' friend, Brian, knows anything, he doesn't seem to have confided in her. So, we just have to wait and in the meantime support Joe and reassure him it is best if Helen goes, and that is who Mrs Faircliff wishes to go."

Later that evening, Monica and Edward had a visit from Jill and Sam Foster and heard all about their unexpected meeting with Mr Faircliff.

"You both must have been shaking in your shoes when you realised Mr Faircliff was standing there, right beside you," Edward said in an understanding voice.

"Well, yes, initially we were, Edward, but he really was such a gentleman throughout the whole saga. He insisted we all go back to his home, and he would learn what was wrong there," Jill answered firmly. "He was not at all what expected, considering what Amy had told me how it was for her mother, or at least, how her mother thought it would be."

Sam intervened, "Yes, Mrs Faircliff told me quite definitely she would never want her husband to know anything about Amy's existence. Yet he was only kindness itself in that street and in their home. So, no one knows how people may react in different and difficult situations."

"Well, hopefully, we'll hear soon from Helen Marks regarding her and Mrs Faircliff's flight and then we can organise some system of contact between us all," Edward said. "I suggest they ring our telephone line here. That might help Joe feel a part of the goings on, rather than using your telephone line, Jill. That's only a suggestion. What do you think?"

"I agree, Edward, and it's not as if it will be Amy herself who will be ringing," Jill said rather sadly. "But at least all of us here will have been brought up to date with what exactly happened to Amy to have brought her to this."

"Your mother is flying out tomorrow from Northern Ireland to stay with you during your trial, Amy." Amy's solicitor had just arrived a short time ago to the interview room and when he saw the young girl, he was struck by the change in her since he had last seen her. She had lost weight, her skin was a dull, ashen colour and her hair clung to the sides of her face in greasy straggles. Looking at her and how wretched she looked, he only hoped the news he had just given her would make some difference. Now he was rewarded when she looked at him directly, her eyes lit up and the glimmer of a smile touched her lips.

"Oh, is she? Isn't that wonderful. But," Amy hesitated and then went on, "it's such a pity she didn't want me to come back home with all my friends. Such a pity."

"I know, I know. But once she realised you were in trouble, everything else was forgotten about. And only how you were seemed to matter to her."

"Yes, I do realise that, and I will be so very glad to see her," Amy said as she took her seat across from her solicitor.

"There is also a friend of yours travelling back here with her. Mr Faircliff did not want his wife travelling so far alone. Her name, I understand, is Helen Marks."

"Oh, is Helen coming? How wonderful to hear that." With that, Amy began to cry, something she had been determined not to do. But hearing this wonderful, so surprising news—that her mother and Helen were coming out to Australia—just overwhelmed her. She was sure they would believe and support her when she told them all that had happened. She fervently hoped so, because she knew with an awful certainty that so many people already believed she was guilty of trying to kill Mrs Reid.

Chapter 85

"Please, I need to speak to the sergeant who is in charge of the Perth Technical School murder case." Molly knew she sounded agitated and distressed as she spoke. And no wonder, she did not know if she should be here at all or not, and for saying anything about Mrs Reid and her house. But she had felt compelled to come and say what she had seen, even if it turned out to be nothing at all to be worrying about.

"The sergeant who was dealing with that case has handed it over to higher authorities, but he will listen to what you have to say, and he'll see that the proper authorities are informed." The policeman behind the desk had remained pleasant and polite as he spoke to Molly. "If you just follow me to his office, then I'll go and fetch him for you." And he smiled warmly at Molly to try to put her at her ease. "By the way, what is your name?" He continued to smile at her because certainly she seemed very stressed and anxious about what she wanted to report and his curiosity was aroused. But sure, wasn't everybody's? Wasn't the whole incident the talk of Perth, and it seemed to be all about the principal of the technical college and one of his students. It would all come out in court and then everyone would hear what had brought Molly Dougan here today. The everybody would know all about it and everyone in this barracks here would have plenty to talk about.

As Molly waited in the sergeant's office for someone to appear, she became more and more agitated. Was she simply being a bit of a gossip here, and nothing else? Was she being disloyal here to her boss, Mrs Reid who had first employed her to do her cleaning some seven years ago? But then, what if there was something serious to report and she had not bothered to do it? What then? She had spent many sleepless nights pondering about what she had seen and now here she was, and she could hear footsteps approaching the office she was seated in. Suddenly, all nervousness and anxiety left Molly and she felt quite calm.

might prove to be nothing, but she must say to this sergeant now entering his office what exactly she had seen. It was the right thing to do.

Now he was extending his hand in greeting. "I'm Sergeant Mitchell, how can I help you, Ms Dougan?" he said encouragingly to her. "I understand it is something to do with the technical school's assault charges, and although I have handed my report to the higher authorities, anything you might have to tell me about it today I will ensure it will be sent to those in authority, Ms Dougan, have my assurance on that."

"Thank you, Sergeant Mitchell," Molly replied. "Perhaps it is nothing to worry about, but I thought I needed to report what I saw on the afternoon of the day the assault took place between the two ladies. So here I am."

Even as Molly started to speak, Sergeant Mitchell was pulling his pen and paper towards him and proceeded to write down very carefully what the young woman sitting before him was now telling him.

When she had finished, there was quite a silence between them, and then Clive Mitchell spoke. "It is imperative that I get this statement to the authorities who are dealing with the case, as soon as possible." And again, he gave her a very encouraging smile. "I must say, it is very brave of you to come, very brave indeed. Someone will be in touch with you regarding this statement. So, if you don't mind giving me a telephone number where we would be able to reach you, and of course, your address."

"Of course," Molly replied quickly, as she wrote her mother's telephone number and address on the page the sergeant slid across the desk to her. Secretly, she was thinking how silly she had been not to think they would certainly want some contact number from her. She hadn't even thought about any of that, but just now, she knew she had covered that fact up very well.

Chapter 86

Molly sat quietly gazing round her in the courtroom where this infamous trial of Amy Matthews was being held. She was stunned by the number of people present here today and it was only then that she realised how important it was that the truth must be told. It was important for Mr and Mrs Reid and their family, and it was so essential for the jury who were just this moment filing into their seats to hear all the evidence. Molly resolved to tell all the details exactly as she remembered them that afternoon when she saw Mrs Reid working at the stair carpet. Now she was filled with a quiet acceptance of how essential it was that she be here. She had no doubt that the quiet manner of both the solicitor and the barrister had made a major contribution to her resolve to tell everything as she remembered it.

She was not the girl who had sat in a state of anxiety and trepidation in the local police station, when she had decided to go there and report what she had seen. The solicitor had stressed how morally right it was for her to present herself as a witness. If she had any doubt about Mrs Reid's evidence it increased her resolve to tell everything, even though initially she had felt guilty saying anything about her employer who had been so good to her during the seven years she had worked for her.

Now, as the judge entered the courtroom, she was so very glad of the legal support Amy had because they certainly gave her added courage. When her name was called, she approached the witness box with a new, calm confidence.

Although she did not expect such a barrage of questions from either Amy' barrister or the barrister for the prosecution, she explained fully how she always gone on a Tuesday afternoon to clean Mr and Mrs Reid's home. How on the evening in question, she was just about to open the door on the landing—the door which separated one set of bedrooms from another. This door had a clear glass panel in it, so she could see quite clearly the area she was now speaking of She had been able to describe in detail what her employer had been wearing that afternoon. Molly told the court how mystified she was that Mrs Reid seemed to be working at the carpet, at the join at the top of the stairs. It had become rather noticeable, Molly stressed, and she thought that perhaps Mrs Reid had decided to repair it herself, even though she was always telling Molly she had asked her husband innumerable times to do it. However, what puzzled Molly was that Mrs Reid seemed to be working at it with a small knife, but surely, Molly decided, her employer must know what she was doing.

It was only after she learnt that Amy had been accused of tampering with the carpet that she firmly decided to report what she had seen.

Now, on her way back to her seat, Molly was relieved when Amy's barrister gave her a discreet smile of encouragement. Amy's solicitor in turn, as Molly took her seat, gave her a brief pat on her hand.

Molly heard very little of the closing summaries of Amy's barrister and the prosecution counsel because she was continually going over in her head what she had said as she stood up there. Had she told all she knew? Had she forgotten anything? Could she have emphasised some of what she had seen more clearly? But it was all too late now, the jury had finished their deliberations and had reached a verdict.

As she watched the jury file into their seats once more, Molly lost her nerve completely and could feel tears welling up in her eyes. How had she come to be here today? And why on earth had she said anything? But just as she looked across to Amy, realising she had been right in all her actions, the head jury announced they had reached a verdict. The judge then asked if it was a unanimous verdict and he was informed that it was. "And how do you find the prisoner, guilty or not guilty?" the judge's voice rang in the courtroom.

"Not guilty, my lord, not guilty."

And then Molly, together with Amy's barrister and solicitor, hugged Amy tightly and wept tears of joy at the news. And Molly knew nothing else mattered, only that Amy had been found innocent.

Chapter 87

"Amy…Mrs Faircliff, I can't begin to tell you how glad I am that I picked up the courage to go to the police station that day and tell them what I had seen."

Shortly after Amy's release from prison, she had contacted Molly and asked her to come to dinner in the hotel where her mum, Helen and Amy were staying.

"You were very brave, Molly, to do what you did. You did run a big risk of not being believed and being snubbed by half of the people in Perth. After all, Mr and Mrs Reid are one of the elite in Perth, and we certainly aren't considered to be in that class. I do believe that's why the prosecution was anxious to find a 'Guilty' verdict for me. So, I knew what I was up against," Amy said quite sardonically.

"I owe everything to you, Molly. And to think I almost fell for that headteacher's charms. But it turned out his good name was more important to him than any romance with me. Do you know, he may well have suspected his wife was the one who had tampered with the carpet, not me. But his good name meant everything to him, so he was never going to say anything."

"Mrs Reid must have forgotten that I had a dental appointment that day and would be a little later in coming to her. She was happy enough about that. But was very lucky she did not see me on the landing," Molly felt she needed to explain to Amy in detail about that afternoon. She had told the solicitor about her change of hours and the barrister's summing up he stressed that because Mr Reid was so intent on making sure that the carpet was now dangerous, she had forgotten all about Molly's change of time that day. As to when and where she thought Amy and her husband met up, she must have decided it was probably in Amy's bedroom in the evenings and this had been confirmed by Amy to her solicitor. There was nowhere else in the house they could have any privacy.

"But you do realise, Amy, that if all this had never happened, you and I would still not be reconciled. I was always so scared of what my husband would think of me, especially keeping such a secret from him for all these years. I felt such

294

fraud, you know, I really did. I am so sorry, darling, for all the hurt I have caused you and everyone else. Unnecessary hurt because he could not be more loving and understanding about all this. He says he can't wait to meet you and make you one of the family." Mrs Faircliff's voice shook. "And that's all I want too, my love."

On hearing her mother's words, Amy burst into tears. To think it was all she had ever wanted but instead she believed she had been unwanted by any of her family. And she knew that in turning to Mr Reid, she had simply been looking for love and acceptance from him. Now Amy's mother hugged her tightly, so aware of what her daughter had been through. Then Helen too, embraced her. "And just think, you will soon see Joe again and I know he seems to be stunned by everything that has happened. But I believe it will take time for him to come to terms with it all."

"I hope so, Helen, I really do. But at least I have been reconciled with my long-lost family and that will do for now."

Molly had been sitting quietly, giving the others time and space to support one another. But now she spoke, "It makes me so very happy to see you all together like this and if I never do anything remotely like what I have done in court, in my life again, I will be very content indeed."

"I should very much think so, Molly. But now let's go into the dining hall where our dinner is waiting to be served to us." And Mrs Faircliff rose from her seat and led the way into the grand dining room of the hotel.

Amy had written to Joe during her time in prison and again when she knew the date of her flight back to Northern Ireland. In her letters, she had begged Joe for his forgiveness and tried her best to explain why she had taken up with her headmaster. But so far, she had received no reply from him and in spite of her happiness at returning home, she was deeply troubled by Joe's silence. She tried to console herself that once he knew when her flight was due in, he would make a point of coming to meet her and all would be well.

Helen was most comforting. "Well, Amy, Christopher is coming to meet me of the flight, so I'm pretty sure your Joe will want to see you after all you have gone through. I'm sure he'll come with Christopher to the airport."

As the plane touched down at Aldergrove Airport, Amy began her search for Joe, but although she could see Christopher very clearly, there was no sign of Joe. Then Amy had her worst fears confirmed—Joe had decided not to meet her—Amy felt her heart was breaking. As she stood on the tarmac waiting for her luggage to arrive, she felt her mother's arms around her, holding her close.

"I'm sorry Joe's not here, Amy, but give him time and space. Your behaviour was so out of character for you, and he still must be shocked by it all."

Amy was so appreciative of her mother's kindness to her at this time. During their time together in the hotel, Amy began to understand what her mother had gone through believing Amy was dead. And worst of all, the fear of her husband's reaction to the whole situation. She was determined then to make both her mother and stepfather proud of her. She intended to finish her teaching course here in Northern Ireland and become a qualified teacher. She also intended to visit Joe and try her best to explain to him why she had behaved as she did.

Amy found her mother's house a warm comforting place with its spacious living room and three bedrooms upstairs. Her two stepbrothers had always shared a bedroom. So, she did not feel she was depriving the two boys of anything. After all the years she had been gone from Northern Ireland, she really had no recollection of the children's home she had been in. She had a vague memory of getting onto a bus one morning with some of the other children from the Home but that was all.

When she mentioned any of these details to her mother, she always hugged her closely and told her not to dwell on the past but to look forward to the future with her family. So, she took her mother's advice except for the memory of Joe. After writing to him on two occasions since she had returned to Northern Ireland and receiving no reply, she resolutely began to enquire at the local colleges how she might complete her teacher training and of what value the qualifications were which she had acquired in Australia. She was delighted when Stranmillis Teacher Training College accepted her, and she was told that a year with them would complete her training. After talking to her mother and stepfather, this assured her of both financial support and moral support.

Chapter 88

While Amy was devoting herself to her studies, Helen Marks had found work again looking after an elderly lady who lived close by. Helen knew it was a position she would love. She felt very settled and content these days and was very happy with her mother and family. But most of all, she was very happy with how Christopher's and her relationship was developing. They were becoming very close and indeed Christopher had mentioned marriage to her on a couple of occasions. But she needed time to become more familiar with everything that was happening round her. Christopher, in turn, wanted to make sure that the boyfriend who had wanted so desperately to marry her, when they were in Australia, would not appear again. Helen had to reassure him that he had already taken up with another girl.

Although Helen knew she loved Christopher and that he returned her feelings, she worried what his parents might think of such a liaison. No doubt they wanted the very best for Christopher after his years of absence from them. So, she was adamant that she must accompany Christopher when he told his parents of their love for one another.

"Oh, how wonderful, Christopher and Helen. We are delighted for you both. Edward and I hope you will be very happy." Monica smiled lovingly at the two young people. "We did suspect, you know, we were more or less expecting this news very soon." As she spoke, Monica rose from her seat and hugged both Christopher and Helen tightly, with Edward behind her doing the same thing.

"Edward, Christopher and I would like to make the celebration for both our wedding and our homecoming. My mother says she would love that but just couldn't have the funds to do it. So, she did wonder if you could make a contribution."

"Well, we would intend to help you with the wedding costs anyway, and certainly we would be delighted to help indulge in a good celebration for our son, daughter and friends who made it safely back to Northern Ireland. We need to think carefully about an appropriate size of venue and all of that."

"Yes, of course, Dad, and I intend to speak to Joe and ask him to be my best man. I mean, who else would I have after all the years we stuck together through thick and thin?"

Monica and Edward looked enquiringly at Helen who said, "I hope to have Amy as my chief bridesmaid. Just like Christopher, I want someone who suffered as I have done, and we understand each other." Helen hesitated, and then went on, "We would also like Faith and Jennie as our bridesmaids, if you are agreeable?"

"We would be delighted both for ourselves and for the girls," Edward was quick to reply.

"I haven't thought of a groomsman yet, but I do think David Gillespie would be a good choice. He shared so much with us in Australia, Dad, but I will let you know what I decide and indeed if David would be willing to take on the job."

"Mrs Wallace, I do need to tell you that Amy seems to have come to terms with Joe's absence from her life and concentrates on her work and her family. I hope to call round with her tomorrow, tell her I need to discuss shopping venues with her. So, I will know better after I talk to her how she is."

Later that evening, Christopher went across to Sara's annexe and over a good cup of tea, he asked Joe if he would honour him by being his best man when he married Helen. Joe immediately rose from his seat at the window and went over and hugged Christopher tightly. "Of course, Christopher, I would be delighted to do so." Joe looked over at his grandma and said, "Isn't this some honour for me, Grandma?"

"Indeed, it is, Joe, it is a very suitable choice Christopher has made. And perhaps some day, he will be able to do the same for you."

Sara's words were followed by a very uncomfortable silence for a moment or two as they all thought of Amy and how things had turned out for Joe and her. Then Christopher lightened the mood by saying, "Well, you never know, Sara, what lovely girl Joe might meet at this celebration. But in the meantime, we have been given the task of finding a suitable venue for everyone—with Edward help, of course. We are going to have a celebration for all those who have come safely back from Australia, as well as Helen's and my wedding."

"Oh, good," Joe replied, just relieved the conversation had turned away from any talk of women. Because, when such a conversation cropped up, he always thought of Amy and his inability to forgive her for what she had done. He had searched his mind so many times. He had after all, long ago, forgiven the priests who had so abused him and who had treated the children in the Swanson home with such disdain and total lack of respect. Even now, throughout the time he and Christopher had worked for the Moores and the last two years since his homecoming, he did not seem able to talk about his experiences, preferring to forget all about them. But why could he not forgive Amy for her one mistake and forget about it?

Now he said to Christopher, "Let's arrange to meet Edward very soon and get going in our search for a good venue."

"Well, first I need to visit David Gillespie at his father's farm and wondered if you would like to come with me, Joe. I would like to ask him if he would be groomsman for me on my wedding day."

"That would be wonderful, Christopher, the three of us together again. I haven't seen David for about a month or even more. He is just so busy helping his father on the farm, but he certainly seems very happy."

"Well, we'll go and see him tomorrow evening. How does that sound?"

"It sounds good, Christopher, and I'm certainly free."

"Good, Joe. I'll pick you up at seven o'clock then. I'll say goodnight now and I'll see you then."

Chapter 89

On her wedding morning, Helen wakened to beautiful early morning sunshine and the sound of birds rendering their early morning chorus. It was such a wonderful feeling to think this was her wedding day and that she was marrying Christopher Scott. Christopher, who, in all the time they had been in Australia, had shown no interest in her, nor indeed any girl. He had always explained briefly to anyone who wondered about this, that he had no intention of settling down with any girl in Australia. His sights were set on finding his way home to Northern Ireland and finding his mother. That was all he wanted, to be able to find his way home to his mother.

Helen, though, had always felt the opposite, believing they ought to settle down in Australia and forget about home. Because how would they ever get there? Where would any of them get that class of money from? That was why she had been determined to marry her super rich boyfriend, settle in Australia, and forget about Northern Ireland.

How wonderful it was now for herself and the others that they had been found after all these years and brought back home to her mother who she had such vague, but warm memories of. She was home, where Christopher and she had gradually become inseparable. Christopher realised from right he had been not to have any romance with anyone in Australia, but to pray for the day he could come home.

Helen intended to look her very best today, not only because it was her wedding day but because she would meet with others who had managed to make their way home from Australia. Thanks to the publicity Edward had given to the press, this day was now possible.

Joe and Christopher had worked so hard in the preparation for today. They had chosen the Conway Hotel with its magnificent entertainment room with conservatory off it, because they knew it should accommodate some one hundred and fifty to one hundred and sixty comfortably.

Joe had designed beautiful posters, giving the reason for the celebration and the venue and date and asked local shopkeepers if they would kindly display them in their windows and Christopher had posted out all the invitations. Helen's mother was still involved with helping Helen chose her dress, her flowers and hairstyle and one of her close friends had offered to bake two cakes.

Every time Helen thought of how all the children, who had boarded that bus some fifteen years ago, would all be together on such an important day, she was overcome with emotion. Now to think they would form such a special bridal party—the only addition being Faith and Jennie. Helen knew her wedding to Christopher could only be a success.

Amy had been delighted when Helen had asked her to be bridesmaid. She felt it was a real honour to be part of the wedding party and to play such a pivotal role for Helen. She had believed she could face Joe and have a natural conversation with him now. It was, after all, over two years since she had seen him, and she had become used to life without him.

But now, with the arrival of Helen and her stepfather in the porch, Amy knew, in her heart, she dreaded seeing him. As she fell into step behind Helen and began adjusting her train, she knew she was faced with the job of doing whatever was necessary to make a success of her role in Helen and Christopher's wedding.

Joe, on hearing the organ music announce the arrival of the bride, turned to look at the procession coming towards him. He did not see Amy at first as she was obscured by Helen and her stepfather, but then, there she was, only a few feet from him. And as he looked at her and saw how beautiful she was despite the look of inordinate sadness in her eyes, he just wanted to reach out and hold her close. He wanted to tell her how sorry he was for the way he had isolated her from him for so long. He had found it impossible to forgive her for her such brief fall from grace with the schoolteacher.

Now, he realised that Amy's behaviour and their subsequent split from each other had simply represented to him all the horrible times he had had in the past fifteen years, thanks to the British and Australian governments and to the weaknesses of the priests he had encountered in Home. How stupid he had been and so full of condemnation for Amy.

Now, as he stood beside Christopher listening to the service and handing over the ring at the appointed time, he knew he must beg Amy for forgiveness for all his arrogance. But apart from seeking Amy's forgiveness, he intended to make sure that Mrs Reid, the headmaster's wife, was brought to trial, just as Amy had been. She needed to be questioned about her actions on the day Molly Dougan had seen her working at the stair carpet. It was over two years now since Amy had been accused and after her acquittal, Joe had assumed Mrs Reid would be questioned about her activities on that awful day when Amy was arrested.

But according to his friend Brian in Australia, whom he wrote to quite often, the whole business seemed to have spluttered out. As for Mrs Reid being questioned about it, Brian believed that had simply never happened. When Joe heard this, he was amazed and infuriated, obviously Mrs Reid's innocence had never been in doubt. What could Joe do about it? Certainly the chance of doing anything about it was very remote but challenge the system he must. He owed it to Amy to do his best for her and if Mrs Reid was guilty of any foul play, she must be held responsible. So, he must return to Australia to get some answers to his questions. When the festivities were over, he would talk to Amy and see what she would think of it all.

"Please, Joe, I don't intend to return to that awful country ever again. Please don't ask me, but if you really feel like going back to have Mrs Reid convicted I can't keep you back." Then Amy smiled at him. "I'll wait for you until you return."

Joe hugged her close. "I promise I won't ask you to wait too long. But intend to have a word with Christopher's father and see what he thinks."

Chapter 90

"Why do you want to do this?" was Edward's first question when Joe and he met in Edward's sitting room the following week and Joe told him that he needed to go back to Australia to do some investigating of his own. He needed to know why Mrs Reid's innocence in the saga had just been assumed.

"I feel I owe it to Amy to solve the case properly," Joe answered, "and I think Mrs Reid's behaviour was never questioned. After all, she might have been tampering with the stair carpet in order to do Amy serious injury which it may well have done. And her actions have never been questioned, as far as I understand. I feel it is morally and criminally wrong to leave the whole thing hanging in the balance."

"Joe, I believe you are right but what chance have you of changing anything?"

"I don't know, Edward, but I do mean to try."

"Well, Joe, if that's the case, I'll do all I can to help you. I will accompany you and I'll talk to the Criminal Justice System. Once they know they are talking to the man who took so many children back to their home country and who made sure the same children were well-compensated for the years they had spent in the wilderness, they will listen to what I have to say."

"You can't come to Australia. I'll manage fine on my own," Joe protested.

"I'm accompanying you, and that's that. Ask Christopher to book two tickets and a hotel for a couple of weeks."

Edward considered what he had just said. "Yes, a couple of weeks should tell us quite a lot, Joe." Edward smiled at him. "You must remember this will be my first visit to Australia. Quite apart from trying to help you, Joe, I am interested in seeing some of the places you have all talked about," Edward said. "Now let Amy know as soon as possible what your plans are and that I will be with you. That will reassure her. Your job will be here for you on your return, so don't worry on that score, Joe, I'll see to that."

"Oh, thank you, Edward." Joe hugged Edward fondly before leaving him to return to Amy.

The very first morning after Edward and Joe had arrived in Australia, Edward began to make telephone calls to the government to arrange relevant meetings regarding the Reid attempted murder case of over two years ago when the jury had found Amy Matthews to be innocent. Joe and Edward attended three meetings when members of the government and the Criminal Justice System were present. Edward stated firmly that the reason for his and Joe's visit was to try to establish if Mrs Reid had faced any charges regarding her use of the penknife on the stair carpet. The men facing Joe and Edward were quick to shake their heads and one man at the centre of the group stated that Mrs Reid had been interviewed and she was found to have no case to answer.

"Edward, I can scarcely believe any of this," Joe said later that evening. They had just finished their evening meal and were now in the hotel lounge contemplating what they had been told about Mrs Reid earlier in the day. "I mean, the woman was seen working at the stair carpet with a penknife, yet Amy was the one charged with attempted murder," Joe said angrily, "and look what it did to our relationship."

"Joe, there is no point dwelling on any of that," Edward said firmly. "There is however, one thing we could try to do. I don't know whether it would work or not, but because we have come so far, it is worth a try. Let's go to our room where I'll explain."

Meekly, Joe followed Edward back to their bedroom, mystified as to what he could possibly be planning next. He felt they had reached the end of the road regarding proving Mrs Reid's culpability. No one in authority was prepared to accept the possibility Mrs Reid had wished Amy to trip on the cut stair carpet and fall down the stairs. When that failed, she had resorted to having her accused of trying to murder her. Only for Mollie Duggan, there was little doubt Amy would have been found guilty and sent to prison.

Now here was Edward, doing his best to help him.

"Right, Joe, there is one last thing we can try and if done properly has the potential to be very effective." Edward hesitated. "You should try interviewing Mrs Reid and find out how she felt about Amy."

"But if I tried to repeat anything she might have said, she would just deny all," Joe argued.

"Not if you could secretly record her words, especially if she speaks ill of Amy," Edward spoke very firmly. "It is up to you, Joe, how you handle the interview. Look, think about it, then let me know in the morning whether you think you could go through with it or not. I happened to bring a small tape recorder with me, and it will fit in your pocket." Edward smiled at Joe now. "You have a lot to think about, so let's get to bed and you can tell me in the morning what your decision is. But I'll tell you this, Joe, you will need to keep a cool head if you are going to do this successfully."

The following morning, Joe confidently told Edward he was prepared to do what was required to get the truth. When he rang the college, he managed to get Mrs Reid's telephone number by explaining he was a past student from college and how Mr and Mrs Reid had helped him so much he would like to organise to meet with them and thank them for all they had done. Mrs Reid answered the telephone and Joe quickly explained who he was and that he was planning on marrying Amy. Before he did so, he would like to know what her behaviour in general had been like in Australia and would prefer to meet in confidence to find out more. If she would like to meet him for a drink in the lounge bar of the Sheridan Hotel, she could tell him how it was when Amy moved into a room in her house and how everything went.

Mrs Reid said she had no objections to meeting him but had no idea how she could be of assistance. Joe said he would appreciate anything at all she might help him with. He would explain how things had been for him since Amy's return.

"Make sure that the recorder is switched on when you see her coming. I have it fully charged, and it will make no noise during the interview. Then when you return, we will tape it back and we will hear how it went." Edward smiled confidently at him because this was some undertaking Joe was contemplating. But if he wanted some proof against Mrs Reid regarding Amy, this was the only way. Meantime, Edward must wait in the bedroom until Joe's return. The first half hour was quite tolerable for Edward, he knew Joe must set the scene in a trustworthy manner, but as time rolled on, he began to get increasingly worried. He had visions of Mrs Reid realising what exactly Joe was at, of finding the recorder and of Joe being beaten up, or perhaps even worse. It was forty-five minutes before the bedroom door opened quietly and Joe stood before him, with a smile on his face.

"I think you will agree with me when you listen to this tape that I have been successful, Edward." Then Joe's brave facade left him, and he broke into tears as he threw himself down on the bed.

Edward quickly went to him and held him close. "Right, Joe, well done but I really need to hear this tape. Where is it?"

Meekly, Joe indicated the pocket of his jacket, the same pocket the tape recorder had been safely stored in on Joe's departure as he went to meet Mrs Reid. Edward quickly retrieved it and switched it on as he started playing the information back to them both. They both listened carefully as Joe introduced himself to Mrs Reid who assured him she knew who he was and that he was the boyfriend of that hussy, Amy Matthews.

"It is so kind of you, Mrs Reid, to even consider seeing me, after all you have been through. I just wondered if you could give me some advice about Amy and my future with her."

"Oh, I don't really mind, gives me a chance to talk about her and how ever thinking about her makes me feel. I'm sure you are as good a listener as anyone How did you even think to have dealings with her after hearing of her cavorting with my husband?" Her voice sounded quite shrill, but Joe knew the importance of being calm and in a quiet voice assured Mrs Reid that it must have been a very difficult time for her when she discovered what was going on. He felt every sympathy for her, he said. He had split from Amy for the last two years but realised that it would not be so easy for Mr and Mrs Reid to split up from on another and he sincerely hoped they could put this all behind them. As for himself, he knew that he still thought a lot of Amy despite her behaviour when she had felt so alone in Australia.

"You what? You still think a lot of her? I think you are so like my husband I believe to be I know, he still thinks about her." And now Mrs Reid had a wild look about her and, Joe knew, she was on the verge of screaming. She said, ' wish I had done the job properly that day with the penknife on the stair carpet but I thought I had done enough to send her crashing down the stairs. It turned out she was too strong for me and managed to fight me off. So now you know Joe Totten, I wanted to kill her that day because of what she had done to my marriage and if I ever had the chance, I would not hesitate to do the same thing again. And with more success."

Joe thanked her very calmly and said that, on consideration of her words, he would have to think very deeply before ever marrying Amy Matthews. "Bu must thank you, Mrs Reid, for all your help this day. I much appreciate you setting time aside and coming to see me," Joe said pleasantly. "I'll show you out now, Mrs Reid, and thank you very much indeed. I will be in touch to let you know what I have decided." Secretly, as he said goodbye, he could scarcely believe it had been so easy. No doubt, she had agreed to meet him out of sheer curiosity. Once she had seen him, however, she had just given vent to her feelings about Amy and what she had actually done on the day Molly Duggan had seen her.

"That's it, Edward, what do you think?"

"What do I think? I think it's very good and should uphold in court," Edward said. "But we must record this on to another recorder. We need to take one to the Criminal Justice System, but we must keep the original for ourselves. And I do know that Mr Todd, the head of criminal justice, will listen to us much more attentively when we have such evidence for him. I'll ring shortly and make another appointment with him. Hopefully, we will see justice done for Amy." Edward just wanted to see this saga through and all thoughts of sightseeing in Perth were forgotten. He just wanted to get Joe safely back to Northern Ireland.

Six months later, Mrs Reid, wife of Mr Reid, headmaster of Perth Technical School, was found guilty of the attempted murder of Amy Matthews and was sentenced to nine years in prison. Shortly after, Joe and Amy were married in Lisburn Cathedral with quite a few of their friends present for the celebration. Amy received substantial compensation from the Perth government for wrongful arrest and the attempted murder charge.

Printed in Great Britain
by Amazon

44680103R00170